CALL ME STAN
A Tragedy in Three Millennia

Essential Prose Series 188

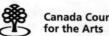

Canada Council **Conseil des Arts**
for the Arts **du Canada**

ONTARIO ARTS COUNCIL
CONSEIL DES ARTS DE L'ONTARIO

an Ontario government agency
un organisme du gouvernement de l'Ontario

Canada

Guernica Editions Inc. acknowledges the support of the Canada Council
for the Arts and the Ontario Arts Council. The Ontario Arts Council
is an agency of the Government of Ontario.

We acknowledge the financial support of the Government of Canada.

CALL ME STAN

A Tragedy in Three Millennia

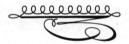

K.R. Wilson

GUERNICA EDITIONS

TORONTO • CHICAGO • BUFFALO • LANCASTER (U.K.)

2021

Michael Mirolla, general editor
Julie Roorda, editor
David Moratto, interior and cover design
Guernica Editions Inc.
287 Templemead Drive, Hamilton, ON L8W 2W4
2250 Military Road, Tonawanda, N.Y. 14150-6000 U.S.A.
www.guernicaeditions.com

Distributors:
Independent Publishers Group (IPG)
600 North Pulaski Road, Chicago IL 60624
University of Toronto Press Distribution (UTP)
5201 Dufferin Street, Toronto (ON), Canada M3H 5T8
Gazelle Book Services, White Cross Mills
High Town, Lancaster LA1 4XS U.K.

First edition.
Printed in Canada.

Legal Deposit—Third Quarter
Library of Congress Catalog Card Number: 2021933086
Library and Archives Canada Cataloguing in Publication
Title: Call me Stan : a tragedy in three millennia / K.R. Wilson.
Names: Wilson, K. R., 1958- author.
Series: Essential prose series ; 188.
Description: Series statement: Essential prose ; 188
Identifiers: Canadiana (print) 20210140348 | Canadiana (ebook) 20210140364 |
ISBN 9781771835985 (softcover) | ISBN 9781771835992 (EPUB) |
ISBN 9781771836005 (Kindle)
Subjects: LCGFT: Novels.
Classification: LCC PS8645.I4695 C35 2021 | DDC C813/.6—dc23

To my father. I think he would've enjoyed it.
And with apologies to Wilhelm Baumgartner.

Contents

Now

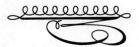

"WANDERING JEW" IS a misnomer. I'm a Hittite. Or I was, when there was such a thing.

Call me Stan.

"Hittite" is a misnomer too. We were the Hatti. But then somebody mixed us up with that Canaanite hill tribe in the King James Bible, and we've been wearing the wrong name ever since.

Names. They're so malleable.

I was originally called Ishtanu, after one of our sun gods. We had a lot of gods. Some were ours; some co-opted from our vassals. We had a lot of vassals.

My life started out like any other bronze age teenager's. Shepherding. Arranged marriage. Military draft. It got more complicated when I realized I didn't die. It got a *lot* more complicated when other people realized it. Pre-modern society may have embraced a lot of theoretical immortals, but it wasn't all that tolerant of actual immortality. Modern society isn't noticeably better.

I cope by changing identities every 20 years or so. That creates its own complications. You think you have trouble keeping track of your online passwords? Try keeping track, over thousands of years, of which name you're using for each eyeblink of your life. I try to keep a common element. I've been Drustan, Constantius, Constanze. You get the idea. Sometimes I can't, so I've also been Olaf, Gestas, Jagdish. I was even Ishmael for a while. But don't call me that.

Yes, Constanze. And Anastasia and Betty. Don't look so puzzled. Change identities often enough and after a while you want to mix it up. Just give me a good razor or a dab of hot wax. I've done it for decades at a time. Eventually it's not just the appearance you want to mix up. With the endless scope of human mating options, would you settle for a steady diet of the same thing century after century? Please. So when you live as long as I have, you eventually try pretty much everything.

I've been warrior and pacifist, ascetic and hedonist, thinker and doer, oppressed and oppressor. I've spied and been spied on, betrayed and been betrayed, killed and been ... well. People have *tried* to kill me. Sometimes they've thought they had. But here I am.

I know that look. I've seen it before. Wondering whether I'm genuinely delusional or just a really brazen liar. Setting up an insanity defence, maybe. But there's another possibility you shouldn't discount so easily: I might be telling the truth.

Which is it?

You're the detective. You figure it out.

You want to know what happened. That's why we're here. Fair enough. But if you want the whole story it could take a while.

Don't say I didn't warn you.

Six Weeks Ago

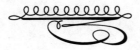

SHE MUST'VE FOLLOWED me to Kyiv.

I was at an umbrella-shaded table in a sculpture park, drinking a Beck's beer with a Cyrillic label. The Chechen geneticist I'd met on the dark net was forty minutes late. There were gold domes in every direction except across the Dnieper, where there were grey Stalinist apartment blocks. Kyiv is the ugliest beautiful city in Europe. I checked my watch again.

The first time I saw Kyiv it was a fenced clutch of huts on a hill. The next time, when the frescos in Saint Sophia were barely dry, the Kyivan Rus dominated the Dnieper basin and Russia was just open space dotted with nomadic horsemen. Now it had German beer and Chechen geneticists.

At my age all journeys are long journeys.

I finished the beer and got another from the tent-like booth beside the path.

You've got, what, ten or fifteen years in as a cop? Seventeen. That's a good long time. Bit of seniority, privileges of rank. History of solid work. Pension on the horizon, not imminent, but there, visible, in the middle distance.

Imagine having to give it all up. Start over. No history, no qualifications. No contacts. No friends. Literally from nothing. Well, some cash, if you've worked out how to hide it away. Build it all up, all over again. Knowing you'll never reach that pension. Knowing that the whole time you're building up all the normal details of your normal life—phone number, library card, car payments, life insurance, internet service contract, the random crap in your glove box and the brand of noodles in your cupboard—you're working out how to dump it all, and when. Dump every detail of your life. Set up a new one up for immediate possession—phone, library card, noodles—while still living the old one, and then disappear without raising too many questions.

So you put it off. Shave your hairline back a half inch, grey the temples. Grab your lower back and wince every once in a while. Complain about the cold. Maybe you extend it five years. Ten if you get really good.

You know that feeling you get on a dark December morning: *Oh God, do I really have to go into work again*?

Imagine that on a scale of lifetimes.

I sipped the Beck's, checked my watch. Then I saw her.

Not the geneticist, who is a flabby young man.

Nicca.

I knew her with certainty in that initial moment, even though the last time I'd seen her was in Paris a century ago. Apart from wavier hair and a waist-length leather jacket, she looked the same. Weary. A long way from the exuberance that defined her when we first met.

South Asian women weren't any more common in twenty-first century Kyiv than in the Paris of the twenties, but there were enough that it didn't have to be her. Only it was. In a left bank coffee house or a Ukrainian park feigning interest in a carving of a round-headed woman in a robe, Nicca was unmistakable.

Do you have a family? You won't tell me, of course. Fair enough. Let's say yes, for the purpose. Wife. Kid or two. See them into the world, grow old together. Two or three weeks in Turkey or Tuscany once the mortgage is paid off. Imagine having to walk out just when things are taking shape.

Not the only option. You could confess your true age and then hang around while they all grow old and die. I've done it both ways. Walking out is the way to go.

But what if they didn't die either?

What would you give for that?

My phone purred. I wouldn't have taken my eyes off her to pick it up, but it might have been the Chechen. It was. An encrypted e-mail, changing the time and place. The park was too isolated. He wanted to meet in a crowd.

I wasn't sure why he was so skittish. There wasn't anything illegal in what we were doing. Well, maybe some of the immigration stuff. But I had enough in the bribery budget for most complications.

He named an outdoor cafe just off the Maidan. One hour.

When I looked up from my phone screen, Nicca was gone.

I wandered around to see if I could find her, but no luck. Not surprising. I'd only find her if she wanted me to. I'd only *seen* her because she'd wanted me to. I walked down to my hotel. A public meeting could go either way. I wanted my passports and my tickets out of town near to hand in case things went sideways.

The hotel was the height of Cold War chic, with caged fluorescent lights and wood panelled corridors. A determined cop could've searched every cranny of my tiny room before the door finished swinging shut. So I only kept one set of tickets and ID there. I had another in a locker at the airport, another at the train station, and another under a planter in the hotel bar, all in different names. You can never be too careful.

I grabbed my shoulder bag from my room, went down to the empty bar, and ordered an espresso. While the barman grudgingly fetched it from the kitchen I tilted the planter back and scooped my documents into my bag. When the coffee arrived I plopped in a sugar cube and drank it slowly enough not to attract attention, but quickly enough to make my meeting on time.

I stopped at a bank machine on Khreshchatyk Street and inserted my card. The account belongs to a Caribbean shell company owned by a Liechtenstein *anhalt*. I took out enough for a night's worth of beer and *holubtsi* and strippers, just in case. I stuffed the documents from the planter into a gap between the ATM and the wall. If the Chechen brought the authorities, it would hardly do to have two sets of ID.

He'd chosen a corner table, where the patio railing met the exterior wall. Good spot. He could see the other tables and the street beyond. But he couldn't see me. He wouldn't unless I wanted him to. I waited until he was gazing down the street to his left. Then I approached the patio from his blind side.

I'm pretty good with languages. I've seen a lot come and go. The Chechen and I had been corresponding in Russian, which I've made a point of keeping up. Along with Latin, strangely. Of course it hasn't evolved much since its big shift from the language I spoke as a Roman soldier to the one I spoke in the monasteries of the Middle Ages. Maybe that's why my brain hangs on to it. Keeping the monastic back door open in case I need a quick getaway.

"Switch chairs," I said in Russian.

He jumped sharply, slopping honey spiced vodka onto the table.
"Switch? Why?"
"I'm better at watching the street than you are."
He moved to the—
Sorry, what? No, I didn't see Nicca again on that trip.
The sword? Fine, I'll tell you about it. But we'll have to go back a bit.

There was this commune in northern Wales in the late sixties. Naive twenty-somethings looking for a simpler life. Raising bees for candle wax. Dying hand-carded wool with berry juice. Some of the men wanted to do bronze castings the old way. Bronze Age old. It was tragic. Their stuff looked like it'd been carved out of dung with a spoon. But one of the weavers was kind of cute, so I decided to join them for a bit and share some of what I'd learned from—

No. We're going to have to go back further than that.

The Hatti

STEPMOTHERS GET A bad rap. I've known wonderful stepmothers. I've even been a couple. Mine, though …

I never knew my mother. I was told she died giving birth to me, when I was told anything. I know she came from somewhere else, to the north. Her name was Tabiti, though Lelwani—who'd been betrothed to my father before my mother turned up—preferred "that foreign tart."

According to Lelwani, my mother was dumped by our troops on their way back from an expedition and seduced my father in one of our shepherds' huts for his lunch of bread and cheese. He never confirmed this, though he never contradicted it. I don't remember him ever contradicting Lelwani.

When my panicking father eventually revealed Tabiti and her belly to my grandparents, there was a swift wedding, followed an unspecified number of months later by my birth, in the fifth year of King Muwattali the Second. My mother's obliging death left Lelwani free to pick up her previously scheduled life with my father, and within the following two years she gave birth to my brothers, Rundas and Telepinu.

Sometimes my mother came to me from the afterlife while I slept. She never spoke. She didn't need to. She was reminding me, simply by appearing, that she was there, on the edge of awareness, keeping me as safe from Lelwani as she could.

Which wasn't much.

Shepherds' sons like my brothers and me helped with the flocks pretty much as soon as we could walk: birthing, tending, milking, shearing and butchering, depending on the season. If we were good with numbers, we helped with the business end as well.

I remember the first time my father asked me how many yearlings we had. I was six or seven. We were gathering our flock from the pasture, just the two of us, and had paused at midday to split a flat loaf and some salt mutton. There was a soft wind, rich with the reassuring smell of the grain ripening in the neighbouring fields, and a light haze on the horizon promising evening rain.

I looked down to the low basin where we'd assembled the flock to be driven down to the pens near our compound, and did a quick count. "Forty."

My father nodded. "What's one third?"

I pictured them in my head, lined up by tens. "Thirteen," I said. "Roughly."

"Yes. Roughly. But why do I ask?"

"Because one third is the King's Portion." Every year my father drove a third of the yearlings into town to the king's military stores. The other men did the same with their grain or their cheese or their heifers.

"Does that change your answer?"

I hesitated. "Fourteen?" It was a little more than a third, but it was the only other possible answer.

"Good. Why?"

I didn't know. Then I remembered something I'd heard him say one year when Lelwani complained that the King took too much.

"Because it is dangerous to risk shortchanging the King?"

He nodded. "Always remember that. One thing you know for sure is that you don't shortchange the King."

We sat in silence and finished our bread. When we were done my father stood and brushed the dust from his tunic. "Want to help me drive them into town in the morning?"

My eyes went wide, and he smiled. Which was nice. I don't remember him smiling much.

Lelwani was less pleased. "You shouldn't indulge him like that," she said to my father with a scowl. He lowered his eyes and didn't respond.

But he still took me.

Whenever I wasn't in the pastures watching our flocks, I was usually hanging out with Halki. Halki's father ran the tavern on the outside of the village wall, near the gate we used when we visited the market or the temple. If Lelwani wasn't with us my father and I would stop there on our way back, and he'd spend a few coins on a dark beverage drunk from a bowl. "Don't tell Lelwani," he'd say sternly. I never did.

When my father and the other men sat at the ale bowl, Halki and I would be sent outside together to amuse ourselves. Halki had an instinct for trouble. If we'd grown up together these days, I probably would've gotten my first cigarette from him. As it was, I got my first broken arm, after he challenged me to climb the village wall. The next time we met after that he looked at me with surprise. "How come your arm isn't still wrapped up?"

I shrugged. "It's all better."

He was impressed. "You heal fast."

When I was old enough to go into town on my own, I went as often as I could, to get away from Lelwani and my brothers and to hang out with Halki. He was daring in a way I wasn't. Not then.

At the far end of the village there was a walled compound, with a wooden door split horizontally across the middle to make a rough counter. "There are soldiers in there," Halki said one lazy afternoon while we wandered the village on our own.

"I know. That's where we take the sheep."

He stopped and smiled. "Want to go in?"

I looked around nervously. "Are we allowed?"

"Who cares? C'mon."

"No!" I grabbed his sleeve. "We can't." I pictured ranks of fierce men waiting for a small boy to put a foot wrong.

He shook me off. "Why not?" He spread his hands to encompass the village. "We can go anywhere else. Why not there?"

"I don't know." I was sweating. "We just can't."

"Well that's not fair. C'mon." He darted toward the door.

"No!" I said again. But it was too late. He was already there, peering through the opening. Then he had a knee over the edge and he was gone.

I looked around in panic. Had anyone seen me with him? Was I going to be in whatever trouble he was in? I pressed myself into the shadow of a nearby shop.

About two minutes later a pair of thick arms stuck Halki through the opening in the door and dropped him in the dust. The door slammed shut, and there was the thunk of a bolt being slammed home. Halki spotted me and walked over. He frowned and shook his head. "Nothing much. Barns and stuff."

One spring, when we drove the yearlings into the village, Halki was crouched outside the gate trying to fry a beetle with sunlight and a piece of broken glass. "Hey," he said happily when he saw us. "What's up? This isn't a market day."

"The King's portion," I said loftily.

"Cool." He dropped the glass and jumped to his feet. "I'll come with you." I looked quickly up at my father, who nodded.

The top half of the door was open when we got there.

"How many?" the duty soldier asked.

"Eleven." We'd had a slower year.

The soldier made a mark on his clay tablet. "Out of how many?"

"Thirty-one."

The soldier's lips moved as he did the calculations. He made some more marks. "And if we checked we'd find twenty still in your pens?"

My father nodded. "Send someone today if you like."

The soldier gave him a weary look. "Let's just take your word for it." He opened the gate and they drove the sheep inside, where presumably some other soldier would know what to do with them.

"What a tool," Halki said as we walked back through the village. "I thought soldiers were supposed to *fight*."

My father roughed up Halki's hair. "I'm happier when they don't."

Halki and his romantic notions. I could tell him so much, now. Three thousand years too late.

By the twentieth year of King Muwattali I'd grown tall and slim, and my voice had deepened as much as it ever would. I was grateful that our custom was to be clean-shaven. My facial hair was the patchiest in our family.

One evening shortly before I turned 15 my father and Lelwani took me aside after dinner. "You're betrothed," Lelwani said. "We made the arrangements this afternoon."

I looked back and forth between them. Just like that? "What?" I finally managed to say. "Who?"

Lelwani looked toward my father. "Ishara," he said. "The oldest daughter of Tilla the cheesemaker."

"It is a good match," Lelwani said. "We produce milk. They make it into cheese. We both profit."

"But I don't even know her. I mean, I may have seen her in the village with her family years ago." I had an image of a wispy thing clinging to her mother's skirts near the leatherworker's stand. "Besides, doesn't Tilla make his cheese with cow's milk?"

Lelwani frowned. "Cheese is cheese."

Our families got together at Tilla's house for what amounted to an engagement party. There was a lot of cheese. After some formalities, they brought Ishara out.

I was grateful for my shoulder satchel, which I quickly shifted around to the front. I was a fifteen-year-old boy. And wispy Ishara had grown into a tall young woman with a body like a bag of basketballs. In our fertility-based culture she was the erotic ideal.

"I'm good with this," I said to Lelwani.

She looked at me like I was a turd she'd found on her sandal.

"This isn't about you. It's about giving the family sons." Her gaze was like the beams of sunlight Halki burned beetles with. "You have no other value. Remember that."

In the run-up to the wedding the local women spent a lot of time preparing the hut where Ishara and I would live. It had belonged to my grandparents, but my grandfather had gone to the afterlife after a long wasting illness, and my grandmother had moved across the compound to live with my father and Lelwani.

One afternoon as I returned from the pasture I saw my grandmother standing outside while the other women remade her conjugal home with scrub brushes and fresh linens and newly carved idols of Aserdus the fertility goddess. I put my arm lightly across her shoulders. It was all I could think to do. What fifteen-year-old boy would know what to say?

My grandmother let out a sigh. "Don't grow old, Ishtanu," she said softly.

"All right." It was a knee-jerk assent to ease the pain in an old woman's eyes.

But I've thought about that exchange a lot in the last three thousand years.

The wedding celebration was an embarrassing mix of high ritual and low innuendo. I didn't care for the attention, but I had to hang in for the prize at the end.

It was held in the all-purpose temple in the village. We had a range of gods, whose lamps we lit or chants we chanted for various purposes at prescribed times through the year, but nothing gathered them together like a wedding.

The whole village attended. There were offerings to Tarhun the storm god and his wife Arinna the sun goddess, our pantheon's chief executives. Aserdus the fertility goddess got a lot of recognition, for obvious reasons. We also gave a prudent nod to all the little industrial demigods we invoked against things like spoiled curds and sheep blight. Eventually we made our vows, and with a loud cheer the ceremony gave way to the party.

At the centre of the room was the communal beer bowl, porridge-thick with fermenting barley and surrounded by waiting villagers. "Here," Halki said with a grin, handing me a long, hollow reed. "Take a deep drink." He raised an eyebrow toward Ishara, at the centre of a cluster of envious younger girls. "It'll make you less nervous for later."

I stuck the reed into the bowl. "Why would I be nervous?"

"Because what if you can't do it?"

That hadn't occurred to me.

I'd seen the rams in rut, of course, so I had a basic idea of the mechanics. But beyond that no one had told me anything. Ishara, on the other hand, had been in long discussions with the village women, which I now realized had probably been for instructional purposes.

I put the reed to my mouth and drew a long draught of the sweet, malty liquid. The men of the village egged me on, chanting as I drank, and when I broke for breath they cheered loudly and plunged their own reeds into the brew.

Halki pounded me on the back. "Attaboy!"

As the party wore on I matched the others drink for drink, but while the rest of them began to slur and stumble I somehow stayed completely clear-headed.

Eventually the party wound down, and we walked back to the compound in the dying daylight. The women carefully installed Ishara in our hut before I was allowed in. They ignored me as they left, apart from my grandmother, who gave me a silent pat on the arm.

The bedchamber was lit by a single oil lamp marked with fertility symbols. Ishara was standing by the bed in a white robe made of the thinnest fabric I'd ever seen. It clung to her like fog. My breath caught in the back of my throat. I walked awkwardly toward her until we were nearly touching. Then, taking my cue from the rams, I turned her around.

"No," she said. "The other way."

I stopped. Really? The one bit I was sure I had right?

"What do you mean 'the other way'?"

"We're supposed to face each other." She lay on the bed on her back. "Like this." She lifted her hands to guide me down.

I did as I was told.

"Wait. Lift up for a second." She hiked her gown to her hips. "OK. Keep going." Again I did as I was told. There was squirming, and a stifled yelp. After a few moments she spoke again.

"Was that it?"

"Um. I guess."

"Oh." She was quiet for a moment. "Can you do it again?"

"I think so. Give me a second."

By morning we pretty much had it mastered.

My days as a new husband were the same as before: in the pasture with the flocks or, depending on the season, in the pen for shearing or the barn for birthing or on the darkened hard-packed earth behind the barn for slaughtering. But my nights were as different as I could have imagined.

During evening meals Ishara and I would exchange what we thought were private, teasing smiles, while my brothers snickered and Lelwani frowned and my father pretended to ignore us. We'd retire early, pleading exhaustion from our work day, and cling damply to each other in the flickering light of the fertility lamp.

After a few months, though, things changed.

I was well aware that Ishara hadn't become pregnant yet, but I didn't realize others were so aware until I overheard a conversation between her mother and Lelwani through the curtain of a cloth stall at the market. I'd just finished selling four dozen balls of yarn to a local weaver, and I was on my way to return the cart I'd borrowed when I heard familiar voices.

"She still bleeds?" Ishara's mother asked.

"As regularly as the moon."

There was a discreet pause.

"And are they ...?"

"Oh yes." Lelwani's tone managed to be both approving and disapproving at the same time. "Some nights I have to stuff wool in my ears." Both women chuckled. I felt my face burn.

"The problem can't be on our side," Ishara's mother said. "Our women barely have to smell a man to conceive."

"Well it can hardly be on *our* side. That foreign tart was obviously as fertile as a whole brace of rabbits."

It must have galled Lelwani to say it, but I guess you take your pride where you can.

As Ishara and I lay curled together that night after yet another attempt, I told her what I'd heard. At first she didn't respond.

"Does it bother you that they're so concerned?" I asked.

She went still in my arms. "It bothers me that you aren't," she finally said.

That surprised me. "You think I'm not concerned?"

"Not that I've noticed."

It took a moment for that to sink in. This marriage thing was turning out to be complicated. But I'd learned a thing or two from watching my father.

"What would you like me to do?" I asked.

I took Ishara to a village wise woman, who prescribed a tea made from one herb and a compress made from another and charged me a whack of money for both. I littered our bedroom with every deity our village's religious marketplace had to offer. I learned all the fertility prayers and chants and prostrations I could find, and performed them every evening before we set to work. Which was exactly what it felt like. And yet every four weeks, there, in Ishara's undergarments, was the stain of our failure.

We were at a complete loss as to what to do next when the soldiers came.

The King's troops usually passed through our village, stopping just long enough to take provisions from the stores. This time something else was up. Helmeted archers on horseback were making the rounds of the pastures and farms, asking to see their young men.

"These are my sons," my father told them after he'd lined us up. "Ishtanu, Rundas and Telepinu."

"How old?"

"Sixteen, fourteen and thirteen."

While the men were conferring a nudge from behind made me stumble forward.

"Take this one," Lelwani said. "The others are too young."

Ishara had been watching from the main hut. When she saw the soldiers send my brothers away she came out and ran to me.

"Ishtanu, what's happening?"

"I don't really know. I think they might want me to be a soldier."

"A *soldier*?" From her expression they might have wanted me to be one of the stars in the sky. "But you *aren't* a soldier, you're a shepherd. And you're my husband. They can't make you be something you aren't." Her face was a heartrending mix of uncertainty and fear. "Can they?"

Lelwani put a hand on Ishara's shoulder. "They can. And they will."

Ishara looked back and forth between the two of us in confusion. "But ... but our child. We have to keep trying, Ishtanu. Tell them." She turned to Lelwani. "Tell them, Lelwani. They can't take him away now."

Lelwani took Ishara by both shoulders. "They don't care about that, Ishara." Her voice was unusually calm and soothing. "The army has its own concerns. Those don't include whether their soldiers are trying for a family or not."

I moved to take Ishara in my arms, but Lelwani was still holding her, so all I could do was stand next to her awkwardly. "Maybe it won't be for long. When I get back we'll keep trying."

Ishara didn't look convinced. But after a long, hard stare from Lelwani, she did manage to look resigned.

The archers escorted me and two other boys about my age into the village and dropped us at the end a long line-up in the marketplace. "Hey, Ishtanu," Halki called from a spot farther along. "Come join me." No one seemed to mind if I jumped the queue, so I moved up. "Exciting, isn't it?"

I shrugged. "I don't even know what it is."

"That's what you get for living in the sticks. The King is bulking up the army to stop the Egyptians from invading."

"Who are they?"

He shook his head at my ignorance. "Another great power. Not as great as us, obviously. They envy us, so they want to take our land."

"What, here?" I looked around anxiously, imagining Egyptians over the next rise.

"No, numb nuts. At the border. At the edge of our empire."

I hadn't realized we had an empire. Or that it had an edge.

"And where is that?"

"No idea. Pretty far away, though, I imagine."

"Then why should we go? What do these Egyptians have to do with us?"

"Keep your voice down, you idiot. We have to go because we're part of the King's Portion, aren't we?" I had nothing to say to that. It had never occurred to me that people could be part of the King's Portion. But now that Halki mentioned it, I didn't see why they couldn't. And one thing I did know was that you didn't shortchange the King.

Halki smiled broadly. "Besides, how else can a couple of hicks like you and me see the world, eh?"

I hadn't realized there was a world, either.

That was a long time ago.

At the front of the line was a long table with two men in clean tunics and polished helmets. Their hair hung in thick braids down their backs. One had a soft clay tablet and a sharpened reed, like we used for the accounts.

"Name?" said the first man.

"Halki."

"Age?"

"Sixteen."

"Are you healthy?"

"Body like a god," he said with a wink. "Ale and mutton every day."

The men weren't amused.

"Lift that," said the one doing the talking. On the table was a squared block of stone no bigger than a newborn lamb. With a small grunt Halki lifted it over his head and held it there. The man at the table started counting. When he got to fifteen he told Halki he could put it down.

"I can go longer."

The man sighed. "Kid, everyone can go longer. Just put it down." He pointed to a wooden crate. "Then pick out a tunic and go take a seat in the temple."

I was put through the same perfunctory test, with the same result and the same instructions. I sat on a bench next to Halki.

"This was the only tunic that looked like it would fit," I said. "But why is it so dark around the neck? The others weren't."

Halki smiled. "Its last owner probably had his throat cut." He wiggled his fingers through a slit in the back of his own tunic. "See? Mine has a spear hole."

By the time the trickle of recruits into the temple stopped there were maybe fifty of us, scattered nervously around the benches in twos and threes. The men from the table came in, with a dozen or more others who'd apparently been killing the time at Halki's father's tavern. The one who'd done the talking before took a position facing us.

"Up front," he said sharply.

Halki looked delighted. "Here we go."

We hustled into a tight group in front of him.

"Line up in tens."

Halki made sure he and I were in the front group. The man walked slowly in front of us. From his expression, we were quite the disappointment.

"Anittas," he said to the nearest other soldier. "Take these piglets away and clean them up." He took a deliberate look at the scruffiest of us: a boy with matted hair and pimples and another with cow dung on his tunic. "Well. Do what you can."

Anittas was a hard-faced man with a broad neck and a malformed ear. He wore the same thick military braid as the other soldiers, but his was shot with grey. He quick-marched us through the village gate to the stream, where he ordered us to strip down, scrub ourselves, and change into our new tunics. When we were done he issued each of us the rest of our kit: boots, a belt, a small satchel with a knife and striking stones for making a fire, a leather helmet and a short, flat sword with a curve at the end. Then he marched us to where a handful of tents had been pitched on the flat ground just outside the village wall.

"Two lines of five," he shouted. There was awkward jostling while we arranged ourselves.

"All right," he said, pacing back and forth. "You are now the newest and most useless part of the army of King Muwattali the Second. But don't go dreaming of glory on the battlefield, boys. That's not for the likes of you." He smiled wearily. "Nor me. The King's army needs all sorts." He raised his hand and held it at his shoulder, palm down. "Some ride in the chariots and slaughter the enemy." He lowered it to his hip. "Some guard the wagons and tend the livestock." He smiled archly. "Which of them do you suppose is you?"

No one answered.

He squared his shoulders and raised his voice. "You have trouble hearing me? Because I thought I asked you a question. Which of them. Do you suppose. Is *you*?"

"Wagon guarders?" ventured the lad with the matted hair.

"Yes!" Anittas stomped the ground for emphasis. "You lot are the *wagon* guarders. Does that sound very glorious to any of you?"

We all mumbled various versions of "no."

"No!" Another stomp. "No, it is bloody well *not* glorious. It is tiring and boring and very, very anonymous. No one will ever sing stirring songs around the campfire about your *glorious* wagon guarding or your *noble* cattle driving. This battle is not your story. Now why am I telling you this?"

The kid with the dung smear cleared his throat. Anittas raised an inquiring eyebrow. "To give us something to aspire to?" the kid said.

Anittas gave him a look of mock amazement. "To *aspire* to? Do you actually imagine there's a bug's chance in a bonfire that someone like you"—he looked the kid up and down—"will *ever* see the inside of a battle chariot?" The boy looked silently down at his feet. "Don't fool yourselves, lads. Conscripts aren't chariot material. So I ask again, why am I telling you this?"

No one spoke. No one knew.

I felt a stirring of awareness, like a mist rising to reveal an unseen road. For maybe the first time in my life I thought I understood something no one else did. It was a giddy, slightly dangerous feeling.

"To keep us in our place," I said.

Anittas turned toward me with a surprised little smile. "Good job, lad. Your pale-skinned little friend here has it exactly right, boys. To keep you in your place. Because that's where we *need* you. You see, what you have to understand is that an army is kind of like a big animal, you know?" He stuck his hands out, an arm's length or so apart, apparently to illustrate what an animal was. Or maybe what "big" was. "The legs need to be the legs, yeah? And the teeth need to be the teeth. What do you suppose happens if the legs try to be the teeth? Eh?"

I was having too much trouble picturing it to come up with an answer. Apparently so was everyone else. So we all stayed silent. Eventually Anittas answered his own question. "A mess, is what happens, let me tell you." He nodded his head. "A big mess."

Not as elegant an answer as I'd been expecting.

He wrapped up. "So. My point. No glory for you. The army *has* people for that. What it needs from you is sheep-herding and wagon guarding. So do that, right? You start doing other things?" He nodded gravely. "That's when people start dying."

It seemed to me that since we were going to war people were going to start dying anyhow, but that didn't feel like something I should bring up.

"Right." Anittas' suddenly relaxed stance said he was moving on. "Any questions so far?"

A muscular boy whose helmet was half-perched on his massive head spoke up from the end of my row. His voice was surprisingly thin.

"Will we be getting any training? In, like, how to fight, and stuff?"

Anittas stared at the boy. "Training? In fighting? Have you been listening at *all*?" He looked down at the ground and shook his head in contrived exasperation. Then he looked back up. "All right, here's some training. See that curved blade you've got stuck in your belt?"

The boy put his hand on his sword-hilt and nodded. "Uh-huh."

"Well," Anittas said. "If you see an Egyptian soldier coming after your sheep, hit him with it. The sharp bit, for preference. Good enough?" He shook his head at the ignorance of conscripts. "Right then. Any other questions?"

Halki had a mischievous smile. "Why are the toes of our boots curled up?" I cringed in anticipation of Anittas' withering answer. But he just nodded appreciatively.

"That's actually a pretty good question," he said. "You'll be glad of that curl on a long march, every time your boots don't catch on a rock or a root." His eyes moved on. "Next question?"

"But sir." Halki again. Uh-oh. I knew that look. He always had to push it. "How can you tell when your boots *don't* do something?" His smile was guileless. "I mean, is there some special way of noticing? Some soldier way?"

Anittas slowly turned back toward him. He'd been waiting for this moment. For the first, inevitable smart-ass to declare himself. He walked calmly to where Halki was standing, until they were almost touching. Then with astonishing swiftness he slapped Halki's face, hard. The sound echoed like a gunshot off the village wall. Halki's head spun sideways.

Yes, I know guns hadn't been invented yet. But I'm telling this now, aren't I?

Anittas' voice was low and deliberate. "The same way you can tell when I'm not smacking your soft little face. Do you think you'll have any trouble noticing *that*?"

Halki straightened and looked him in the eye. His cheek was bright from the blow. "No, sir," he said evenly. His expression said something very different.

If Anittas noticed, he didn't seem to care. "Good. Now come with me to your tent, all of you."

As we followed, Halki leaned toward me and spoke so that only I could hear. "Bugger wagon guarding. I'm finding my way into a battle chariot."

Hattusha, the capital, was unimaginably exotic and impossibly distant. No one I knew had ever been there. Sometimes traders would tell stories of towers as tall as ten men, or vast chambers carved into the rock, or water that came right to your hut through a long clay tube. Nonsense tales to dazzle the yokels. For the people of our village Hattusha might've been the moon.

Now we were going there.

The career soldiers and the local garrison spent most of the following day organizing the wagon train. That happened mainly in the King's Stores. We weren't part of it, but we were intensely aware of it: the shouts and bleats as carts were loaded and sheep were shorn, and the all-day, achingly delicious aromas of baking bread and smoking mutton.

We weren't part of it because, despite Anittas' earlier dismissal of the training question, we spent the day doing military drills. He walked us through formations for attack and defence, he taught us the basics of swordcraft—using sticks rather than our actual swords—and, late in the afternoon, as something to look forward to, he handed out genuine military bows and arrows for an hour or so of archery practice. The arrows were light and straight, with reed shafts and tapered bronze heads, and the bows were supple and strong.

Halki grinned as he seized his. "This is the coolest thing I've ever seen. The only bow I ever had was basically a stick with a string on it. My whole life I only managed to get two rabbits with it."

"Not so rough," Anittas said. "It's a delicate instrument. Handle it like you'd handle a woman." He looked at Halki and snorted. "If your imagination will extend that far." He held his own bow up to demonstrate. "Your grip should be light." He waggled the fingers of his bow hand and then curved them in with exaggerated gentleness. "Keep it light and she'll respond like she's part of you." He tightened his grip, and the bow visibly shook from the tension in his arm and hand. "Too firm and she'll fight you. You don't want that, believe me." He notched an arrow and took aim at a stack of hay bales against the village wall, fifty paces away. Someone had sketched the rough outline of a man on it, with a tall headdress that was presumably meant to look Egyptian. "Breathe out gently as you release." The arrow left his bow, arced swiftly toward the bales, and stuck in the Egyptian's thigh.

We all whooped at the shot, but Anittas just shook his head. "Don't get too excited, lads. Time was I would've hit the rotten bugger's eye six shots out of seven, and no worse than his neck on the seventh." He sighed and handed the bow to the next boy. "See how you manage with her."

That was the end of our instruction. We goofed around with the bows until the light started to fade—most of us hitting the bales most of the time, but few of us managing any real damage to our cartoon enemy—while Anittas sat next to our tent and worked his way through a pot of ale.

At dawn on the day we left, a dozen ox-drawn baggage carts—simple, two-wheeled platforms with fence-like frames of rough posts—emerged from the King's Stores loaded with sacks of grain and baskets of smoked meats and heavy soldier-bread. They were followed by fifty sheep, two dozen cattle, and fifteen newly-broken horses.

The carts were the vanguard. We conscripts followed, in long lines on either side of the parade of livestock, with two soldiers on horseback at the end. The rest of the career soldiers rode the new horses in turns, patrolling the length of the train and scouting ahead and on either side.

It took us two days at a slow march to get to Hattusha, across low hills of green pasture and brown scrub land. When it first came into sight I thought it was an unusually regular rock formation. No wall could be so long, or so high. But it was. And the nearer we got, the more preposterous it became.

"There aren't enough people in the world to fill a compound that big," I said to Halki as we gazed toward it from a rise a mile or more away.

"And how would *you* know how many people there are in the world?"

"Well. Um. There just can't be. I mean *look* at it. It's bigger than ... than ... damn it, Halki, it's so big I don't have anything to *compare* it to."

Anittas was next to us on one of the new horses. "It's so big you couldn't walk all the way around it in a day." He winked. "I know, because I tried it once. I had to beg a ride back to my encampment on a timber merchant's cart."

I must have gaped, because Halki shook his head at me and chuckled. "He's winding you up, Ishtanu. Sure, it's big. But I bet I could walk around it in an afternoon."

We ended up getting plenty of chances to find out.

We were camped outside Hattusha for more than a month, while chariots and troops from our Great King's northern allies joined us and set up their own camps on the increasingly crowded plain surrounding the city. The King himself wasn't there. He'd already moved his base south to Tarhuntasha.

We had basic duties—tending the livestock, repeating our military drills, even disassembling war chariots and stacking their parts onto wagons for transport, which Halki particularly seemed to enjoy—but there was always more time on hand than work to fill it with. And for teenage boys that means boredom. So we filled the balance of our days with what mischief we could find, which meant wandering through the lower city visiting the taverns or bartering with the stall-keepers or flirting with the girls. There were whole streets of temples, where, in a riot of languages and pictures and smells, people in strange outfits were roasting things and burning things and chanting things. Basic international relations, I now realize. All vassal states got spots in the capital for their temples.

By week four I started taking an interest in the horses.

A stretch of plain had been set aside for chariot training. Scheduling must've been a bugger, with hundreds of new charioteers arriving daily from all directions. Not that I got near them. They were the elite. The fighter pilots. But I managed to hang out at one of the stables for a while. I just turned up and started to help. Tentatively at first. Stroking a horse's mane. Carrying a sack of feed from a cart. Then, once it seemed the stable master didn't mind, with more confidence.

"You've worked with horses, have you?"

I shook my head. "Not really. Sheep, though."

The stable master wrinkled his nose. "Nothing like." But he let me help walk them down to the stream that afternoon. And the next day. A few days later when a couple of them got skittish at the sight of a bull being butchered on the other side of the stream, he showed me how to calm them.

"Here, you wave your hands like so, and do this whistle." Just two descending notes, but together with the hand gesture it brought the horses back in line.

"Wow. That's magic!"

"No, lad. That's just trainin'. Chariot horses got to learn to follow orders, just like any other soldier."

I practised the wave and the whistle, and on the following day when one of the stallions tried to scamper toward a passing mare he let me try. It didn't work at first.

"A little higher on the bottom note," he said, and when I tried again the stallion actually steadied. "There you go." He smiled. "You've got a knack."

I was delighted. "I felt like a sorcerer," I told Halki later.

He wasn't impressed. "More like a horse-erer," he said.

All right, I made that part up. It wouldn't have worked in our language.

But I'd learned something useful. Something powerful.

And in a way I'd also had what amounted to my first music lesson.

That was my last afternoon with the horses. We were about to leave for the battle. By that point you could scarcely see the ground. Encampments with tents and tunics of various colours filled every field and valley as far as I could see. There was barely space for the chariot drills.

The afternoon and evening before our departure were spent offering sacrifices to various gods. We each got a portion of roast mutton and two cups of wine. In the morning, when the command came to depart, it took hours before our group began to move. We had to wait our turn, and there were thousands ahead of us. It was slow going, and it got slower once we moved from the plateau into the long valleys and winding passes of the mountains.

"Nice braid," Halki said, marching behind me. His hair had been longer than mine to start with, so his braid was in reasonable shape. Mine didn't reach my tunic yet.

"It'll get there."

The distance we covered in a day was determined by the horses. Men might collapse and be dragged to their feet to keep marching, but the horses were indulged. They got the best drinking spots at each stream and the choicest grain for their feed, and their grooms rubbed them down each evening to sooth their tired muscles. On the road we sang marching songs about loose women and cowardly enemies, and in the evenings we played a board game with multi-sided dice and black and white markers on a grid. My feet were raw by the end of the day, though they always healed by morning. Within a few days they were hard and resilient, and my leg muscles were lean and taut. Every few days we stopped at a village like our own to replenish our supplies from the King's Stores.

Two weeks in there was a commotion down the line. Anittas went to check in with his commander. When he came back he looked sombre.

"What's up?" asked Halki.

"Deserter."

"Really? Now?" I'd figured if anyone would run it'd be on the eve of battle.

Anittas shrugged. "His friends say he kept talking about how he missed his family." Which I understood. I missed my father and Ishara.

"Is that why he did it? Did they ask him?"

Anittas raised an eyebrow at me.

"What?"

"No one cares why, son," he said. "The sentries called out twice, and when he didn't stop, they put an arrow in his back."

About a month into our march we arrived at Tarhuntasha, where the Great King and his southern allies joined us. Ten days later we emerged onto a broad coastal plain and made camp near a sea port. Ten days after that we reached our main interim destination, the Kingdom of Ugarit. Apart from Hattusha itself, I'd never seen anything as impressive as Ugarit. It was nearly as big, and every bit as crowded. And it had ships.

I'd only ever seen small river-going boats. The ships were impossibly huge. Too big to float on water, I was sure. But they did. It was like they were powered by sorcery, or by the gods themselves. They were coming and going, loading and unloading the entire time we were there. Crates and bundles and bales, in and out and around, *en route* to and from places I couldn't even imagine.

"Is that the palace?" I pointed to a grand structure on the city's highest point.

Anittas shook his head. "Nope. Temple of Baal." I must have looked puzzled. "Local god," he added. "Big noise in these parts, they say."

I'd seen temples to a gazillion gods in Hattusha, and yet here was an apparently important one I'd never heard of. New gods and sea-going boats. The world was bigger than I'd imagined.

"No wonder Egypt wants our land," Halki said. "They can't possibly have anything this cool."

On our last day of marching we entered a flat scrub plain. Nothing to see for miles except smelly men and endless horizon. By mid-day the boredom had reached a whole new level. Then a murmur spread. Someone had seen something. No one was sure what. That's not how murmurs work. But the possibility of anything other than flat horizon was enough to create a relieving sense of interest.

An hour or so later we could just make it out: a flat bump on the edge of vision.

"Qadesh," Anittas said.

"Doesn't look like much," Halki said.

Anittas gave him his *you know it all, don't you?* look. "Long way off yet."

Gradually it took shape. A broad bluff, rising above the flat plain like a ship on the sea. Yes, I know how tired a metaphor that is now, but try to imagine how fresh it was to me, just out of Ugarit. Dominating the bluff were the city walls of Qadesh.

"You could see for *miles* from there," Halki said.

I nodded. "We'll be able to spot the Egyptians a whole day before they arrive."

Anittas shook his head. "We're not going in."

Halki looked shocked. "Why not? It's our city. It's the best view."

"It's our city today. Maybe not tomorrow." Anittas' mouth was grim. "The King of Qadesh has to allow for both possibilities."

"He's not helping us?"

"He'd be a fool to. If he does, and Egypt wins, his city gets sacked. This way he has an even chance."

"Then why are we even here defending him?"

Anittas sighed. "We aren't defending *him*, you idiot. We're maintaining the authority of the Great King against Egyptian aggression." He said this last bit with the flat tone of a functionary repeating his talking points. Then he smiled at us indulgently. "Qadesh isn't a player here, boys. It's the game board."

We picked up a brush-lined river on our right and followed it upstream to a lake. We paused to drink and water the horses, then pressed on. When we'd rounded the lake, the troops ahead of us stopped in the angle between the lake and the river that fed it, with the city ahead and to the right.

"Why are we stopping here?" Halki asked.

"Nowhere better," Anittas said. "Flat land. Water for men and horses."

"But we can't see anything." He pointed toward the bluff. "Isn't that the direction the Egyptians will come from?"

"Yes."

"How will we see them?"

"Wrong question."

"How is that the wrong question? Don't we need to see them to fight them?"

"First, my lad, let me remind you that you aren't fighting anyone. You're guarding the camp and the wagons. If we get to the point where we need you to join in, we've already lost. And second, what's more important than seeing the Egyptians?"

Halki looked blank. But I knew what Anittas meant. "Not letting them see us."

"Bang on. They come up from the south, the city is in the way." He pointed to the right. "They come around it from the west, they can't see us for the vegetation along the riverbank."

"Then how do we join battle with them?"

"The Kings'll work it out. Decide on a place to line up and then have at it."

"Then what's the point of not being seen?"

"Rest, my boy. Food and rest." Halki still looked puzzled. "Look," Anittas said. "The Egyptians turn up, today, say, or tomorrow, at the end of a long march. They're tired. Their horses are tired. They look around. No sign of us. 'Good job,' thinks their Great King. 'We'll catch our breath and then start drawing up the battle lines.' But then *our* Great King trots us out from behind the city, rested and fed and ready to go. Mister Egypt can't put it off, can he? Bit embarrassing. So just when his men think they're getting a nice rest at the end of a long day's marching, they have to line up and fight." He smiled and tapped his head. "The surprise messes with their heads."

"All right," Halki said, shrugging off his kit. "So we rest and get fed now. Cool."

Anittas' smile broadened. "Not you. Its the charioteers and infantry getting fed and rested. There's still a perimeter to build and tents to pitch and chariots to assemble. None of that's going to do itself, is it?"

The surprise messed with Halki's head.

"Trench digging," he grumbled as we dug. I stomped my wooden shovel into the bottom of the ditch and levered out a damp clod while he stood and ranted. "I never signed up for trench digging."

I plopped the clod onto the growing rampart along the outer edge of the trench. "You never signed up at all. You were conscripted, like the rest of us. Conscripts get scut work."

"And I will get the whip, if I have to," Anittas said from his spot two men over. He could've gotten away with standing and supervising, but he'd picked up a shovel and pitched in. I admired him for that.

"Couldn't we at least have done the chariots? We've been guarding their parts since we left Hattusha. I know them better than the men who designed them by now."

"That's skilled labour. You'd have the horses in the back if we left it to you." Anittas waggled his shovel. "But even you can't get one of these wrong way 'round."

By nightfall the tents were pitched and the chariots assembled, and there was a defensible rampart around the encampment. My shoulders ached and I had blisters on my hands, but there was a feeling of accomplishment after weeks of one-foot-in-front-of-the-other. Not all of us were feeling it, though.

"Dig the trenches," Halki muttered. "Watch the wagons." He glared toward Anittas, a hundred paces or so away, in conversation with his commander. "Don't get smart or I'll smack your face." Not even our extra rations of beer and salt beef had cheered him up.

"He hasn't smacked your face since that day outside the village wall."

"There's a huge battle coming, and we're being left out. I can watch wagons back home."

Anittas came and sat with us. "It's confirmed. No fires. Not likely they'd attack by night, but we're playing it safe."

"So what happens next?"

"We get what sleep we can and see where we are in the morning. Which for us is here watching the wagons. But them there—" he gestured toward the Great King's tent and the hundreds of chariots next to it "—will have some figuring out to do." He bit off a chunk of beef and chewed it slowly.

I watched him. "You seem to know a lot about ... about strategy and stuff," I said. "Chariots. The planning they'll be doing."

He swallowed and nodded, staring into the night. "That I do."

"But. Um." I wasn't sure how to ask what I wanted to ask.

"But what?" He turned. "Something's giving you an itch. Scratch it."

"Well. It's like. I mean, how do you know? If you're, well ..." I gestured around feebly. I was getting this badly wrong.

Anittas just smiled. "Wasn't always a wagon watcher, was I?" His voice was soft, and a little sad. He nodded his head toward the masses of chariots. "Used to be one of them."

That got Halki's attention. "A charioteer? You?"

Anittas nodded. "Not a bowman, mind. Held the shield to protect the bowman and the driver. But I was good at it." He took a long draw on his ration of beer. "Better than some who are still at it, I expect."

"Then why aren't you still doing it?" I was too young to recognize that it was possible to ask one question too many. But Anittas didn't seem to mind.

"I got old, son." He tipped his beer, took a swallow, and stared into the night.

I woke to the stirring of horses. Not close, but a lot of them, and by the sound of it all getting into harness. I rolled into a sitting position and rubbed my eyes.

"Morning Ishtanu," Anittas said. He was coming back from the officers' tents, his bow and quiver slung over his shoulder. "Give the rest of 'em a kick. Briefing in five minutes."

I shook the others awake and then took my razor down to the river. By the time I got back to the tent they were gathered around Anittas.

"Right, lads. Probably not much will happen today. Our chariot-eers will do a little wander to see what's what. The Great King and his little buddy kings will go there—" he pointed upriver to the base of the bluff "—with their personal troops to set up an observation post. For now the infantry and our allies' chariots are staying here. And us, of course." He glared pointedly at Halki. "So hit the mess tent for some porridge, then come back and feed the oxen."

As we got our breakfast we could see ranks of chariots forming up for the reconnaissance run around the city. "That should be us," Halki said sourly.

"In what world should that be us? A pair of untrained nobodies from a village no one ever heard of."

"In the world I want to live in."

We took our porridge to our tent and ate in silence, watching the progress of the troops upstream. The river forked around the bluff, with its main branch on the near side. Beyond the bluff our chariots were pushing through the brush on the near bank to what was presum-ably a ford. Nearer to us the kings and their retinues—including a modest few dozen charioteers—had started down the riverbank to their observation post. When we'd eaten, Halki, Anittas and I went to the river to wash our bowls. I was drying mine on the edge of my tunic when Halki perked up.

"What was that?"

"I didn't hear anything."

"No, listen." I did. And I heard it.

"Trumpets?"

Anittas nodded. "War trumpets. Egyptian, probably."

"But the Great King is still just over there. How could he have worked out the battle plan yet?"

"Buggered if I know. But then that's not our business, is it? Our business is to get back to those wagons and keep an eye."

We were half way back when we heard a commotion in the distance, on the other side of the bluff.

"That sounds like a battle," Halki said.

Anittas furrowed his brow. "Shouldn't be. Skirmish with our chariots, maybe. Can't be a battle. We haven't even lined up our infantry yet."

Halki stared at the ground. He seemed to be making a decision. "I'm going to check it out," he said. He handed me his bowl.

"The hell you are," Anittas said. "You're coming back to the wagons."

Halki turned on him. "I didn't come all this way to babysit wagons." He pointed in the direction of the bluff. "There's a battle going on over there. You're a soldier. Don't you want to be part of it?"

"Not my place anymore, son. Nor yours. Come back to the wagons."

Halki turned and trotted off down the riverbank.

Anittas' face went tight. "You're deserting your post!"

Halki didn't reply.

Anittas unslung his bow. "You know what happens to deserters, boy. Don't make me do this."

I was frozen in my spot. What was happening? We were rinsing our bowls, and now suddenly Anittas was levelling an arrow at Halki's back. "Last chance," he shouted.

I put my hand on his arm. "No, please. Let me get him. He'll listen to me."

"I don't have a choice. It's discipline. You desert your post, you die."

"But he isn't deserting. Not really." I was pleading. "He's just ... trying to gather some information."

"Not his job."

"You're right. Not his job. But not worth killing him for. Right?" Anittas' eyes softened. He didn't want to take the shot. Maybe I had a way for him not to. "Just order me to go after him. That way I can get him without deserting *my* post. Please. I'll get him back. Please."

Anittas shook me off. But he sighed and lowered his bow.

"Off you go. But bring him straight back."

I took off at a sprint.

The kings' observation post was in the angle where the river forked around the bluff. A hundred paces this side of it Halki disappeared into the brush. When I got to the same spot I went in after him. He'd found an animal trail. I couldn't see more than a few paces in any direction. The cries beyond the bluff were louder now, but I could only hear them occasionally over the rustle of leaves and the rumble of the river. I followed the trail. When I spotted a flash of white to my left, I picked up my pace.

Halki was crouched by the riverbank. He didn't notice me until I got within ten paces and whispered his name. He didn't hear me the first time—the last thing I wanted to do was surprise him into a shout—but the second time he did. He smiled and waved me over. He spoke so softly I could hardly hear him. At least he was being cautious.

"The Great King just sent two men across. I was about to go myself."

"Don't be an idiot. Come back to the tent. If the Great King's men spot us we'll be tortured as spies."

"We're in uniform." He flipped his hair with his hand. "We have braids. They'll think we're enterprising."

"You think Egyptian spies couldn't grow braids?"

"You worry too much. I'm going across." He waded into the water.

"Get back here," I whispered as harshly as I could. "You'll be killed as a deserter."

He grinned at me. "Not after I triumph in battle." He slogged through the current with surprising speed, and disappeared into the brush on the other side.

I should've let him go. Things might've worked out better. But he was my friend. All we had to do was go back to our wagons and wait it out, and then we could go home and get back to our lives. They were good lives. I could make him see that. I hadn't learned yet that there are things you can fix and things you can't.

"Damn you," I muttered as I followed him into the river.

I caught up to him at the far edge of the brush on the other side, his eyes glittering, his voice quiet. "Look." He pointed across the scrub land.

I looked. "What?" Just open land and blowing dust.

"Wait for the dust to clear."

The wind dropped, and I glimpsed something. A smudge on the far side of the plain. "What is it?"

Halki sounded almost feverish with excitement. "I think it's the Egyptian camp."

I felt a chill. "You're not thinking of trying to surprise them, are you?"

He gave me a dismissive scowl. "I'm not a fool. Their archers would have me before I got within two hundred paces." He stared across the plain. "I'm just going to have to wait for my opportunity."

I grabbed his arm. "No. There won't be one. You're coming back to the tent, and then back home." My voice was trembling. "You're marrying a plump girl from another village and taking over your father's tavern one day, and our sons are breaking their arms climbing the village wall together."

Halki placed his hand gently on mine and looked into my eyes. "That's not my life. Yours, maybe." He looked back toward the Egyptian camp. "This is mine. I'm going to *make* it mine."

I should have gone back. But I decided to wait with him. I'm not sure why. Maybe I was hoping I'd be the one whose opportunity would come. The opportunity to get Halki back to camp.

It didn't.

The sun was high when I felt him tense. "Something's happening." I followed his gaze. Through wisps of blown dust we could see movement at the near edge of the camp. Sunlight on metal. The rumble of hooves and wheels.

"Chariots." Halki's tone was reverent. Dozens of them, maybe hundreds, pouring from the Egyptian camp and wheeling southward, around the bluff toward the battle. "They're leaving their camp defenceless!"

"No they aren't. They haven't sent out any infantry. There are probably still thousands of bowmen in there."

His shoulders sagged. "Fine. That wasn't my opportunity. But it's coming."

I didn't respond. All I could do was wait him out. Maybe once the battle had run its course without presenting his make-believe opportunity I could get him back to camp and persuade Anittas to let him off.

Then we heard a commotion to our left, on the far bank. By the time we'd scampered back down to the water for a look, the kings' chariots were half way across.

Halki grinned. "Now we're getting somewhere." We ran back to our spot and crouched there, marvelling. "That's the Great King himself. In his own chariot!"

So it was. And the king of Ishuwa. And the king of Mitanni. Not that I knew who they all were at the time. Each king had his own escort of chariots—magnificent two-wheeled platforms with three men each—all charging the Egyptian camp at full gallop, their bronze scale-armour shimmering like water. There weren't many of them. Just each king's own personal guard. Behind them, clambering from the riverbank and forming into ranks, came the infantry. Again, not many. The kings' personal troops.

"They're crazy," I said. "There aren't enough of them to take on that whole encampment."

"They're glorious," Halki said.

I now know their strategy was just to draw the Egyptian chariots back to defend their camp. At the time, though, it just seemed foolhardy.

But not as foolhardy as Halki. He sprang from the brush and ran toward the forming ranks of infantry.

"Come back! You don't know what you're doing."

"Yes I do!"

I scanned the plain, trying to spot the dangers he was rushing into. Like there was anything I could do. It looked comparatively safe. Scrub plain. Camp well in the distance. Maybe he'd blend in with the infantry until I could somehow get him back.

Then my gut went cold.

To the right, to the north of the Egyptian camp, was a column of dust. Sunlight glinting. Distant hoofbeats. Chariots. A lot of chariots. And from that direction they couldn't be ours. I screamed Halki's name. But by then he was too far away.

It was a rout. The Egyptian reinforcements charged into the plain with such force that the Great King and his allies quickly turned back, but it was too late. The lighter two-man Egyptian chariots spread out to fill the field and advanced with breathtaking speed, their arrows dropping into our ranks with stomach-turning thuds. Horses went down screaming. Men spun and dropped from their platforms, hands clutching their chests or their faces, and were trampled by their own comrades. Our chariots retreated to the river with the Egyptians in tight pursuit. In the middle distance I could make out Halki—the only unhelmeted head among our troops—still advancing. I screamed at him, but my voice vanished into the chaos. Out of the confusion a panicked team of horses ran toward me, their empty chariot bouncing wildly across the uneven field.

I ran toward them from the brush, waving my hand and whistling the two note command I'd learned from the stable master. It took a moment to get their attention, but soon they'd settled enough for me to gather their reins and mount the platform. I had no idea what to do next. I yanked the reins, and managed to get them facing back toward the melee. Apparently that was enough. They were a well-trained war team. With a driver in the back and a battle before them they knew what to do even if I didn't. Before I could consider how stupid this was, they were off.

I aimed them at Halki as best I could. I screamed his name as I bounced along, clutching the edge of the cab with my free hand. There's something about your own name that cuts through surrounding noise. His eyes went wide when he saw me. "Where'd you get that?" he shouted as I approached. He had a spear now.

"Get on."

"Damn right!"

I managed to rein in the horses enough for Halki to swing aboard. "Yes!" he shouted. "*So* much better than walking. Let's go." He waved his spear toward the Egyptian camp.

"That's not where we're going," I said, reining the team around. "The kings' charioteers are going back. So are we."

"But this is my chance!"

"No. This is *my* chance."

His voice was almost a shriek. "We're not going back!" He grabbed the reins. I tried to pull them away. The horses balked. The chariot tilted. I lost my balance. Halki shoved me with his elbow and snatched the reins.

I fell backward from the platform. As I hit the ground I saw him pull away into the battle, his head lifted in a war-crazed whoop of joy. "Whoo-ooo!" he hollered, waving his spear.

The Egyptian arrow took him just under the jaw.

"Halki!"

He landed twenty paces from me, the bloodied arrow sticking out of the back of his head. I scrambled toward him, but an Egyptian chariot cut between us. I rolled away sharply. A spear scuffed the dirt inches from my shoulder. A wheel grazed my hip. The Egyptians were coming thicker and faster. I saw own troops frantically making for the river. I took a last look at my dead friend and ran as fast as I could to join them.

The Egyptians were faster. They had chariots.

I was a half-dozen strides from the brush when a powerful blow to the middle of my back drove me to my knees. Hooves clattered by my head as the Egyptian yanked out the spear. It happened so fast I didn't even scream. I rolled over and watched the charioteers drive away. They didn't look at me. Things to do.

I got to my feet and stumbled toward the brush. My tunic felt warm and wet against the backs of my legs. The ground lurched and spun. My shoulder smacked a tree. I half fell into the bushes. Branches scraped my legs and my face as I pressed on toward the water, no longer a thinking human being, just a blundering animal desperate not to die. When I broke through I collapsed into the cool water and rolled over, face toward the sky. The current carried me northward, away from the battle.

Away from everything.

I don't heal instantly. My life isn't a Marvel comic. It takes time. Not as much as for you, but time. Cut me now and I'd bleed. Just not a lot, and not for long. By morning I'd have a light scar. A week later, no sign at all. That's for a basic cut. The more serious the injury, the longer it takes.

An Egyptian spear to the back is a serious injury.

When I washed up in the mud near the mouth of the river I expected to die there. The pain of my injury ran right through me. Like the spear head had. When the Egyptian pulled it out, it was bloody down to its base. That's a deep wound.

My childhood broken arm had healed pretty fast, as had a lifetime of other minor scrapes. But I knew this was different. The Egyptian had just driven away. He didn't linger to finish the job. He knew he'd delivered a killing blow.

So I lay there in the mud and waited to die.

The sun worked its way across the sky. It baked my face. Dried the parts of me that weren't in the water. I didn't move. I couldn't. Plus there was no point. The sun was nearing the treetops. I'd be in shade soon. Unless I died first. Then I'd be in a different kind of shade. I laughed. It hurt. Time passed.

We see what's in front of us. In front of me was the sun. Arinna, the sun goddess, baking my dying face. *Hi Arinna*, I thought. It made me feel less alone. Arinna would guide me to the next life.

Arinna's husband was Tarhun, the storm god. Tarhun brought rain. Rain sounded good. *Hi Tarhun*, I thought. *A little rain would be nice just now. Just until I make it to the next life.* No clouds came. No rain. Just sun. Arinna. Tarhun's wife.

Minds drift. Mine drifted to my own wife. Ishara had no idea where I was. That I wasn't coming back. The pain of that knowledge was almost as sharp as my wound's. I asked Arinna to keep an eye on Ishara for me.

I dozed. Night came. I dozed some more. The moon was out, so I talked to the moon gods. *Ease my passage to the next life,* I asked. *Take care of Ishara.* I had nothing else to do. And there were plenty of gods to talk to. I avoided the war gods. They couldn't be trusted. Halki had—

I winced.

He came to me as I slept. His eyes were shadows. He didn't speak. He seemed lost. I woke with a chill. It took me a while to sleep again.

Morning came. Minds drift. Mine drifted to the ships at Ugarit. The high temple of Baal. I talked to Baal. *Ease my passage.* Maybe there was something he could do. After all, he was local. *Take care of Ishara. Look after Halki.*

The sun rose higher.

Hi Arinna.

It wasn't until the evening of the second day that it occurred to me I might not die. My mind seemed clearer. I could roll over enough to drink from the river. It still hurt, but not like my liver was being ripped out.

I started talking to the healing gods.

By the morning of the third day I was hungry. I was sitting up by then. I'd done an inventory. I had my sword and my shoulder bag with my striking stones for making fire. I tried to make one, but the twigs and grasses I could reach were too damp.

I discovered I could stand. Walking was a struggle, but I had to find something to eat. I made a crude staff from a sapling and started back toward camp. If there still was a camp.

I listened for the sounds of combat. I hadn't heard anything since I'd washed up in the mud. I didn't know if the battle was still going on, or, if it was over, who had won. But I had to go somewhere. And if the camp was still there, they'd have food. Plus I owed it to Halki.

I followed the bank of the river toward the bluff. Still no battle sounds. Just birdsong and the murmur of the river.

I reached what was left of the camp at midday. The ramparts were intact, but apart from odds and ends—a collapsed tent, a cart with a broken axle—it was empty. No dead. No blood. No breaches. All the signs of a peaceful departure.

We must have won. Won and gone home.

Without me.

The cart was all but empty—no baskets or barrels or sacks of grain—but in one corner I found a smashed loaf of bread only partially picked away by birds. I brushed it off and ate it.

I followed the river to the Great King's observation post. It had been completely cleared. I followed the chariot tracks to the river and looked through the flattened brush to the plain beyond. It looked empty. It gave me a chill. I wanted to run. But I couldn't.

Steadying myself against the current with my staff, I waded across. On the far bank a shoulder bag had been crushed into the dirt. I pulled it loose. In a cloth bundle were a strip of smoked mutton and a half loaf of soldier bread. I took a bite of the mutton and put the rest into my own bag.

The field was scarred with chariot tracks and littered with arrows and stained with blood. There were no bodies, but it was obvious where they'd gone. I followed the smell. The north edge of the battlefield was lined with fresh ash pits and the remnants of makeshift pyres. Stray wisps of smoke drifted across the plain and up to the sky. "Safe passage, my friend," I said softly. I eased myself to the empty ground with my staff and began to cry.

I made my way to the Egyptian camp. Again, signs of peaceful with-drawal. Which made no sense. Somebody must've won. But who? And why hadn't they sacked the other side's camp? I was baffled. Baffled and unsure what to do.

I couldn't go to the city. If the Egyptians had won, Qadesh wouldn't look kindly on a Hittite soldier at its gate. But where else was there to go?

There was only one answer. I didn't much care for it.

Home.

Alone.

I retraced the route we'd taken from Ugarit. I ate the mutton and some of the bread, and drank as much water as I could hold. By the time I'd put the lake behind me I was feeling strong enough to toss my staff aside. My back was stiff, but there was hardly any pain. I continued along the rough road north, my curl-toed boots slipping lightly over the roots and rocks. I felt them. Every single time.

By dark I couldn't see any signs of settlement, so I took shelter at the base of a small rise and built a fire. I ate the last of my bread and drank water from a stream at the bottom of a nearby gully, then curled up next to my fire to sleep. I was just dozing off when the bandits came.

I jerked into alertness at the sound of something over the top of the rise. A scuff, a rattle of pebbles. I sat up and reached for my sword.

Too late.

They dropped from the rise. Fierce eyes in the firelight. A club swinging toward my face. Then nothing.

I woke up naked at dawn, at the bottom of the gully, with my right shoulder and arm in the stream. There was a sharp pain in my head. My breathing was ragged. When I blinked to clear my eyes I felt some-thing crusty on one of the lids.

I rolled toward the stream. It hurt, but no bones were broken.

I checked my reflection in the water. My scalp was split, the left side of my face caked with dried blood. I touched my lips to the water and took a sip. My stomach seized. I waited a bit, then took another. Better. I dunked my face. The cold against the wound sent a shock down into my shoulders. I drew myself to my knees, scooped some water and scrubbed my face. The stream ran pink. I waited until it cleared. Took another sip. Scrubbed some more.

The wound was tender, but not bleeding. I looked around. Stream. Gully. The rise where I'd lit my fire, flagging my location for anyone within an hour's walk. I stood. Wobbly, but steady enough. I climbed out of the gully to the dead remains of my fire. Footprints. Lots of them. Nothing else. No bag, no boots, no sword. No tunic.

I sat against the rise and sighed. Hell of a few days.

The first signs of human life turned up mid-morning. A murmur of voices on the wind, there and gone, somewhere to the north. I might've imagined it. But a few minutes later I heard it again. And what might have been hooves. The creak of a wagon.

They came around the rise a few minutes later. Eight armed guards, flanking a four-wheeled cart enclosed with thick timber. Not soldiers. Plain clothes. Scraps of leather or bronze for armour. A mismatched assortment of axes and swords. Plus they didn't have the discipline of soldiers. They were chatting and laughing. The cart's driver, a dozy man in a dark tunic, wasn't joining in.

The lead guard was the first to notice me. Not that I was a threat. There just wasn't much else to notice. He called out, and his comrades snapped into formation, weapons at the ready. "Hands where we can see them," the driver said.

I lifted them slowly. It was all I had the energy for.

The driver looked around. "Anyone else with you?"

I shook my head. "This is it."

"Check," the driver said. The lead guard did. "No one," he said. The driver nodded, and the other guards relaxed.

The driver looked me over. "Bandits, I suppose?"

I nodded.

"You were alone?"

I nodded again.

"You're very confident or very foolish. Headed where?"

"Hattusha."

"By yourself? On foot?"

"No other choice."

"There's always another choice."

"Didn't see it that way."

"Seeing it differently now?"

I didn't feel the need to answer.

He gestured at my wrecked camp. "You made a fire?"

"Keeps the animals away."

"Not the human ones. But you know that now." He turned to the lead guard. "Get him a tunic out of my bag. Not one of the good ones. The one I wear in the smithy." The guard stuck his hand into a sack on the side of the wagon and pulled out something faded and frayed and speckled with burn holes. He tossed it to me. I put it on. It was coarse and baggy. But I wasn't naked.

"Thanks. You know I don't have anything to pay you with, right?"

"Oh, I'm not letting you keep it. And yes, you do."

His name was Yassib. He was a merchant and a metalworker, and he offered me a deal. He'd take me to his warehouse in Qadesh, where I'd work for him doing whatever needed doing until his next trip to Ugarit, and then he and his guards would let me travel there with them. It sounded promising. But there were a few loose ends that need-ed clearing up.

"Who won?"

"Excuse me?"

"The battle."

"Battle?"

"A few days ago. At Qadesh."

"Ah. That explains the army." He shrugged. "Don't know. Wasn't there."

"Army?"

"We had to detour around a big army, day before yesterday. Seemed in good shape. Orderly. Not hurrying. Maybe they won."

"Did they have hair like this?" I lifted my braid and let it flop back down.

Yassib looked at his lead guard, who nodded. He looked back at me. "You part of that army?"

"I was."

"You a deserter? Not wise to help deserters."

"They left without me." Yassib looked skeptical. "I was hurt."

"Seems to happen to you a lot. If you're trying to catch up, you're two or three days behind them. On your own I don't care for your chances. You're safer taking my offer."

"You're probably right. But if Egypt won the battle, then—" I lifted my braid again "—I may not be so safe in Qadesh either."

He tilted his head to one side and squinted. "You really *need* the braid?"

I looked myself up and down. Plain tunic. No boots. Without the braid I could be anybody. And I was travelling with a local. "Fair enough." I reached behind my head and started undoing my hair. I'd borrow a knife and cut it shorter along the way. "There's just one more thing."

"What's that?"

"How long until your trip back to Ugarit?"

"Six weeks, give or take."

"Six *weeks*?"

"Or you can give me my tunic back, and we part friends."

So I went to Qadesh.

Yassib got my answer about the battle from the guards at the gate. "Things look pretty calm here," he said casually. "You'd hardly know there was a battle."

The chief guard shrugged. "Didn't affect us." He pointed to the southwest, past the smaller of the forked rivers. "They bashed about a bit down there." He swung his arm north, toward the empty Egyptian camp. "And then over there. Next morning the two Great Kings were chatting away up here in our man's palace, and then off they all marched."

"That's the way with Great Kings, isn't it?" Yassib said, smiling wryly. "Make a big fuss over who's in charge, get some good men killed, and then wander off home."

Yassib only kept four guards on strength while he was in town, including the two who guarded the warehouse. The rest were part-timers he brought in to travel with his shipments. The full-timers were responsible for carting and stacking and securing the inventory—mainly ingots of bronze or copper or lead—and I was responsible for whatever else needed doing. Mucking out the stalls. Washing tunics and blankets down at the river. Bringing back water in heavy wooden buckets to fill the cistern. Every few days I went to Yassib's forge to clean out the ashes and stack the firewood, which the guards brought in by cart and dumped near the door.

"I like having a servant," Danel, the youngest of them, said one evening as he took his plate. Until my arrival the grunt work had probably fallen to him.

I got my meals, barn-straw to sleep on, two worn tunics, a pair of sandals, and the promise of a safe trip to Ugarit.

The shipment Yassib was bringing to Qadesh when he found me was silver from Hatti. Silver was important. But not as important as tin.

Yassib kept a chunk of tin ore on a shelf in his forge. I took it down one afternoon after I'd helped him cast some bronze arrowheads. "I don't see what the big deal is." It was chunky and shiny, but more rock than metal.

Yassib arranged the moulds on a table to cool. "That's because you don't understand it."

I turned it over. "What don't I understand?"

"That not everything that's useful is beautiful."

"I understand that. But how is this rock useful?"

"You're a soldier. Ever use a copper sword?"

"Of course not. Copper's too soft."

"What was your sword made of, then?"

"Bronze."

"And what is bronze?"

I shrugged. "A metal."

"A useful one?"

"The most useful."

"What makes it more useful than copper?"

"It's stronger. It doesn't tarnish as fast."

"That's *how* it's more useful. What *makes* it more useful?"

"Same thing."

"No, it isn't."

He put some shavings of copper and a fragment of the rock into a stone bowl and heated them until the copper melted. A silvery smear spread across the surface. He swirled the liquid with a stone rod and poured it into an arrowhead mould.

"So what—"

"Shh."

We sat in silence until the mixture began to solidify.

"That looks kind of like bronze," I said absently.

Yassib raised an eyebrow.

My eyes went wide.

According to Yassib, the other thing that made tin valuable was that not many places had it. "There's a kingdom to the east where ours comes from. We can't get it from anywhere else. So our king gives their king a gift of silver, or cloth, or ebony, and their king gives him a gift of tin. Then our king gives the king of Ugarit a gift of tin, and he gives our king a gift of olive oil, or wool, or barley. The kings divide up what they get among their brothers and sons. Eventually it trickles down to the marketplace. Everybody wins."

One of the bigger winners was Yassib of Qadesh. Because all these gifts had to get where they were going, which meant the kings had to rely on trusted intermediaries. Who received a cut.

The shipment I was going to be travelling to Ugarit with was one of those gifts.

In my sixth week with Yassib, a man in an elegant robe came to the warehouse. The next morning he came again, with an escort of soldiers and a dozen wooden crates. Yassib's men—apart from Danel, who, oddly, wasn't there—started stacking them in the wagon.

"Ishtanu. Come with me to the forge, please."

By then I'd spent a lot of time in the forge helping with the smelting and casting. But that wasn't why we were there this time. "I have another deal to offer you," Yassib said once we were alone.

"I'm not staying longer. I need to get back to my wife."

"No, not that. You'll like this. Danel got into a tavern fight last night. I had to put fifty stitches in the shoulder of his sword arm. He'll be fine, but he's no use right now. And we have to leave today."

I looked at him warily. "How does that affect our deal?"

"What have I done to deserve such suspicion? I told you, you'll like this." He lifted a long cloth-wrapped bundle from a chest against the wall, and opened it on the table. Its blade was longer and straighter than my old sword. It had some nicks, and the leather grip had cracked, but it looked like a decent weapon. "Take Danel's place in my guard as far as Ugarit, and when we get there you can keep the sword."

I stared at him. He laughed and cuffed my head. "And you all suspicious."

The trip to Ugarit was less eventful than my first attempt. Professional help makes a difference. It took more than two weeks, which was fine because that was what safety called for, but it was also that much more time away from Ishara, who probably thought I was dead.

The rest of the trip home was just as uneventful. In Ugarit Yassib convinced a friend who ran cargo to Hattusha that he could use another sword arm.

I don't know why Yassib was so kind to me. Maybe it was something his gods encouraged. Maybe I was so pathetic he couldn't help himself. Maybe he was just a decent man. I've run into a handful like him in my life, and I'm grateful to all of them.

Only a handful, mind you.

By the time we reached Hattusha I'd been away more than seven months. I walked through the night to our village, and practically ran the rest of the way to our compound. I saw my father crouched at the threshold of my hut, making repairs to the stonework. "Hey," I shouted. He spun sharply, startled. It wasn't my father. It was my brother Rundas, taller and sturdier than when I'd seen him last. He looked as surprised as I felt. "Looking after things for me in my absence?" I asked.

The door swung open. Ishara came out, squinting in the sudden daylight, with her wrist draped protectively across her slightly rounded belly.

My father was in the main hut. "You *permitted* this?" I shouted when I saw him. Pleasantries seemed beside the point. "You let Rundas take my place in Ishara's bed?"

"We thought you were dead. The soldiers came back. You weren't with them. We thought ..." He trailed off.

Ishara came in cautiously, followed by Rundas. I ignored them. They were the battlefield, not the battle. Lelwani put down the wool she'd been spinning and rose to face me. "You couldn't give Ishara a child. Your marriage had no purpose. And you were gone. So we had it annulled." She might've been describing the purchase of a cabbage from the market.

"But it might not have been *me*. It might've been Ishara who couldn't have a child." Lelwani simply gestured toward Ishara's belly. "You didn't know that at the time," I said. I looked over at my father. His eyes were on the ground.

Lelwani's smile was small but satisfied. "That doesn't matter anymore. We know it now. Rundas is Ishara's husband. Together they'll give us sons."

I looked at each of them in turn—Ishara red-faced but resolute, her hands folded in front of her growing child; Rundas smug but wary, his eyes darting to the sword at my hip; my father outmanoeuvred and broken in front of his eldest son; and Lelwani, glowing with triumph, her family now pure, the last trace of the foreign tart sidelined.

I stood shaking and silent. I fiddled with the hilt of my sword. I saw a satisfying flash of fear on Rundas' face, so I fiddled with it some more. Then I stormed out and ran into the hills.

I butchered a yearling with my sword and built a fire by the shepherd's hut. They owed me that much. I ate greedily, defiantly, until I was so full my stomach rebelled and I threw it all up. I was crouched by the stream, rinsing my mouth, when my father came over the rise. He approached slowly.

"Followed the smoke from the fire." I didn't reply. I wiped my mouth on my sleeve.

He sat next to me, arms crossed on raised knees. Neither of us spoke. I was too angry. He was probably too baffled. But he was the one who finally broke the silence. "Your mother," he said. I stared. He'd never talked about her. He seemed far away.

"My mother?"

He drew a long breath. Looked over his shoulder, as if expecting Lelwani to pop up behind the nearest rise. Looked back at me. "She was kind." He stared into the sky. "Sometimes I miss that. Sometimes I miss *her*." He shook his head. "All behind us." The fire crackled and popped. A curl of smoke rose and drifted off. "I hate this, you know. I do. But I can't find a way to make it wrong."

"Of course, it's wrong." The bitterness in my voice surprised me. I'd never spoken like this to my father. Never had reason to. "I'm your eldest. You don't just replace me."

"I know. But that's what I have to do. I have no choice."

"Of course, you have a *choice*." He looked down and shook his head. I gritted my teeth. "Because of Lelwani. Because she decides."

"No," he said softly. Then he snorted. "Well. Yes, she does. But that isn't why." He looked up into my eyes with agonizing sympathy. "And you know that."

There it was. The thing that was more important than his son. More sons. The next generation of sons.

I looked into my father's eyes, silently begging him to let there be another way. But there wasn't. Then his tears ran down his face and he held me while I howled at the pain and the betrayal and the injustice and the inevitability of it. My cries echoed off the hillside. They could probably hear me down at the compound. I didn't care. The cries were bigger than I was. Bigger than Ishara and Rundas. Bigger than bandits. Bigger than Halki. The cries had to have their day.

The cries turned to sobs, and then to heaving, snotty gasps, and eventually to a long sigh and a kind of calm. My father and I sat there by the stream, his arm still around me, breathing together.

"Where will I stay?"

He paused. "Not at the compound."

"No, of course not."

"You could probably find work in the village."

"All I know is how to care for sheep."

He paused again. "They have sheep in the village," he finally said.

I lifted my head. "The King's Stores?"

"You're a soldier, after all."

We went straight there, bypassing the compound. The soldier at the gate—a middle-aged lifer named Astabis, who we knew from our annual deliveries—greeted us cheerfully. "Afternoon, boys. What can I do for you?" He peered theatrically at the empty ground behind us. "No sheep today?"

My father chuckled obligingly. "Wrong time of year, Astabis."

Astabis chuckled back. "Mind like a fish net. Only the big stuff sticks." Pleasantries done, his tone grew more earnest. "What brings you here today, then?"

"Well." My father looked uncertain as to how to proceed. "We were hoping you'd be able to give my boy here some work."

Astabis looked puzzled. "Don't you need him in the pasture?"

My father rubbed his jaw. He was a simple man, accustomed to quiet days in the fields with his flocks. He didn't know how to deal with delicate social issues.

"I can't stay there," I said.

"Why not?" No edge. Just a request for information. It needed an answer.

"There isn't a place for me there anymore. My brother has ... replaced me."

Astabis looked a little stunned as he put the pieces together. Another simple man accustomed to quiet days with his flocks. He puffed his cheeks and blew out a long breath. "Sorry to hear that. But this is a soldiers' barracks. We're not here to give work to civilians."

This bit my father could handle. "But Ishtanu isn't a civilian. He was conscripted eight months ago to fight the Egyptians." He gestured through the gate, toward the shed where the clay tablets were kept. "You can check your records."

And so thanks to meticulous Hittite bureaucracy, I had a place to live.

"You know it isn't my call, right?" Astabis wanted to be sure there were no misunderstandings. "The regional commander will have to confirm it his next time through."

"But in the meantime I'll have work, and meals?"

"That you will, lad. Let's find you a bunk."

The storehouse took up more space than I'd imagined. Behind its high walls were four barns—sheep, cattle, horses and mules—and four deep, well-sealed grain pits, plus the records shed, kitchen and pantry, a small dining hall, a smithy, a locked warehouse filled with weapons, uniforms, chariot parts and stacked bronze ingots, and a barracks with half a dozen straw mattresses.

"Full complement is six, but we're running on three. That's your bed there. Peg on the wall for belt and clothes. Sword and other personals go in the wooden chest."

"Thanks. Um … so what do I actually do?"

"You can replace Hazzi on shepherding. He's better with the cattle anyhow. Runs in his family. We've had Sharuma on cattle, but only because he's getting on and has a hard time ranging as far as the sheep. I'll put him on kitchen duty. Nice break for him, and spare the rest of us pitching in on the cooking. Frankly I could do without Hazzi's charred mutton."

After I joined the garrison my father stopped bringing the King's portion. Rundas did it instead. With Rundas it was strictly business. At first I just saw him from a distance, dealing with Astabis at the gate, but after Astabis taught me the record-keeping we had to deal with each other directly. Directly, not personally. There was nothing personal about it. For all anyone knew he was another random shepherd and I was another random grunt.

Years came and went. My braid grew back. Sometimes troops passed through and replenished their supplies. More often we sent the bulk to Hattusha, keeping just enough to feed ourselves and help the area's needy. One winter Sharuma passed in his sleep. He wasn't replaced, so we were back to three.

Somewhere in my twenties something happened. Or didn't happen. If it hadn't been for Rundas and his son I might not have noticed it. Well, I would've eventually. But not that day.

It was during the first famine. Rundas had been bringing the boy for ten years or more by then. I don't remember his name. I'm sure he didn't know who I was. Rundas had never made the introduction. I was just the soldier who took their sheep every year.

They'd brought fewer, but we'd expected that. There'd been fewer of all the animals. And less grain. And less cheese. Less of everything. Because there was less rain. We didn't have big rivers or complicated irrigation systems. Our agricultural model was simple: if we had rain, we had food. That year we didn't have much rain.

I filled a fresh tablet with clay to document the six yearlings Rundas and his son had brought. "It's the right number," the boy said, though I hadn't asked. "We're short of feed. Had to cull the flock." He eyed me warily. There was something of Lelwani in the curl of his brow.

"Don't worry about it." I pressed the entry into the damp clay. "Everyone's portion is down."

"Are you the same soldier who was here last year?"

I didn't look up. "I am."

He looked from me to his father and then back again. "And the year before? And before that?"

I set the stylus and tablet aside and unlatched the gate. "Every year you've been coming. And well before that." I swung the gate open.

The boy looked puzzled. "I thought he was older than you," he said to Rundas. "Hasn't he always been older than you?"

"He is." Rundas' voice was gruff.

"But he isn't. Look at him."

Rundas looked at me, maybe for the first time in years. I looked at him. The odd strand of grey. Creases around the eyes. The usual signs of approaching middle age. With a twinge, I realized what the boy was seeing. I'd seen my own face that morning, in the bronze mirror as I'd shaved. I'd seen none of those signs. "Mind your business," Rundas growled. "Let's get to the tavern."

We rode that year out, and the next one brought good rain and good crops. People rebuilt their flocks and herds. Relief showed on everyone's face. It was a blip. We'd had worse. We'd have worse again.

We got seven fat years that time. Then the lean years came again. Hard.

The drought was so bad that by the end of the first year we were doling out more from the stores than we were taking in. Most of our grain came on ships from Syria or Egypt, and then overland from our port towns under heavy guard.

The second year was worse. Two cowherds didn't bring us anything. They'd butchered the last of their herds for lack of anything else to eat. That troubled Hazzi, the son of a cowherd. "We never had it that bad. You need enough stock to rebuild." He was in command by then. Astabis had died of a wasting sickness two years earlier, and had been replaced by the third son of a local bean farmer.

The shipments of imported grain continued, but the demand was always greater than the supply. Tensions grew. As a result, so did the garrison.

"This barracks is built for six," Hazzi said when the word came from the capital. "How we're going to fit twelve I can't imagine."

The new men were veteran combat soldiers, not stylus-pushers like us, which they clearly felt put them in authority. They quickly worked out how to fit twelve into barracks built for six. "Not the first time I've bunked in a barn," I said. Hazzi didn't take much comfort from that.

Two of the new soldiers manned the gate when people came for their allotment of food, and they challenged every claim down to the individual grain of barley. When Rundas and his son—now a grown man—came with only three yearlings I accepted their count, as usual, but the hard-ass at my shoulder overruled me.

"Let's go check your flock." He fixed his helmet onto his bullet head.

Rundas went red. "This is the full amount. We have no feed. We have almost no flock. Even with this you're taking food from our mouths."

I tried to calm things. "I know these men. They wouldn't short us."

"Get your helmet on," the bullet-head said.

I hadn't been to the compound since I'd first returned from Qadesh. There was a new hut, presumably for my brother Telepinu and his family, but otherwise it looked the same. And yet not. Its spirit was different. The still air seemed almost brittle. The effect of the famine, probably. As we approached the main hut an old man came out, hunched and grey and listing to one side. It took me a moment to recognize my father. He didn't recognize me at all, at first.

"What's this?" he asked. His voice was thin.

"We've come to check your flocks," the bullet-head said.

"Check my flocks? Since when?"

"Since you only brought three yearlings."

"But that's the full portion."

"I don't think so."

"Feel free to look. Rundas, show them to the pasture. Telepinu and his boy are up there."

"I'll take him," I said. I didn't trust Rundas to keep his temper once they were in the hills. Not that I had any use for him, but I didn't want him getting his throat cut.

My father's face went slack. He'd recognized my voice. "Oh." Nothing else. We all just stood there. Then the door to the main hut opened and three women came out. I didn't know the third one. Telepinu's wife, presumably. But I knew the other two. Ishara had grown rounder in middle age. She stopped when she saw me. "Ishtanu?" Her voice was so soft I could hardly hear her. But there's something about your own name. "You can't ... can it be you? You're ... you look so young."

"It's him, all right," Lelwani said. Her hair was shorter and greyer, her skin less taut, but she was as tall and wiry and commanding as ever.

"I've been saying that," Rundas' son said. His expression made him look more like Lelwani than ever. "I said that two famines ago."

"How have you managed that, Ishtanu?" Lelwani's eyes were dark. "What foreign sorcery keeps you so young?"

Rundas' boy realized they were calling me by name. "Wait, you know this man?"

"Just from seeing him in town," Lelwani said. Ishara's eyes looked pained. My father lowered his head. Neither of them said anything.

I took the bullet-head to the pasture. I counted the sheep for him and did the percentages. "They could've hid some," he said. So we went back to the compound and he searched the huts and outbuildings. He didn't find anything. I knew he wouldn't. You don't shortchange the King.

Rundas' son watched as we walked away toward town. Our visit had stirred up some secrets. But at least none of them had been sheep.

On our way back the bullet-head examined me carefully. "How old are you, anyhow?" I didn't answer. After our meagre dinner that night I saw him and two of his colleagues whispering together near the barns.

By the third year of famine people were desperate to understand why. It wasn't enough to know it was from lack of rain. They needed to know *why* there was a lack of rain. Not a meteorological reason. A moral reason. A reason they could control.

Most put it down to the gods. We'd offended Tarhun somehow, and he was responding by withholding rain. Or he'd gone off in a huff, leaving his wife the sun goddess in charge, so we were getting too much sun.

Opinions varied as to what we'd done wrong. Most people felt we hadn't given him enough offerings of livestock and grain. But surely a god wouldn't be foolish enough to respond to inadequate offerings by cutting back on the things we offered.

Some thought he was jealous of the attention we were paying to the other gods. Some thought he was the wrong god, and that we should divert our offerings to someone else. But the thing with gods was that you asked them for stuff, and they answered or they didn't. If they didn't, there wasn't much else you could do. I think that's why the talk about gods dropped off that year. It made people feel too helpless. And I think that's why, when people started wondering aloud about sorcery, the idea caught on pretty fast. A sorcerer was something you could do something about.

Or to.

For a few weeks after our visit to the compound nothing out of the ordinary happened, apart from the odd suspicious look from the bullet-head and his mates. Then I had a bit of an accident. We were shearing what wool there was from the few sheep we had—a task beneath the newbies—and a slip of the blade left a gash down my calf. It wasn't deep, but it bled quite a bit so I wrapped it in some clean bandages and lay down for the rest of the day to let it heal. By morning it was just a pale line on the skin.

"You back at it already?" Hazzi asked. "Shouldn't you be resting that leg?"

"It's fine." We'd had this conversation before. But this time the bullet-head was nearby. "Let me see," he said.

"It's fine, really." I thought he was concerned.

"Let me see."

I showed him. I remember thinking it was strange for a hardened campaigner to be so troubled by an innocuous wound. But the innocuousness was the problem. He looked puzzled, but didn't say anything.

Maybe his puzzlement nagged at him. Or maybe Lelwani or her grandson stirred things up. They could easily have dropped a word in someone's ear in town. Whatever the reason, the bullet-head checked the records. He cornered me in the kitchen while I was cleaning the breakfast bowls. "The tablets say you was born the fifth year of King Muwattalli."

"If you say so."

"Now it's the twentieth year of King Hattushili."

"Can't argue with that."

"Which makes you more than forty years old." Someone had done his sums for him. I just shrugged. "But you look younger." The suspicion in his voice seemed to be wrestling with something like awe. "A *lot* younger."

I finished wiping a bowl and put on a stack of others. "Some people do."

"Not like you." His voice was steadier now. Suspicion had awe pinned to the mat. "You have all your *teeth*."

"I take care of myself. Exercise. Plenty of water."

He leaned close. "I take care of myself. But I look ten years older than you. And I'm almost ten years younger."

"I guess you've lived a rougher life than I have."

He gave me a long, hard look, but didn't say anything else.

My knees gave out as soon as he was out of view.

It all fell apart the day of the riot.

Our bins were empty. There'd been no shipments from Egypt or Syria in months, but the people didn't believe it. They kept coming to the gate with lethargic toddlers and slack-jawed babies. "We're starving," they'd say. They'd hold up their children. "He's going to die." It broke my heart. But there was nothing we could do.

"We're starving too," Hazzi would tell them. His face was sunken and grey. "There's nothing here. The grain is all gone. The animals are all slaughtered."

It was repeated endlessly.

Then one day a voice from the back called out: "That one looks healthy enough. He's getting food from somewhere." A woman's voice. I don't know whose. But I've always had a suspicion.

Everyone looked at me.

"Yeah," another said. "The soldiers are getting fed. Why not our kids?"

The crowd pressed against the gate. "Feed our kids," they chanted. "Feed our *kids*. Feed our *kids*."

"There's no food!" But Hazzi's voice was lost in the din.

The chanting grew louder. The gate began to crack. "Feed our *kids!* Feed our *kids!*" Even the bullet-head looked concerned.

The gate gave way. People stumbled through, then stopped, startled at their success, unsure what to do next. They looked around. Time froze. A breathing space, but not much of one. There were too many to control, and they were too desperate.

"It's him," the bullet-head cried. He was pointing at me. "He isn't eating. None of us is. There really is no food. But he's fine. I think he's a sorcerer."

That stopped the crowd. They murmured among themselves.

"They say a sorcerer brought the famine," a voice called. There were murmurs of approval. "It must be him," another said. The murmurs grew louder.

I went cold. I was in sandals and a tunic. No sword. No armour. About as vulnerable as I could be.

It was inevitable that someone would say it. And someone did.

"Kill him!"

The crowd surged forward.

Before I knew what I was doing I was on top of the empty sheep barn. It was a hop skip from there to the back wall. Down I went, and into the brush along the stream.

I didn't stop running until the sound of the mob had receded into silence.

The Aesir

I HEADED WEST. WE had a client kingdom called Wilusa on the sea coast. One of their tribute missions had passed our village when I was a boy. Halki had said—

I squeezed my eyes tight.

One foot in front of the other.

On the third day I came upon one of our outposts. Two soldiers and four empty barns, the tiny settlement around it deserted. My braid and tunic got me a bowl of soup made from endlessly re-boiled bones.

"Why are you out here alone?" the older of the two asked.

"Scout. One of the Great King's nephews is on his way to Wilusa with a force of a hundred to ask for aid. I'm two days ahead of them."

The soldier frowned. "We weren't told."

"I'm telling you now."

The younger one looked at my feet. "They sent you scouting in sandals?"

"Boots are in short supply. Men are boiling them for whatever nourishment is left in the leather." It was a thin excuse, but the boy brightened.

"We must have a dozen pair in our stores!" They might have been a dozen fat heifers. It broke my heart.

Not enough to knock me off my game, though.

"Got any size nines?"

I woke in the night to the tinkling of crockery. The ground was vibrating. It only lasted moments, but it took me a while to get back to sleep. By morning I'd all but forgotten it, as I set out in my new boots under a clear sky.

With proper footwear I made better time. Wilusa was the perfect place to make a new start. By all reports it was a proper city, so it would be easy for me to blend in and find work. I was young—as far as anyone could tell—and fit, and had some marketable skills. If I'd known what an oyster was, the world would've been mine.

Yeah. Would've.

Not making the connection? Wilusa? Twelfth century BC?

Ah. You won't know it by that name.

You call it Troy.

The refugees fleeing the other way should have been a clue. There were only a few at first—I took them for ordinary travellers—but soon there was a steady flow. Before long every settlement I passed was thick with them. I assumed it was the famine. Wrong horseman, as it turned out.

Three days before I arrived at Wilusa I saw the drifting column of smoke. Two days later I smelled the rot of the dead. I was tempted to go back, but by then my curiosity outweighed my gag reflex.

I arrived at dawn the next day. Wilusa was massive. The first thing you noticed was the high-walled fortress on its promontory, overlooking a large, marshy harbour. And while that bit was impressive enough on its own, it was dwarfed by the city that had grown up around it. Intricate streets of houses and shops and gardens and squares wound down the hillside and out onto the edge of the plain, where they were surrounded by another, lower wall. The kind of development only an imperial capital or major trading centre could manage. It was magnificent. And empty.

I'd never seen devastation on such a scale.

It was the silence that was the most unsettling. Even from this distance I should have been hearing the squeals of children, the cries of vendors, the thump of cargo being loaded into ships. Nothing. Not a sound. Not even from the scavenging birds that dotted the ruined landscape. They didn't have to squabble. There was plenty for everyone.

Multiple breaches scarred the city walls: huge gaps surrounded by rubble and rotting bodies, as if clawed loose by giants. No human—or human device, even—could have caused it. It was something only the gods could have done.

I remembered the vibrating earth at the outpost, during the night. Had that been some god knocking down these walls? And if so, why?

I realized I'd never actually seen a god. Never expected to. When we prayed to ours, it was for stuff that could happen anyhow. Good health. Rain for the crops. We expected them to act behind the scenes. The rains came. The sick recovered. We didn't expect them to march across a battlefield like plus-sized soldiers. But maybe I'd been thinking too small. Or maybe whoever had attacked Wilusa just had bigger gods than we did.

I saw a flicker of movement on the plain. A hunched figure, face wrapped in cloth, picking at the carnage. Once I'd seen it, I noticed others. Only a few, here and there across the battlefield and between the buildings of the town. None in groups. Desperate loners, salvaging what they could find.

I realized how hungry I was. How exposed. I was pretty desperate myself. And pretty alone.

The town first, or the battlefield? One might have food. The other might have weapons. Not a tough choice. I'd been weaponless long enough. And if I did find food, I might have to fight for it.

The edge of the battlefield had been stripped clean. I moved deeper into the rot and stink, picking my way around pale bodies and ruts of dried mud, keeping my distance from the others. Safest to avoid conflict until I was armed.

I saw a body with a single boot. Another with a torn but mendable tunic. Nothing I needed, but good signs. Then a breakthrough: a knob of bronze, shining through the cracked mud. The pommel of a sword. I chipped the weapon loose with the heel of my boot. It had a leaf-shaped blade, and a leather-wrapped grip that nicely fit my hand. I stood a little taller. I was armed now.

A hundred paces later I saw the edge of a shield under a rotting horse and a crushed one-man chariot. Using the chariot's snapped draught pole as a lever I raised it enough to get the shield out. It was round and small, made of layers of bull-hide over a wooden frame. The bronze boss at its centre was dented, but it was otherwise intact. Now I had defence as well as offence. I picked up my pace and headed for the nearest breach in the lower wall.

The wreckage was overwhelming once I was next to it. Chunks of masonry as tall as I was were piled one on the other, their ragged edges raw against their flat, painted surfaces, the gaps between them weirdly lit by the low morning sun. In one gap something gleamed. I shifted some smaller bits of rubble and discovered the body of an almost fully equipped soldier, apparently untouched since he'd fallen. I had no idea which side he'd been on, but that hardly mattered. I stripped him of his belt and corselet and greaves. I didn't take his helmet, but only because I couldn't find his head.

Food was harder to come by. I went house to house and shop to shop without finding anything other than dead Wilusans. Then around mid-morning, while searching a mercifully corpse-free house, I saw something I hadn't noticed before. One corner of the flagstone floor had been pulled up, exposing a cool, dry space filled with empty clay pots. I sniffed them. Despite the ambient stench I smelled grain. They'd stored it under the floor.

In the next house the floor was intact. I worked my way along the floor, tapping each flagstone with the pommel of my sword. There was a hollow sound at the second corner. The stone pulled up easily. The space below it was filled with clay pots. These weren't empty. One held stacks of flat bread. Another held barley. Cheese. Dried beans. Hard-cooked eggs. I almost cried.

I ate until my jaw ached from chewing. Then I rested, and ate some more. Then I made a sling from a blanket and filled it with as much food as I could carry.

I stepped back into the sunlight and looked across the ruined city. There were more scavengers now, some in groups. Gangs, even. Time to get out of Dodge. But in which direction? I'd come from the east. To the west was only water. My mother had supposedly come from the north.

It was as good a direction as any.

I skirted the coastal wetlands and crossed a broad, rush-lined river, which I followed inland to a tributary with a wide, walkable bank. The perfect northbound highway. The walking was easy, though my greaves chafed and my scale-armoured corselet was heavy. I kept to the edge of the trees and moved as silently as I could. By early evening I decided to make camp in a small clearing.

I spread the corselet as a ground sheet and unlaced the greaves. My chafed shins had bled onto them. I went back to the river to give them a rinse. As I swirled water in the first one I realized that the hollow where it broadened out was like a shallow bowl. That gave me an idea.

Back at the clearing I built a small fire and banked it with fist-sized rocks. I took one of the greaves to the river and brought it back sloshing with water. When the coals were right, I propped the greave over them, tipped in a handful of dried beans and cooked them until they softened. The other greave was my soup cup. I made four servings. I'd have done a fifth, but dusk was approaching and I had to kill the fire.

I set off again just after dawn, still moving quietly. I felt a little foolish being so cautious, since I hadn't seen anyone since I'd left Wilusa, but then I hadn't seen the bandits on the road to Ugarit either. So I stayed alert. Not long after the sun cleared the treetops my caution was rewarded. In the forest, not ten paces away, I heard a grunt. I dropped to a crouch, shield and sword ready, and listened.

Nothing.

I listened a while longer. Still nothing.

I was standing to continue when I heard it again. A stifled grunt, like someone in pain trying to stay quiet. A wounded soldier, hiding in the trees.

The fact that he was trying to stay quiet meant he knew I was there.

I looked down at my armour. Which side was it from? The same as the soldier, or the other? My choice of arms—random at the time—took on deadly significance.

My heart thumped in my chest. There were only two possibilities. I was dressed as his enemy, in which case he either didn't have a bow or was too wounded to use it, or else I'd already be dead. And he was probably alone, or his companions would've killed me. Meaning the smart thing to do was keep moving. Or I was dressed as his ally, in which case he'd expect me to help him. But if I did, he'd know I was a fake. Which took us back to the first possibility, where the smart thing was to keep moving.

He grunted again, and again immediately muffled it.

I tried to see into the trees. Nothing. No apparent threat.

Right. I should go.

Instead I walked toward the forest. Slowly. Shield up, grip tight on my sword. Curiosity outweighing self-preservation. Or maybe not just curiosity. I was alone in a strange place, with no real destination. I knew the dangers of travelling alone. If I got a chance to explain myself, maybe we could travel together.

In for a penny. If we'd had pennies.

I stuck the sword into my belt and raised my empty hand. "Friend," I called out in my language. My only language, at that point. "Friend." I hoped he would understand. And believe me.

I was such an idiot.

She understood me, as it turned out. Our languages were as similar as, say, German and Dutch. But she didn't believe me. She tried to stay quiet as I approached. But her circumstances soon made that impossible.

She wasn't a soldier. And she wasn't wounded. She was in labour.

She was also armed. She pointed a well-polished sword toward me, holding it absolutely still, and said through gritted teeth: "If you come any closer I will disembowel you and make a cradle for my child out of your entrails."

Women can be a bit tetchy when they're in labour.

"Sword down," she said.

I kept my hands up and took a slow step. "I can—"

"Sword down!"

"All right, all right." I reached for it.

"Other hand. Two fingers. *Uunnghhh!*"

Contraction. Her body tensed and her face contorted. But her sword never wavered and her eyes never left my hands.

I did as she said. I took the pommel with the thumb and middle finger of the wrong hand, slid the sword from my belt, and dropped it in the leaves behind me.

"Shield too."

"Why the—"

"Shield too!"

It joined my sword.

"Now step away from them."

I did as I was told.

She nodded. "All right. You can pick them up again. I'm satisfied."

I must have looked puzzled.

"You aren't a threat. How dangerous can you be if a woman in labour can disarm you that easily? Now pick up your weapon and go back to the river."

"Fine," I said, a little petulantly. "I'm leaving."

"No, you fool, not leaving! Just going to the river. You'll need your weapon in case we aren't alone."

"Why am I going back to the river? To stand watch?"

She looked up toward the gods and muttered something, then gave me an exasperated look. "No, not to stand watch. To wash your hands. All the way to the elbows."

I must have looked puzzled again.

"As you may have noticed, I'm about to have a child. I could use some help. And apparently you are all the gods have bothered to send me."

When I got back from the river, she was breathing sharply but not in visible pain. I took my first good look at her. Earlier my focus had been on the sword levelled at my nethers. Fine linen robe. Mussed hair with traces of an intricate style. Full set of teeth. Minor princess, maybe. Overlooked when the real nobles were stampeding to safety, or being cut down.

"Who are you?"

Her glare had a single-minded ferocity. "Never mind who I am. Get over here and be ready."

"You look high-born." There was a flicker of a smile. The vanity of nobles. Pleased to be recognized, even *in extremis*. "Where I'm from, commoners like me don't touch the high-born." I didn't know if that was true, but it sounded right. "If I'm going to deliver your baby, I need to know."

She considered this. I waited. She was on her back in a forest with her knees up and a baby coming. Could telling me her name make her any more vulnerable?

"Fine. I'm high born. And you can touch me." She waggled the sword. "Only as much as the task requires."

"Understood."

She grimaced as another contraction seized her. It passed.

"All right," she said. "Your turn."

"My turn?"

"Tell me who you are."

"Me? I'm no one."

"Not good enough." She squirmed. "I need you to distract me. I haven't had anything to focus on for hours other than the wrenching in my belly. It's getting tiresome." She took a sharp breath. "So talk to me. Who are you?" The contraction hit. Her face contorted. She reached out a hand, and I took it. Her grip was like the jaws of a lion. If I'd ever seen a lion.

"All right." I didn't know what she needed. I'd birthed plenty of lambs, but I knew from my wedding night that sheep husbandry wasn't a reliable guide to how things worked with people. I had to take my cue from her. And if she needed me to make chit-chat while she ground my knuckles to powder, then that was what we were going to do. "My name is Ishtanu. I'm of the Hatti. That way." I pointed vaguely east with the hand that wasn't being pulverized.

The contraction ended. "I know who." Long breath. "The Hatti are." She smiled as her breathing settled. "You're our tame neighbours."

I bristled. "Your masters, you mean. Your king rules on behalf of our Great King."

"That's what your king believes."

"He believes it because it's true. Your king sends an emissary every spring, to bring tribute and pledge fealty."

"Our king sends a soft man in soft clothes with soft noises and trinkets, and for a year our border is secure. Simpler and cheaper than maintaining garrisons." Her face dimmed. "Not the border we needed to worry about, as it turned out."

"Your king must have exaggerated his own power. The Great King leaves the day-to-day running of his empire to his client kings."

"*Client* kings?" She nodded toward the ruins to the south. "If this is part of your *Great* King's empire, where were his *great* armies when the Achaeans came?"

"Um. Did he know they were attacking?"

"Did he know?" Her eyes blazed. "Did he *know*? We sent word to Hattusha when we saw Achaean sails on the horizon. He knew before we were even sure who they were."

"And he didn't send help?" That didn't seem likely. Sure, no one had stopped at our village for supplies. But they might not have bothered. Why would they expect us to have any?

"He sent a few men. Thin. Weak. They died early." She turned her head and spat. She picked up the gourd and took a sip. "After that he didn't send more."

I had no answer. What did I know about geopolitics?

She, on the other hand, seemed very well informed.

"Who are you?" I asked again.

She looked away. "I told you. A noble."

"How noble? Enough to be in on your kingdom's diplomatic arrangements, apparently. How noble is that, then?"

"That's not your business."

"I think it is. Right now my safety is tied to yours. I need to know what that means." I stood. "Or I may have to leave you to birth that baby with whoever else the gods bother to send."

"No!" It was the first sign of vulnerability I'd seen. "You can't leave."

"That depends on you. Can telling me your name make you any more vulnerable than this?"

"It can, actually. You see, our king ..." She stopped.

"What about him?"

"He was my father."

That couldn't be right. A king's pregnant daughter wouldn't be alone in the woods. She'd have armed guards and a brace of midwives. "Out here, like this? I don't buy it."

Her eyes went cold. "*You* don't question my royalty. I am Tróán, daughter of Priam, king of Troia. While you—" she jabbed the sword in my direction "—are a common subject of the so-called 'Great King' of the Hatti." She spat on the ground. "Thank the gods my father was never so great that the slaughter of his allies was so beneath his notice."

Now I bought it. That kind of privileged bearing you couldn't fake.

Well, you could. I've done it myself since then, dozens of times. But it was plenty convincing at that point.

"I'm probably not actually his subject anymore."

She wasn't listening. "I watched my husband die in single combat. I begged him not to go. *Begged* him, for the sake of our child. 'Don't worry,' he said 'This man Achilles is all boast.'" Her voice was starting to break. "I saw a barbarian chariot drag my dead brother around our walls while its driver waggled his bare buttocks at us and laughed." Her eyes glistened. "I saw the two soldiers who escorted me out through the back gate cut down by Achaean arrows from our own ramparts." She was silent for a while. When she spoke again her voice was low and hard. "They sent a single man with a sword to finish me off, you know. Because I'm a woman."

I looked up, alarmed. "Is he still following you?" Suddenly every shifting branch was an imminent ambush.

She laughed darkly. "If he's following anyone it's his dead comrades." She held up her sword and tilted it this way and that, watching the play of light on its blade. "When I left him he was crying to his gods to help him push his guts back into his belly." She looked me in the eyes and gave a small shrug. "He underestimated me."

Princesses were less dainty in those days.

In space between contractions I asked about the battle. I couldn't grasp how such a well-defended city could have been sacked so thoroughly.

"We were fine. Our walls were strong. We were well-provisioned. We could have outlasted them. It never got worse than skirmishing. Our chariots trying to harass them into leaving. A small team setting fire to their boats in the night." Her eyes drifted off. "An over-proud warrior deciding he could take one of their champions in single combat."

I gave her a moment with that. But I still had to ask.

"What happened to the walls?"

She came back into focus. "The earth shook. It woke us just before dawn. Bounced our beds across our rooms." She smiled, just a little. "My father said it felt like the hoofbeats of Poseidon's own horse." She placed her hand on her belly and adjusted her position. "It was only when we heard the screaming below that we realized the worst of it."

"The breaches?"

She nodded.

"I wondered. If maybe it had been a god."

Tróán smirked. "Or a god's horse?" She shrugged. "I can only tell you what I saw, and it wasn't horses or gods. It was Achaeans." She picked at a thread on her gown. "Hundreds of them. Thousands, maybe. Swarming into our streets, into our homes. Jabbing spears into every doorway." She smoothed the thread into place and shook her head. "I don't care if Poseidon's horse brought them into Troia in her belly and shat them into the square. It doesn't matter how they got in." Her lips were taut. "What matters is what they did." The pain that flickered across her face might have been another contraction.

Close to dusk, in another lull between, she asked how I came to be in Wilusa. "You're a long way from home."

"I was hoping to live and work there. Make a new start."

"Are you a carrion bird? That's the only work available in Troia now." She stared quietly into the forest. "Plenty of it, though."

Before long the contractions came closer together. "Do as I tell you." Her ferocity would not be disobeyed. "I've attended a lot of births, and asked the midwives plenty of questions."

"Did they teach you swordplay, too?" Her nobler-than-thou attitude was starting to wear on me.

"Focus on my baby, Hatti, or I'll teach *you* swordplay." Her tone was as serious as a burning city. I did as I was told.

She took her gown by the hem and, after a pause and a resigned scowl—*oh, the things we nobles have to do*—she lifted it to her hips. Her back arched. She screamed something obscene at a whole assortment of her gods. It was starting. I'd been right. It wasn't like birthing lambs. It was noisier and angrier.

I remember it mostly as a series of sharp commands alternating with the foulest language I'd ever heard. And I'd been a soldier.

"Press there. No, *there*, you [some Wilusan word I didn't know, but which seemed to encompass both idiocy and excrement]. Right *there*."

"Hold its head. Wipe its face. *Gently.*"

"Ease the shoulders out. *Ease*, not tug. Do you know what 'ease' means, you [Wilusan word apparently referring to unnatural relations with livestock]?"

And finally, after the baby slid free and started to howl:

"What is it? Boy or girl? What *is* it?" The key question for all royalty.

"Boy." I wiped away the rest of the guck, wrapped him in a bit of clean cloth, and handed him to his mother. "A strong, healthy boy."

Tróán smiled at him. She was sweaty and puffy and her hair was a damp, tangled mess, and in that moment she was the most beautiful woman I'd ever seen.

There were other logistical bits I won't trouble you with. Let's just say they were messy. Once we'd sorted those out, I left the pair of them together in the dappled light and went to the river to wash my arms and rinse out Tróán's guck-covered linens.

When I got back she was nursing him. "You will not look at my breast," she said automatically, although her heart didn't seem to be in it.

"Cover it, then."

She frowned, but drew a fold of her gown loosely over her son's head.

I draped the linens on some bushes to dry, and then sat next to her on the ground. "Have you thought about a name yet?"

She nodded. "Mennon and I agreed on one before he went to battle the Achaean. In case what happened happened." She adjusted the cloth. "His name is Tror."

Evening fell. A fire might draw attention, so we did without. Of course anyone within a day's march would have heard her snarling at her gods all afternoon, but I didn't mention that. I gave her some of the flatbread and hard-cooked eggs, and she ate them delicately while her baby slept at her breast. "We'll have to make an early start in the morning," she said. "Sunup or earlier."

"We?"

"I just gave birth. I'm going to need help travelling. Besides, aren't you going to want some kind of reward?"

That hadn't occurred to me. First I'd been too busy not getting gutted by a pregnant princess, and then the whole childbirth thing had kind of taken over. Now that she mentioned it, though, a reward sounded nice.

"From where?" I looked around at the empty forest. "Did you bring your bank manager with you?" I would've used a more bronze-age-appropriate term, obviously.

"From Loricus." As if I should know who that was.

"I'm not from around here. Who's Loricus?"

"One of my father's allies. A Thracian chieftain."

There was apparently a land to the north called Thrace, where her father had had trading partnerships. When Wilusa and its seafaring commerce were threatened by the Achaeans, a few Thracian kings and their lesser chieftains—including this Loricus—had brought men and ships to help defend their economic interests.

"When the walls fell, my father asked Loricus to be ready to evacuate our family. His ship is small enough that it didn't make much difference to the sea battle, and most of its crew were still alive. Father showed us a small cove on a map—it's hidden from view until you're nearly upon it—and asked Loricus to take his ship there to pick up whoever could get away."

"And how many of you are there?"

"More than me, I hope. But I don't know."

She knew the route to the cove exactly, and walked us straight there. Her father must have had remarkable mapmakers. It took a day and a half, which was impressive for a woman who'd just had a baby. Tróán was formidably strong. Her son inherited that strength, and then some. But her intelligence and judgment skipped a generation.

When we made camp along the way, we risked a small fire. I banked it with rocks as I had before, and cooked us bean soup in my greaves.

"Very resourceful, Hatti." I smiled. High praise from the nobility. Once we'd eaten we propped ourselves against a fallen tree while she nursed Tror, our bellies full, savouring the smell of the wood smoke and the sound of the leaves in the breeze. Soon Tror was asleep. Tróán pulled her gown up over her breast and looked at me. "Why did you say yesterday that you aren't the Hatti king's subject anymore?"

I paused. "Another man took my wife while I was away at war. There wasn't room for me anymore." Not the whole story. But a truth.

"You were at war?" The surprise in her tone stung. It must have shown. "I apologize. That was unkind. But a soldier home from war, replaced by a man who stayed behind? Why didn't you just kill him, or drive him away?"

I tugged the swaddling cloth a little higher on the sleeping baby's head, and then lightly rested my hand there. My voice was so soft I could barely hear it. "He was my brother. He was able to give my wife a child." I stroked the down on the baby's head with my thumb. "Had done, by the time I returned."

Tróán's face softened a little. "You hadn't?"

I shook my head. I don't think I could have spoken.

She placed a hand on mine. It was the first time she'd touched me. "There will be other women, Ishtanu of the Hatti. Fine Thracian women who'll bear you armies of sons."

We emerged from a grove of trees and saw the ship, anchored in a teardrop-shaped cove. Tróán was in the lead. I had the baby against my chest in an improvised cloth sling. He was asleep, as he often was when we were on the move. The ship was maybe fifty paces long, with a single sail and a tall prow and stern. "What are those rows of poles sticking up along the sides?" I asked.

"Oars, sheep farmer. Warships need to move even when there's no wind."

I counted the poles. "A ship couldn't have twenty rowers. It would be chaos."

"Believe what you want." She carried on walking. "But let's go."

The cove was screened by trees, and had a narrow dogleg inlet at its north end. It would have been all but invisible from outside. There were a dozen or so men in a rough camp on the shore. Some were throwing dice. Some were tending a bronze pot over a bank of coals. Some were quietly doing combat drills, the heads of their axes wrapped in cloth.

Some had set up a perimeter.

I barely had time to notice the rustle in the trees when my arms were pinned behind me and I felt a knife at my throat. If Tror hadn't been secure in his sling he would've fallen. As it was, he barely stirred.

You know the term "raised by wolves"? You've probably used it yourself, to refer to someone brutal or uncivilized. If wolves had that concept, it would be "raised by Thracians."

The sentries marched us to the camp. A large, bearded man in a fine tunic and leather greaves rose from his dice game. "Tróán," he called out with a smile.

"Loricus."

He embraced her roughly. She turned to me, lifted the baby from his sling, and held him toward Loricus. "Tror. My son." She spoke loudly and precisely. I realized that Loricus probably didn't speak Wilusan, and apparently Tróán didn't speak whatever Thracians spoke.

Loricus placed a hand on the baby's head and smiled. Then he looked at me and said something in a language I didn't understand. The Thracians all laughed. Loricus loudest of all.

"He ask if this you wet-nurse," a man at Loricus' shoulder said, in something approximating Wilusan. Loricus' brother-in-law Dryas, I later learned.

Tróán simply smiled. The composure of the nobility. "This is Ishtanu of the Hatti. He helps with baby." She was doing that thing you do when someone doesn't speak your language well, where you start speaking it badly too, like that'll help somehow.

Dryas translated. Loricus nodded and said something back.

"He no Troian," Dryas said. "We kill now?"

"No!" Tróán stretched an arm in front of me. "He is my helper and my guest. We reward him and let him go." Dryas translated. Loricus shook his head. He and Dryas conferred. "He no go. He go, he tell Achaeans."

"No, I don't," I said. I was doing the language thing too, now.

Tróán saw their point. "Then we take him."

Dryas and Loricus spoke quietly. When Loricus turned back, he was smiling. Not a friendly smile. He walked over until we were barely a pace apart and he struck my face with the back of his hand. Hard. My vision blurred. It was such a shock I didn't even think: my hand went for my sword.

"No!" Tróán screamed.

Loricus raised a reassuring palm. While I was busy noticing that, he kicked me sharply in the nuts. Pain blazed all the way to my eyeballs. I doubled over, as Loricus knew I would. Up came his knee. I heard my nose crunch. I screamed and spun around, instinctively pulling my face out of the fray. As Loricus knew I would. He gave my backside a kick that sent me sprawling into the dirt. There was laughter all around. I heard Loricus call out something to his brother-in-law.

"He need to be train," Dryas said, translating. "But we do." I looked up to see him gesture toward the ship. "He start by row."

Tróán was frowning. "He's my guest."

Dryas didn't bother conferring with his chieftain. "Yes. So we no kill."

I never figured out how someone who spoke such crappy Wilusan knew the term "wet-nurse."

I learned a lot on the voyage to Thrace. Rudimentary Thracian, for a start, from my fellow rowers. Not systematic instruction. More of an intensive immersion program. You receive enough mockery and abuse and pretty soon you want to figure out why, and how to respond.

At first the mockery was about my seasickness. I managed to more or less hold it together while I was rowing, but at every rest break I'd be gagging over the gunwales. To my shipmates it was like television. Really hilarious reality television.

And yet after the dry heaving stopped, the laughing continued. Now it was just about other stuff, but that stuff was hidden inside their warty language. So I made the effort to puzzle it out. By the third day, when we passed out of a wide channel and into what I assumed was a sea, I managed a comeback.

"He thinks this is a sea," said the buck-toothed rower to my left. "What a big [I didn't understand the word's specific meaning, but it plainly impugned my intelligence]. The rowers laughed at their colleague's wit, and my apparent idiocy.

So I tried something. I gave bucktooth a disdainful look. "Yes. I be [I used the same word, trusting I had the context right]. Because I think you *man*."

I didn't say it was a very good comeback.

There was a long, dangerous silence. Then everyone laughed, louder than before. Everyone except buck-tooth. It was his response that mattered. He was right beside me. And he had an axe. But all I saw on his face was surprise, like he'd just seen a horse sing Happy Birthday.

Then he laughed along with everyone else. And then so did I. From relief, mostly.

Another thing I learned was how twenty rowers managed to row together. By singing. Like our Hatti marching songs, but with more purpose. And with a drummer. And in a language I didn't really get. Though I was still expected to join in. So another thing I learned was singing.

We had to sing a lot, because on the other side of not-a-sea was another channel, with a fierce current we had to fight all the way to its end. Rowing and singing. By the time we made it—into what I gathered was an actual sea, I was more exhausted than I'd been in my life, but I could fluently sing a dozen Thracian rowing songs.

"Good voice," buck-tooth, whose name I now knew was Mukabur, said. "Bit like woman, though."

"Like your little woman hands."

And we all laughed.

Thankfully, once we were out into what we now call the Black Sea, the ship could travel under sail. I gorged myself on grain porridge and I drank my entire ration of ale in a single draught.

"Careful, Aesir," Mukabur said. "You'll be sick again."

"I am called Ishtanu. How you not know this by now?"

"I know what you are called, Aesir."

"Then why call me other thing?"

"Not an insult. Like if you call me 'Thracian'. You are from Aesia. You are Aesir."

"Aesir." I tried it out. "And what's 'Aesia'?"

Mukabur gestured vaguely south and east. "That way. Where we came."

"You mean Wilusa?" He looked puzzled. "Sorry. Troia."

"Not Troia only. Troia, and everything after." He flapped his hand to the east, as if to indicate some unfathomable distance.

The ship was roomy for the thirty men it carried. It had probably held more on the way down. Not everyone makes it home from war. In physical terms, Tróán and her baby didn't take much accommodating. In psychological terms they dominated the ship.

They spent most of the journey in a tent-like structure near the stern, which I took to be Loricus' cabin. The first night I heard a yelp, then the sound of a hand on flesh, then low, intense voices. Too low to make out. After that, Loricus slept on deck with the rest of us. There was a new, thin scab just below the corner of his jaw.

Every so often as we made our way along the Black Sea coast Loricus ordered his men ashore to take on provisions. Which meant plundering a village. During one of these stops I caught up with Tróán. Loricus' men were roasting some pigs in the square of an empty village whose inhabitants had fled into the hills. Tróán was sitting on a log

near the water, gazing at the sea. I was standing next to her, holding
Tror in his sling. Loricus had enough men without me, and Tróán, like
all new moms, needed the break.

"So," I said as I swayed from side to side in a baby-soothing rhythm,
"I see you and your little man here have the stateroom to yourselves."

A smile touched the corner of her mouth. "Loricus had ideas about
the sleeping arrangements. Mine were different." She toyed with the
pommel of her sword. "We came to an agreement."

With no rowing, I had more free time, so I started hanging out with
Byzo, the steersman. By the time we reached our destination I'd learned basics of piloting and navigating, and a rich vocabulary of Thracian
curse words. Every half hidden rock or unexpected shift in the current
drew an inventive obscenity, usually connected with illegitimacy or
excrement, though sometimes with the Thracian gods. Which was how
I got to know a little about them, too.

Eventually the ship turned inland at a broad delta, and headed
west. The current was comparatively gentle, but it meant we were back
at our oarlocks.

"Another channel?" I asked Mukabur.

"No, fool. A river."

I shook my head. "Not a chance." I'd fallen for that one before. "It's
too wide." But Byzo confirmed that it was. These days it's called the
Danube.

After three more days on the river—singing, rowing, raiding—we
turned north up a tributary with forest down to its banks. At midday
that day there was a call from the trees, which the watchmen at the
bow answered. That set off a sequence of calls upstream into the distance. An hour or so later the forest on the port bank opened into a
wide meadow dotted with grazing horses and ringed with stone sentry
huts. Men with helmets and drawn bows jeered good-naturedly at the
crew, who jeered back. They exchanged a few lighthearted arrows, to
great merriment and almost no injury.

At the far end of the meadow was a small cove. Three small ships were moored there, with space for the one we were on, and a few smaller boats were drawn ashore at the base of a guard house. A half-mile or so inland the meadow rose to a bare hill with a log palisade.

A skeleton crew of rowers eased the ship into its spot. A crewman at the bow threw a rope to a man on the shore, who hooked it to a team of horses and dragged the ship up onto the soft earth.

"Home," Mukabur said.

And for me it was. For twenty years.

An escort of twenty horsemen had ridden down with extra mounts for everyone. I was the only one who'd never been on a horse. Even Tróán rode at a comfortable trot, with Tror bouncing delightedly against her chest in his sling. And since these horses didn't respond to Hatti commands, it was like the seasickness hilarity all over again, all the way to the palisade.

Loricus' wife Lori met us at the gate. No, really, that was her name. What can I say? It's not like she dotted the "i" with a heart. Though she probably would've, if that had been a thing. She wore her entitlement like a diamond bracelet, bobbing her hand in limp command at anyone within range until everything met her fastidious needs, oblivious to the eye-rolling once she turned away. She hated Tróán on sight. "Princess," she said, in the same tone Lelwani used when referring to my mother. Her nod was so slight it barely qualified as movement.

Tróán was more gracious, in keeping with her guest status. "Dearest sister," she replied, clasping Lori in a hug that made her rigid with discomfort.

It was all lost on Loricus. "I knew you'd be just like family."

Lori was a genius at passive-aggressive social arrangements. She put Tróán and Tror in a hut as far from the one she shared with Loricus as you could get and still be inside the palisade. For the next twenty years she and her personal guards made sure Loricus and Tróán were never alone together. Which was probably best for everyone. Especially Loricus. If he'd tried to renegotiate their shipboard sleeping arrangements, he might have died sooner than he did. And which woman would've done it is an even bet.

Most of my basic combat skills go back to Thrace. Fists. Knives. Axes. Bows. They drilled me hard, but no harder than they drilled their own. It was necessary. I had a lot of catching up to do. Swordplay I learned from Tróán. Swords were rare in Thrace. Not even Loricus had one. I think it was only because of my status as Tróán's attendant that they let me keep mine.

The Thracians also taught me horsemanship. They were great riders. They put lot of time into their horses. Breeding them. Training them. Racing them. Stealing them from their neighbours. Next to riding, nothing gave them more pleasure than raiding.

"Come on," Mukabur said one drizzly morning after I'd demonstrated some basic archery skills. "It's time you joined us on a raid."

"But, um … Tróán needs me to watch Tror later on."

"Are all Aesir men such babies?" He nodded at the bow in my hand. "Why all this training if you don't use it?"

So I went. Not my favourite part of the story. Thracian brutality is legendary for a reason. Let's just say I tried to do less than my share, and leave it at that.

For all their brutality, they were also very cultured. I first developed my singing voice there, and not just at the oarlocks. They sang constantly —at work, at play, around the fire. Through their deep back catalogue of tales and ballads and bawdy nonsense songs, I learned who they were. Stories of brave warriors and capricious gods, and fools who accepted gifts from mysterious strangers without considering their inevitable tragic price. I had a knack for it. Before long I was skilled enough to take the lead in some call-and-response pieces. My finest memories of Thrace are of evenings around the fire, just singing.

They didn't only breed horses, either. The cove where the ships were moored was at the mouth of a gentle river, which snaked through a valley where they grew flax and barley and wine grapes, and raised pigs.

Young Tror grew fast, and grew up strong. Loricus took a special interest in his upbringing, which was fine with Lori as long as it didn't directly involve Tróán. She seemed to appreciate that Loricus' relationship with Tror filled a need. Tror had no father, and Loricus had no sons. Three daughters. But Thracians *really* valued sons.

Loricus' sister Bendidra had sons. Her husband Dryas, who'd done the clunky Wilusan interpreting that first day, was effectively Loricus' chief of staff. Their eldest boy, Pytros, who was four when we arrived, was Loricus' heir apparent. At that point.

Time passed. My skills at riding and combat improved, but I was never fully accepted by the other warriors. No doubt there was some xenophobia to it, but it probably had more to do with the privileges my connection with Tróán gave me. Little things, like fewer nights in the sentry huts, but enough to mark me out.

Time passed.

One summer morning Dryas and his personal guard rode out on what could loosely be called a diplomatic mission to a more or less friendly tribe two valleys over. They returned the following afternoon with two new horses, each laden with dark furs.

"Bear skins," he told Loricus. "Tribute. Hoping to buy us off so we don't raid them before harvest. Maybe we shouldn't. They're nice skins."

Loricus ran his fingers through the fur. "Good bedding. How many?"

"Ten. Five on each horse. Plus we keep the horses."

Loricus examined the horses. His lip curled. "I know their stock. These are middling. Maybe we should raid them after all."

"Up to you. I didn't give them any guarantees. Probably better if we don't, though. They make a nice buffer with the next valley. Where do you want the skins?"

"Six to my hut and four to yours. Distribute yours as you see fit."

Dryas nodded and prodded his horse forward.

"Wait." Loricus smiled. "Let's let Tror put them away." The boy was barely ten. He was tall and muscular for his age, but the skins were huge.

"Tror? It'll take him all afternoon."

"What else does he have to do?"

Loricus called Tror's name loudly. The boy came out of the hut where his friend Taruthin lived.

"What?"

"Put these skins away." He nodded toward the loaded horses. "Six to my hut and four to Dryas'." He seemed to be trying not to grin.

Tror thought for a moment. "All right." He undid the ropes on the first horse. The skins tumbled to the ground. He did the same with the second horse. Then he gathered the skins into a pile and tied them into a single bundle.

"Whoa, boy," Dryas said, laughing. "One or two at a time. They're heavier than you think."

"Mind your business, uncle." Tror tilted the bundle onto its edge and slid his arms under the ropes. He leaned forward and lifted with his legs.

"Take care," Loricus said. "You'll injure yourself."

Tror didn't even look at him. With a barely audible sigh he lifted the bundle and shifted it until it was balanced. Then he looked Loricus in the eye. "Six to your hut?" His voice was strained, but defiant.

Loricus laughed. "Five. Keep one for yourself."

At that point Tror still shared quarters with Tróán. She lived in relative comfort, but resented how marginalized she was. Tror was her only real source of information. She exploited that source to its fullest. I added what I could, but I was hardly at the centre of things myself.

"Tell me," she said as she examined the bear skin, "is Pytros still expected to marry Sura when she comes of age?" Loricus' eldest daughter was a year older than Tror.

"I don't see them together so much anymore. They say she might become a seeress."

"That wouldn't stop them marrying, would it?" I asked.

"I don't think so," Tróán said, running her fingers through the rough fur. She looked at her son with a smile that managed to be both loving and calculating. "But then it wouldn't stop her marrying someone else, either."

Tror began to go along on raids. At twelve he had the height and strength of a full grown man. At fourteen he was a head taller and wider across the shoulders than the largest of the other warriors. Experienced warriors who fought him in training sessions came away bruised, or even broken. When Dryas asked Tror to rein it in for the safety of the others, he laughed. "Tell them they should fight harder."

As Tror did more soldiering, Tróán had less to occupy her time. The other women tried to help, but they didn't grasp with whom they were dealing. "They want me to join in making copper trinkets!" From the look on her face they might have wanted her to make them out of dung. By chewing.

I tried not to grin. "They're nice."

"Pfah! Of course they're *nice*. I'm wearing one." She held up her wrist to reveal a hammered bangle. "But can you imagine me sitting in a circle *making* them?"

I had to laugh. "What will you do to occupy your time, then?"

"Explore. Mothering has made my life narrow." She saw my look, and quickly added: "It's had its rewards. Still does. But I haven't done much else since we got here. It's time to spread my wings again."

"How?"

"Riding. This place is a rider's paradise. I want to see it all."

"I'll come with you, then. For your safety."

She pulled the bangle off and threw it at me. It bounced off my head. "Have you forgotten who taught you to use a sword?"

Tror arranged a mount, and she spent her days exploring the valleys. Sometimes Tror or I would go with her, or she'd take one or two of the few women who didn't much care what Lori thought. Mostly she went on her own.

Tror and I were out with her one afternoon, traversing a sunlit ridge with a view of a neighbouring valley. We pulled up to give our mounts a breather, and I poured cups of wine from a skin. Tróán took a long draught. "Have you hinted to Loricus that you might be interested in Sura?" she asked her son.

Tror drained his cup in one go. "I've more than hinted. I've asked to marry her."

Tróán smiled. She liked his forthrightness. "And?"

"He's thinking about it."

This could have dynastic consequences. "What does Pytros think?" I asked.

Tror sneered. "Who cares about Pytros?" Then he gave it some thought, for maybe the first time. "If Pytros has a problem, we can settle it with axes."

Tror and Sura were married just after she turned fourteen. In a transparent bit of horse-trading, Pytros was betrothed to Loricus' second daughter, Dhrenis. No one had had to settle anything with axes, though Pytros' expression said he might still be up for it if pushed. His mother didn't look much happier. Neither did Lori. No doubt the sisters-in-law had spent years firming up Pytros' claim to the chieftainship through marriage to Sura. They couldn't have foreseen some musclebound foreigner complicating the succession. Their frustration showed on their faces.

Tróán was radiant.

Tror continued to grow. At his full height he could wear his bear skin as a cloak. Which he did. Proudly. As his strength grew, so did his enjoyment of it. Stories began to come back from his raids, of a level of brutality that made hardened campaigners shudder. Tror just laughed. "What good is strength if you don't use it?"

Raised by Thracians.

Sura gave birth to a son. They named him Woden. He had a surprisingly even temperament for a child of Tror. "Has Loricus said anything more about who'll be his heir?" Tróán asked as she rocked her grandchild.

The new parents had come for a visit. The birth of Loricus' first grand-child had given Tróán's standing a boost, but she still had to rely on her son for intel.

"He's being cagey. Too many support Pytros. He doesn't want to alienate them."

"He'll have to decide eventually, won't he, Woden?" Tróán rubbed her nose against the baby's. "*Won't* he? Yes, he *will*." I'd never seen her act like that with her own child. Grandparent thing, I guess.

Sura was a mystery to me. I'm not sure even Tror had a deep sense of her, and not just because he couldn't bother having a sense of anyone other than himself. Sura spent a lot of time with the older women who knew the goddess ceremonies and the uses of healing herbs. More than once Tróán had to look after Woden overnight while Sura went with them to some secret place in the woods.

One day Tróán didn't come back from her ride. She hadn't planned to go far, or anywhere particularly dangerous, but when night fell she hadn't returned. The next day searchers found her horse in a patch of woodland, killed by an arrow, but no sign of Tróán. The archer had retrieved the arrow, so we couldn't tell where he was from.

Tror went nuts. "She's been taken by another tribe," he shouted at Loricus. "Find out which one." He whacked his axe into the log where I was sitting for emphasis.

Dryas did his best to calm him. "Let me do a tour and meet with their chiefs. I'll know if they're hiding anything." For two weeks he made the rounds while Tror seethed in his hut. "No one's seen her," he said when he came back.

Tror's expression was the coldest I'd seen it. "Then it's time for *my* tour." He and his friend Taruthin, a smiling sociopath who'd grown into a formidable soldier himself, took raiding parties in every direc-tion. They came back with gold and horses and livestock, and some-times with blood to their elbows. But not with Tróán.

Dryas appealed to Loricus to stop the raids. "I've spent *years* build-ing these alliances, and this boy has gutted them in days."

"He won't listen to me." Loricus gazed in the direction where Tror and his raiders had most recently gone. "In his position I probably wouldn't either."

I didn't join the raids. Not because I didn't want justice for Tróán. I just didn't think Tror was looking in the right place.

I had no evidence, or I would've passed it on. But there was a man on Lori's personal guard who I'd been on good terms with who hadn't met my eyes since Tróán disappeared. I couldn't say anything, because I couldn't be sure. And she was the chieftain's wife. And if it was true, it would lead to a bloody civil war.

Which we almost ended up with anyhow. But don't let me get ahead of myself.

Eventually Tror's raids ended, although his rage continued to simmer and sentiment in the neighbouring valleys remained grim. Dryas made overtures to the other tribes, but they weren't having. One sent his emissary back without his eyes.

Loricus stayed cagey about his succession plan for another five years. Tror was too preoccupied with his anger and ambition to have much time for his son, so I tried to take up the slack. When Woden was three or four he was watching me replace a splintered axe handle, and I was so busy narrating what I was doing that I lost my focus and the axe-head slipped from my hand. It hit my foot—the blunt end, thankfully —but it stung enough that I cursed in Hatti. Woden looked puzzled. "I didn't hear *those* words before. What are those words?"

I gave him the age-appropriate truth. "My old language. The one I spoke before I came here."

He considered that. "Is it Grandma Tróán's old language too?" Tróán had spoken Wilusan to Woden when he was a baby, but surely he couldn't remember that.

"Sort of."

"Can you teach me?"

I didn't see why not. So Woden grew up bilingual. Not that Hatti was ever any use to him. Well, once. But maybe it primed the pump, since he always had a knack for new languages. And that was seriously useful later on.

Loricus' caginess served him well, until he took an arrow to the shoulder on a raiding trip up the Danube. The wound festered to the point where Dryas was seriously worried, so we left off plundering and headed for home. As the current carried us back downstream we gathered around Loricus in his tent. His skin was pale, his eyes watery.

"The tribe needs certainty," Dryas said, kneeling at his chieftain's side. "You have to name an heir." He lowered his voice. "What if you named me, just for now? As a temporary measure."

Loricus' watery eyes sharpened up. "Naming you would be naming your son."

Dryas's raised eyebrow said: *Would that really be so bad?*

Loricus turned to his other side and reached out his hand. "Tror ...?" Then a shift in the current rocked the ship and wrenched his wounded shoulder. He gasped and lost consciousness. Through the canvas above us I heard Byzo the steersman bark something nasty about some goddess's nethers.

Tror straightened up. "He named me. You all heard it."

"He *asked* for you," Dryas said. "He hasn't named anyone."

"He *named* me. You're only denying it because you want it yourself."

"I'm denying it because it isn't true. Anyhow, he'll make it clear when he wakes up. Let's just get him home."

Loricus was unconscious all the way back. The heat around his wound spread to his whole body. When we disembarked, Tror took him to the palisade on horseback, to spare him the indignity of being carried in a wagon. Dryas rode as near as he could.

Lori screeched when she saw him, then briskly took charge. The wound was cleaned and fresh dressings applied. Not by Lori, of course, but at the direction of her bobbing hand. No one saw Loricus for ten days. Only Lori and her servants and two members of her personal guard were allowed into the hut. She came out every day at dusk with an update. "He kept down some soup this afternoon. He's been trying to speak. But it tires him." She was visibly tired herself. "Maybe tomorrow. One more good night's sleep."

"What's he been trying to say?" Pytros asked. A murmur moved through the crowd. Everyone knew what his question meant.

Lori gave Pytros a fierce look. She turned and gave the same look to Tror. "Loricus will still be your ruler when your children have children. Let him rest so he can get back to it."

Lori was never more impressive to me than in those final days. And remember, I suspected her of having had Tróán killed. So that's saying something.

It was the screaming of Lori's servants that woke the settlement.

During Loricus' convalescence they'd been going in every morning at dawn with clean cloths and herb poultices. I woke instantly and ran to the hut. One of Lori's newer serving women—no more than thirteen—was outside, heaving with frightened sobs, at the end of a trail of dark footprints. I stepped into the hut.

Dryas was there in his night clothes, his hair matted from sleep. He raised his sword as I entered. When he recognized me he relaxed, but only a little. "See this treachery," he said.

I saw. They'd been quick and efficient. Two of them, at least. One to deal with Lori, the other with the lone guard. Otherwise they might've cried out. There could've been a third man, but it wouldn't have been necessary. Loricus couldn't have raised his hand, let alone an alarm. Now none of them would raise so much as a breath, ever again.

"Knife," Dryas said.

"Probably. A sword would've cut deeper."

"No, an actual knife. Next to Loricus."

It was bronze, with a bone handle, entirely coated in blood. Dryas wiped it off. I'd never seen it. Neither had he. As it turned out, neither had anyone else in the tribe. Or no one who'd admit it.

"It's obvious," cried Tror to the crowd later that morning. We were in the space between the gate and the stables, which functioned as a public square. He pointed at Dryas and Pytros. "Loricus was about to confirm me as heir, so they killed him. And Lori, too. A *woman*." There were murmurs of disgust.

We had about two hundred warriors at that point. Twenty or so had family connections to Dryas and Pytros. About a dozen were personally loyal to Tror. The rest were just loyal to the tribe.

"This is ridiculous," Dryas said. "You all know me, and my son. We're Loricus's family." He put his hand on Pytros' shoulder. "Pytros was always meant to be his heir."

"Maybe once," Tror said. "But if Pytros was to be heir, why did Loricus give him his *second* daughter?" There were scattered murmurs of assent. "I'm the husband of his eldest, and the father of his first grandchild."

"And a foreigner." Pytros gave Tror a defiant look from the safety of his kinsmen's axes. He spat. "Aesir." Tror took a half-step in his direction, making him jump. But Pytros' outburst had drawn supportive nods.

Tror looked back out over the crowd. "I had no motive to kill Loricus. He named me his heir, on the way back from his last battle." Dryas tried to interject, but Tror talked over him. "Ishtanu heard it. Didn't you?"

"Well, I heard him say your name—"

"See? I was named." Dryas tried again, but Tror just raised his voice. "Loricus' death doesn't benefit me. It pains me. Not only because I loved him like the father I never knew." He lowered his eyes, then raised them again. "But because he was taken from *all* of us before he could confirm me in front of you." He pointed again toward Dryas and his son. "By them. To create doubt. To steal Loricus' rule from his chosen heir."

The speechifying went on until midday without resolving anything. Finally my buck-toothed oar mate Mukabur—a respected commander by then, and no one's particular loyalist—called for quiet. "Let's go to our huts until after the evening meal and discuss this with our families. When we come back we'll form two groups, based on where we place our loyalties."

There was a rumbling through the crowd as the men—he only meant the men, of course—checked with their friends to see if that sounded right. To most it seemed to. Then Dryas pointed out the flaw in the plan. "What if the two groups are the same size?"

Mukabur looked between Pytros and Tror. "Then I guess they settle it with axes."

The rumbling in response to that idea seemed more enthusiastic. After all, not even the Greeks had democracy at that point.

I followed Tror to his hut. "Did you?"

He spun at me, wide-eyed. "Kill them? Of course not." His face was earnest. "Loricus really was the nearest thing I had to a father. He was about to confirm me as ruler. I'd have to be both cold-hearted and stupid to kill him. You might think I'm one or the other, Ishtanu, but you have to admit I'm not both." He had a point.

"You're right. It doesn't make sense. But did killing him benefit Dryas either?"

"It created enough uncertainty to give him his shot. He still has to persuade the tribe that Pytros is the true heir, of course. Or at least swing enough his way." He snorted. "Or there's a third way, I suppose. Pytros could defeat me in single combat."

Even in the circumstances I couldn't help chuckling. Tror was a head taller than Pytros, with twice his muscle mass. It was hard to imagine a more uneven contest. I went to my own hut and left Tror with his family.

When I went back to the square after dinner Tror was there with his core loyalists. Dryas arrived moments later, leading Pytros like a pony. Once the village was assembled, Mukabur addressed the men. "Show your loyalties." Most already had. There was a large group behind each man. Not all that different in size.

Mukabur studied them carefully. Not tallying them. It wasn't a vote. I think he'd hoped there'd be an acclamation, or at least a decent consensus. But neither man had a marked advantage. "Right then. Axes it is."

There were cheers on Tror's side, and chatter on both. People backed away to clear a space.

"Not tonight," Mukabur shouted over the crowd noise. "The light's fading. It'll be too dark to see. We pick this up at dawn. Agreed?"

"Agreed," Tror said. Pytros just nodded. Once again we all retreated to our huts.

I went to Tror's, along with his retinue of fellow raiders. He was jubilant. "Sura! Wine! And meat. We'll feast into the night." Sura looked pale as she strode to their pantry. She was supposed to be a seeress. What did she know that she wasn't telling?

"Before you get started," I said. "You might want to take a few precautions."

Tror glared at me. "Are you my mother?" Then he laughed. "Oh, no, I forgot. You're my wet-nurse." The laughter spread around the room.

"Never mind me. Think about Dryas." A couple of men settled down a bit and listened. "His scrawny son has to take on a man twice his size at dawn. Do you think he's feasting right now?" More men started listening. "No. He's looking for a way out. The simplest way would be to send a team of cutthroats in the night, like he did with Loricus." Now I had everyone's attention. "Do you want to be drunk and snoring when they come?" Not that Tror's assassination would necessarily be bad for the tribe. Dryas had been a skilled number two for decades, and would guide his son well. We could do worse. With Tror we might. But that morning we'd seen how Dryas dealt with loose ends. Lori was as dead as her husband. I wasn't about to see that happen to Sura and Woden.

We divided ourselves into teams to stand sentry.

Nothing happened. Or at least no attack. There were footsteps and hushed voices outside, but no one tried to enter Tror's hut.

When Tror woke up he cuffed the back of my head. "Fearful old woman. You killed a great party." He roused his dozing men. "Up! Come on. Today's the day."

But as it turned out, today was not the day. Or not the day we thought. Mukabur was in the square. So were quite a few others. But some key men weren't.

Tror looked around. "Where's Pytros?"

Mukabur shook his head. "Gone."

"Gone? Gone where?"

"No one knows. Dryas, too. Their wives. Their horses. Most of their belongings."

Tror walked over to the stables. "Not just *their* horses. There must be twenty or more missing."

Mukabur nodded. "Twenty or more soldiers, too. With their families. Too soon to know exactly how many, but we can do a hut-to-hut if need be."

Tror ambled back with a smile. "Then I guess that's that, isn't it?"

The general mood when Tror took power was more stoic than joyful. There was a feast, and a complicated ceremony, and everyone came. But by the time the chants and sacrifices were over most of the attendees were essentially looking at their watches and muttering about having to give the babysitter a ride home.

The gods didn't seem much more enthusiastic. From the moment Tror and his family moved into Loricus's hut, no rain fell.

The harvest was poor, despite the wise women's best efforts to appease the gods. The farm workers did what they could, carrying buckets of water to moisten the soil enough for the grain to mature, but it wasn't enough. What little grain grew was patchy and stunted. The grape harvest was slightly better. A little dryness late in the season could be good for wine grapes. But there was more than a little dryness that year. And the tribe couldn't live on wine.

The workers spent long days salvaging what they could from the fields, but in the end the grain bins were about a third as full as usual. Some of the people grumbled about the gods. More of them grumbled about Tror.

On a chilly fall day six weeks into the Tror administration, workers started trickling through the palisade gate around noon. Mukabur and I were throwing axes at a target on the stable wall. "That's odd," he said. The workers lived where they farmed, in huts by the fields. They only came in for feasts and rituals, or to take shelter from raiders. And during raids they rushed through the gate in a screaming panic. This time they were calm and orderly. Mukabur pulled his axe from the target and slipped its handle into the loop at his belt. "Better see what's up."

He spoke to some older men in wide straw hats. When he came back he looked concerned. "They're all coming in. You tell Tror while I organize the men."

"Tell Tror what?"

"There's a body of men crossing from the north, an hour or so upriver."

"How big a body?"

"Pretty big, they say."

"Armed?"

"Presumably."

I looked to where the workers were chatting in small groups. "They don't look very alarmed."

"That's because the men at the front are ours. The ones who left with Dryas."

"I thought you said it was a large body."

"That's what they say. At least a hundred."

"But Dryas only took twenty-four warriors with him."

Mukabur nodded gravely. "That's part of what you need to tell Tror."

The whole tribe was safely inside with the gates barred when the men came into view. Tror had even called up the sentries from their huts and the guardhouse. With a hundred men advancing, everyone was safer in here. I was on the rampart with Tror and Taruthin, his sociopathic raiding buddy, who had famously keen eyesight.

"Definitely Dryas at the head," Taruthin said. "Pytros beside him." He was jittery with excitement. He always seemed jittery to me. "I'm guessing three hundred. Fifty or so on horses, including most of ours. The rest on foot."

"What weapons can you make out?" Tror's tone was grim.

"Axes. Knives. Couple of swords. Quite a few bows."

Tror stroked his beard. "What are you bringing upon us, Dryas?" he said softly.

As the group got nearer the question answered itself. I saw bear-claw necklaces from two valleys over, and boar tusk helmets from the valley beyond that. Tribes from all around us. Tribes Dryas had built workable relationships with. Tribes with a bone to pick with Tror. They spread out along the north wall of the palisade, five or six deep, their horsemen at the front.

"Dryas," Tror said companionably. "We thought you'd left us."

"Only temporarily," Dryas said. "Things to do. You understand."

Tror's smile didn't waver. "I'm sure we can still find a place for you. Maybe not for all your guests, though. Why so many?"

"I thought that would be obvious. They're here to help us conclude our agreement."

"Agreement?" Tror frowned. "What agreement?"

"The one you made with Mukabur. And with my boy." He swept an arm back toward Pytros, but his eyes never left Tror. "To settle it with axes."

Tror's smile wavered. Just a little, and not for long. "The agreement was for a one-on-one contest, Dryas. Your boy forfeited."

Dryas shook his head. "I don't recall anyone saying it had to be one-on-one. And there was no forfeit. We just withdrew to prepare. Now here we are. Prepared."

"Outside."

"For now."

Tror laughed. "You think I can't trust my gates?"

"I'm sure you can. I helped build them. It's your men I'm not as sure about." He spread his arms to both sides, toward the warriors from our own tribe he'd positioned there. Good men. Popular men. "Be realistic, Tror. If it comes to a siege, will your men fight their neighbours and friends? For you?" He paused. "For an Aesir?"

Tror kept his cool. But a rumble spread through the crowd as everyone took in the situation. Eventually all eyes turned to Mukabur, who was down in the square with them, not on the rampart with Tror.

Mukabur the respected commander. The voice of reason. He looked up at Tror and Taruthin. He looked around. He stood in silence a moment. Then he crossed his arms. "I'm not raising my axe against my own." The atmosphere in the palisade shifted.

Tror pitched his voice so only I could hear him. "Get Sura and the boy to the boats. Now."

As I scrambled down the ladder he addressed Dryas as calmly as if they were discussing how much flax to plant in which field. "So what do you propose, then?"

"What's happening?" Sura asked.

"I'll tell you on the way." I threw Woden over my shoulder. "Gather what's most important and come quickly." I had my sword in my belt and not much else.

She threw some clothes and jewellery and Woden's little wooden axe into a linen bag and slung it over her shoulder. "All right. Let's go."

We went out through the palisade's small south gate. Dryas had posted two horsemen there. I reached for my sword, but they nodded us through. We weren't the droids they were looking for. Even so, we took a forest path toward the river and ducked along the bank from hut to hut until we reached the cove. "This one." One of the smaller ones. We couldn't be sure we'd have enough men to row the big one. We sat on a pair of seats to wait for whatever happened next, and I caught her up. She nodded like none of it was a huge surprise. "Did you foresee this?" I asked.

"That's not what seeing is like. It isn't all 'ooh, magic visions of the future'." She bugged her eyes and waggled her hands beside her head.

Wait. Wasn't that a seeress' job description? "Then what is it?"

Sura gave me a look a physicist might give a file clerk who'd asked her to explain quantum theory. Not unsympathetic, but not flattering. "It's not that I see things others can't. I just notice things others don't." She smiled. "You, for example."

I was about to ask what she meant when she looked toward the palisade. "Movement." I followed her gaze. The gate was open. Dryas had drawn back. A group of horsemen came out and turned toward the cove. "Twenty-five, maybe thirty. "Tror. Taruthin." An edge of distaste. "Some of the younger men who've been sucking up since Tror took power. No one I'd want to have to rely on. Other than Tror." She sighed. "But that's not up to me."

We watched the group make its way down. "What's that?" Sura asked when they'd made it about half way.

"What?"

"Back at the palisade. Looks like an argument."

I looked. Shoving. Maybe blows. About a dozen horsemen—I couldn't tell who they were, other than that they weren't ours—broke toward Tror and his men. Apparently not everyone was prepared to sign off on a resolution that left Tror alive.

I heard Taruthin shout. The men in Tror's group kicked their horses into flight. Tror screamed a command. A dozen warriors rounded to face their pursuers, and unslung their bows.

The pursuers had bowmen too. More of them, and already in position. But it's hard to shoot from a moving horse unless you practise regularly, which none of them apparently did. Their first volley went wide. The second, by the time they managed it, wasn't much better. Only two arrows found their marks, in the same flank of the same horse. It screamed and bucked. Its rider fell to the ground. He got up quickly, only to take a pursuer's axe in the chest.

The rest of Tror's group was pulling away. Taruthin was in the lead, screaming something about fire.

I bracketed my mouth with my hands. "What?"

This time I heard. "Fire the other ships."

I leapt down. Thanks to the drought there was no shortage of flammable material. I gathered an armload of brittle grass from the edge of the guard house and piled it into the other small ship. Taruthin reined his horse to a halt next to the bow. "Get more."

"I was about to."

"And twigs. Dry twigs."

I'd been building fires before his parents were born, but there wasn't time to get my back up. I gathered more grass while Taruthin struck sparks from his flint and blew them into a small flame. Tror's party was almost at the cove. Only two of the men who'd stayed back were still mounted and still fighting. They were delaying the pursuers, but not all of them, and not enough.

I was passing an armload of twigs to Taruthin when Tror rode up. "Into the boat! Leave the horses!" He scrambled from his mount and ran to the bow of the boat Sura and Woden were in.

"What about the big boat?" Taruthin had a nice blaze going in the smaller one.

"There isn't time." Tror braced his back against the bow and pushed.

"You need horses for that," I shouted.

"No time." He strained against the shore, feet planted in the damp soil, leg muscles quivering.

"I'll hitch the team."

"I've got this. Get the men into the boat!"

We were going to die. Our pursuers were going to find us neatly arranged in the boat while Tror strained at the impossible task of launching it.

Then it moved. Just a shudder. But movement.

People sloshed through the water toward the gunwales. I helped them climb up. Warriors, mostly. Some had brought their wives. No children. I hoped that meant none of them had any. Our pursuers were a couple of hundred paces away.

The boat shuddered again. Then it shifted, just a hand's breadth.

Taruthin splashed over to Tror. "Let me help."

"I have this. Get in." An arrow hit the hull near his shoulder. Tror's ego was going to get us killed. Then the boat started to slide. Slowly. Then faster. The stern rose. Taruthin scrambled up over the bow. I was right behind him. "Man the oars," he yelled.

There were five oarlocks to a side. Those of us nearest the seats took our places. Two oars fell overboard in the scramble.

Four pursuers arrived at the cove. Taruthin and two other men with bows notched arrows. Their aim was good. Two pursuers fell. The other two waded into the water, axes raised.

The boat was now fully afloat. Tror was in the water to his waist.

He gave the prow a sideways heave, and it turned lazily toward the mouth of the cove. He spun to face the pursuers. I don't know what atrocities they'd seen Tror perform in their villages, but I'd never seen men more determined to kill someone. And they were going to. Tror didn't have time to draw his axe. The men were almost within axe-swinging range.

Almost. Which made the difference. Because almost within axe-swinging range is well within oar-swinging range.

In a single movement Tror plucked a floating oar from the water and swung it in an arc that smashed both men's faces into mush. He sprang over the side just as the prow lined up with our line of escape. "Row!" he screamed.

We already were. Hard. In perfect unison.

Without even singing.

We weren't entirely out of the woods. We took a volley of arrows as we left the cove. One caught a starboard rower behind the ear. Tror tossed him over before he stopped twitching and took his place.

Our speed was good, but we were drifting toward to the far shore of the cove, where group of mounted archers was headed. "Ishtanu," Tror shouted. "You can steer, yes?"

"Well enough."

"Up you go."

Woden was at my heels, as usual. "Can I watch?"

"Sure. Just keep your head down."

We made it out of arrow range without any more casualties. The pursuers launched the big ship, but there were too few of them and they were poorly organized. The last we saw they were grounded on a marshy bank, their shouts carrying over the calm surface of the river. At the Danube, Tror chose upstream rather than down. "They won't expect that. Plus we can do better against the current than they can."

"We can do better in a *duck* pond than they can," Woden said excitedly. "They can't row at *all*." The innocent triumphalism of small boys. Tror gave his son a curious look, like he'd never quite seen him before. Then he laughed.

"You heard it, boys." He pointed deeper into Europe. "Up the duck pond."

If you're expecting a story of happy migration to fertile new lands, you'll be disappointed. For the next four years we were basically pirates. We'd find an cove and set up an encampment. We'd raid neighbouring villages or passing boats and take what we could carry. The locals would raise enough men to drive us out. We'd move upstream and start again. Sometimes there would be casualties. Sometimes we'd get recruits. Farm boys looking for excitement, usually. But however the roster shifted, we were always called the Aesir.

I hated being a bandit. I still had nightmares about being on the other side. "Why not just settle some place where we can plant crops and raise horses?" I asked Tror, more than once.

"Every good spot is occupied, and we don't have the manpower to take them."

I could've left, but that would have meant leaving Woden with Tror and his savage friends as the boy's only role models. Plus I was a little in love with Sura by then. I never laid a hand on her. I wanted to keep my hands. Tror was fiercely possessive of his property. Not that I would have tried. What hope would I have had? She was the alpha dog's wife.

Soon after we set up our first settlement, Sura went herb hunting. I went along for her protection. Mostly. It was the first time we'd been alone together since our escape.

"We need an open space with plenty of sun," she said. "Look for a plant about as high as my shoulders, with reddish stems and clusters of yellow flowers."

"What is it?"

"Wormwood."

"What's it for?"

"Intestinal worms. General digestion. Brewers use it to flavour ale." She paused.

"And?"

"What makes you think there's something else?"

"There's always something else. Plus the way you paused."

She turned away. "I can't tell you."

"You have to, now."

"I really can't. It's part of the secret teachings." I started to protest, but she raised her hand. "However. Suppose there was an herb that could end an ... inconvenient pregnancy."

"How could a pregnancy be inconvenient?" I thought of Ishara crying in the night. "Every man wants children."

"Yes. Every man does."

The significance of what she was saying sank in. "This herb can do that?"

"No, of course not. Why would the gods let something like that exist?" She turned back to the path. "Though if they did, maybe they'd allow even more effective ones." She pushed back a branch and ducked under it. "On a different subject, if you see a waist-high plant with frilly leaves and yellow flowers at the top, let me know."

The trees opened onto a sunlit meadow. Sura walked slowly, forehead creased in concentration. She spotted something to her right. "Fleawort. Excellent." She opened her linen bag. The leaves she picked didn't look much different from the rest of the meadow. They were green. They had a bumpy stalk up the middle.

"What's it for?"

She kept picking as she spoke. "It has different uses. Poultices for cuts and rashes. Tea for coughs. You could help pick, you know." I bent next to her. She smelled of earth and sun-warmed skin. I tore loose a handful of leaves. "Not so rough. Pinch them off at the base, like this." I followed her example. They gave off a pleasantly astringent scent. "Much better. You learn quickly."

Soon her bag of leaves was the size of my head. "That'll do for now. Remember this place. We'll want to come back."

By the time we were done we had a fair assortment, including the waist-high plant with the yellow flowers. Though all Sura would admit it was good for was headache and joint pain.

"I have a question," I said as we walked back to camp.

"You're very curious today."

"Not about herbs. About something you said when we fled. In the boat."

Her eyes narrowed. "Yes?"

"Um. Well. You, ah …"

"I said I noticed things. About you. Things no one else notices."

"Um. Yeah."

"You want to know what they are."

"Well yeah, I've been wondering. If you wouldn't mind."

There was a curl of amusement to her smile. "Are you sure?"

It hadn't occurred to me I wouldn't be. Now I wondered. "Why? Is it bad?"

She laughed. She had a captivating laugh. "Not exactly bad. But I see a lot. I wonder if you really want to know how much."

"Well I can't *not* go there now, can I?" How bad could it be?

I thought I knew, actually. But I hoped I was wrong.

"All right. What I notice is that you don't get older."

There it was. But I had my talking points ready.

"Sure I do. It just doesn't show much yet. My father was exactly—"

"No, Ishtanu. You don't get older, and you don't get sick, and your wounds heal overnight. Or was your father exactly like that, too?"

"Sure he was. Amazingly resilient, my dad …" But I could see from her smile that I wasn't getting anywhere. "Does anyone else know? I try to be discreet. Walk like I'm older. Keep my hair covered."

"I can help with that. Add some grey to the beard. The temples too. There are tinctures."

I felt an rush of warmth, like a bucket of sun-heated water sluicing grime from the deck of a boat. She could help with that. This wonderful, fragrant woman wanted to help with the deadening load I carried on my own. It wasn't until she said the words that I realized how big a load it had been. I felt dizzy.

"Whoa." She steadied me. "Sit for a second." She guided me to a flat boulder. "Deep breath. That's it. Another." Gradually the dizziness passed.

"Do the others know?"

She laughed out loud. "Are you kidding?"

"This could be serious. We run with a dangerous crowd. Who knows what they'd do if they knew?"

She put a hand on my cheek. "They don't. Noticing doesn't serve their interests."

"Why not?"

She patted my cheek and took her hand away. "They only notice what Tror wants them to notice."

"And Tror?"

Her jaw tensed. "Tror only notices Tror."

We were silent for a bit. Then we got up and continued toward camp. After a few paces Sura stopped and looked at me. "So how old are you, anyhow?"

"I miss our home," Woden said, about four years into our exile.

I put my arm around his little shoulders. "Me too, bud." We were sitting by a marsh-lined eddy near our current anchorage, tossing pebbles to startle the little fish that browsed there. "What do you miss most?" His hut, I assumed, or his friends. He surprised me.

"Having our own stuff. Instead of taking it from other people."

I nodded. He was too young to realize his stuff had always been taken from other people. But that was okay. I tossed a pebble. Tiny fish scattered.

"When I'm leader, we're going back to that." The earnestness of a privileged nine-year-old.

"To our old home? I don't think we can do that."

He gave me a look. "I'm nine, not stupid. Back to *having* a home. To making our own stuff."

I looked around at our scruffy encampment. "I hope you do, bud. I hope you do."

Woden had always spent a lot of his time drawing pictures in the dirt. Animals. Weapons. Battles. Like kids do. One morning I saw him by the shore drawing our ship in the wet dirt with his finger. He was getting frustrated because little waves kept lapping up and rubbing parts of it out.

"Why don't you do it farther up?"

"The dirt's too dry. The lines are too crumbly."

As he patiently fixed his drawing, I had a thought. "Let me try something."

That afternoon I found a flat piece of driftwood, and hollowed out a shallow cavity as wide as my hand. Then I dug into the earth deep enough to find something like clay, and filled the space with it, smoothing it until it was even.

"What's this?" Woden asked.

"A place to make drawings." I gave him a stylus I'd carved from a broken arrow shaft. "With this you can probably even get pretty good detail."

His face lit up. Then he frowned slightly. "Won't the clay dry out?"

"Then wet it again." I nodded at the river. "You expecting a water shortage?"

Soon it was hard to separate him from his drawing tablet. Whenever he wasn't learning ship maintenance or combat skills from Tror, he was making increasingly intricate drawings. Soon I'd made him half a dozen tablets, so he could keep some of his pictures.

Tror thought it was pointless. "He spends too much time on those toys. It doesn't help feed us or defend us."

"Singing doesn't feed or defend us, but we do a lot of that."

"Singing defends us. It organizes our rowers. Frightens our enemies." A reflective expression crossed his face. "It helps us remember who we are."

"A lot of Woden's drawings are of our ship and our camp. Maybe they help him remember who we are."

Tror grunted. But he didn't take Woden's tablets away.

A lot of languages flowed up and down the river. We met plenty of Thracian-speakers, especially in the early years, but the farther inland we went the more people we encountered from an entirely different language group. If we spent enough time with any of them—usually through conscripting them or occupying their farmsteads—I made the effort to learn their languages. I assumed it would come in handy. It did.

Toward the end of that year we camped near where, five or six centuries later, a tribe of Celts would set up the village that would become Vienna. Back then, though, that stretch of the Danube was farms and fishing camps and sometimes a grubby pop-up market.

"How do people know when it'll be there?" Woden asked once.

"I don't know." It wasn't like the vendors could tuck flyers under people's windshield wipers. And yet there it would be, bustling away.

We were in uneasy demand at these markets. We had good merchandise, and bartered fairly. Experience had taught Tror the wisdom of honest dealing. But a day later and an hour downstream, we might take it all back from you as you sailed home. Not deliberately. We didn't *target* our trading partners. It was just the nature of our job.

The market was as illicit as a market could be. Pork from stolen pigs. Timber from some poor villager's knocked-down hut or boat. The ale in the ale-hut brewed from whatever spilled grains the aleman had picked out of the cart tracks.

The vendors were a rough mix of bandits and brawlers. They kept us fed with the things we couldn't grow or forage for, and accepted the clothing and cookware that were often all we had to trade. Sometimes we managed to loot a trading ship. Then Tror and his closest followers would blow the profits on fatty meats and rough wine and the women at the edge of the market who hired themselves out by the hour.

With the market already so disreputable, you can imagine what we thought of the hunched little man who set up on the riverbank beyond its fringe. How degraded did you have to be to be unwelcome in that pit?

Tror strolled up to him gaily, clearly meaning mischief. "What's for sale, then?" He gestured at the man's dirt-smeared woollen sack.

The man peered from under the hood of his cloak. "Who's asking?" He spoke a kind of Thracian, but it wasn't his first language.

"You must be new." Tror stood straight and squared his shoulders. "I'm Tror of the Aesir." He waited for a response.

"Oh. Right."

Tror looked a little hurt. While he was stirring his mind for a reply, Taruthin cuffed the man. "Show some respect. Tror's an important man."

The man held his arms up defensively. "Sorry. I didn't know." He shuffled back a pace. "I just got here."

"From where?" No doubt Tror was hoping for the name of some town fabled for its riches, which this grimy fellow might have run off with.

The man waved a nervous arm northward. "Other side of those mountains."

"What town?"

"Not a town. A mine."

"Gold?"

The man shook his head.

Taruthin kicked the bag. Its contents clunked together heavily. "What's in there?"

"Better than gold."

"Better than gold? Like what? Self-filling wine cup? Unicorn steak?"

The man opened the mouth of the sack. Taruthin peered inside and laughed. "Rocks. Plain old rocks!"

Tror reached in and pulled out a fist-sized lump of rough grey stone. He shook it in the man's face. "Better than gold? When I can find a hundred like it anywhere along this riverbank? What, does it have magic powers? Heals wounds? Neutralizes poisons? I've heard them all."

Heard them and fell for them, I thought. But the thought was fleeting, because I couldn't take my eyes off the rock. "Can I have a look?" Tror tossed it to me. I caught it and held it to the light. I was right.

So was the little man.

"You may find it hard to believe, but this *is* better than gold." I held it toward the man. "Is this from the mine you mentioned?" He nodded. I turned and held it toward Tror. "This could be a game-changer."

The man's name was Rhaskos. The tin mine was a three-day walk through the mountains and another three days by boat down a river he didn't know the name of.

Tror was looking at the rock sceptically. "Explain how this is more valuable than gold?"

"Could you use a copper axe?"

"Of course not."

"What about a bronze axe?"

"They're all bronze. What's your point?"

"This rock turns copper into bronze."

"So it's magic?"

"No. You melt them together."

"Melt a rock?"

"Yes. Well, no. Not exactly."

I began to appreciate how patient Yassib had been with me in Qadesh.

We took Rhaskos and his bag of ore to our camp. Tror didn't want the market bandits to know what we had. When Rhaskos resisted, Tror had Taruthin do some persuading.

I found a flat rock with a thumb-sized depression and heated it on banked coals to melt a small copper amulet. I added a chunk of one of the rocks. The tin bled out, as it had when Yassib showed the process to me. I muddled the liquids together with a water-soaked stick.

Tror watched carefully. "Now what?"

"We let it harden."

We shifted the makeshift crucible out of the coals and watched it as it cooled. Rhaskos sat apart, on a fallen tree three or four paces away. When we eventually pried out the rough bronze disc it had sharp edges from the shape of the depression. Tror tapped it on the rock. "Nice and hard." He scraped it along a branch, and grinned as it peeled the bark away. "Not bad, Ishtanu. Who knew you could be useful?" Then an idea seemed to take him. With a flick of his wrist he sent the disk sailing toward Rhaskos. It buried itself an inch deep in the log next to the man's hip. Rhaskos yelped. Tror laughed. "Rhaskos my friend. Take us to your mine."

Rhaskos glanced at Taruthin, who smiled wetly.

"Happy to."

The planning started the next morning, and immediately got complicated.

"Three days through the mountains?"

"Yes."

"With our boat?"

Rhaskos shook his head. "Oh, no. You couldn't haul that boat through the mountains."

"That's my point." Tror was already losing patience. "But we'll need a boat on the other side, yes?"

There was a sheen of sweat on Rhaskos' forehead despite the cool breeze from the river. "Yes."

"So you see the problem." Tror cocked his head to one side and stared at Rhaskos. So did Taruthin. Rhaskos went pale as he realized that they were expecting *him* to solve it.

"Um. Well." He blinked sweat from his eyes. "You could sell this boat and buy another one on the other side?"

"Sell the boat? Have you *seen* the market? The biggest thing they've ever handled was a haunch of venison."

Rhaskos was starting to tremble. "Um … leave the boat here and steal one on the other side?"

That was on brand, but risky. It would mean giving up an actual boat for one we might not find. Still, Tror was considering it when Woden spoke.

"We take it apart and then put it back together."

Tror cuffed him. "Don't be an idiot, boy. Leave the thinking to the men." He shook his head and chuckled. "Take it *apart*."

Woden didn't give up. "Let me show you." He went to the linen bag where he kept his few personal things, and came back with one of his larger drawing tablets. "Look. The ship is made of parts." I bent over the tablet. It wasn't just a drawing. It was practically a blueprint. If we'd had blueprints. "You see how the hull fits together here, and here?" Over the next twenty minutes or so, the boy explained in detail how the ship could be taken apart, transported on wagons, and reassembled. "We'd need to find pitch somewhere, of course, to make it watertight. But it can be done." We all stared at him. "And wagons, of course."

We'd need at least a dozen, plus horses to pull them.

"Or men," Tror said.

Taruthin shook his head. "Hard work. I can't see our men agreeing to it."

"I wasn't thinking of using *our* men."

So our raids took on a new focus: wagons, horses and conscripts.

It took about a month, but eventually we'd stolen or built enough carts for the task—by luck one of our new conscripts was a wheelwright—and horses for about half of them. After one last push we had men for the rest.

Under nine-year-old Woden's direction the men broke the boat into its parts and loaded them for transport. Rhaskos' three-day hike took five with loaded carts. Along the way I got to know him a bit.

"Tough work, mining. That's why I left. Dawn 'til bedtime, seven days. Hammering, mostly. I'm not a big man." He smiled weakly. "Took a rock here and a rock there, not enough to be noticed. Figured I could buy my way onto a boat and get to one of the big kingdoms down the coast." He frowned. "Made a good start."

"You're returning in force, now."

"Not to that mine."

Wait, what? "Then where are you taking us?"

He realized what he'd said. "No no, don't worry. There are dozens of mines there. I'll get you to one. Just not that one. Please."

It wasn't hard to imagine what might be waiting for him there.

Eventually the mountains tapered to a river valley. We passed a couple of villages until we found one with signs of shipbuilding. Its shipwrights enthusiastically helped us rebuild the boat on the sensible understanding that once we were back on the water we'd stop beating them up and taking their stuff.

When we left I covertly paid them for their time in tin ore. If Rhaskos was right, we'd soon have plenty. We also left them our carts and horses. A pony on a boat isn't as much fun as it sounds.

We made easy progress after that, downstream all the way. The morning of our third day the river flowed into a larger one, and that afternoon Rhaskos pointed to a green ridge in the distance to our left. "The ore mountains. Tin mines all over 'em."

At the edge of the tin mountains we passed a town with a series of wharves, a market square, and a cart track into the surrounding forest. We carried on beyond it to a secluded cove where we beached the boat. Tror took Rhaskos and half a dozen warriors into the mountains to find a suitable mine. They were back the following day. "Flat ground for huts," Tror said. "Stream for water. Kids fishing, so it could be a food source. Clay pit with a potter's hut. At least I took the smoke to be from a kiln fire."

"What about the tin?" I asked.

"Production looked good," Rhaskos said. "Two large horse carts. Both looked well used, and one was about half full of ore."

"Population?"

Tror smiled. "Small enough to take. Large enough to do the work."

At dawn the next day our warriors dressed in what armour we had and filed through the forest. We could hear it before we could see it: a rhythmic pounding of hammers on rock. Rhaskos pointed. "See that cliff face above those trees?" I nodded. "The mine is at its base."

The village was in a clearing a hundred paces from the cliff. I counted a dozen huts before I lost track. There were fewer than twenty of us, but we were well-armed. "Spread out," Tror said as we left the cover of the trees. We approached in two lines with Tror at the centre. A villager cried an alarm. People scrambled from their huts to see what was wrong. Mothers held children close. The few men not at the mine faced us sternly, the women and children behind them.

A man with receding hair and a salt-and-pepper beard stepped forward. "Who are you?" he asked. His language was near enough to the one I'd picked up on the Danube, so I translated.

Tror ignored the question. "Who's in charge?" I translated.

"I am," the bearded man said.

Tror didn't wait for my translation. He nodded. Taruthin raised his bow and shot the man in the eye.

And so we became miners. Well, mining executives. The villagers did the work. We lived off the profits. It was a simple enough business model: build a big fire against the cliff face until the rock grows fragile, hammer out the ore with mallets, and take it to the river market to trade. When the rock gets too resistant, build another fire.

Before our arrival the villagers had made a decent subsistence living. Tin was valuable enough that they could live well without overdoing it, with plenty of leisure time for fishing and family and handicrafts. Their pottery was quite lovely.

Tror changed all that.

Now the men put in longer hours quarrying, plus Tror had them working on new buildings. A large hut with a stone foundation and brick walls for him and his family. Another like it, but smaller, for Taruthin, who had no family. He'd been betrothed more than once, but they always seemed to run off before the wedding. And at the edge of the clearing, a barn-like structure was taking shape.

"What's it for? Crops?"

"We're not here to grow crops, Ishtanu. Or to be tin miners."

"It's a tin mine. That's kind of why we came."

"It isn't the tin that matters, though, is it? It's the bronze." He lingered over the last word the way a pantomime miser might linger over the word "gold" while dribbling coins through his fingers.

"And so this building ...?"

"Is where you're going to make bronze for me."

He knew exactly what he wanted. Knives. Arrowheads. Axes. Militarization on a large bronze-age scale. And that was as far as he needed to think it through. My job was to figure out how to give it to him. What I might've wanted didn't figure into it.

Again, I could have left. Again, Woden. And Sura.

First we needed copper. I asked at the riverside market. Boatloads of ingots came upriver from the south every couple of months. "We can probably make a trade when they stop at the village," I told Tror.

He smiled at Taruthin. "Or we could do it another way." Six weeks later, when the two of them and half a dozen others turned up with blood-spattered tunics and a cartload of copper ingots, I didn't need to ask.

We also needed moulds.

"Clay will work, but stone is better if we're going to reuse them." Within the week Tror brought me a stonemason. He was scared speechless and bruised all over his neck and face, but he was magic with a chisel. The arrowheads from his moulds were so precise they'd make you weep—which he did pretty much the whole time he was with us. He also made the stone crucibles I used for blending the alloy, the stone rods I used for stirring, and the stone clamps I used when I tipped the molten bronze into the moulds.

With help from some of the villagers, I cranked out thousands of arrowheads and hundreds of axes and knives in a matter of weeks. We built a forge, where I hammered the knives and axe blades to razor sharpness. The woodworkers fitted the axe heads to their handles and the arrowheads to their shafts, and carved bone handles for the knives. Tror stored a few crates of each in his hut, but kept most of them on our boat, which was guarded day and night in its hidden cove.

The larger our arsenal grew, the tighter Tror's grip got.

We started making talismans for trade. Indistinct faces of inter-changeable gods. They pulled in money from travellers on the river who wanted protection from storms or bandits—usually too late and after the fact. By the end we were experimenting with bronze bowls and drinking cups, cast, like the talismans, in clay moulds. For the more intricate pieces we used a technique Yassib had described to me, where you made a wax model, fashioned a clay mould around it, and melted the wax back out. It worked brilliantly once we mastered it. We didn't use it often, since the resulting pieces had to be smashed free. Reusable stone moulds were more cost-effective. We also made bronze ingots. They were more valuable than the ore, being refined and ready to go.

Profits rolled in: gold coin and fine wine and an array of luxury goods. But the more the profits accumulated, the less the workers saw of them. So a rumbling began.

Continued, really. There'd been rumbling against us from the start. Their dead leader's son was rumoured to be hiding in the moun-tains, though I seemed to be the only one who found that worrying. But so far the rumbles hadn't been open.

In the meantime we had more immediate concerns. "I don't think we're ending up with all the tin we mine," I said to Tror.

"How do you mean?"

"I mean that for the amount of ore coming out of this mountain, we should have more finished bronze. Not a lot, maybe. But more."

"What do you mean 'finished'? Axes? Ingots?"

"Everything."

"How do you know?"

"I don't. Not for sure. It's a feeling. I have a sense of how much tin goes into how much bronze. And I think some of it is going missing."

"How could it go missing?" He held one hand toward the cliff face and the other toward the smelting hut. "It goes from there to there."

"But no one keeps track. When we hammer out the ore we pile it where we can. When we move it to the smelting hut we pile it differently. When we break it up for smelting, the smaller pieces go into different piles again."

"You think someone is stealing it? Like Rhaskos did from his old mine?"

"Could be."

Tror's face went hard. "I'll have Taruthin torture them until they confess."

"We wouldn't know where to start. Too many workers at too many stages. Plus Taruthin's tortures are too effective to be useful. He'd have every worker here confessing to the sack of Troia if that was what you wanted."

"He *can* be a bit enthusiastic. So what do we do?"

"We need to keep better track of how much there is at each stage. Then if some goes missing, we'll know where, and when, and who could've taken it."

"So first we need a way to measure the amounts. Then we need someone who can remember them. Do we have anyone we can trust with that?"

"I have a more reliable way."

I'd had the woodworkers make a shallow box which I'd filled with clay. Tror sniffed. "That looks like one of Woden's drawing toys."

"It is, kind of. But this one is for writing." I had to use the Hatti word. The concept didn't exist in Thracian.

"What does that mean?"

"I'll show you." I'd trimmed a reed into a stylus. "Give me some numbers of things."

"What kinds of things?"

"Anything. Boots. Chickens. The more the better. Make the numbers as mixed up as you can."

"You mean like, 'six pairs of boots, twenty-one cups of beans', that kind of thing?"

"Exactly." I noted both in Hatti cuneiform. "More. As many as you like."

"Um. Four hundred and eleven arrowheads."

"Good." Into the clay they went.

"Fifty-eight mares."

"Keep going."

We ended up with a list of twenty things, no two the same quantity.

"All right," I said, tucking my stylus behind my ear. "Let me read that back."

By the end of the list Tror's eyes were practically bugging out of his head.

"These marks tell you everything I said?"

"Yes."

"But ... but how can they *do* that?"

"A lot of men can do this where I come from. We learn it so we can keep track of things. Like we can do with the ore, now. I can teach you, if you like."

"No!" He took a step back. "This is a strange power. I don't like it. It's beyond my understanding." It occurred to me that if Tror got creeped out by everything beyond his understanding, he'd never crawl out from under his blanket. "I understand *things*, Ishtanu. Things I can hold, or throw, or crush. But marks that *mean* things?" He shook his head with a shudder, as if the very idea of abstract representation might already have infected him through his eyes.

Which it kind of had, as it turned out.

A pleasant realization spread through me. Tror was *scared*. For him the written word was a kind of magic, a power he didn't understand and couldn't control. And, more importantly, didn't want to. Because he'd grown up singing tales that told him strange powers always came with a horrible cost. He looked at me warily. "But if *you're* okay using them ..."

I restrained a chuckle. There it was. Tror was fine with taking the benefit of this strange power, as long as the cost fell to someone else.

We started tracking our ore. We did it transparently, so everyone at every stage of the process knew it was happening. And although ore production stayed about the same, bronze production went up.

Tror was delighted. "Your odd marks have power, Ishtanu."

"You sure you don't want to learn them yourself?"

I might have suggested he drink his own urine. "No, I'll leave them to you." I knew he wouldn't have changed his mind. I just liked winding him up.

Pretty much everyone involved was happy with our foundry's new efficiencies, with one exception. Rhaskos seemed a little crestfallen.

I don't think Tror noticed. If he had, Rhaskos would have been given an appointment with Taruthin. And all of us would've noticed that.

"Make me a war hammer," Tror said a few days later.

"What's wrong with your axe?"

"It's too clean. It *slices*." Like slicing was a defect in an axe. "I want a weapon that *crushes*." He smiled to himself. "In fact that'll be its name. Crusher." He glared at me. "Make it."

I made a model hammerhead out of wax. It would be a one-off, so I wouldn't need a re-usable mould. When I showed him the model, he frowned. "Too small." I'd scaled it up from the largest war hammer I'd seen. The palm of my hand barely covered it. But if Tror wanted something bigger, then fine.

I made another model, half again as long. "Still too small." He drew a rough rectangle in the dirt with his finger. "This big." It was the size of my forearm. It was preposterous. I didn't know if it was possible to cast something that big.

"That'll take enough bronze to make five hundred arrowheads. Or a dozen axes. It'll be too heavy to lift."

"Never mind how much bronze it takes. We have plenty. And let me worry about lifting it."

This time he was satisfied with the model.

"Right. I'll cast the mould." I started toward the path to the clay pits.

"Wait."

Oh gods, what now? I turned back.

"You know those marks you make? The ones that mean things?"

"Yes?"

"Put some on the hammer. Its name. Crusher. And words of power. Calling down the aid of the gods. That sort of thing. All over it."

Tror had found the magic of the written word too hard to resist.

"Will do."

By the time I gave the model to the potters it was covered in cuneiform. Across the top I'd put "Crusher," as I'd said I would. The rest I don't remember exactly, but instead of invoking the gods I'd decided to have some fun. After all, I was the only one who knew what any of it meant. So it was mostly stuff like "If you think I'm a huge tool, you should meet the guy who wields me." That sort of thing.

Tror loved it.

"And this one?"

"A traditional invocation to the Hatti storm gods." If I remember it right, it was actually an unflattering description of Tror's backside.

"This will do nicely. Have the clay workers make the mould."

If archeologists ever recover that hammer from the bottom of the North Sea, they're going to go batshit over those inscriptions.

The final product came out beautifully. I cleaned the burrs from its edges and polished it to a fine glow. The woodworkers made a long handle from a length of walnut, and I secured them together myself. When it was finished I set it on my worktable and looked it over carefully. I was kind of impressed with myself. It was a unique and noble weapon. Almost fit for a god. If you ignored all the scatological inscriptions.

Tror gripped it by its handle and raised it over his head, laughing. His instincts had been right. The weight wasn't a problem for him. He had Sura perform a blessing ceremony for it in front of the community, with chanting and herb burning and water sprinkling. At the end he held it up to the sky in both hands.

"This is now the emblem of my rule. Crusher, vanquisher of foes. May all our enemies flee or fall before you."

Yeah, whatever, you big knob. It was still just a hammer.

Although Tror and his warriors were fascinated by the cuneiform characters, none of them expressed any interest in learning to read or write. The only one who ever did was—unsurprisingly—Woden. "Can you teach me those marks?" he asked one evening as I recorded that day's ore production.

I considered the range of obscenities about his father that were now cast in bronze on our tribe's most prized artifact. "Another time," I said.

Somehow I never got around to it.

Tror's tragic flaw—apart from his ignorance, his vanity, his brutality, his greed, his licentiousness, and his overarching inability to treat others as human beings—was that, for all his skill at capturing places, he was rubbish at holding them. Wherever we went, our days were always numbered. Including our days at the tin mine.

"Warriors!" cried one of our sentries one day during the morning meal.

Tror sprang to his feet. "Where? How many?"

The sentry pointed inland. "That way. Dozens. Well-armed. Mercenaries, by the look of them." The former leader's son hadn't just been hiding. He'd been watching. And recruiting. You could pay a lot of mercenaries with the kind of wealth we'd accumulated.

Tror sighed. "It's Dryas all over again, isn't it, Ishtanu? Only this time we don't have a palisade." Part of the initial attraction of the place had been how poorly defended it was. Maybe if we'd been there longer Tror would have done something about that. But probably not. There was always too much meat to be eaten and wine to be drunk for him to bother with follow through. "Right," he said, more resigned than angry. "Anyone leaving with us follow me to the boat. Up the duck pond."

He'd seen it coming. That was why most of our weapons were already on board.

As we marched into the woods I saw Rhaskos slip furtively away in another direction. I hoped he'd cached enough pilfered ore to get him to that coastal kingdom he'd always dreamed of.

Our experience at the tin mine set the pattern for the next fifteen years, all the way to the North Sea. We'd take over a village with our superior war tech. Tror would kill their leaders and force our ways on them. Eventually they'd rally the neighbours and force us farther north.

The farther we went the more the languages changed. I made the effort to learn every new variant. So did Woden. Sura always picked up enough to be able to compare notes with other wise women. No one else could be bothered. Especially not Tror.

"They'll learn our language. Otherwise what's the point of conquering them?"

Sometimes a child was born into our group, but not often. For a while I didn't give it much thought. The longer it went on, though …

I usually went with Sura when she scouted each new location for herbs. She always looked for pretty much the same ones. Including the one with the yellow flowers. "I've told you, Ishtanu, it's good for headaches and joint pain." She sounded a little irritated when I brought it up near our latest new village.

"We've gathered bushels of the stuff. I have a hard time believing our people get that many headaches."

"How would you know? Are you our healer? Wait, no. That's me."

She was going to make me ask her outright. "Fine. Here it is. Our women don't produce many babies. Some none at all. I have to wonder."

Her face was impassive. "Wonder what?"

"You told me something years ago. Well, you didn't exactly tell me."

"Leave it, Ishtanu. I told you there is no such thing. And if Tror even suspected there was, can you imagine what he'd do?"

There it was. She didn't trust me. Not with this. Despite all we'd shared, on this she saw me as part of Tror's camp. His steersman. His armourer. It kind of hurt. We stood in awkward silence for a moment, the only sounds the buzzing of insects and the breeze rippling the grasses. Then I had an idea.

"Can I tell you something in confidence? It's about Tror's hammer."

By the time she stopped laughing the atmosphere had changed.

"There are ways to prevent a child from taking root at all, too, but they don't always work. The herb with the yellow flowers is a last resort. Most of the time it really is for headaches." There was a pleasant lull. Then her face went dead serious. "You understand how important it is that no one finds out, right?"

"Yes, I know. Especially Tror. I just don't understand why it's necessary."

"You're not a woman. Have you ever thought what it's like for one of our women to have a baby while living hand to mouth on plunder? Knowing she might be uprooted at any moment and shifted to some empty cove two days downriver?"

I hadn't. Though if I had, my benchmark for how women handle pregnancy would probably have been Tróán. And since she'd disembowelled an Achaean soldier at nine months, I might not have seen the problem.

"But the men will eventually suspect. And if there are no babies, our tribe will die out."

"Our women aren't planning never to have babies, Ishtanu. They're just waiting until we're more settled."

They might wait too long if Tror's pattern of conquest and flight continued, but I didn't mention that. Sura was as aware of that as anyone. Plus I had a question I wanted to ask instead. "Including you?"

"Including me what?"

She understood. She was just hoping I meant something else. I didn't. Woden was still Sura's only child.

"Waiting until we're settled?"

Her voice went tight. "No. Not including me. No matter how settled we get, Tror is never having more children by me."

Wow, I thought.

Sura damn sure trusted me now.

When Woden was twelve or thirteen I found him in his hut with a sharpened reed and an old goat skin scraped clean of its wool. He was pricking a design into the skin using dark berry juice. "I didn't know you did handicrafts."

He scrunched his pimply face in adolescent disdain. "It's the boat design." His old clay tablet with its rendering of our ship was on the ground next to him. I took a closer look. He was reproducing it on the goat skin. "The clay is deteriorating. If it gets smashed or wet, we'll lose the plans. This way I can roll it up and keep it safe."

I rarely regretted not teaching Woden cuneiform, but that day I did. If he'd learned to write, imagine the ripples it might've sent through the next two thousand years of Nordic culture. The Vikings might've invented the steam engine.

I try not to let my mind go too far down that sort of path.

Somewhere to the north we moved into a new language group. I pieced it together through negotiations in trading towns and post-coital chats with sex workers from so far north their hair was as yellow as grain.

Eventually the river ran out, and we found ourselves on a chilly sea coast. Tror, flabby and forty but still in charge, decided we should follow it north east until we located a suitable village.

We camped in a cove at the base of a long ridge. Tror sent Woden —now grown to full, tall manhood—on foot along the ridge line to scout for settlements. Sura went with him to look for herbs. I went as an extra sword arm. After an hour's walk, with stops for Sura to gather some plant or root, the ridge tapered toward the sea. Woden and I trudged downhill through long grasses that swished around our legs, while Sura followed a finger of cliff to search a small copse. We heard her call out a few moments later. She waved to us. We trudged back up.

From the cliff-edge we had a two or three mile view along the coast to a broad harbour with a rocky beach and a gentle river valley. Stone huts above the tide line were separated by chicken pens and green rows of vegetables. Farther up the valley the breeze rippled through fields of what smelled like barley. Fishing boats lined the beach and dotted the glistening waters of the bay.

"It's perfect," Woden said. "Open land. Healthy crops. The sea, for fishing." He gazed over the low hills further inland. "We could even raise horses here."

"And children," Sura said quietly.

Yes. In a place like this we could truly, finally be settled. But I shook my head. "It wouldn't last. They'd eventually drive us out like they always do." We stood in silence.

Then Woden spoke. "It doesn't have to be that way."

We looked at him. "Why not?" his mother asked.

He explained.

Woden could say anything in front of me and trust me with it. He knew my secret. I don't mean he held it over my head. I mean that by then our trust ran that deep. It was Sura who'd told him. I'd asked her not to, but he was a smart kid and was starting to notice on his own. Better to tell him than have him ask awkward questions in front of his father. He had questions, of course. I couldn't answer most of them. But I let him cut me lightly and watch it heal.

The problem, Woden said, was that we always imposed our language and ways on other villages. "What if we let them keep their own? Their language. Their laws."

Villages this far north weren't led by warrior chieftains, but by someone they called the lawspeaker, who kept their rules and traditions in his head and ritually recited them on special occasions. It was impressively civilized. So every time we took a village, Tror killed the lawspeaker.

"We'd leave the lawspeaker in place?" I asked.

"We'd have to."

Sura looked thoughtful. "And our traditions?"

"They could co-exist. Over time maybe the others would adopt them, or some of them. But we wouldn't force them to. The more familiar things stay, the less reason they have to want us gone. It's the forced change that's the problem."

"That and the brutality," I said. "If a man's whipping me bloody, I probably don't much care whose rule he thinks I've broken or what language he's cursing me in."

"Yeah, we'd have to rein that in."

"Though if we kept things more or less as they were," Sura said, "presumably the work would get done the way it always has. Maybe that would be enough. Maybe there'd be less need for ... discipline."

We stood in silence again. Finally I said what we were all thinking. "Tror would never go for it."

"No," Sura said. "He wouldn't."

Woden didn't say anything. But the gears were turning in his head. If we'd had gears.

Tror was excited at our find. "All right. Let's pick our moment." He was the master of the choreographed conquest by then. "What can we make use of?"

Taruthin eyed the clouds at sea. "Storm coming."

"Excellent. Let's see how it shapes up." He waved a commanding arm. "Up the duck pond."

The storm shaped up to Tror's liking. Rain not too heavy, plenty of lightning over the water. We rowed hard without singing. Woden steered. A couple of hundred yards off shore he pointed our prow directly at the rocky beach, and at Tror's command we rowed at maximum power, this time singing a fearsome war chant. Tror stood in the bow, his hammer raised overhead in both hands.

His timing was spot on. As the first villagers came out of their huts, a brilliant flash of lightning backlit Tror and his hammer in otherworldly silhouette. Its thunderclap hit the downbeat of our war chant. The boat crunched to a halt on the beach. To the villagers it must have looked like a visit from the gods. Which was the idea.

They didn't cave, though. As we leapt over the gunwales and ran through the surf, they launched a volley of arrows. It was brave but futile. The wind of the storm blew most of the arrows wide, and before they could reload our bowmen were close enough to take two of them down.

Not all of the villagers' arrows went wide, though. A lucky shot—for the villager, not for me—drifted wide of Taruthin and took me hard in the left shoulder, spinning me toward where Woden was advancing with his axe. I cried out and grabbed the shaft with my hand. "Leave it!" Woden shouted. In Hatti.

That stopped me. More than the arrow. "Excuse me?" I said, also in Hatti.

"Leave it. Keep going like it isn't there. I have an idea."

No one else seemed to notice our exchange. I squared my shoulders and walked up the beach as steadily as I could, stepping over a dead villager. It wasn't easy. But whatever his idea was, I trusted it.

Our warriors quickly put an end to the resistance. They gathered the villagers on the beach in the rain, then parted to let Tror come forward. He loved an entrance. "Which of you is the lawspeaker?" He said it in Thracian, of course. I was about to translate when Woden held up a hand. "Let me," he said. Still in Hatti.

Fine by me. I was tired of drawing lawspeakers out to their deaths. Plus my shoulder hurt like blazes. I hoped he'd tell me when we could do something about it.

Woden spoke loudly and clearly. "If you are the lawspeaker, do not identify yourself to the man with the hammer."

Wait, what?

I looked at him, puzzled. "Follow my lead," he said. He turned back to the crowd. "Our leader wants to kill the lawspeaker." A balding man near the centre looked apprehensive. "But I want the lawspeaker to live."

Tror was impatient. "How long does it take to ask who the lawspeaker is? It can't be that complicated a language."

"They don't understand the question. I'm trying it in different ways."

Tror waved a hand. "Go on, then."

Woden addressed the villagers again. "I suggest that one of your women tell me that you have no lawspeaker."

A stout woman with serious eyes stepped forward. "I don't know what you're doing, but somehow I trust you more than I trust the man with the hammer. So I'll tell you what you want to hear. We have no lawspeaker."

Woden turned to Tror. "They have no lawspeaker."

"Well ask who their leader is, then. I need to execute *somebody*."

I could see Woden's gears turning. He addressed the woman again. "Point to the oldest dead bowman on the beach and tell me his name."

The woman looked back and forth between Tror and Woden. Her choice was clear, and she knew it. She pointed to the nearest body. "His name was Alfhildr. We were cousins."

Woden turned to Tror. "That simplifies things. We've already killed him."

Tror grinned. "I love it when a plan comes together."

While our crew hauled the boat up the beach and started unpacking our goods, Woden told Tror he was going to see if they had a healer who could look at my wound. Tror looked at the arrow in my shoulder like he was seeing it for the first time. "Is that still in there?" He laughed and shook his head. "All right, get it seen to."

We walked toward the balding man. He looked uneasy, but didn't avoid us. Woden smiled kindly. "You're the lawspeaker, aren't you?"

He only hesitated for an instant. "Yes."

"Your name?"

"Meinrad."

"Good to meet you, Meinrad. Sorry about the circumstances. My name is Woden, and this is Ishtanu." Tentative nods of greeting all around. "I've told our leader we're looking for a healer. We're going to pretend that's you. Agreed?"

"Agreed." There weren't many options.

"Do you have a cloth we can use to staunch Ishtanu's wound?"

"I can get one." He called to the woman who'd spoken earlier. She ducked into a hut and came out with a square of folded wool.

"My wife, Brynja," Meinrad said. "She's the healer."

Woden smiled at her. She didn't smile back. "Good. Our story will be that you are both healers, together."

Brynja scowled. "Why don't you just leave us? We've done nothing to you."

"That's not going to happen, Brynja. We're here. You're going to have to adjust. My hope is that we can make that adjustment easier than if we left it to my father."

"The man with the hammer?"

Woden nodded. "Tror. His views of leadership aren't as … inclusive. I'm hoping to find a way around that, if you'll help me."

"Um …?" I pointed to the arrow in my shoulder.

"Yes, Ishtanu. We'll get to it. This is important."

Fine. I knew where my shoulder and I stood.

Woden quickly explained his plan. Meinrad would continue as lawspeaker, but covertly. Normal village life would also continue as much as we could manage it, except in direct interaction with us.

"How do we keep that balance, with two separate systems?" Meinrad asked.

Woden thought. "Is there somewhere secluded where we can meet?"

Meinrad and Brynja looked at each other. "Our cove?" he said.

She nodded. "Half a mile north there's a tiny inlet, surrounded by boulders. It's all but impossible to get to by land." They shared a wistful smile. "It's very private."

Woden smiled too. "Thanks for sharing it with us."

Woden and Meinrad agreed to meet there every ten days, or more often if needed.

"Um …?" I said again, looking at the arrow. "Our cover is that we're tending to my wound, right?" My shoulder was throbbing horribly.

Woden gave me a strangely serious look. "All right, Ishtanu. If we must. Not like it matters, though." *Play along*, said his tone. So I did.

Woden spoke to the couple more formally now. "There's something else you should know. Something that will explain why you have no choice." He gestured toward our warriors and our women. "You see, we aren't ordinary people. We are the Aesir. We have great power. And great gifts." He turned to me and spoke quietly in Hatti. "Grit your teeth."

He gripped the arrow with one hand, placed the other flat against my chest, and pulled. It came out cleanly, I'll give him that. But it still felt like being run through with molten copper. My eyes watered, but I didn't scream. Playing along, wasn't I?

Woden turned back my tunic to expose the wound, which was bleeding freely. "Bind it. We'll look at it again tomorrow. Then you'll know our power." Meinrad pressed the square of cloth against the wound, and Brynja bound it in place.

"Smart plan," I said under my breath as we walked away. "You couldn't have let me in on it earlier?"

"I was improvising."

The following afternoon my wound was just a fading scar. Brynja's face went ashen. "This is sorcery."

"No," Woden said. "It is the power of the Aesir. Teach your people to respect it."

"Our power?" I said under my breath as we walked away.

"Whatever keeps the peace."

Forced adjustments were made to the living arrangements. The largest hut—essentially a kind of community hall—went to Tror and Sura. Woden took the hut where Meinrad and Brynja and their children lived, bumping them to Alfhildr's. Their eldest, eleven-year-old Hrodulf, treated the move as an adventure—which it was, since it broke up the usual routines. Plus the notion that we were magical beings had spread among the villagers—especially the children—after Woden's pantomime with my shoulder.

"Can I help you move your things in?" Hrodulf asked Woden.

"I don't have much, but sure." I stuck around to watch. My few things were already in the grain shed Tror had designated as the new forge.

While Woden was arranging his armour in a wooden chest, Hrodulf unrolled the old goat skin with Woden's diagram of our boat.

"What's this?" he asked eagerly. He'd obviously never seen anything like it. Few people had.

Woden looked over his shoulder. "Oh. That's just my boat."

Hrodulf's eyes went wide. "You have an animal skin that can become a *boat*?"

Woden laughed. "No, I just—" He stopped himself. The gears were turning. Whatever keeps the peace. He lowered his voice confidentially. "Only in times of great need."

As soon as they were done unpacking, Hrodulf flew out the door to tell his friends about Woden's magic goat skin that could turn into a boat.

The arrangement with Meinrad worked well. He and Woden met regularly at the cove to discuss routine village management. Sometimes I went along. He appreciated the back up, since, apart from Brynja and Sura, I was the only other person in the loop. The brutal discipline that had characterized our previous occupations started to feel like a thing of the past. Meinrad resolved most disputes in the privacy of his hut, while we gave Tror the odd minor scuffle to decide, just to keep him believing he was in charge. Which he did.

Until he didn't.

"The grain harvest was a bit thin, I think," Woden said as we rowed into the cove, toward the patch of shingle where Meinrad's boat was already beached. "I'll have Meinrad look into hoarding. It must be tempting, when we take so much more than we let the villagers have." The bow scraped onto the shore, and Woden hopped out to pull it up farther.

"Be careful how you pitch it to Tror if they are. Our delicate balance—"

"How you pitch *what* to Tror?" said an unexpected voice from behind the rocks.

My guts went wobbly. Woden stayed poised.

"Father," he said brightly as he turned. "Why are you here?" He might've been asking why he'd chosen ale over wine for his lunch.

Tror strode casually down to the beach. He seized the prow of our boat with one hand and hauled it halfway up the rocks. He had his hammer in the other. He dropped the boat with a crash. I was still in it. It rattled my teeth.

"Don't piss around with me, boy. Your friend Meinrad is enjoying Taruthin's company in the forge at the moment, waiting on my word. When I left, Taruthin was heating his knife in the coals." He smiled. It wasn't a nice smile. His rarely were, but this one was particularly not nice. "You have about two minutes to explain these secret meetings. Depending on how satisfied I am, I may have him limit himself to the man's face." His smile dimmed. "But I doubt I'll be that satisfied."

Woden barely blinked. "Meinrad's the healer. He's a good source of information. We're just sparing you the day to day trivia."

I swung out of the boat and moved toward Tror's opposite side, my hand on my sword. Tror pointed his hammer at me. "Stop right there, Hatti, before I crush you." I held up my hands. Tror turned to his son. "Meinrad isn't the healer. His wife is the healer. Meinrad's the lawspeaker. The one you said they didn't have."

Woden tried to look like this was news to him, but he couldn't quite pull it off. "That's what they told me. You remember—"

"I remember you having a long conversation with the wife. You were cooking up this betrayal even then, weren't you?"

"Nobody has betrayed you, Tror," I said. "This is just—"

"This is between me and my son." He tossed his hammer lightly from hand to hand. "Who seems to have forgotten who the leader is. Who thinks he can rule in secret through whispers and trickery."

"Not trickery." I couldn't believe how calm Woden was. "Through understanding. It's working pretty well."

"It's indulgent. Worse, it's *weak*. You lead through strength, not through ... through *talking*." He shook his head in disgust. "That's what Dryas never understood. Always going around to the other tribes, talking and talking, like women at their weaving. Making us look *weak*. That's why I had to stop Loricus from handing the tribe over to him and his idiot boy."

Wait, what?

"But Dryas killed Loricus. Or had him killed. Because he was going to confirm you."

Tror looked at me with disdain. "Do you really think Lori would've let him do that? Turn the tribe over to a foreigner? To Tróán's son?" He stretched his free hand toward the ground as if Loricus' hut were there in front of us, across the years and the miles. "She was alone with him, day after day. Whispering to him. Working him." His lip curled at the injustice of it. "She would've kept him there until she got what she wanted, one way or the other. Either he'd make Pyotr his heir, or, if he died first, she'd tell us he did." He shrugged. "I had to find another way."

I felt sick. "You can't know what Lori was doing. No one was allowed in there."

He shook his head. "Honestly, it's like talking to a child. Lori's handmaidens were in and out all the time." I thought about the young women outside the hut that morning, howling in shock and fear. Bile burned my throat.

"You told me you didn't do it!"

"And you believed me! Taruthin and I still laugh about that."

Dryas said there'd been at least two killers.

I stared into Tror's eyes. He stared back. Not defiantly. Just amused.

I looked away. "That's it. I'm done."

"Done? Done with what, exactly?"

I looked around at the rough patch of beach. The boulders around us. The two little boats. "All of it. All of you." I shook my head. "I can't stay. Not anymore."

His amusement took on a menacing intensity. "You're right about that, at least."

"What's that supposed to mean?"

"I can hardly keep you around now, can I? Not after this. But if I let you go, what's to stop you from coming back one day and upsetting our little village with these pointless old stories? Upsetting my wife." Beautiful, fragrant Sura. Loricus' daughter. And Lori's.

I looked toward Woden. He was motionless. I looked back at Tror. "You can't kill me in front of your boy."

"My *boy*?" He laughed. "My *boy* will do as I tell him. If he doesn't, I'll skin his mother in the square." It was his offhand tone that did it as much as anything.

My sword was out before I sprang. Tror's eyes glinted as he raised his hammer to crush my skull. The hammer I'd made for him. He'd enjoy the irony in that, if anyone pointed it out to him. And explained to him what irony was. He was so confident he didn't even bother using both hands.

But he wasn't as quick as he'd once been. Or as young.

I was. I was still sharp. And so was my sword. When the hammer paused at the top of its swing, I took Tror's hand off at the wrist.

Hammer and hand dropped together onto the rocks beside him. He stared down at them in disbelief, leaving the side of his neck exposed. I took his head off on the backswing. My sword buried itself in his collarbone and stuck there. His head rolled around it and landed at his feet. He toppled sideways, wrenching my sword free.

There was a long beat of silence. Not even the sea made a sound.

"Wow," Woden said. "That was harsh."

I may be paraphrasing.

I bent double and threw up. My whole body was trembling. My sword slipped from my fingers and clattered on the rocks. I turned toward Woden in a panic. "How do we explain this?"

He looked at me calmly. "Explain what? To whom?"

"This!" I gestured at the headless corpse. "To the people. How it happened. Why it happened. What happens next. All of it."

Woden took me by the shoulders. "What happens next, Ishtanu, is that we carry on as we have, but with me as leader. Which makes it easier, obviously. The rest, no one needs to know."

"But Tror is *dead*. They'll notice. And I did it. We have to explain it to them."

"Explain what? That he was in our way? That he would've driven the people to rebellion? That he was killed by one of his own people while his own son stood by?"

That stopped me. I hadn't grasped the size of the mess I'd created, or that it could only get messier. "But it's the truth," I said weakly.

Woden squeezed my shoulders. "You don't rule by telling people the truth, Ishtanu. You rule by telling them what they need to hear."

What our people apparently needed to hear was that Tror had died slaying a giant sea serpent. "It had killed hundreds of people," Woden told them. The fact that there'd been violent thunderstorms to the north gave the story a ring of plausibility, if anyone asked around. A big storm could be relied on to kill a few people. The numbers didn't matter. People expected a little hyperbole from their leaders. "After battling the creature all day and night, your King, my father, finally slew it, but his own wounds were too great to bear. So instead of returning to you, he has gone on in glory to the Hall of the Fallen, in the world to come." He smiled. "Some of you may join him there one day."

That was the first I'd heard of any such place. I think Woden improvised it.

He was pretty shrewd at reading an audience.

What actually happened to Tror was less glorious. Once Woden convinced me we had to get rid of the body, we couldn't decide whether to burn it or push it out to sea in a boat. So we did both. The last I saw of Tror was a smudge of dark smoke near the horizon, drifting toward the approaching storm.

His hammer will still be out there, at the bottom of the North Sea.

Sura never questioned the story of her husband's death. And when Taruthin went missing from the forge that same day, she didn't question that either. No one did. Which was no surprise. Most of the village would've happily drowned him in a ditch once he lost Tror's protection. And if anyone noticed that Meinrad's new boots looked a lot like the ones Taruthin used to wear, they never mentioned it to me.

I stayed on a while longer, but my relationships with Woden and Sura never felt quite right after that. One morning I just left. I took a small boat and rowed north, from village to village and tribe to tribe, learning their ways, living their lives, moving on. Sometimes I became their lawspeaker. Sometimes when tales were told around the fire I added a few about Woden the wise or Tror the hammer-wielder, or the others I'd travelled with across what wasn't quite Europe yet.

When I got so far north that the villages ran out, I stopped. I'd never been so tired. I stayed there for years—I have no idea how many—entirely on my own, living on river water and reindeer meat.

It was the first of what I call my retreats.

Have you ever been bedridden for a long time, recovering from something? Really? You have my sympathy. I've been shot myself, more than once. Let me ask you this. While you were recovering, were there whole afternoons, whole days even, when you just weren't interested in reading, or listening to music, or doing anything at all other than existing in a bed? Awake, but in a kind of stand-by mode, and fine with that?

Don't look so surprised. It's common enough. Mind and body too busy healing to bother about stimulation of any kind.

Every so often I seem to run out of something. Life force. Will. Something. The brain can't go on, so it shuts down its higher systems. Tells the body to find a shelter and a food source and to pack the rest in. Basic life-sustaining activities only until further notice. Like that sick bed, but for years instead of days.

This was like that.

When I felt rested, I worked my way back south.

In the places I'd known, I was a stranger again. Anyone who might've remembered me was generations gone. But their descendants were still telling stories of Woden and Tror and the other Aesir. They weren't just my stories. Other versions had drifted up from the south, carried by merchants and raiders and nomads. Tror the tyrant and thug had become Thor, a dim Norse version of my old Hatti storm god. And Woden, strangely, had become his father, Wotan. I had to restrain a smile when someone told me, in all seriousness, that Wotan had a magic animal hide that could turn into a boat.

Woden's new status as Tror's father struck me as a good sign. There's something encouraging in the mythic instinct to put wisdom over brute strength.

Or if not wisdom, at least cunning.

Four Weeks Ago

I WAS WAITING for one of my logistics guys in an ironic bar where they only play Barry Manilow, and the cocktails are named for cartoons. The walls were covered in *Caillou* and *George of the Jungle*, and the bar painted to look like The Magic School Bus. I was at a corner booth sipping a Super Friends when he ambled in, lean and insolent and forty minutes late. Eleven O'Moron is a genial hoodlum who'll do pretty much anything as long as it isn't too violent and there's a buck or two for him at the end. He has a shaved head, a short ginger goatee, and inch-long sideburns hovering aimlessly in front of his ears. He thinks my name is Murray.

He winked at the sullen woman in the limp singlet behind the bar. "Bring us a Dora, love," he said, not slowing down on his way to my table.

"What's in a Dora?"

Eleven slapped his phone onto the table. "Tequila, guava *agua fresca* and Quick Brown Fox liqueur. Served in a beer boot."

"Is it as strange as a Super Friends?"

"Never had one. Saw it on blogTO. Can't be worse than the beer, though." He nodded toward an interior window, where a copper tank brewed pale liquid that tasted like crabgrass.

"Remind me why we meet here?"

"Hipster bar." He glanced at the empty tables. "Never anyone here 'til after ten."

The bartender brought him his drink. It looked like diluted gravy.

"Thanks, Angela."

She held out her hand. "It's Artura." Her voice had the kind of lassitude that took practice. Maybe in the mirror behind the bar. She'd have the time.

"Like there's a difference." Eleven handed her a ten.

Artura sighed elaborately. "Eleven sixty-five with the tax." We went through this every time. I think he was hoping if he did it often enough, I'd start picking up the cheque.

Eleven gave her a smile so thin you could open an envelope with it. "We're calling it ten today, yeah? And your tip can come out of that, too."

"Eleven sixty-five. With the tax."

He dug out another five. "Fine." When she reached into her apron for change he waved her off, suddenly magnanimous. "No, that's all set." She turned to go, still expressionless. "But I expect pretzels."

He turned back to me. "So. We have two distinct realities unfolding in real time."

"Without the bureaucrap." He does it to wind me up.

"I've got a bent immigration consultant for your Chechen's paperwork. Chap from back home. We were at magistrate's court together."

"I don't need his personal history. How soon can he get it done?"

Eleven sipped his drink. From his face it might've been prune vinegar. "I'll have to get back to you on the timing. Contingencies."

"Meaning he's squeezing us?"

He nodded slowly, like the thought was only just entering his mind. "Couple hundred. Maybe three." Which meant one. If anything.

I took a billfold from my jacket and handed him two US hundred dollar bills. The international currency of dodgy transactions. "No more contingencies. And your tip can come out of that, too."

He stuffed the bills into his shirt. "The equipment should be easier, if that helps."

"How's that coming?"

"Order's in. Invoiced to the numbered company in Germy's name. Waiting on a shipping date." He held up a hand. "Not a contingency. Just the way of these things."

"And Customs?"

"Should sail right through. Once it's clear I'll send Weiner to the broker's with the van."

I don't know if he thinks his pseudonyms for Jeremy and Wayne fool me, or if he's just mocking my circumspection. It doesn't matter. What matters is that he doesn't know anything about me. I have centuries of experience in counter-surveillance. Eleven couldn't follow me to the washroom unless I wanted him to.

"Anything else?" he asked.

"I need a lab. For the equipment."

He picked up his phone. "Any particular specs?"

"Water and power." He typed on the screen with his thumbs. "Sanitary surfaces. Space for the equipment. Fridge and stove. Separate room for a cot."

"Long or short term?"

"Try to make it month to month. I'll know more when I talk to the Chechen again."

The Dharma

THIS I HAVE heard. Suddhodana of the Shakya clan was the most overprotective parent ever. He raised his boy entirely inside the Gautama family compound, feeding him on caviar and Cornish hen—or whatever the aristocrats of the Himalayan foothills fed their princes—and somehow kept him from ever hearing about aging, or illness, or death. Don't ask how that's possible. Savour the legend.

He also kept him from learning any religion, which presumably left the young prince a comfortably shallow thinker who never wondered about anything deeper than his next lobster salad or lute recital, or—once they'd married him to his cousin—his next lie-down. Not an auspicious beginning for the founding of a major religion. Just goes to show.

I never met the Buddha. We didn't travel in the same circles. But eventually his ideas moved far enough west and I moved far enough east that we overlapped for a while. Not long. A few lifetimes. But he had a lasting impact on me.

According to the legend, it was his surprise discovery of suffering that drove him to develop a new way of living. I imagine it was quite a shock. Thirty years of perfect comfort, and then one day you and Alfred finally slip out of Wayne manor and *kapow*! Poverty and misery, right outside your walls.

What I admire most about him is that his reaction, right there at the beginning, was compassion. He could've gone a very different way. A lot of men would have.

I came to his ideas from the other direction.

Don't worry, I'm not going to tell you my whole life story. I assume you've been given a limited amount of time to get what you can from me, so I'll try to stick to the relevant bits. You'll just have to trust me that they're relevant. But what other choice do you have?

After the North Sea I was a lot of people in a lot of places. Eventually I felt a need to go back to Hattusha, just to see how the old place was getting on.

I couldn't find it.

A lot can change in a thousand years.

I couldn't be sure where anything was anymore. I found some stones that might have been part of the Great King's city, though they might just as easily have been the remains of some sheep farmer's hut. Ours, even. I couldn't even place the landscape.

It didn't help that entirely different groups were living there, with different languages and clothes, and different ideas about what gave offence. I spent a whole morning running from a stick-wielding mob just because I'd asked a young woman where the well was. Mind you, my Cappadocian was pretty rudimentary. I may have missed some subtleties.

I worked my way south toward Syria. I had the idea I might be able to find Halki's grave. Surely the bluff where Qadesh had been would look the same. Maybe Qadesh itself would still be there. Sometimes in towns along the way I'd get temporary work in a smithy, though I had to re-learn a lot of things. It was all about iron by then. Bronze was so last epoch. With work opportunities that tight, you take what you can. So I did. Even though it meant postponing Qadesh.

It started with a bowl of lentils and a headscarf.

I'd made it as far as Antioch. I decided to spend my last few coins on a decent meal before making the rounds of the smithies. The aromas from the food stalls in the market were making me so hungry it felt like my stomach was trying to claw its way out to get at them.

I settled on the stall with the prettiest server. The bench at the counter was empty. The young woman—she couldn't have been more than sixteen—was rinsing bowls in a bucket. She smiled tentatively. Three copper pots simmered on an iron grill over a brick-enclosed fire of banked coals. I sat on the bench and took a lingering sniff.

"How can food possibly smell so good?" I smiled my most charming smile. "That smell is easily the second best reason to come to this stall."

"The first being our food's taste?"

"I can't possibly know that yet, can I? What do you recommend?"

"The lamb stew."

"Done." I held out my palm with my few copper coins.

She laughed out loud. "I can maybe do you the lentils for that. A small serving."

"Oh, come on. You can upgrade a weary traveller to the lamb." I winked. "Special case?"

An older man with a badly trimmed beard stepped through the back curtain and set a cloth bag on the ground. "Don't be taken in by the likes of him." He looked me up and down. "Nothing special there that I can see." He took a fat onion from the bag.

The woman adjusted her rough woollen head scarf. "I wasn't *about* to." The universal tone of the long-suffering teenager. "Why do you assume I'll fall for every wink from a stranger?"

The man sliced the onion into one of the pots. "Don't pretend you haven't given me reason to."

She sighed theatrically. "Jonah isn't a *stranger*, father. And it was just a scarf."

The man started on another onion. "Yeah," he said, half to himself. "That's how it starts."

The woman snatched the coppers from my hand and stuffed them into a pocket on her father's apron without looking at him. Then she ladled a bowl of lentils and banged it on the counter in front of me. It looked pretty full for a small serving. Civil disobedience. The man kept slicing onions.

The smell of the food was mesmerizing. "What kind of lentils are these, that smell this good?"

"It isn't the lentils, fool. It's the spices."

"The what?"

She stared at me like I'd asked what the sun in the sky was. "The spices?" The insolence in her look was remarkable, even for a teenager. "The things that, like, flavour the food?"

"I thought food just had its own flavour."

She shook her head and went back to rinsing bowls. I tasted the stew.

I actually stopped breathing. Despite the aromas, I'd been expecting the slightly earthy flavour of your basic lentil. And it was there, but not as a solo voice. More like a reassuring bass under a riot of woodwinds and strings.

You've grown up with spices. Dried oregano in the spaghetti sauce. Salt and pepper at the table. Try to imagine first tasting any spice—*any* spice, of any kind—as a grown man. You can't. It would be like imagining your first breath.

I had no words. My mouth trembled. I held the stew there, savouring it. I swallowed almost reluctantly. "What's *in* this?"

The young woman looked up from her rinsing, irritated. "Just garlic and a bit of cardamom."

Garlic I'd heard of. Cardamom was new to me. "Where do you get it?"

She shook the water from her hands. "Every lane here has at least one spice stall. She looked my dusty clothes up and down. "But trust me, you can't afford it."

She'd missed my point. "But where does it *come* from?"

"Traders bring it in."

"From where?"

"From wherever traders *go*." She turned back to her rinsing.

I nursed the stew as long as I could. The man finished with his onions and began grinding seeds in a small pestle. The woman stacked the bowls, then scooped some lentils from a sack into the pot my meal had come from and added water from a jug. When her father was done grinding he sprinkled the ground seeds into each of the pots. A new, marvellous smell rose to my nostrils. "Mind the stall," he said to his daughter. "I have to go back to the house for a bit."

She dropped her shoulders. "What *else* would I do?"

He didn't get drawn in. He just parted the curtain and disappeared. A moment later his daughter peered around the front, making sure he was gone, and folded back her headscarf to reveal another one underneath. It was the blue of an evening sky, and so unexpectedly fine and light that for the moment I forgot about my food.

"What kind of cloth is that?" I reached to touch it.

She snatched it back. "Don't get out much, do you? 'What are spices?' 'What's silk?' You'll want me to explain water next."

"I'm—" I hesitated. "I've just come from the north. A lot here is new to me."

She softened a little. My ignorance had an explanation. Sometimes that's all it takes. "Traders bring it in too." She rubbed the cloth lightly between her thumb and finger and stared out into the market with a tiny smile. "It's from far away." The wistfulness of the small-town teenager. Dreaming of some vague elsewhere she'll never see, but thinks she might. It always breaks my heart.

"Aren't you worried your father will come back from the house and see you wearing it?"

She hadn't expected me to be paying attention. I get that a lot. It can be useful. "He isn't at the house. He's at the tavern. He'll be the rest of the afternoon."

I finished my stew, wiping the last of it from the bowl with my finger. "So this Jonah is a trader?"

"You weren't supposed to hear that."

"I was sitting right here." I put on my sympathetic uncle face. "That's why your father doesn't like you wearing the scarf? Because Jonah's a trader?"

She pulled it tightly around her jaw and frowned. "Because he's a Judean."

"What's a Judean?"

"I should start charging you for information. I would, if I hadn't already taken all of your money for the stew."

"Last topic, I promise."

"I think they're some sort of tribe. They're from the south, but

Jonah says they're all along the trade routes. He and his family only go from here to Baghdad. Others do the next part, and others the part after that."

"There are communities like that on most trade routes. Why would your father particularly mind about these Judeans?"

"I'm not sure. But I think it's because they only have one god."

I wasn't sure I'd heard her right. "One god? How can that be enough? It'd get lost among all the rest."

"No, not just one god for them. One god, period."

"What, for *everyone*?" I looked around. I saw three idol stalls in that lane alone. "There are other gods everywhere. Do they just pretend they don't see them?"

"How would *I* know?" she said. We'd reached her theological limits. "I think they just say they're false gods or something."

False gods? That wouldn't go down well. I was starting to see her father's concern.

It wasn't my concern, though. I wanted to know more about spices and silks. After a touch of cajoling, she directed me to the storehouse Jonah's family owned. "He's not in Antioch right now, though."

"But someone from his family should be there?"

"I guess."

Jonah actually was in Antioch. I saw him later that day in the storehouse's courtyard, with his hand in the skirts of a plump serving-girl. But that wasn't until I'd talked my way past four armed guards and Jonah's father, Elias.

"What's your interest?" Elias asked, after my persistence had convinced the guards to go get him. We were standing in the street outside his thick cedar gates, his guards flanking him on both sides.

"Curiosity."

"Right. And you'd climb a mountain because you were curious about the sky."

"I might, if I hadn't seen the sky before."

"You're saying you haven't seen silks before?"

"Or spices."

"Or spices. Or sand, maybe? No. Only a competitor or a thief would come here pretending curiosity. And I know all my competitors."

The guards, picking up on his tone, stepped toward me.

I took a step back. "I'm from far to the north. Spices might be common as sand to you, but they're practically sorcery to me."

Elias halted his guards' advance. He took a closer look at my rough woollens. "That certainly isn't local weaving." It didn't seem to be a compliment. "Cappadocian?"

"Farther north."

"Thracian?" he asked, tentatively. I was about to say 'farther north' again, when he added, "Supposed to be good warriors, Thracians."

So they still had that reputation. Good to know.

I spread my hands in mock submission. "You've found me out."

Elias's eyes moved from my clothes to my sword. It was a sturdy, iron blade. Better than I could have made myself. I'd taken it three summers earlier from the corpse of a Scythian horseman who, as near as I could tell, had been thrown by his mount and landed head first on a sharp-edged boulder. I'd traded his horse to a Bithynian farmer for two months' worth of dried meat and beans. It was more horse than he could handle, but that wasn't my problem.

"Good blade," Elias said. "You know how to use it?"

I jerked my head toward his guards. "Better than any of them." A couple bristled. The younger ones. I filed that away. "Why do you ask?"

"We ship expensive goods through rough country. A good sword arm pays for itself." His eyes narrowed. "If it's genuinely good. And can be trusted."

"I'm not looking for work. I really am just curious."

"Suit yourself. But I pay in silver."

I could barely remember the last time I'd seen silver. "Trust takes time to earn. But I can show you some skill right now if you like."

"How?"

I nodded toward the two younger guards. The ones who'd bristled. Who wouldn't have the calm control of the older ones.

"Have these two try to take my sword from me."

Fifteen minutes later Elias was laughingly pouring me a cup of wine while a healer from down the street looked after the guards' injuries. I'd been careful not to do too much damage. Elias still needed them both. "Shall I just leave their swords here?" I asked as he waved me to a seat at a polished wooden table.

He shook his head. "Jonah!" he called toward a sunlit door. "Make yourself useful." Through the door I saw the boy lift his head from the serving girl's neck and scowl.

"Now? Really?" His tone was just like the food-stall girl's. All teen derision has a kind of sameness.

"Now," his father said, laughing. He turned back to me and spoke more quietly. "That's the problem with boys his age who have access to expensive things. Most have to work to win a girl over. This one—" he nodded toward the door, where his son was now approaching "—just has to wave a bit of silk."

Jonah came to the table, trying to hide an awkward kink in his trousers. "Take these back to the armoury," his father said. "Then go down to the docks and see if there's any word on that ivory shipment."

The boy looked toward the courtyard door. "But—"

"Ivory."

The boy flushed, and took the swords. He paused to glare at Elias—an act of rebellion, however minor, was required—and stomped off in what I assumed was the direction of the armoury.

I worked the Antioch to Baghdad run for Elias—and when he died, for Jonah, who, like most teenaged boys, grew up to be a decent man—until my cover wouldn't hold anymore. It was a good long run. After a thousand years of faking my own aging, I was pretty good at it. When I left Jonah, I worked Baghdad to Marv for a Sogdian named Ghurak, and after that Marv to Samarqand for another Sogdian, also named Ghurak. One day I'll write a paper on the Great Bactrian Name Shortage.

It was hot, brutal work. The terrain was rough and infested with bandits, drawn by the luxury goods strapped to our horses or mules, or—in the deserts to the east—to our camels. But it paid well. By the time I left the second Ghurak in Bukhara I'd accumulated quite a pile. Which I then gave away. *Dana*, the Buddhists call it.

But I'm getting ahead of myself.

Antioch to Baghdad was the most pleasant section. It followed the Euphrates valley, which meant moderate temperatures, plentiful water and station stops well-provisioned with fresh foods. Baghdad to Marv was mountains followed by deserts, which meant relying on our own supplies or on the overpriced crap at the *caravanserai*. Think plastic-wrapped ham and cheese at a highway gas station.

Marv to Samarqand was more arable and more populated. The foods were richer, the clothes wilder, and the trade goods more varied than anything I'd seen anywhere: gemstones and glassware from the west, incense from the south, silks and spices from the east. Dates and dyes, sugars and scents, pressed oils of a dozen kinds. The luxury goods market being what it always is, there was money sloshing all over, and a decent chunk of it went to the skilled professionals like me who protected the goods-owners from the goods-coveters. These days it's cybersecurity. Back then it was a sharp blade and a watchful eye. I had both. I was as valuable a commodity as walnuts or cinnamon.

As you might expect from a melting pot like that, the religious climate was wildly diverse. I was in the constant company of men from every region of Asia, each carrying his home gods with him. More and more, down every valley and around every bend.

Or sometimes fewer.

Second Ghurak only had two: a good one and a bad one, in eternal combat. "How else do you explain all the rot in the world?" he said to me one afternoon as our cart rocked along a shady river valley. "Ahura Mazda gives us sunshine and good meat, and Ahriman comes along behind with hailstorms and maggots."

Elias, the Judean, only had the one. "When the Babylonians took our country they dragged us to their homeland. Yahweh held us together." The Babylonians were apparently an empire I'd missed. But empires were like phases of the moon. Unless you were actively watching, who could keep track?

"What happened to the Babylonians?"

"They fell. They always do, in the end."

"Why didn't your people just go back then?"

"Some did. Some didn't." He gestured at the road. "Worked out fine for me."

The theological extreme came years later, after I'd quit the trade routes.

"*No* gods?" I said to Alexandros. "But where did—" I looked around at the river and the hills and the sky "—I mean how could ... who ...?"

He held out a calming hand.

"Bring your gods with you, if you like, Have as many as you want. The how and the who are up to you. We're more about the what."

But again, I'm getting ahead of myself.

Private security is a pretty wearing gig unless you have the temperament for it. I do and I don't. I can manage just fine for a conventional lifetime or two, but any longer and I find myself waking in the night, haunted by the faces of the gutted and beheaded. Or worse, by the fact that I can't *remember* their faces. The dead start weighing me down like an iron tunic.

"You just need another cup of wine," second Ghurak said at our final meal together, in the Bukharan equivalent of a beer hall. He signalled to our server, who was putting a loaf and some cheese in front of a slim man at the other end of our table.

I swirled what was left in my current cup, which was most of it. "No thanks. Doesn't have its usual appeal, somehow."

"A holiday, then." He leaned in. He smelled of campfire smoke. "Finish this trip, and when we get to Samarqand I'll give you a bonus. Enough to stay there until we come back through. Do whatever you like in the meantime."

Whatever I liked. Whatever that was. I genuinely couldn't think of anything.

I could think of plenty of things I didn't like, though. At the top of the list was carrying on to Samarqand.

I shook my head. "That's very generous, Ghurak, but—."

"And—" he pulled out his camel skin coin pouch and rattled it "—enough for all the wine and women you want while you're there?" He really didn't want to let me go.

Not that I could blame him. I was good at my job. It'd been six years since our last lost-goods incident, and even that one was a military confiscation. Ghurak himself had waved our swords down that day. "When you're outnumbered four to one by disciplined soldiers, your goods are already gone," he said afterward. "No point in losing your men too."

He wasn't being sentimental. Guards were an investment, like horses or storage space. Discretion was just the better part of business. His bonus would pay for itself if it kept me on staff for another year or two.

I was tempted. Not by the women and wine. Not even necessarily by the break. A few weeks in Samarqand was an eyeblink, not a proper retreat. And even a longer retreat somehow felt pointless. Nothing about any of it appealed to me. But a change was a change. Maybe a self-indulgent shake up would help me see things differently. I doubted it. But what other options were there?

"Or ..." the slim man at the end of our table said through a mouthful of bread.

Ghurak turned and glared at him. "Mind your business, bhikkhu." The man shrugged and took a bite of cheese. The server topped up our wine.

I dropped my voice. "What's a bhikkhu?"

Ghurak's look reminded me of a time he'd found maggots in a cask of poorly-cured mutton. "Nothing to concern yourself about." He took a deep gulp of wine.

"Seriously, tell me." I nodded down the table. "If you won't, I'll have to ask him." The thought of drawing the other man into our conversation pried a bit more out of Ghurak.

"Misfits. Men who withdraw from the world." He raised his voice enough to carry down the table. "Live in their own heads. Spend their lives thinking instead of doing."

There was a beat of silence as the slim man chewed and swallowed. "And who sometimes find a peace other men don't," he said. He didn't look at us. He might've been talking to the tabletop.

Peace.

That sounded good.

I stayed there with Alexandros the rest of the afternoon. Ghurak hung on for a bit, scowling. Then he sighed and took my elbow and tried to get me to leave, but I wasn't going anywhere. He could see that. He was a realist. "I'll bring you your savings on our next trip," he murmured close to my ear as he left. It was nearly dusk before I realized he'd looped his camel skin coin pouch around the hilt of my sword.

"I see anguish," Alexandros said.

I looked away and shrugged. Tough guy, me.

"Troubling thoughts. You shoo them away, but they don't go."

"Fine. I have anguish."

"Big whoop for you. All of *life* is anguish." He waved an arm. "Everyone in this room is in anguish. Everyone in this town."

That took it a bit far, I thought. I nodded toward a young couple in a dim corner, wrapped so tightly around each other it was hard to tell where one stopped and the other began. "What about those two? They aren't in anguish."

He took a glance, then tilted his head side to side in a *comme ci, comme ça* motion. "Right now, maybe. But in a few minutes she goes back to her father's house, and they both ache with longing."

"And then they get together again."

"And then they're apart. Or then they stay together, but the longing stops. He gets lazy. His eye wanders. She becomes suspicious. He feels caged." Alexandros smiled sadly. "Anguish."

"Or maybe they actually have a happy life together."

"Maybe. But they worry about their safety. About their children. About rain for the crops. In the end one of them dies, and the other grieves, and in the meantime they worry about which of them it will be, and when, and how."

Two tables down there was a burst of laughter. A group of young traders was ordering another jug, flirting with the server and shoving one another like puppies. I nodded toward them. "The gods have given us wine to smooth those harsh edges."

"A hiding place. The wine wears off, and the anguish finds us again."

"I can't say I'm finding much peace here, Alexandros." I started to stand. "I should probably just get back to Ghurak."

He clasped my forearm. "Peace comes from truth. The first truth is that life is anguish." He drew me back down to the bench. "Before you treat an illness, you have to identify it."

I sat. Alexandros didn't let go of my arm. "First truth?"

"The next tells us where the anguish comes from."

"It's obvious where it comes from. Hunger. Illness. Death." I thought of the faces that haunted my sleep. "Memory."

"No, Ishtanu." He tightened his grip on my arm. "It comes from holding on."

That was new.

It was a half hour's walk to Alexandros' community, a compound of huts and sheep pens that housed fifty or so men of various ages. "No women?"

"Not here. They have their own community inside the town walls. For safety."

"Wouldn't they be safe here with you?"

"Safe, maybe. But distracting. And distracted."

"Distracted from what?"

"From the dharma."

The working language was Greek, though a lot of them spoke a Sogdian dialect similar to Ghurak's. They looked at me uneasily when I arrived. Their suspicions lifted when they heard me speak their language, and vanished entirely when they learned I had experience with sheep. I was on the duty roster before they even showed me where I would sleep.

Fitting in with the dharma took a little longer.

The dharma was what they called the teachings of the Tathagata, the Shakya prince who'd been gobsmacked as a young man by the anguish of the world outside his father's walls. "He overcompensated at first," Alexandros said. "Followed a path of strict ascetic renunciation. But it didn't solve the problem of anguish."

"You seem pretty ascetic here."

"Not really. Simple, yes. I'm talking about an asceticism where eating a grain of rice is seen as a failure of will. The Tathagata eventually realized that living that way was as self-indulgent as his earlier life of rich foods and soft beds. Just as distracting."

"Aren't there always distractions?"

"Yes and no. Some you can avoid. Women, for example. Or us for them, probably. Wealth. The rest of it is just finding a way down the middle. Not getting distracted by the desires of the world or by the desire to eliminate them. Just letting them all go."

Like all simple ideas, it was a lot more complicated than that.

For a start there were two more truths about anguish: ending it, and the path to ending it. And then that path had eight parts, and each of those parts left plenty of room for debate. "How do I know if what I say is right speech?" I asked one day. "Who decides that?"

"No one *decides* it, Ishtanu. Not in the imposing-it-on-you sense. It isn't a rule. We have rules to encourage it, of course." He'd already started teaching me some of these *vinaya*, which were basically common sense principles for keeping the peace in a close group. "But the point isn't whether your speech—or your actions, or your livelihood—accord with some rule. It's whether they develop your compassionate heart."

Just like right concentration wasn't about ticking some practice box; it was about moving toward a clean awareness where anguish and indulgence—and eventually, somehow, even the self itself—just drifted away, irrelevant.

It was a lot to take in. I struggled. Alexandros smiled.

"You'll see it more easily as you go. If you decide to stay."

Which he never pressured me to do.

I wrestled with their lack of interest in the gods. "Shouldn't your teachings include something about where the world came from? Or who's in charge?"

"How would that help with our sufferings?"

I wasn't sure. "Um. Wouldn't it be comforting to know?"

Alexandros settled his face into its familiar pedagogical expression.

"You've been a warrior, yes?"

I nodded.

"Suppose you're shot with a poisoned arrow. I'm there to pull it out and apply the antidote. What do you do?"

"I let you get on with it. What else would I do?"

He feigned surprise. "Really? You don't grab my wrist and say no, first you need to know the archer's name? Where he was born? Who his people are?"

"But that's not the priority at that—" Oh. "Never mind."

I knew Ghurak's caravan schedule like my own breathing. When the time for him to pass through Bukhara again, I asked Alexandros if I could go into town to see him.

"He has some things of mine."

"Your money."

"Yes."

"You'd like to collect it."

"Yes."

"Of course."

Ghurak slipped it to me discreetly in the beer hall. "Don't spend it all in one place." He looked me up and down. "Found peace yet?"

"Working on it. I get a glimpse sometimes."

"Hmm. Then maybe there's something to this bhikkhu stuff after all, if the likes of you sees something in it."

That was the highest praise I ever got from him.

Alexandros never showed any interest in my money. We put it in a separate bag in the secure chest where the community's few valuables were kept, and as far as I could tell he never gave it another thought. But I did.

"You understand that I may need it again one day, right?"

"Of course."

The more I progressed, the more it worried me. "There are things the community could use. What if we took some of—"

"We're fine."

"But I keep thinking of the things I could—"

"Let it go."

"My money?"

"Your *thoughts* about your money."

Easier said than done. I worked on it, but before long I was back again.

"Divide it among the poor families in the town, then," Alexandros said. "Or fling it in the river. Whatever lets you let it go. If that's what you need."

In the end I gave it to the community. Which was kind of notional, since it stayed where it was. But it wasn't mine anymore. And once I let it go like that, it let me go, too.

That was a very different time for me.

Alexandros thanked me, though he didn't seem to care much.

"You should spend it carefully," I said.

"On what?"

"On ... I don't know, on things we need."

"Needing is clinging."

And clinging was anguish. "All right, then. On things to keep us from slipping too far into asceticism."

"Like what?"

"You really have no idea, do you?"

"And I don't want to."

So I took on the role of managing the community's finances. Carefully. Nothing to shift us out of the middle way. Getting the wool shears sharpened. Laying in a few extra sacks of beans in case of lean times. The lessons of the Hatti famine hadn't left me.

The bulk of the money was still there when I left.

There was memorizing, which wasn't that hard for me after hundreds of years among the pre-literate. But sweet Yeshu, there was a lot of it. The twelve links of this, and the sixteen aspects of that. Factors and afflictions by the cartload. It made my brain hurt. But I took it all in. The whole blessed, convoluted path. And in the end, its essence really was pretty simple. Nothing stays put. Including you, smart guy.

Yeah, you. You think you're one, singular thing. Separate. Permanent. Of course you do. But your thoughts come and go. Your breath comes and goes. Physical bits of you come and go. You start out small and get bigger. You absorb food and dump waste. You cut your hair, scrape off your whiskers, trim your nails. You lose some teeth in a fight. You bleed. You sneeze. You get fat. You get thin. You get a tattoo. You learn stuff. You forget stuff. One day you die, and your body breaks down to dust. Where, in all that mess, is the one, singular, separate 'you'? Let go of the 'you,' and let go of the anguish.

Simple.

I saw it work splendidly for dozens of men. I thought it would work for me. Not singular? Got it. Not separate? Done. Not permanent?

Ah.

The part of the dharma I found the strangest was, strangely, the most familiar. It came up early on, when I was still grappling with the pervasive definition of anguish.

"Fine," I'd said. "Suppose I accept that in this life there's no escape from pain and longing and fear of losing. At least it ends with death, right?"

Alexandros shook his head. "Death isn't an end, Ishtanu."

"Of course it's an end. Kind of the definitive one."

"No. It's just a marker, in the cycle of death and rebirth."

Death and *what*? "Rebirth? Seriously?"

Seriously.

Which was preposterous, of course. And yet ... been there, done that. Skipped the dying part, was all.

According to Alexandros, the path ultimately led to a way off the death-birth merry-go-round, but I never quite grasped how. Oh, he explained it me. Many times, over many years. So did his successors in other dharma communities. The goal that wasn't a goal. The non-duality beyond all non-dualities. After many years I'm pretty sure I understood it intellectually. I just never quite *grasped* it.

But then grasping is clinging, isn't it?

Starting to see the problem?

The compassion part was easier.

Every so often we took our sheep cheeses or our bales of wool to the market in Bukhara to trade for grain or melons or cloth. When we did, I'd also take a couple of silver coins from my former wages. There was a stall where you could exchange them for coppers, which we distributed to beggars. Enough for a meal or two.

Some of the other bhikkhus would make them listen to a pitch about right thought or no-self first, but Alexandros never did. I asked him about it.

"Our brothers offer them the dharma out of compassion. That's a good thing, from a good place. But for the beggar, right now, is the dharma a good, or just a string attached to a more immediate need?" He smiled. "Judgment call."

The community changed. Men left or died. Others joined. That's how impermanence works. Eventually I found myself in a position of seniority. Which really just meant not having left for long enough. Oh, I was a capable enough teacher of the *vinaya* by then, but that was memorization. I didn't feel very senior in terms of practice. Despite hundreds of hours spent refining my concentration, I hadn't managed to let go of much of my self, or of its anguish. Sure, the dead weren't visiting my sleep as often. But the peace I'd been looking for seemed a long way off. I felt I was on the right path, though, and I was determined to stick to it.

Then along came a complication. The usual one. I'd kind of forgotten about it.

"You don't age," Alexandros said.

I froze. I thought I'd been managing my appearance with my usual skill.

"What do you mean?"

"You know what I mean."

I was silent for a moment. "Where does that leave us?"

"It means you can't stay much longer. Others will notice. It will be distracting."

"But I have more to learn."

Alexandros smiled. "I know a guy."

So that was how my next few lifetimes played out. I crossed Greek Bactria from dharma community to dharma community, learning what I could before I moved on. My teachers were fine men, and some of them deeply wise, but no one after Alexandros ever spotted my secret. A secret as inconsequential to him as the silver I'd given to his community. "For me, rebirth requires death," he said. "For you, maybe not. But we're both stuck on the wheel, and the path is the only way off for either of us."

That may have been true for him. I don't think it was for me. Believe me, I tried.

I don't know if Alexandros ever made it off the wheel. I hope so. He deserved to.

The most physically beautiful dharma community I ever lived in was the last one. The Varmayana valley—you'd call it Bamiyan these days, if you called it anything—was lush, green and flat, with rugged cliffs along its north edge and snow-capped peaks a half day's walk along the river. We raised barley and beans and goats. The climate was temperate, we had adequate food and water, and there was plenty of time for dharma study. Yet for all the richness of the setting, there were never more than a dozen of us.

Our teacher—a vague old boy named Bhurz who'd lived there his whole life—didn't seem to mind. "Better a few of us properly following the path than a crowd of indifferent hangers on, eh Ishtanu?" he said one lazy afternoon as we rested against the base of the sun-warmed cliffs. His presumptive successor Philippos, on the other hand, had a grander-is-better mentality that didn't quite line up with how I understood the dharma. In another time he might have been a capable Renaissance Pope, or a modern American anything. His father had been a well-to-do Greek sculptor. Philippos had a genuine gift for carving the footprints and empty seats that our communities used to symbolize the Tathagata's transcendence.

"But think of the suffering minds we're leaving behind if we don't expand," he said as he squirmed against the rock. Idleness made him uncomfortable, even for a few minutes. "We need a better way to get the word out."

One of my great pleasures in Bamiyan was winding Philippos up. That pettiness was probably an early sign that my heart just wasn't in it anymore. I tipped my head back to stare up at the cliffs above us. "Well, Philippos. You could always carve a big *bas relief* of the Tathagata in this cliff face. That'd get people's attention."

Bhurz pursed his lips. "Oh come, dear boy. We don't do representations of the Tathagata. It wouldn't be proper."

Philippos followed my gaze up the cliff. He looked thoughtful for a moment, as if he were doing a mental preliminary sketch. Then he smiled sadly and shook his head.

It took more than half a millennium for the Bamiyan community to get around to carving its massive Buddhas into that cliff face. So I probably can't take credit for the idea. But sometimes I wonder.

I walked away from the Bamiyan valley that summer, and from the Tathagata's teachings as well. Not that I rejected them. I have enormous respect for the dharma. I just don't have the patience. Not on my timeline.

I came back six centuries later, when I'd returned to the spice trade for a while. By then the village was a thriving trading centre, and the dharma community had grown beyond all recognition. The cliff face was dotted with caves full of bhikkhus and bhikkhunis in their hundreds, studying and reciting and debating. Philippos' expansive vision had come about. And yet as impressive as the caves were, they looked like gnats swarming around two massive—multi-story-car-park massive—statues of the Tathagata that had been carved into the rock. Ideas of what's proper don't stay put either.

Nothing I'd seen outside Egypt compared to them. They didn't just dominate the valley, they overwhelmed it. They were Buddha billboards on a scale that not even my provocative joke at Philippos' expense had imagined. If their sculptors' point had been to keep the dharma in the public consciousness, then done and dusted. No matter where you went—farm, pasture, riverbank, marketplace—you could always see at least one of them, smiling over at you. Well, sort of smiling. Bactrian cliff carving hadn't reached Rushmore-level facial subtlety.

I had a clear view of the taller one from my seat at a wine stall in the market, next to a tinker's tent with strings of pans clattering in the breeze. Although alcohol doesn't affect me, it affects other people so marvellously that wine stalls and beer halls and bars are my venue of choice when I want to learn about a place.

"Lot of carving there," I said to the stallholder, nodding toward the statue.

He glanced up at it as he wiped a wine cup. "Brings in the tourists."

"Not a follower, then?"

"Don't know much about it. Good as any other teaching, I imagine."

"Not something you'd spend your days chipping rock out of a wall for?"

"Got to make a living, don't I?" He set the cup under the counter and held up the wine jug. "Same again?" I nodded. He poured. It was a vile red that burned my nostrils, but it was cheap. And it came with local knowledge.

"Don't the bhikkhus have to make a living too?" I thought of the long hours I'd spent milking goats and weeding rows of beans.

"Some do. Others beg." He wrinkled his nose.

"You don't approve?"

"It's fine, I guess," he said, worried now that he might have offended a paying customer. "They don't ask for much. Scraps of food. Good for the community, probably, folks like them." He looked past my shoulder. "There you go. Here's a bunch of 'em now." I turned. A half-dozen women in simple woollens emerged from between the tinker's tent and the cheese stall, smiling softly and holding out wooden begging bowls. They weren't overtly asking for anything. Just walking and smiling and holding their bowls. A vendor with some aging goat kebabs on his grill waved them over and scraped a couple of lumps of the overcooked meat into each bowl.

The last women to receive her food stood out from her companions. Not just because her skin was slightly darker. Her eyes were brighter. Her complexion clearer. It wasn't just her youth. Youth was cheap. This was something other. Life's rigours lay on her more lightly, like they were incidental to some deeper vitality. I'd never seen anyone so untouched by the passage of time. With one exception.

I caught my own reflection in one of the hammered pans hanging in the tinker's tent. And in the blazing afternoon sun, I felt a chill.

The Teacher

WHEN I LEFT Bamiyan the first time, I went back to the trade routes and worked my way west. I was thinking about Halki and Syria again. The caravans were good places to catch up on politics and to pick up new languages. The starter set for where I was going now included Latin—from some new empire out of a place called Rome—and Aramaic, so I focused on them.

I arrived at night in a fishing town called Capernaum, on the Sea of Galilee. The first thing I learned about Capernaum was that it was dead after dark. No light burned, no dog barked. It might have been abandoned. But then as I passed an area of jetties and storage buildings, I heard singing. Not raucous, drunken singing, which I might have expected on a working waterfront. More like some sort of devotional chant. A dozen or more men and women, maybe half of them with a decent sense of pitch. A call-and-response structure, back and forth between groups. I followed it down a narrow passage to a warehouse door and stood in the dark street, listening. It was rough and ragged and beautiful. Organized human voices. What a thing.

I had to know who they were, why they were here, singing at night in a warehouse in a comatose town. I tapped on the door. The singing stopped.

There was an urgent murmuring. Then footsteps. Then a man's voice saying something I didn't quite catch. Asking who I was, probably. That's what I would've asked. I answered in Latin. "I'm a traveller." Silence. "I like your singing," I added.

More murmuring. Then the same voice, in Latin. "We sing for Yahweh. Leave us." Elias' Judean god. Silence again. Waiting for me to go.

Not that easily. "Why sing at night? Wouldn't Yahweh hear you just as well during the day, and let you sleep at night?"

"Not *at* night. Through the night."

"All night long?"

"Apart from this interruption."

"When do you sleep?"

I could hear him sigh through the door. "We don't do this every night. That would be impossible. Every seventh week. A special cere- mony. Which you're interrupting."

"If you'd let me come in and listen, the interruption would be over."

"Our ceremony isn't for listening. It's our community."

"What if I wanted to join your community?" Wait, what? What did I just say?

It made the man behind the door pause. "It isn't an easy life. We're very disciplined."

But I had him there. "I've spent many years in disciplined com- munities." More than I'd care to mention. "But there wasn't any sing- ing. I miss it." I hadn't realized it until I heard myself say it. How long since I'd really sung, with others?

"You sing?"

"I do."

The murmuring resumed. Then the man spoke again. "Sing some- thing for us."

And so I joined the Therapeutae. Because my voice won them over. Because I was tired of travelling. Because my hunger for singing over- came the hindrances. And oh, there were hindrances. For a start, there was the monotheism, which didn't make any more sense to me than it had all those years ago in Antioch. But it was a deal breaker, so I sucked it up. Plus they really were *very* disciplined. Ascetic. Caves in the desert ascetic. They didn't own property. They fasted a lot. They didn't drink anything stronger than water. But discipline was old hat.

Then there were the scriptures I had to learn. A lot of them. In an- other new language, which I also had to learn. Histories and rules and songs and sayings. Abraham and Moses and Solomon. They recited them and debated them and endlessly drew out their hidden meanings. But I knew about learning scriptures, too. The stories and players were new, but the way they *lived* them was a lot like life in Bactria.

Everyone had their individual cell, carved into the cave wall and closed with a reed curtain. From dawn to sunset we sat in silent prayer or read and reflected on passages of scripture. There was a comforting feeling of continuity. And after the adversities of the caravan roads, something safe and reasonably familiar was welcome. Let me correct myself, though. Monotheism wasn't the biggest hindrance. Circumcision was. It was new to me too. And something I wouldn't care to repeat. But it was standard across the Yahwist communities, and, again, it was a deal breaker. So on one of our trips into town one of the elders borrowed a knife, and got a clean cloth ready, and gave me a stick to bite down on ...

Actually, I'd rather not talk about it.

Let's just say that's when I learned that my ability to heal doesn't include growing things back. Once something's gone, it's gone. And it leaves a scar. It's my only one.

Our community was one of half a dozen around Capernaum. Every seven days we gathered in the storage building, which was owned by a pock-faced olive merchant who let us use it as a way of laying up merit with God. Men on one side of a dividing cloth, women on the other. Every seventh gathering started with an evening meal, which the merchant provided—presumably in exchange for extra merit, though I often wondered how much he deserved for his stale loaves and off-batch olives—followed by singing through the night. Naphtali, the man I'd been speaking with that first night, led the singing. At the end, a member of each community would gather a share of whatever food was left over. That fell to newbies like me. Even communal organizations have hierarchies. There was never much, but it was a welcome addition to our diet of wild succulents and insects.

The morning after one vigil I was walking back alone. I had four small loaves and a pound of raisins in a cloth bag, and a goatskin of water for the journey. The sun was punishing. By the time I reached the shade of a low ridge my clothes were soaked and I'd drunk more than half my water. I sat in the shade of the ridge. The slight breeze felt like cooling ointment. I leaned against the ridge wall and sipped from my goatskin, resting in the present, pleasant moment.

I heard a moan from above. A bird, I told myself, not wanting the moment interrupted. A breeze in the thistle bushes. Then I heard it again. Someone was up there, in the direct sun. I climbed up. It wasn't far. A thin, almost naked man was on his back near the edge, arms wavering in the air above his chest. Dark curls. Thick beard. Small, vacant smile.

Great. A mystic. Close to the forty-day mark, by the look of him. As a short-cut to revelation, fasting in the sun was up there with certain rare mushrooms and grain fungi. Whatever gets you through the dark night, as long as you don't die of heat stroke. Which looked like a concern here.

"Hey," I said. No response. I knelt beside him. "You all right?" I put the a hand on his cheek. He was burning up. His eyes were watery and unfocused. "I think you're done. Let's leave off and have some water." I tipped my goatskin to his lips. The thin smile didn't change, but he took the water. Then some more. His eyes focused a little.

"Here." I lifted his head and slid a flattish rock under it. "Let's prop you on this stone and get a little bread into you."

"Stones."

"Yeah. Rest your head on this stone."

"Bread." The word was barely a breath.

"That's right." I took a loaf from the bag. "A bit of bread. Get some strength back." I tore off a scrap. He whispered something.

"Sorry, what was that?"

"You can't tempt me."

"It's just bread." I held it to his mouth.

"You want me to make bread from stones." Mystics and their *non sequiturs.*

"No, this bread is already bread. I just want you to try to eat it. Then we'll get you back to town. The stones can stay stones."

"You tempt me with dominion over the town?" Temptation was big with this one.

"Let's get you out of the sun." I sat him up, slowly. "Down this ridge to the shade."

He jerked away. "You tempt me to fly?" His eyes were wide and wobbly. "You think I can command angels to fly me down this cliff?" The ridge was maybe ten feet.

"Flying won't be necessary, with or without angels. There's a way down, right there." I turned and gestured toward where I had come up.

In the moment before I turned back he picked up the flat rock. "You tempt me with dominion over the *Temple?*" he said as he swung it. And on the word "Temple" it connected with mine.

I can't have been out for long. When I woke up the sun was still high, but the mystic was gone. He hadn't taken anything. I still had my goatskin, and my bag of loaves and raisins. Even the scrap of bread was still there, on the ground next to me. I took the bread and ate it.

Bloody mystics.

Years passed. Contemplation. Meetings. Feasts. Singing. Oh, the singing.

They were simple tunes with simple devotional texts, but that was just fine. There's something about singing in a group that nothing else can match. How had I gone without it for so long?

I learned the Yahwist texts and debated them with authority, but I never quite accepted them. I liked a range of gods. It was what I'd grown up with. But I carried on. Mainly because the discussions were so stimulating. Unlike the mainstream Yahwists in the villages and towns, for the Therapeutae the literal stories were less important than the signposts to the infinite hidden inside them—the infinite being always and only literally Yahweh, not some abstract principle. You didn't make that mistake more than once with Naphtali. Teasing out the "aha" moment when a surface story opened into something transcendent was probably what kept me there so long.

And the singing. Have I mentioned the singing?

One day on our way into Capernaum we saw a group of revellers on the waterfront. A dozen or so men and a handful of women, grilling fish over a low fire, gathering driftwood, splashing and laughing at the water's edge. At their centre, sitting on a weathered log, was my desert mystic.

Naphtali tightened his lips. "Keep moving."

"Who are they?"

"Ignore them."

Ezra, from one of our brother communities, was more forthcoming. "That's Yeshu the Nazarene. He's a bit ... controversial."

"Controversial?"

Ezra lowered his voice. "They say he claims he's the *mashiach*."

I'd seen the term in the texts. "An anointed one?"

"Not *an* anointed one. *The* anointed one." His tone was dismissive. "The twig from the root of Jesse." We'd discussed the books of Isaiah a few weeks earlier. Naphtali said the root of Jesse bits were a metaphor. Most of the community agreed with him. One didn't. I looked around. Where *was* Thaddaeus, anyhow? When had I last seen him at all, come to that?

I pictured the group at the waterfront. Grilling fish. Gathering wood. Barefoot in the surf, laughing and splashing. One of the laughers had been a squat, balding man. Thaddaeus was a squat, balding man. Thaddaeus liked to laugh.

There wasn't a lot of laughing in our community.

A few days later Naphtali and I had a surprising conversation. I was sitting in my cell and heard feet shuffling beyond the curtain. "Gestas?" My current name, which I'd picked up on the road. Naphtali's voice was almost a whisper.

I uncrossed my legs and rotated my head to stretch out my neck muscles. I poured two beakers of water from a jug and invited him in. He angled himself in next to me. The cells were too low to stand in and barely large enough for one person to sit. That suited Naphtali's purpose. His voice was a bare murmur. "That man Yeshu from the waterfront worries me."

"Because of Thaddaeus?"

"Not just that. People say—" He hesitated. "They say he claims to be the *mashiach*."

"I've heard that."

"That's a serious claim. If too many accept it and follow him, it could bring down the wrath of Yahweh. Like in Ezekiel, or Hosea, or—"

"I know the texts. I thought we didn't take them literally."

"You think we should ignore the plain meaning just because there's a deeper one?" This Nazarene had him rattled. "If this man is really claiming to be the *mashiach,* we have to do something about it." He didn't specify what. Send a message to the Temple in Jerusalem, probably. "If not, no need to worry."

"Why come to me?"

"We only know what people say. We don't know what he actually claims."

"And?"

"And I need someone to find out."

But to avoid creating a stir in our community, he needed someone to do it covertly, on the pretence of a forty-day fast. Someone he could trust to come back with the truth, but who was flexible enough to go along with the duplicity.

He was a shrewd judge of character, Naphtali.

The listening stage was a bust. I went into the desert as we'd planned, then doubled back toward town. I stayed a week, sleeping in doorways and begging for bread in the market. I heard Yeshu speak three times: once in the synagogue and twice in the public garden. He was magnetic, but not especially controversial. Well-versed in scripture. Conservative in debate. Maybe he took a more mystical approach to Yahweh than most scholars, but who was a Therapeutae spy to judge him for that? He didn't claim to be the *mashiach*. Not in my hearing.

"Maybe he's just publically discreet," Naphtali said when I came back a week later, claiming illness. "We really need to know what he says to his followers."

Which is how I became one.

This time our story was that I was going to convince Thaddaeus to come back. As far as our group was concerned, I would then seemingly be persuaded to become one of Yeshu's followers. Only Naphtali and I would know I was there undercover.

And only I would know even that was a pretext. Because I didn't share Naphtali's concerns about Yahweh's wrath. Why would a god of the whole world care what some backwater preacher said? I agreed to Naphtali's plan because Yeshu intrigued me. I agreed because I wanted to know more. I agreed because roasted fish and laughing in the surf would be a nice break from locusts and dourness.

I found them on the shore, crouched in the shallows washing their clothes. They watched me warily. Thaddaeus waded toward me, wringing out a tunic and pulling it over his head as he came.

"Gestas."

"Thaddaeus."

"What brings you here?"

"Lovely to see you, too."

He didn't smile. "If you've come to take me back, you can turn around."

"I haven't. Unless someone from the old community asks. Then I have."

"Which is it?"

The problem with duplicity is keeping the stories straight. I decided to keep it simple. "They think I've come to bring you back. But I think I've come to join you."

We walked up the strand to where Yeshu was smoothing a woollen robe across a flat rock. Another, larger man joined us. A fisherman, by the look of him. He had the broad back you get hauling heavy nets of carp. He took a position behind my right shoulder. I was being treated as a threat.

Yeshu stood as we neared him. Our eyes met, and he smiled. "I know you." His voice was warm and welcoming. But how could he know me?

Not from the desert. He'd been barely coherent. His hands were slim and sturdy. A worker's hands, and a scholar's. He grasped my shoulders. "You came to hear me speak three times. Twice in the garden and once at the synagogue. You wore a hood, like you didn't want to be known." His gaze hadn't left my eyes.

"This is Gestas," Thaddaeus said. "From my old community."

"A good man, your Naphtali, from what I hear. Maybe a bit severe." Thaddaeus grunted. Yeshu chuckled. "Forgive Thaddaeus. He's still adjusting." He let go of me and bent back to the robe on the rock. I nearly lost my balance. I looked around, startled. Everything was still. The ground was level. Nothing had changed. Nothing but that gaze. I hadn't noticed its power until he released me from it. It was like being released from shackles.

"Have you eaten?" Yeshu had finished with the robe and was ready to move on to the next thing. "We have figs, and smoked fish, and an urn of well water." The fisherman started to protest, but Yeshu held up a hand. "I know, Andreas, our stores are low. But we can spare a bite of fish and a cup of water for a man who came to hear me three times in a week. If only in compensation." He took my arm. "Come with me, Gestas. We have temporary space a short walk from here." I glanced toward the others. "They'll find their own way back. Let's feed you, and you can tell me why you've come to me four times."

Five, counting the time you brained me with a rock in the desert. But I didn't say anything.

The space was small but sufficient. Not all of them lived there. A core group of ten or twelve men followed Yeshu full time. The larger group, men and women, had homes, and work, and families. They came when they had time, and brought food when they could. Their stores really were getting low. I couldn't bring myself to take more than a single fig and a thumb-sized piece of fish. They had plenty of water, though, which I took advantage of. The walk from the desert had been parching. After I'd eaten, Yeshu came to the point. "Your Naphtali is worried about me." I tried not to react, but the glint in his eye told me I'd failed. "It's all right. He isn't the first. Others worry too. They worry because people say I claim to be the *mashiach*."

So there we were, already. "And do you?"

He waved a dismissive hand. "Talk about the *mashiach* misses the point." Not a clear denial.

"In what way?"

He picked a date from the dish and looked at it closely, turning it between his fingers. "People say a lot of things about the *mashiach*. He'll unite the world. He'll defeat our enemies." He shook his head. "All of that is just government." He took a bite of the date and chewed it thoughtfully. "I'm no governor, Gestas."

He dipped his cup into the urn. "Others say that the *mashiach* will defeat death." He dried the base of the cup with the hem of his robe. "That may be closer to the mark, but it still misses the point." He took a sip, smiling, savouring the tepid water. Was he edging closer to an admission? I hoped not. A single afternoon was hardly the breather I'd been looking forward to.

"Why does that miss the point?"

He finished the date and dropped the pit into his cup with a soft *plop*. "Because, Gestas, if you really understand the Father, then you know there already *is* no death."

The rest of the group arrived. Andreas the fisherman. His brother Shimon, called Petrus, who seemed to be a kind of second-in-command. Two more brothers, Yacobus and Yochanan, also fisherman. Thaddaeus, of course. You've heard the list.

"This is Gestas," Yeshu said. "He'll be with us for a while."

I hadn't said so. He just knew.

Life with Yeshu wasn't leisurely, though it was more leisurely than life with Naphtali. There was study and contemplation. There was food to be gathered, from donors or through casual labour. And of course there was teaching. Yeshu loved to teach. It was an unspoken rule that we'd go with him when he did.

Study. Prayer. Work. Teaching. Week after week. It was nice.

Once Yeshu accepted me, Thaddaeus did too. "I'm happy you're here, Gestas. This is a good community."

"It seems to be." I decided to probe a little. Might as well give Naphtali his lack-of-money's worth. "But what made you come in the first place? You seemed content enough in the desert."

"I came because of Yeshu."

"Anything in particular?" Something starting with "m," maybe?

"Of course. You're here now. You must see it, too."

I hedged. "But what is it, exactly, that makes him different from, say, Naphtali?"

Thaddaeus snorted. "Naphtali? Naphtali's an administrator. Yeshu's a leader."

Naphtali and I had arranged to meet after a week at a rocky inlet. It felt like our old meetings with Meinrad the lawspeaker.

"Is it true? Does Yeshu say in private that he's the *mashiach*?"

"Maybe. There are hints. Too soon to tell."

"Keep at it."

We agreed to meet each week at the same spot.

Study. Prayer. Work. Teaching. But after a while, whenever Yeshu went out to teach it was always the same twenty or thirty people who turned up.

"You've reached everyone in Capernaum who's prepared to listen," Shimon Petrus said. "We should take your teachings into the country."

Naphtali and I met at the prescribed time and place.

"They're moving on. Touring the villages. Spreading the word."

"Is that word that Yeshu is the *mashiach*?"

"Still too soon to tell."

Naphtali sighed. "Go with them."

We went south along the Jordan and the Sea of Galilee, staying in fishing villages and shepherds' encampments. We ate what we could beg, and Yeshu spoke to whoever would listen. Sometimes young people from smaller communities joined us, though they tended to drift back home once the excitement of leaving turned into the drudgery of hungry walking. Occasionally we'd fall in with a travelling trader or merchant, which meant eating a little better for a while.

One night we camped in a range of low hills. After we'd eaten, Yeshu moved away from the fire, to a hillock wild with lilies. I joined him. He was crumbling bits of bread and tossing them to the sparrows.

"They love me," he said.

"The sparrows?"

"My followers. They love me."

"They're loyal. You're lucky."

"I don't mean it that way." He tossed another crumb. "Look at them." He gestured toward the camp. I looked. Thomas leaned a branch against a boulder and stomped on it, breaking it up for firewood. Yacobus placed the wood in a pile. Andreas added some to the fire. Yochanan sat by the fire and peeled a fig.

Yeshu leaned slightly closer. "They love *me*. They follow *me*. They don't always follow what I *say*."

"They follow your word without question."

"Not follow as in *obey*. Follow as in *grasp*."

"But surely Shimon Petrus—"

"No. He's a good man, Petrus. Excellent with the working people. He lives their life. He knows how remote the Temple officials seem from a life of drought or sheep ailments or the prices fish fetch in the markets. He'll be a fine leader and a capable teacher."

A sparrow landed. It snatched a bread crumb and flew quickly away.

Yeshu gestured toward the fire, where Shimon Petrus was adjusting the wood with a stick, making tiny, efficient spaces for the air to feed the flames. "See there. Petrus understands the wood, and the fire, and the air. Make the right space, and the air flows the right way to make the right flame. That's Yahweh's law for fire. It doesn't change, and Petrus understands it perfectly. And I *need* people who understand the importance of Yahweh's laws. I'm not here to tamper with the Law."

His gaze moved upward, following the flames and the shimmering warm air above them, up, up, until he was gazing into the sky. "But there's something more than the Law. Something *behind* the Law." He paused a moment, eyes skyward. "My Father," he said softly. Then he looked back down at me and laughed. "And *your* Father." He swept an arm toward his disciples. "And their Father, and *everyone's* Father. The Father behind all fathers." He shook his head again, smiling this time. "I don't always have words for it, Gestas. But I *know* it." There was wonder in his eyes. "I've known it since my time in the wilderness." He grinned. "Sorry for hitting you with that rock, by the way."

I felt my jaw drop, and he laughed again at the sight of me. "Of course I remember. That dribble of water brought me back to reality. Without it I wouldn't have made it back to town."

"Maybe you shouldn't have been out there in the first place."

"No, you're wrong, Gestas. That was where I needed to be. It cleared away the inessentials. Burned everything back to basics."

"Which are?"

He looked into the distance. Beyond the camp. Beyond the hills. "That there's more to the Father than how air flows through a fire, or whether people eat pigs. You just have to find a way to *see* it." He gave a soft snort of amused frustration. A sparrow darted in for a crumb and darted away again. "And then you have to find a way to explain it. To help *others* see it. That's the hardest part. Laws are easy. Easy to teach. Easy to follow, mostly. But *this*." He held out his right hand, palm cupped like he was holding something delicate and priceless, and a bit dangerous. "This ... thing, this thing beyond all things. This thing *behind* all things." He stared with an intensity that made me squirm. "How do I teach people that, Gestas?" His gaze on mine. Riveting. It was a rhetorical question.

Or was it? I thought about my dharma training.

"I think people have to experience it, Yeshu. Like you did."

"I can't ask people to starve themselves in the wilderness so they can experience the Father. I did that *for* them. It's my job to bring it *back* to them."

"You're right, starving in the desert is too much for most people. It was nearly too much for *you*." He had the grace to look a little chagrined.

"So what then?"

"Well, there's Naphtali's approach. Study and contemplation." Our approach in Bactria, too. "But not everyone has the time or the inclination to sit in a cave waiting to open up to … the Father."

Something simple. Something accessible. I thought about Alexandros' example of the poisoned arrow. How it cut through the cobwebs. "Maybe if you put it into a small story."

Yeshu cocked his head. "A story?"

"Something simple, but with deeper meaning. Like with scripture, but from people's common experience."

He sat a little straighter. "Such as?"

Exactly. For a warrior, a story about an arrow. For a subsistence agricultural community, a story about what? "Something everyday. About fishing, or raising sheep. Or planting crops." Another sparrow landed. It took two hops and cocked its head. "Or sparrows."

"Sparrows?"

"Why not? If the Father has a law for fire, and a Law for man, he must have a law for sparrows." I looked around us. "Or for lilies. Anything, really. Use the laws of ordinary things to get at the bigger thing behind them."

Yeshu thought for a moment. "That could work." He plucked a lily and looked at it, as if seeing one for the first time. "Look how beautifully our Father dresses these flowers. They don't have to make an effort. They just follow the law of flowers. And aren't we more precious to Him than they are?" The sparrow took another hop. Yeshu broke off a crumb of bread held it out. "Or than this sparrow, who follows the law of sparrows?"

The sparrow snatched the crumb and flew off.

Yeshu laughed and twirled the lily between his fingers. "What makes it so hard for us to trust in the Father, when it's so easy for this lily, or that sparrow? What sense does that make?"

He was on his way.

We carried on from village to town, eventually to the port at Tiberias. At a wine stall there I met a tin merchant from Ha-ramathaim, in Judea, whose small fleet was on its way south with a cargo of earthenware casks.

Yusuf was a well-fed, bearded man in early middle-age, with the shrewd grin of someone who knows his sensual pleasures.

"I sell most of my tin in Jerusalem," he said over a cup of honeyed wine, "but I keep a little to trade to wholesalers here for olives and oil." He drained his cup and set it on the counter. "Which I then also sell in Jerusalem." He laughed. It was deep and throaty. He dipped his cup back into the jug.

I was interested in anything he had to say. The wine was on him. Plus, if I could swing it, a ride down the coast in his little fleet would be a welcome break from walking.

"And where does the tin come from?"

He lifted the dripping cup and waved it vaguely northward. "From the ass end of the bloody world. A freezing dungheap of cliffs and pit mines the Romans call Britannia." He mimed a shudder. "Years ago they pretended it was part of their empire by dotting it with frightened little garrisons of the worn-out and the beardless. No offence," he added, gesturing with his cup at my smooth cheeks.

"None taken." I waggled my empty cup. He chuckled and refilled it.

I hadn't had wine in ages. Lifetimes. The Bactrian communities didn't allow it, and the Therapeutae forbade it with a holy vengeance. Drinking was an expellable offence, which was a nasty punishment in an isolated desert community. But any Therapeutae near here wouldn't have known who I was.

Still, the fact that I was so breezily breaking their rules should have told me something was up.

Yeshu and the others were camped on the beach not far from the pier. They'd caught or cadged a half-dozen fish, and Shimon Petrus was spearing them on sticks for roasting when Yusuf and I stumbled down with a sack of honeyed dates, two shanks of mutton and an amphora of red wine.

I think Yeshu only agreed to accept the ride because it would give him a chance to work on Yusuf. "The wealthy are the toughest," he said to me over the roar of the salt breeze, as we sat near the aft end of one of Yusuf's small cargo boats. The fishermen in our group were helping the crew, and the rest of us were doing what we could. Yeshu was braiding a length of *gamla*, a thick rope. I was mending a sail. "They find the Law manageable, and they take their riches as evidence that the Father is pleased with how they follow it. Why would they look past that?"

"Maybe wealth is a sign of the Father's approval."

"Have you seen some of the wealthy? No. Wealth is just a sign of wealth."

I pulled the end of a thread into a tight knot and bit it off. "You should come up with one of your stories, then. To help them see." I shifted the sail across my lap until I came to another tear, and drew out a fresh length of thread.

Yeshu stared out at the water. "In my experience, they can't be bothered seeing past their rich meats and soft beds." He shook his head. Then he turned back, saw me, and laughed. I was peering closely at the needle, struggling to thread it. He held out the rope he was working on. "In fact it would probably be easier to get this *gamla* through the eye of that needle than to get the rich to see the Father's kingdom right here in front of them."

I smiled. "There you go."

Yusuf dropped us at the south tip of the Sea of Galilee and carried on down the Jordan toward Jerusalem. He provisioned us with bread, dates, salt fish, and three amphorae of wine, which we carried in rope slings rigged by Yochanan, who was clever with knots. We followed the river southward, stopping in communities on both sides. On the whole things went smoothly. There was an incident near Gadara when a madman drove a herd of swine into a creek, but Yeshu calmed him down and the rest of us managed to save most of the pigs from drowning.

By the time we reached Nain, near Mount Tabor, word of Yeshu's teaching had begun to spread, and we were expected. The local teachers were impressed by his scholarship. The more humble folk were drawn by his welcoming manner and by rumours that he was a great healer. He did his best to oblige. He sat up all night with a young man whose fever had left him all but dead, feeding him sips of water and cooling him with compresses. By morning the man was sitting up and making conversation. To his overjoyed mother, who thought she'd lost him, this was nothing short of miraculous.

Over the course of our travels I told Yeshu about what I'd learned in Bactria. He was taken aback, but intrigued. We'd withdraw from the others for a half hour or so every two or three nights to talk. It wasn't always easy, especially at the beginning. No matter how carefully I tiptoed around the non-duality beyond all non-dualities, Yeshu refused to associate the Father with anything that impersonal. Duh. But because the rest of the dharma resonated with him, he decided to treat it as an innocent lapse on the Tathagata's part. After that we were fine.

On a typical evening I'd say something like: "There's the everyday world, and then there's the world of release from suffering. What you might call the world of the Father. But they're the same world. The difference is just in how you see them."

And Yeshu would say: "Yes, exactly! Lift a rock, and there's the Father. Split a piece of firewood, and there He is again! And in the axe, and the chopping, and the flame. And the food it cooks, and the warmth it provides. You just have to know how to look." He was uncovering a vocabulary for his understanding. It was a joy to see.

He went *ballistic* over the stuff on compassion.

In most places the people saw Yeshu as the charismatic teacher he was becoming. Nazareth was a different story. There the people still saw him as that carpenter's boy who went off north and left his mum. To be fair, the local officials did let him speak in the synagogue on the Sabbath, as others had in other towns. But in Nazareth it didn't go so well.

He opened, as he often did, with a passage from Isaiah. The one about being anointed to bring good news to the meek, and so on. Solid choice. It placed his calling in a familiar context before he moved on to his more challenging ideas. But already the people were having none of it.

"So who anointed *you*, then?" called out a ropey-shouldered labourer. "Wasn't it that nut case in the desert who was living off bugs?" His companions nudged him and laughed. There were murmurs of approval in the crowd.

Yeshu smiled gently. "Try not to take Isaiah too literally. Remember, this is a spiritual text." He held out his left hand, palm up, as if cradling something precious. He'd been using that gesture since our talk about the sparrows. "On one level, sure, he's talking about physical anointing, with water or oil. On the head. By an official." He tightened his grip on the unseen precious thing, still smiling. "And you're right, he does mean that." Then he held out his right hand, also palm up. "But for those with ears to hear, as they say, there's more to it than that."

"You saying I don't have ears?"

"Not if you keep listening I'm not."

This exchange had happened a couple of times in other towns. It usually got a chuckle. This time it got silence. Yeshu pressed on. "As I was saying, Isaiah also means something more." He raised his right hand a little higher and tightened its grip to match the left. "Anointing in the spirit. Not on the head, with oil. In the heart. With *fire*." He paused a beat. Some of the congregants looked puzzled, wondering if he meant actual fire. There were always a couple. "And not from a human official." Two robed elders frowned as if slighted. "From the Father."

The man who'd spoken out wasn't smiling anymore. But I was. I'd seen it a dozen times by then, and it still impressed me. He was bringing them around.

Then one of the frowning elders spoke. "Do you mean to tell this assembly that you have been *specially anointed* by Yahweh? With *fire*?" The the room went silent, waiting for Yeshu's response. He thought for a moment.

"All that I mean to tell this assembly is that I've received a *calling* from the Father. To bring to all—"

But the elder interrupted him. "Are you saying this calling makes you the *fulfillment* of Isaiah's words?"

"That isn't *quite* what I said." The murmurings resumed.

The elder raised his voice. "But you described yourself in Isaiah's words. Are *you* Isaiah?" He looked at Yeshu in mock puzzlement. A few men near him chuckled.

"No, I—"

"Are you *like* Isaiah, then? You, a carpenter's boy? Are you a prophet?"

The crowd held its breath. "Well," said Yeshu, "that depends on—"

That was as far as he got before they shouted him down. His answer wasn't a flat "no." Beyond that, nothing mattered. The carpenter's boy thought he was a prophet. The nerve.

Yeshu kept trying to make himself heard, but he'd lost them. He retreated to where the rest of us were standing. We pressed through the crowd into the street and didn't stop until we were well beyond the limits of the town.

The elder hadn't even mentioned the *mashiach*. He hadn't needed to.

Nazareth was our only real disaster. In most places Yeshu was well received. At Cana he made such an impression that a local dignitary invited us to his daughter's wedding feast. I don't know when I'd last eaten so well. Endless platters of roast lamb, endless baskets of fresh bread, endless strings of dried figs and honeyed dates. The only thing that wasn't endless, apparently, was the wine. It ran out unexpectedly early.

The panicking steward was about to send a boy to a nearby winemaker for more when he spotted the amphora beside me. He stopped. "What do you have here?" he asked.

I hesitated. It was the last of the wine Yusuf had given us. "Water," I said.

The steward raised an eyebrow. "Water?"

I nodded. "Fresh water. From a well. At, um." Where had we last stayed? "At Rumah." I was pretty sure it had been Rumah.

"Water from Rumah."

I nodded harder. "Very good water in Rumah. Very nice well. Hard to know when you'll find good water again when you're travelling. Always best to carry some."

"It sounds quite remarkable," said the steward. "May I taste some?"

One day I just told him. On the march between one scrubby village and another I got him on his own and told him. I told Yeshu I don't die. He slowed his pace and looked at me, the corner of his mouth curling to join in the anticipated joke. When he saw my solemn expression, the curl faded. I could see him working out what this new thing might mean. How to respond. Was I mistaken? Was I mocking him? Was I nuts? Then the wariness turned to sympathy. That was so Yeshu.

"They say things like that about me, sometimes," he said. "You've heard them. That I'll defeat death itself." He smiled shyly, like the idea was too embarrassing to entertain. "I try not to encourage it." He was going with *mistaken*. Sensible choice. Might've gone with it myself in his position.

"No, it's not that I *won't* die. I *don't* die. I've lived the way you see me now for generations. For more than a thousand years. I marched against Egypt for a people who no longer exist. I've travelled north to where the water turns solid from the cold. I've starved, and frozen and been pierced by arrows and split with axes and I *don't die*." There was a pounding in my chest and a burning along my arms. The bewilderment of a hundred lifetimes. Six paces ahead of us Thomas turned his head with a puzzled scowl.

Yeshu placed a gentle hand on my shoulder. "I'm here. You can tell me. But for now only me. And a bit more softly."

Why that day?

Damned if I know.

Why Yeshu?

Because I trusted him. Completely.

That evening, after a meal of nuts and stream water, Yeshu and I walked to a low hillside where we could talk privately. "I've been thinking about what you told me," he said as we climbed. "That you've lived so long." Like we needed to clear up what the topic was. We sat within view of the camp, but well out of earshot. "It's unusual. But not unprecedented." Had he decided to believe me? Or was he indulging me for some therapeutic reason? Whichever it was, he was taking me seriously, and trying to help. I loved him for it.

He lowered his head and closed his eyes, the way he did when he was recalling things he'd been taught. "The Books of Moses mention elders who lived for hundreds of years. Jared and Methuselah almost a thousand years each. Noah more than nine hundred." He opened his eyes. "It's only more recently that lives have been shorter."

"I know the texts, Yeshu. I know the numbers. I'm not an ancient in a book." I put his hand on my forearm and pressed his fingers around it tightly, making white marks in the skin. "I'm real flesh, right now." I held my arm up to show him the marks. "At a time when men rarely live to fifty. In all my life I've never seen anyone live to a hundred. I've never heard of anyone who's lived as long as I have."

Yeshu's eyes were warm. He turned my forearm over, exposing its pale underside. "Methuselah and Noah were real flesh too, in their time. But that isn't my point."

"Which is?"

"The Father had a plan for Noah. And for Methuselah." He patted my arm. "Maybe He has a plan for you, too, Gestas. Maybe that's why you don't die."

It was an explanation. One that made sense, or at least the kind of sense I needed it to make at the time. Because it had also started to make sense to me that the multiple old gods were just stories. War gods for soldiers. Rain gods for farmers. Sky gods for nomads. Whatever the people in a given region cobbled together to suit their needs. And if they were only stories, then it made sense that the one god of Yeshu's people was story behind all those stories. The one that was true. The one that made sense of my longevity.

And He had a plan for me.

I slept well that night.

By the time we got back to Capernaum, Yeshu was drawing good crowds. Some came for the healing. Some came for the novelty. But a lot of people—especially among the less well-off—were genuinely interested in what he had to say. There was enough interest that Yeshu decided to find some high ground where he could easily be seen and address whoever from the area was interested.

There were more than we had anticipated. Hundreds. "What if they expect us to feed them?" Yacobus asked, looking out over the gathering crowd. "We're down to our last loaves and a couple of dried fish."

"Don't worry about it. People always bring their own food to these things."

Our travels had polished Yeshu's timing to perfection. When the buzz of the crowd was at its height, just before its predictable slide into impatient grumbling, he climbed the hillside to a broad ledge and stood there, alone and exposed. He spread his arms wide. The buzz died almost instantly. Every eye in the valley was on him.

He wore a simple woollen robe, newly washed and hung to dry without creases. His hair was loose against his neck, and stirred slightly in the breeze. He opened by confronting his critics. No *good morning*, or *how was the journey* or *I trust everyone slept well*. Straight to the point.

"Some people say. That what I teach. Goes against the Law." Short, punchy phrases to carry across a river valley. He paused, just for a beat. "Maybe some of you here have said that." A few older men in the crowd looked down or away. Yeshu knew his people. "Well I tell you here today. Whoever says that. Is mistaken. The Law is our bones and our breath. The Law is who we are. As a community. As a people. I follow the Law. I preach the Law. I'm not here to destroy the smallest particle of the Law."

There was a low stirring in the crowd. Acknowledgement, mostly. Surprise from some. Disbelief from those who'd come with minds made up. Yeshu waited for it to subside.

"But here's the thing. The Law tells us what *pleases* our Father. But if you want to *experience* our Father. To experience Him in his fullness. Then the Law, on its own, won't get you there." He dropped his head, took a breath, and then raised it again. His voice went up a notch. "The Law looks after our day to day. Our going out, and our coming in. This is important. But if you truly want to *know* our Father. To know His Kingdom. Then you have to both follow the Law and go *further* than the Law." He swept his hand up and out toward them as if urging them onward. "To the depths of yourselves. To the places beyond the Law. To the places beyond your *selves*."

The murmuring grew again. Was this some verbal trick to get around the Law while professing the opposite? He needed to bring it down. To make it real. So he did.

"The Law tells us not to kill. That's a pretty good rule. It's hard for us to live together peacefully if we go around killing one another."

There were a few nervous chuckles. "That's the *Law*. The going out and coming in. The day to day. Let go of killing. I have no problem with that." He raised a forefinger. "But." He paused. His expression was earnest. The crowd paused with him. Then his face relaxed. "If you want to do *better* than the day to day." He swept his forefinger around. "If you want to experience the truth of the Father, then you need to do more than just let go of the killing. You need to let go of the *anger*." There was a silent, collective *huh?* from the crowd. "Well," he added with a self-effacing shrug, "at least unless there's a *really* good reason for it." There was a mild ripple of laughter. "Anger gets in the *way*. To know the Father, let go of telling your brother he's worthless, or your sister that she's a fool. Let it *all* go." He threw both hands up. "*That's* how you start to experience our Father."

The murmuring grew more positive.

"You are what you do, sure. That's why our Father gave us the Law. To help us manage what we *do*. But that isn't the whole story. You aren't just what you do. You're what you *think*. You're what you *feel*. Who you are isn't just in your actions. It's in your *heart*." He pressed his fist against his chest.

The abstract.

Then the concrete.

"For example. The Law says not to commit adultery. Again, a pretty good rule if we want to live together in a community. But." The forefinger again. "If you want to know the Father, it isn't enough just to not do it out here, in the world." Waving one hand loosely toward the valley. He made eye contact with a burly man near the front. "No, or behind a curtain either." The man flushed and smiled, and Yeshu smiled back. He looked up again. "If you want to know the Father then I say you shouldn't even commit adultery in your *hearts*." He paused for a beat. "It's distracting."

This time the laughter was relaxed and hearty.

He had them.

Yeshu was spellbinding.

No, that isn't it. He was always spellbinding. This was on another level entirely. He was taking the confusions and contradictions of everyone there, all those lives, all those goings out and comings in, and he was owning it, owning it all. He was making it all theirs, and making it all his, and making it all part of some greater whole they might vaguely have imagined but had never truly felt until that day, in that little river valley, in the presence of that one miraculous man. They hung on his every turn of phrase.

"If you want to experience the Father, purify your heart. Then you'll be blessed. If you show mercy, you'll receive mercy. If you hunger for righteousness, righteousness will fill you up. If you make peace in your villages you can truly be called our Father's children."

Each new phrase drew an enthusiastic response. A few of the literate listeners were trying to write some of it down, on their hands, or on the wrappings of their lunches or the hems of their robes.

"You." Yeshu's voice, even louder now, echoed across the valley. "Are the light. Of the *world*." The crowd cheered. "You. Are a city. On a *hill*. You can't be hidden. Your light will shine. Before all men. To the glory of our *Father*."

The crowd erupted. Yeshu could scarcely make himself heard anymore.

It was time to wrap it up.

"Remember, you are what you *think*. And you are what you *do*. My words are just words. On their own they'll wash away, like a sandcastle in the rain. But if you think about them. And follow them to the Father. Then they'll shelter you like a castle of well-hewn stone."

And he stepped down from the ledge and out of their sight.

I took his hand to help him down the last few steps. He would have fallen if I hadn't. It was like he didn't even know there was ground under his feet. He was practically vibrating, his eyes wide, his smile otherworldly.

Predictably, people with various ailments pressed forward toward where they'd last seen him. As the rest of the crowd started to disperse I saw Matthaeas direct several of the disciples to go in among them with baskets. "Excuse me," I heard Thomas say to a prosperous-looking family as their servant folded their sitting-blanket into a satchel. "If you have any food left you could spare, we'd be grateful."

The husband hesitated, scowling slightly. "Ah ..." he started.

"Or if not for us, then maybe for those here who don't have your good fortune." He nodded to where an empty-handed family of six in patched woollens was stirring itself for the long walk home. The man sighed. Then he nodded to his servant, who dipped into the satchel and came out with a flat loaf and a string of dates.

"May the Father bless your house," Thomas said, bowing gently to the man as he accepted the food. He put it into his basket and moved on to the next well-to-do family. I looked around. The other disciples were also filling their baskets with offerings. And Matthaeas was quietly asking the poorer folk if they would mind remaining a moment, as there would be food for those in need.

Shimon Petrus directed the ailing into a queue and showed them through to Yeshu one by one. Yeshu spoke to them kindly, gently placing his hand on their foreheads or shoulders or across their eyes. Each came away a little taller, a little stronger, a little less troubled, after just a few moments of personal attention from this simple, radiant man. Andreas guided the poorer of them onward to the accumulating food stocks.

After a while the ailing gave way to the merely curious. Yeshu was just as kind and patient with them. Toward the end, squeezed to the back by the stronger, was a dusty young boy. "Master," he said, "is it true you will defeat death?" His words were so formal they had to be something that was making the rounds. "That you will return to redeem us from its sway?"

Yeshu smiled the same smile I'd seen when we'd talked about those rumours. He looked up and noticed me, and his smile grew warmer. "Well." He put a hand on the boy's head. "If it is, then maybe there's someone here who'll stay until I come back."

The boy looked over his shoulder, following Yeshu's gaze, and saw me. His eyes widened in awe. "Do you mean this man won't die before then?" He was cleverer than he looked. Yeshu, realizing his mistake, held up a hand. "That isn't *quite* what I said."

But it was too late.

From little acorns mighty legends grow.

When the last meal had been handed out and most of the stragglers had gone, Matthaeas gave Yeshu his summary. He was standing by two cloth-draped mounds. Matthaeas liked to make a bit of a show. "We came here with five loaves of bread and two dried fish," he said, reading from a slate. There were nods and groans. We all knew our provisions had been nearing their end. "We received contributions from about twenty percent of the crowd, which wasn't bad." He seemed to be ticking off items as he went. "From those, we were able to give meals to everyone who wanted one, which was about a hundred and fifty families. And remaining for our own use we have—"

He put his hand on the larger cloth, paused for effect, and snatched it up.

A couple of us gasped.

"Twenty-two loaves. About four pounds of salt mutton. Two baskets of fresh fruit. And—" He lifted the second, smaller cloth. A small amphora was wedged into the dirt. Matthaeas smiled triumphantly. "Enough wine for about two cups each." There was a ragged cheer. If food had been thin lately, wine had been nonexistent.

Yeshu embraced Matthaeas warmly. "Thank you, Matthaeas. Well co-ordinated, as always." He turned to the rest of us. "Take your portions and enjoy. Today has been a good day."

Matthaeas divided the food, and we sat in small groups to eat. There wasn't much conversation at first. Soon, though, when our bellies were happier, we started discussing Yeshu's speech and the crowd who'd attended it. *The bit about the meek was nice. Guess you're out of luck then, snort snort. Even that group of Samaritans at the back seemed to like it all well enough.*

I was chuckling at Thomas' mock-surly impression of the Roman soldiers who'd been watching from the fringes when I caught a flash of movement in the corner of my eye. One of the stragglers, no doubt, looking for healing.

"Gestas," a sharp voice said.

I looked up. It was Naphtali.

My wine-cup stopped halfway to my lips.

Our return to the community was brisk and silent. Naphtali could've expelled me. Instead he knocked me back to a kind of probationary status. I wasn't allowed into town for our weekly meetings or our periodic musical vigils, until some unspecified time when it would be decided that I'd redeemed myself. Which meant no singing.

I hadn't wanted to go back. Yeshu had persuaded me. "Maybe this is part of the Father's plan. Why else would Naphtali have come at just that moment?"

Yeah, well. That part of the Father's plan lasted about a month.

As I said, my breezy breach of the rules should've tipped me that something was off. Now I could see it: I just wasn't into them anymore. Besides, I start over often enough on my own. Why let someone impose it on me?

I tried to find Yeshu's group, but they were back on the road. Stories varied as to where they were. After a while I gave up. Apparently the Father's plan didn't include finding Yeshu again. I was starting over after all.

The action was apparently in Rome. Maybe I should go there.

A journey to Rome isn't built in a day. I'd need money for passage. The nearest place to make decent money was probably Jerusalem.

Plus I'd heard the Father had a house there.

The first thing you noticed about Jerusalem was the Temple. That was no accident. The Temple was the calculated effort of two generations of Herods to buy their puppet regime some legitimacy with the people, so a big part of the point was to make it conspicuous. *See how pious we are? See what an impressive palace we've built to glorify Yahweh?* Even some of the priests thought it was overblown.

There had already been a Temple there, on and off, for centuries. The Herods could just have done some re-mortaring and thrown on a fresh coat of paint. But when you've handed your country to an invading empire in exchange for a comfy client kingship, bigger ameliotory

gestures are called for. And the Temple reno was nothing if not big. By
the time I got there the construction of the larger complex was in its
fifth decade under its second Herod and it still wasn't done, although,
wisely, they'd prioritized the Temple building itself and finished it in
the first year and a half. It dominated what we'd now call the skyline,
its marble façade and gold-topped pilasters rising high above the walls
of the surrounding compound-in-progress, dwarfing even the towers of
the Herods' own nearby palace. (*See how pious we are?*) I noticed it long
before I arrived at the city walls.

Job done, Herods.

But the Temple wasn't where I was going. Not yet. A stranger from
the sticks wasn't likely to find money-making opportunities among the
priests and nobles of the upper town. I followed my usual routine.

At a wine stall in the lower town I cadged a cup of red from a
chatty Roman named Silvius Constantius, who'd come to Jerusalem
with a cohort of the First Augusta, married a local girl, left soldiering,
and set up as a dove merchant near the Temple. When his wife died
delivering a stillborn child, Silvius coped with his loss by getting rich.
He expanded into money changing, extended his operations into the
surrounding area, and soon had a modest villa in the upper town with
marble walls and a brace of servants.

I'm good at talking to soldiers. Especially soldiers who like to
drink and brag. By our second cup I was coyly admitting to being new
in town and looking for work. By our fourth I had an entry-level job in
the quiet suburb of Bethany, near the Mount of Olives.

The Temple drew pilgrims. Most of them needed animals for the
sacrifices, but very few arrived with the Tyrian *sheqels* the Temple required. They also had to stay somewhere, and for those who couldn't
afford Jerusalem, suburbs like Bethany were an affordable option. And
if they didn't have *sheqels*, there I was to provide them, taking their
prutah or *denarii* in fair exchange. And if they weren't entirely clear on
the *rate* of exchange, who was I to correct them?

The work wasn't as profitable as I'd expected. Silvius was tight with
a *sheqel*. At his rates, Rome was going to take a while. But it wasn't
demanding work, and I was good at it. So good that by Passover of my

second year Silvius had moved me to the prime spot at the Temple, where I ran the cash table and oversaw two teams of dove-sellers. I did well. I took my growing wealth as a sign of the Father's approval.

What a noob.

In addition to the currency exchange, the Temple operation offered small loans to pilgrims who hadn't allowed for the inflated city prices of sacrificial animals. Because of my new responsibilities, Silvius entrusted me with the keys to the dovecote in the lower town where he kept the floats of cash for all of his Jerusalem operations.

Our table was in the Court of the Gentiles, a colonnaded commercial area around the Temple proper. It was the noisiest, smelliest, most congested market I'd ever seen. You could get pretty much anything there short of actual prostitutes: flatbread fresh from the pan, or mutton warm from the coals, or crumbly white cheese cut from thick blocks in barrels of cloudy water. There were garish tents hawking crude images of priests in their robes, or leather wristlets with "Jerusalem" branded on them, or badly carved *bas reliefs* of the Temple façade. There were crammed pens of calves and lambs, and stacked cages of doves. There were beggars, and beggars, and more beggars.

And of course there was money. Money passing between grubby hands. Money slapped onto rough wooden tables. Money traded for other money. Money in pouches and purses and locked hardwood chests. Because there was money, there were thieves. And because there were thieves, there were Roman soldiers. They wandered in small patrols through the narrow spaces between the stalls. Most of them were conscripted auxiliaries from Samaria, though every once in a while you'd see an actual Roman citizen of the officer class. A deterrent, mainly. A symbol of the civil peace. With polished swords, just in case.

Business in the Court was highly competitive compared to the virtual monopoly we had in Bethany, but we were well-positioned. We had two of the five largest dove-selling operations, and our currency exchange table was in a prime spot next to the Beautiful Gate. Silvius encouraged the perception that the closer you were to the Holy of Holies the more blessed your money was.

I was just getting the hang of things when Yeshu turned up.

I heard him before I saw him. I was busy counting out a few too few *shequels* for the number of *denarii* a grey-haired grain farmer from Sepphoris had given me.

"Gestas."

I knew his voice instantly. I looked up.

He'd aged a little, but not much. Shimon Petrus was on his right. Andreas on his left. Yacobus and Thomas. Matthaeas the former tax gatherer. The whole band was still together. I nodded deferentially. "Yeshu."

The grain farmer started to step away, but Matthaeas stopped him, took two additional *shequels* from my table, and put them gently into the farmer's still-outstretched hand.

"Did we take a wrong turn?" I'd never seen Yeshu's face so stern. I looked down, away from his eyes. They were still on me, though. I could feel them on my head like the sun of the desert wilderness. His voice coiled like an adder. "We meant to go to the Temple. But it must be easy for country folk like us to get lost in the big city, mustn't it, Gestas?"

I didn't respond. At the edge of my vision I saw him straighten, lift his head, raise his arms. Some of the people at neighbouring tables looked over. His voice grew louder.

Always so good with a crowd.

"We must have taken a wrong turn, mustn't we?" I glanced up. He was looking around at his disciples in mock bafflement. A couple of them shrugged theatrically. Yeshu spread his arms to encompass the surrounding tables and stalls, the cages and the money chests, the buyers and sellers, the gougers and profiteers. "Can this place be the Temple of Jerusalem?" He was using his crowd voice now. Everyone within view could hear him, and they all seemed to be listening. "The holiest of our Father's places?" He dropped his arms and shook his head. "Doesn't seem likely."

I glanced around nervously. A hundred feet away two Roman auxiliaries had stopped to watch. Four more lounged at a nearby wine stall.

Yeshu looked down at me again. He lifted his right foot, and rested it gently on the front of my table. He looked back out at the crowd. "This place." He flexed his right knee. The table creaked. "Seems more like." He waited. Scanned the crowd. Noticed the soldiers. Made sure he had everyone's attention. Held it. Held it. Drew it out to *just* that moment when the anticipation peaked. And then, into the clenched silence... "A nest of *thieves*." And on the last word he straightened his leg.

My table tipped over and onto me, knocking me from my stool. Loose coins scattered. As I scrambled to catch them, I saw Yeshu nod to his followers. They spread through the crowd, upending tables, opening cages, breaking open sacks of coins and flinging them into the crowd. Surprised traders and merchants shouted their outrage, or swung at them with fists or clubs. Bystanders scrambled to grab the suddenly free cash from the cobbles.

As the uproar spread I gave up on Silvius' money and covered my head with my hands. The last thing I saw was one of the auxiliaries signalling his colleagues at the wine stall. I crouched by the overturned table with my face against my knees and my arms around my ears. Something hard hit the table. Someone's knee hit my back. It went on for a while.

As these things go, there was eventually a lull around my table. I looked up. Yeshu was still there. He reached a hand toward me.

"Get up, Gestas." His voice was gentle. I took his hand, and he helped me to my feet. Around us people were chasing livestock or stuffing their purses or just trying to get to safety. The soldiers, mired in the chaos, had barely moved. Yeshu glanced at them, then turned back to me. His eyes were sad. "Leave this place."

I shook my head. "It's people's livelihood, Yeshu."

He glanced at the soldiers again, and slipped away through the crowd.

A larger force of armed Romans eventually arrived and restored order. But by then Yeshu and his followers had gone.

I gathered what coins I could. It wasn't much. The crowd had made off with whatever was in reach. It got worse when I checked with the dove-sellers. Dozens of cages smashed to scraps. More than half of our inventory flown off or trampled.

At the dovecote that evening Silvius was unsympathetic. "All I'm hearing is that you lost my money," he said, scooping seed from a sack with a small flat dish and sliding it into a cage. He took another dish from a pouch at his waist. He turned to me and held it out. "Each has his portion, Gestas. And only his portion." He smiled grimly. "Do you take my meaning?"

I didn't. Not everyone had Yeshu's gift for metaphor. I shook my head.

He waggled the dish at me, then dipped it into the sack and turned back to the row of cages. "I mean that your losses will come out of your savings." He slid the dish into the next cage. "Leave the chest on the counting table. I'll do the calculation."

The next morning Silvius introduced me to a thickly muscled Thracian gladiator he'd hired to accompany me to the Temple as security. "Just until we're sure this, ah, *crisis* has passed." His tone said it wasn't *really* a crisis. Or it wouldn't have been if *he'd* been at the Temple yesterday. "The cost of the Thracian will come out of your wages," he added as he ducked back through the door of the dovecote.

Life at the Temple was soon back to normal. We repaired the tables and cages, replenished our inventory, and went back to making money. Apart from my reduced circumstances and the Thracian over my shoulder, it might never have happened. Then one day one of the other money changers approached me at my table with a smile and a nudge. "I guess you'll be able to get rid of your Thracian now," he said cheerfully.

"What? Why?" Had Silvius had a change of heart?

The man smiled a gap-toothed smile. "They got the bastard."

"What bastard?"

"You know." He put his foot on my table and jiggled it. "That one. The Galilean. Who started the riot." He backed toward his own table, pointing a happy finger at me. "You'll have your satisfaction now."

Rumours about Yeshu raced through the town, in the markets and at the wine stalls and wherever else two or three people gathered. He was the leader of a group of violent rebels. No, it was an army. An *army*? Well, a small one then. He was the true King of Judea. Really? Well, so he *said*. He'd been sent to Herod for trial. He'd been sent to Pilate himself. He'd been banished. He'd been made a galley slave. He was to be crucified.

This last one turned out to be true.

Yeshu was being kept in the upper city, in an outbuilding of the palace compound of Yusuf Caiaphas, Rome's puppet High Priest. Caiaphas was famously jittery about any threat—real or imagined—to the political structure that fed and gowned him so well, and he had Pilate's ear. It was just like him to make an example of a gentle soul like Yeshu in the hope that any genuine rebels would take the message.

It was near dawn when I climbed the wall of Caiaphas' compound. The outbuilding was in the corner of two exterior walls. It was guarded by a single soldier, which said a lot about how big a threat they really thought Yeshu was. The soldier was on a stool by the door. From the look of his uniform in the torchlight he was a local auxiliary. Probably some farm boy from Samaria who'd thought soldiering would be a great adventure. Judging by his girth—and by the wine pot in his hand—that had been a long time ago, the dream long dissipated.

I was about to drop down when I noticed two figures below me at the edge of the torch light. The soldier noticed them too. "Hey." His voice was slurred. He drew his sword. "Who's there?"

The figures cowered out of the light.

"Oh no you don't." The soldier jiggled his sword toward them. "Come where I can see you." The figures moved gingerly forward. Shimon Petrus and his brother Andreas. "Hey," said the soldier brightly. "I know you. You were with this one." He waved his sword toward Yeshu's prison. "When we took him. At that garden."

Shimon Petrus' eyes widened in fear. "No. You're wrong."

"Yeah, I remember you." The soldier chuckled. "You tried to cut off poor Annas' ear. Would've, too, if your master hadn't stopped you." A glow of realization lit his face. "You're here to get him out, aren't you? Free your master?"

Shimon Petrus shook his head in fear. "No."

The soldier slid his sword back into its scabbard and, looking around a bit, moved closer to the brothers. "You know," he said softly, "there could be a way." The disciples were rooted to the spot. The soldier lowered his head toward them. "Say a fellow were to have enough money to move on to someplace else. Start over, like. A fellow like that might be able to convince folks he'd been overpowered by a band of thugs." He lifted his hand. Something jingled in the torch light. "Thugs who took his keys, say."

"No." Shimon Petrus was physically shaking. "I told you, I don't even know this man."

"And besides," Andreas said, "where would we get that kind of money?"

The soldier's face grew hard. "Bastards." He stepped back, drew his sword again and swung it in front of them in a wobbling arc. "Off with you then. Go on, get out before I call the Romans down from the house."

They vanished into the dark. The soldier returned to his stool and his wine pot, muttering to himself. I dropped to the ground and approached him slowly. When he saw me he jerked to his feet and reached for his sword, but I raised my hands. "I heard you with the others."

His eyes grew fearful. "I ain't said anything to anyone. You can't prove I did." He slid the sword out a couple of inches, his hand shaking. The blade rattled in its scabbard.

I smiled reassuringly, my hands still raised. "I'm not an official. I was just ... intrigued, let's say. By the story. About the fellow with the keys?" I eased toward him, slowly, unthreateningly. The blade continued to rattle. Otherwise he didn't move. His face was badly shaved. He smelled of old leather and fear. I gently touched his sword hand. "That story left me wondering about something." I eased his blade back into its scabbard. The rattling stopped. I spoke softly. Barely a breath. "How much money would a fellow like that need?"

He drew back to study my face. I did my best to look benign. I must've succeeded. His eyes brightened. "Well now," he said. And he gave me a figure.

It was a lot.

I could've afforded it if Silvius hadn't bitten into my savings. I didn't have that kind of money anymore. But I knew where I could get it. And then Yeshu would be saved. According to the Father's plan.

A rooster crowed. It was dawn.

I'd have to be quick.

The caged doves coo'd softly.

I took only enough for the bribe, plus my passage to Rome. I could hardly stay. Silvius would know it'd been an inside job. I tucked the bag of coins into my tunic. I was re-locking the chest when Silvius and the Thracian came in.

"I paid you well, Gestas." I was on my knees on the dirt floor of the dovecote, my forearms tied behind my back with stout knots. The Thracian was waiting outside. "You had savings, and an income, a good one, for as long as you wanted. Why would you throw that away for this?" He tossed the bag of coins onto the counting table as if it were inconsequential. It probably was, to him. Except in principle.

He lifted a short leather whip from the table and held it to my face. It had a blunt, bound handle and short, bronze-tipped leather thongs. He drew it back.

"You dare to break into my building." He struck me across the cheek. I clamped my eyes shut and gritted my teeth. It was only pain. Pain was transient. "You dare to take my *money.*" He whipped my other cheek with his backhand. I felt the skin split over the cheekbone. Pain was empty, I told myself. Pain was an illusion. "Why, Gestas?"

I didn't answer. I kept not answering until my face and neck and shoulders were raw. I kept not answering as long as I could, until the thongs of the whip were red and sodden and I could barely see through my swollen eyelids. But eventually I answered. I always do. I always say I'll hold out, but in the end I always answer. Pain may ultimately be illusory, but conventionally it still hurts like blazes.

"The Galilean."

Silvius leaned close. "Excuse me?"

"The Galilean."

"The Galilean?" Puzzled, as if the words were just animal sounds. "What Galilean?"

I hung my head. My laboured breathing stirred feathers on the floor. Blood dripped from my face. "The one who started the riot at the Temple. The one they're going to crucify." I looked up at Silvius and mustered a little bravado. "The one that idiot Pilate thinks is trying to start a rebellion."

Silvius' face was still close. His breath reeked of garlic. "What of him?"

I shook my head. Silvius lifted the whip to my nose. I smelled my own blood. He pressed it into my nostrils, forcing my head back.

"What of him?" he asked again, almost growling.

And I told him.

And he smiled and went to the door.

"Not just a thief, as it turns out," Silvius said as the soldiers dragged me from the room by the arms. "A traitor to Rome." He was enjoying himself. "In league with the rebel leader Yeshu of Galilee, who is to be crucified. On Pilate's orders."

"That so?" one of the soldiers said dully. From his tone, traitors to Rome were a *denarius* a dozen in Jerusalem, and wasn't it just his bad luck to stumble upon another one this morning.

"Make sure that goes into your report," Silvius said, arm outstretched and finger pointing downward, as if the report were there in front of them. "A rebel and a traitor."

The soldiers flung me onto a cart and started up toward the upper town.

"One more for the cross," Silvius called out as we rounded a corner.

We rattled on in silence for a while. Then one of the soldiers spoke.

"Think I'll retire and become a cross-builder," he said dryly to his companion. "That's where the real money seems to be these days."

There was a trial, of sorts. I was taken to a side door in Caiaphas' palace. It led to a small stone room with a table and a stool and a heavy, iron-reinforced door in the interior wall. A man was propped in a corner, bruised and unconscious. When the Roman officer next to him saw we weren't officials he relaxed a little. "What've you got there?"

"Rebel," my prospective cross-builder said. "Mixed up with that other one. You?"

"Bandit. Cut two throats on the road to Jericho."

That was it. No further conversation. I wasn't in the mood to start one.

A little while later a harried-looking official came through the reinforced door, tugging a robe over his shoulder. He sat on the stool, set a wax tablet on the table and squinted at it. "Which one's Dismas?"

"This one," the other officer said, tapping the unconscious man with the butt of his spear. The man stirred slightly.

The official didn't look up from his tablet. "Bandit? Two dead?"

"Yes."

"Your identification?"

The officer drew out a small wooden diptych and opened it. His *testatio*, his proof of Roman citizenship. The official peered at it, took out a stylus, and made some marks in the wax. "And you attest to this crime?"

The officer nodded. "I do. Spoke to someone who survived the attack."

The official made another mark in the wax. "Guilty," he said. "In the name of Caiaphas our High Priest and Pilate our Prefect I sentence this man Dismas to crucifixion." The officer dragged the man out by the arms.

The official peered back at his tablet. "This one's Gestas?"

"Yes," my guard said.

"Rebel against Rome?"

"Yes. I attest to it. I spoke to the man he confessed to. Here's my identification." He showed the official his *testatio*.

The official made more marks. "Guilty," he said.

There wasn't much point to crucifying someone if you didn't make a display of it. What kind of deterrent would that be? In Jerusalem the display took place at Golgotha, a hill outside of the city wall near the Joppa road. The crosses were simple and sturdy: rough timber crosspieces on rough timber uprights. The uprights were durable enough, but the crosspieces tended to rot, from the blood that soaked into all the overlapping nail holes. Once a crosspiece deteriorated beyond further use, the soldiers had the next condemned man carry up a replacement. They probably considered it efficient. Which it was. But still.

Not that anyone asked me. Or that it happened to me. But it happened to Yeshu. That wasn't all. Because of the cooked-up story that he claimed to be King of Judea, some Roman wit had twisted some thorns into a rough crown and jammed it onto his head. Blood from the deep scratches trickled down his forehead.

We made a pathetic procession on our way from Caiaphas' compound to the hill. The bandit and I, chained together at the ankles, led the way, whipped by soldiers and spat on by the crowds. Yeshu came behind with his crosspiece on his shoulders. The jeering the bandit and I received was nothing to how that crowd treated him. Between his presumed blasphemy and his presumed claim to kingship, the crowd gave him their worst. Some just cursed, or threw stones. Not that stones aren't nasty. A jagged one caught his scalp and drew blood. Others mock-bowed with exaggerated flourishes, and then flashed their bare backsides. Others threw buckets of urine, or kitchen filth. I was glad to pass through the city gate and start up the hill. Briefly.

When we got to the top I saw two crosses and one empty upright, all laid out flat. The soldiers took the crosspiece from Yeshu, notched it into its upright, and secured it with ropes and nails.

When they dragged me to my cross I started to struggle and scream. It's impossible not to. It doesn't matter how dignified you've resolved to remain. Once the reality of what's about to happen is there in front of you, you turn into a flailing, spitting animal. I begged for mercy, from the soldiers, from the crowd, from Yahweh and the Tathagata and Tarhun the thunder god and anyone else I could think of. I apologized. I promised. I railed. I shrieked invective. Nothing made it stop.

It took five of them to hold me down, but they did. They were ready for it. They'd had plenty of experience. But I didn't stop struggling and I didn't stop screaming. If anything, I struggled harder and screamed louder when the nails started going in. I've never experienced such pain in my life, before or since. They drove them in at the wrists, between the bones. The flesh of the hand won't take the weight. The one at the feet went through the heel bones. Basic carpentry, really.

Bones hold nails better. It made a nice solid sound. They might have been building a cabinet if it hadn't been so excruciating. I actually tried to twist my own leg away at the ankle.

Let me correct one thing, though. I said that it was impossible not to scream and struggle, but that isn't quite right. Yeshu didn't. Yeshu stepped slowly and calmly toward the middle cross, to my right. He lay where they directed him to. He spread his arms when they asked him to. There was hammering, and sharp intakes of breath. But no screaming.

The discipline. Honestly. I've never witnessed anything like it.

Not that I witnessed much of it. By the time they propped up my cross in its hole in the ground, I'd blacked out.

When I woke it was night. There was a moon, but it was behind clouds. The bandit on the far side of Yeshu was babbling in the dark. I couldn't make it out. I don't think it was words.

Yeshu was speaking quietly. I couldn't make it out either, but it was words. It sounded like one side of a strangely calm conversation. I don't think he was talking to the bandit, though. To the Father, maybe. The one with the plan.

"Yeshu." My voice was thin. Hard to draw breath.

He stopped. His head turned toward me. "Gestas." There was warmth in his voice. He may even have been smiling. It was hard to know in that dark. But it sounded like it.

I strained to draw enough breath to speak. "I'm sorry about the Temple."

There was silence for a moment. Had he heard me? Then he spoke. "The Temple?" He sounded puzzled.

"The money. If it hadn't been me at that table—"

"Shhhhhhhh." It was a cool, reassuring sound. A man dying painfully on a cross was taking the trouble to reassure me. The discipline. Honestly. "If it hadn't been you I would've kicked over some other man's table. There were plenty."

I shook my head, winced. Even that small movement brought screaming pain. "No. If it hadn't been me." I swallowed. It was hard. My throat had never been so dry. "If it hadn't been me. Who travelled with you. Listened to your words. Shared your food." I swallowed again. "Things might have been different. You might not be here now. Here at your death."

Another silence.

"Oh Gestas." Yeshu's voice was gentle, like he was speaking to a slow child. The clouds stirred in the breeze. A fragment of moonlight lit his face. I was right. He was smiling. Looking over at me from his cross and smiling, with the affection I remembered so well. Then he turned back, leaned his head against the cross and closed his eyes. "There is no death."

I awoke again near dawn.

Still crucified. Damn.

There was a murmur of voices.

I looked to my right. Yeshu and the other man were both still.

I heard the voices again. Coming up the hill. Moving quietly enough not to have awoken the guards but noisily enough to have awoken me. The nails pulled at my wrists like burning knives. My wrenched chest strained for even a wisp of breath. Noisy bastards. I'd rather have stayed unconscious, thanks very much.

I squinted into the dimness. Five figures. All men. One of them, heavier than the others, seemed to be their leader. The way his robe stirred in the morning breeze suggested fine linen. The others wore rough tunics. One held some sort of bundle. Another carried what looked like a ladder. "Here," said the leader, pointing to the ground. The one with the bundle spread it out. A piece of cloth, the length of a man and about an arm's length wide. The leader gestured. "That one." The man with the ladder carried it to Yeshu's cross and leaned it against the back. The leader climbed up. He was carrying some sort of tool. "One of you under each arm," he whispered. His voice sounded familiar. But after a thousand years all voices sound kind of familiar.

Two men took up positions at Yeshu's sides. The other two kept watch over the sleeping guards. The man in the robe reached around the crosspiece to Yeshu's right wrist. There was the creaking sound of metal against wood, and then Yeshu's right arm hung down. One of the men reached up to support him. More creaking, and his left arm was free. The two men held him up while the leader climbed down and freed his feet. "Gently," the leader said as they lowered Yeshu from the cross and carried him to the cloth. His voice was deep and resonant, even when whispering. Then it came to me. Yusuf. "Gather the edges," he said. "Carefully." The leader was Yusuf, the tin merchant from Haramathaim.

The men took the cloth by its corners and lifted. Yeshu's body hung slackly between them. Yusuf started back down the way they had come. He beckoned the others. "Quickly."

I cleared my throat. "Um. Excuse me?"

Crucifixion changes a man.

Yusuf put me in a hidden cellar under one of his warehouses. He brought me food and water every morning. It took me more than a week to heal, and longer than that to lose my limp. The damage to my heel bones had been extensive. When I was able to move about, I disguised myself as a beggar and started following Silvius. It was painstaking work. When he went out it was usually in crowded public spaces, and when he carried money—which was most of the time—he was with the Thracian gladiator, who he'd kept on as a bodyguard.

But I was patient.

After two weeks everything came together. He was strolling tipsily home at dusk down an empty street, without his Thracian. He passed me without seeing me, as his kind do with beggars. I rose up quietly behind him. My right hand covered his mouth while my left stuck a dagger under his shoulder blade and into his heart. He barely made a sound. I lowered him to the ground, my hand still over his mouth, and pulled back my hood. When he saw my face his eyes went wide and he tried to speak, but I kept my hand tight against his lips. I watched the life leave his face. Then I dragged him into a dim alcove, out of sight.

I counted the money in his purse. Not enough for Rome, but enough to get as far as Cyprus. The only other thing in the purse was a small wooden diptych. I felt a tingle. A wooden diptych. I took it out and opened it. Silvius' *testatio*. His proof of Roman citizenship. *Silvius Constantius Flaccus. Born at Salona in Illyricum*. I snapped it shut and pressed it against my lips. The wood was still warm from Silvius' body. Did I dare? The penalties for falsely claiming citizenship were famously severe. Then I smiled grimly. Worse than crucifixion?

I thought it through. Silvius had no family in Judea. He had two sisters in Illyricum, married to minor officials, but he hadn't been in touch with them in years. The First Augusta cohort where he'd served was now in Caesarea. It could work. The Empire was a big place. As long as I stayed out of Illyricum and avoided the First Augusta ...

I stripped him of his clothes and jewellery. Then, as quietly as I could, I smashed his face against the cobbles until it was unrecognizable.

Crucifixion changes a man.

The Roman Governor of Cyprus was recruiting soldiers. As a citizen I could expect an officer position. It might not get me to Rome right away, but I was in no great rush. Ever, really.

There's a postscript to my experiences in Galilee and Judea.

Two decades and three legions later I was with the Second Augusta when they occupied Britannia. The local tribesmen fought hard, but they were overmatched. Say what you like about elephants, they make a difference when your opponents' idea of a great beast is a particularly large stag. The Emperor Claudius declared Britannia a province, and we set about the drudgery of building roads and forts. The glories of war.

We were still at it more than ten years later. At that point my cohort was building the fortress at our westernmost outpost, a trading town called Isca Dumnoniorum. Isca was remote even by Britannian standards. It was about four days' march from the nearest cantonal capital and two weeks from the provincial capital at Camulodunum, not allowing for raids by local tribesmen along the way. It was important, though, because it was the centre of the tin trade. Which is why I shouldn't have been surprised.

I'd risen to the rank of Decurion by then, and was treating my troops to a cup of ale at a Dumnonii tavern when a puzzled voice over my shoulder said: "Gestas?"

I turned.

Yusuf. The tin merchant.

He'd grown thicker with the years and his beard and hair were now fully white, but otherwise he looked just the same. Tall and broad and vital.

"Bugger off," one of my troops said. "There's no Gerstis at this table. You, sir, are addressing the Decurion Silvius Constantius Flaccus of the Second bloody Augusta, and I'll thank you to accord him the proper respect." He laughed and clinked cups with his mates, in the slightly smug camaraderie of military regiments everywhere.

I stood, and put my hand on my soldier's shoulder. "I'll sort this out." I dropped some coins on the table. "Order another round."

I used my rank to clear two Dumnonii stone masons from a corner table and sat Yusuf down. "It can't really be you, can it? You haven't changed at all." He kept his voice low, which I was glad of.

"My people age well. Granddad still has all his hair. Listen, Yusuf, I have a good thing here, and I'd be grateful if you could just play along, all right?"

His face opened into a broad grin. "So it *is* you." Then, bowing his head in mock solemnity, "But of course, Decurion, as you wish, De-curion." He looked up and winked. "Soul of discretion." He drew an elaborate cup from his shoulder bag. "Is there a chance the Decurion might spot me an ale, since he's buying rounds?" He smiled gleefully. The richest man in the room, tapping me for a drink. But I bought him one. More than one. I kind of owed him.

I was delighted to see him after so many years. I gave him a sani-tized version of how I'd come to be a Decurion in a Roman backwater. He talked about the tin trade. Booming due to the *Pax Romana,* for which he thanked me. He caught me up on Judean politics. Herod and Caiaphas had been deposed, but the latest of Herod's descendants, Agrippa, still ruled as puppet. I sent a third round of ale to keep my puzzled troops happy.

After a while there was a lull, as there always is, and to keep the conversation going I asked Yusuf about his odd drinking cup. He held it up and looked at it. "What, this?" It was a grey goblet with a thick stem and a pattern of vines and flowers. The workmanship was extraordinary. It looked like some sort of metal, but with a rich, subtle sheen. It stood out from the mismatched crockery in the rest of the tavern like ... well, like a Roman fort in a Britannian village. "Gift from a client. Pewter. Mostly tin, with a bit of copper and whatnot. Nice stuff." He grinned and waggled the cup. "I use it to wind up the Chrestiani. I tell them he and his followers used it at their last meal before ... well, you know."

"Wind up who?"

He looked at me, puzzled. "The Chrestiani. You know. The worshippers?"

I had no idea what he was talking about. "Worshippers? Of what?"

Yusuf sat back and shook his head. "You really are at the edge of the world here, aren't you my friend? Of our Yeshu. Haven't you heard? Yeshu is now a god!"

The Abbot

IT WAS THE Thracian rowing songs that got me started as a singer. Music was functional in those days. Rowing songs. Marching songs. Drinking songs. Not lifted out of daily life and refined. That isn't a criticism. I've spent half my life in the refined arts. In fact you'll notice three recurring enthusiasms in my life: singing, soldiering and contemplation. But soldiering gets tiring, and contemplation eventually makes me restless. Singing is limitless. And past a certain point on the History of Europe timeline, there were often a lot of opportunities for a capable singer. Paid work, even. At least room and board.

In the early years those opportunities tended to be in the Christian church. Same with contemplation. Christian monasticism was the only game in the European town for a *very* long time. Put the two together, and it'll be no surprise that I've spent quite a chunk of the past couple of thousand years in the service of the Church. So let's deal with the Messiah in the room: Did Yeshu die and come back?

Well, if he did, I didn't see it. But then in the weeks after the crucifixion I'd had other things on my mind. Learning to walk again, for example. How could I have known that the most influential event in western civilization may have been happening almost at my elbow? All I can safely say is that I've never seen an actual resurrection, before or since. But then at that point I hadn't seen anyone else like me either. So I don't rule it out.

Was Yeshu God made flesh, then? Which isn't quite the same question.

I don't have any special knowledge about that. After all my lives I still can't say whether there is a God, or a godhead, or whatever you want to call it. What I *can* say, though, is this: Of everyone I've ever met, the person who most embodied one? Yeshu the Galilean. And that may have to do.

It was odd, at first, to join what I'd thought of as the cult of Yeshu. To espouse what they espoused. They had a certainty I could only pretend to, though over time that pretence became sincere in a way. Because I believed in Yeshu. Probably not the same way the others did. But ... duh.

My Christian monasticism and my formal singing career started at pretty much the same time. I was pissed because I'd missed the fall of Rome. You know how it is. You get caught up doing one thing or another, and before you know it that Empire you'd been meaning to visit has gone and collapsed on you. I hate that.

To be fair, I had been kind of busy. When my fake Roman ID was finally discovered in Britannia, I'd had to make myself scarce, so I'd ended up spending the Empire's dying centuries among Picts and Slavs and other peoples for whom Rome was barely a rumour. When the Empire split in two, I was with a community of Balts on the coast of what is now Latvia. While the Vandals and Visigoths dismembered the Western bit, I was retreating with the butt-end of dead Attila's once feared Huns to a scrap of land in Ukraine. Through it all I remained determined to make it to Rome one day.

This seemed like a good time. Years had passed. Risks had abated. Borders were porous, and record-keeping less rigorous. So from a Hun outpost on the Black Sea I worked my passage down through Constantinople, across the Mediterranean and up the Italian coast to the port at Ostia. Then I walked inland to Rome itself. I'd made it. Five hundred years late. And more than a hundred years *too* late.

When I'd set out from Jerusalem, Rome was the centre of the universe. Now it was a crumbling barbarian town in the Kingdom of the Ostrogoths. Suddenly I felt very tired. I needed a retreat. A big one. Enter the Church.

In my formative centuries religion was a local, personal thing. You had your gods, and the guys over the mountain had theirs. If you were a trader you might take yours with you on the road, or you might make nice with your customers by adopting theirs. Or both. Oh, sure, an empire might impose its gods on its conquered neighbours, but the old gods wouldn't have to up and leave. We've talked about all this. Plurality. Streets of temples in Hattusha. But that all changed with monotheism.

During the dying days of its power, Rome had formally endorsed Christianity. In fits and starts, mind you, but eventually it took. And there's nothing like political patronage to turn an artisanal belief system into a multinational religion. Ashoka the Great with Buddhism. Constantine with his cross. Try to imagine how little room Rome's imperial monotheism left for the old gods. Oh, wait. You don't have to, do you?

So although the Empire was in political shards when I arrived in Rome, each shard was still dominated by its official religion. What had started as a offbeat variant of Judaism had grown into a vast international network of communities and temples supported by a bureaucracy centred in—you guessed it—Rome. The city was buzzing with basilicas and monasteries named for wealthy patrons or dead heroes of the religious revolution. But buzz wasn't what I needed. Not for a retreat.

"Well," said a grey-haired man through the portal in the door of Sancta Anastasiae sub Palatio, "there's a chap called Benedictus. Runs a community in the countryside somewhere. Can't think where. Hang on." He closed the portal. A couple of minutes later he opened it again. "Right. The place is called Monte Cassino. Follow the Via Appia south for two or three days, then ask around."

Monastic communities are good places for retreats. Prostrate yourself as required, pick the grapes or stir the barley-pot or sweep the sanctuary floor as directed and there's a bowl of something warm and nourishing morning and evening. They generally don't even care if you're mute, or seem to be. Sometimes that's practically part of the job description. Benedictus's place at Monte Cassino was the archetype. Literally. He wrote the rules monks would live by for the next sixteen hundred years.

And those ruled included singing.

If I hadn't been so desperate for a refuge, I wouldn't have made it through their screening process. I arrived in the middle of the afternoon, exhausted and footsore. When I first saw the monastery in the distance, my shoulders sagged. It was at the top of a rocky hill. But at least it was in sight. I pressed on, keeping my eyes on the gate at the end of the path. When I finally reached it I sighed with relief and knocked.

"Yes?" the porter said.

"I've come to join your community."

"Go away."

"I've come a long distance. I'm very tired."

"Go away."

I spent the night in the woods. The next day I tried again. Maybe there'd be a different porter. There wasn't.

"Go away."

"Can I speak to your manager, please?" Something like that.

"No. Go away."

Four days of this. I had nowhere else to be. On the fifth day, things changed. "Right, then." The porter stood aside. "In you come."

They put me in a guest room with a thin straw mattress, and brought me vegetable soup and a cup of wine. I heard singing in the distance. After it stopped, the door opened and an earnest man in his early forties came in. "I'm Brother Constantinus."

I bowed. "Faustinus."

"I hear you want to join us."

"Yes."

"Why?"

"To glorify God in all the things of my life."

I'd done my homework in the taverns along the road. You'd be surprised how much intel about a supposedly closed community can leak into the neighbourhood.

"There are strict rules. A brother will read them to you. Then we'll see."

"I'm literate. I can read them myself."

Constantinus frowned as if I'd asked to borrow his sister. "Forgive me, Faustinus, but we're hardly going to trust a stranger with a manuscript." Fair enough. It was right there in the name. Books had to be written manually. They were the community's most valuable possessions. "Plus if we read them to you, we know you've heard them."

So a pimply young brother read me Benedict's Rule. It went on forever. It was a disciplinary code wrapped in a day planner inside a series of job descriptions. It was pretty demanding. But I still clicked "accept."

Later that day Abbot Benedict himself came to see me. "There are vows, you know. Poverty, chastity and obedience." He was lean and grey and hard. The portrait Fra Angelico painted 900 years later only captures a whiff of his intensity, and nothing of the rest of him. But then the Angelic Friar would've been working from a model in his own community. Benedictus was a one-off. With his severe black cloak and sizzling grey eyes, he commanded respect and obedience, and no small amount of fear.

Ho hum. I was seventeen hundred years old. Insert mic drop here.

"I understand."

He looked me up and down. Embroidered tunic. Finely woven knee breeches. Polished leather boots. "You have money." It wasn't a question.

"Yes." In a pouch on my belt. And more buried in a wood a mile away.

He spread his hands, as if in, er … benediction. "Vow of poverty." I untied the pouch and handed it over. I'd calculated it carefully. Enough to allay suspicions that I'd held any back. Benedict weighed it briefly, seemed satisfied. "You'll stay in the guest area for now. We'll see how you feel after a few days of reflection." He hefted the pouch. "If you decide to leave, you'll get this back. If you stay, it goes to the community." He looked me up and down again. "Your clothes, too."

"Fine." It had been a long time since I'd bothered getting attached to clothes.

He examined my face. "You've experienced the world." Again, not a question. "Women. Maybe men." I nodded. I wasn't about to admit to more specifics than I had to. "No more. Vow of chastity."

"I understand."

"And the vow of obedience. Obedience nurtures humility. It can be a challenge for men of the world. Can you manage it?"

"Piece of cake." How hard could it be?

It was hard. Have you *seen* Benedictus's rule book? Pull it up online if you don't believe me. In the abstract it had sounded demanding. In practice it was punishing. Our days were rigidly scheduled, hour by hour. Take a moment to think about that. We didn't have reliable clocks, but each day was as crammed with back-to-back duties as an ad salesman's appointment app.

Ora et labora. Pray and work. We did plenty of both. Long days in study—or the fields, or the kitchen, or the scriptorium—were broken up every few hours by formal worship services called Offices. You've probably heard some of the names. Vespers, the evening office, say. They happened all day, including twice during the night. Every day. Every. Day. Even the Therapeutae weren't this rigorous.

At first it grated. In time I came to see how perfect it was. My retreats were about down time, and the Rule meant never having to make a decision about anything. It was all laid out, all day and all night. What we wore. When we ate. When we could speak. Once I was in the rhythm, I could basically shut down my higher cognitive functions and coast. It was like drifting below the surface of a tranquil sea, only coming up to sing.

When I graduated from the guest room, I was put with the other novices, some of whom were boys barely out of diapers who'd basically been donated to the Church by their families. We were on probation until we proved we could adapt. Senior brothers taught us to read and write—using a popular Latin translation of a collection of texts called the *Biblia Sacra*—and instructed us in basic theology.

Benedictus hadn't been kidding about the obedience. Even asking questions about the party line was frowned upon. "But how can the Christ be both perfect god and perfect man?" I asked Constantinus one morning during lessons.

"Because the Church tells us so."

"But can you explain how that works? I don't understand it."

"You're a novice, Brother Faustinus. It isn't your place to understand it. It's your place to accept it. If our Lord wills, your understanding may come later."

"But I—"

"Remember the Rule, Brother. Accept this admonishment with humility."

I clenched my teeth. I had agreed to the Rule. Admonishment was just the first stage. More serious infractions—including failing to respond to admonishment—drew more serious penalties. Ritual shunning, for example, which brothers only earned their way back from by lying on the floor in penitence while the rest of us stepped over them on our way to the refectory. In extreme cases, like blasphemy, there was public flogging. It happened more often than you might think. You only had to see it once to realize the importance of keeping your head down. Below the surface.

Brother Rufus was the singing master. I adored that man. He was my first proper music teacher. "You have lovely tone, Brother Faustinus. And a fine sense of pitch. Have you had training?"

"None to speak of." Apart from the mockery of a boatload of Thracian rowers.

"Well bless our Lord for bringing you here."

"Bless our Lord," I said in rote response.

The Rule told us what to sing at which points in which Offices in which seasons. It told us which hymns to frame with an antiphon or follow with an alleluia. It told us when to sing a responsory after a lesson and when not to. Benedictus was *that* meticulous.

If the point was uniformity and discipline, job done. Most armies I've fought with could've taken lessons in orderliness from Benedictus. Even the Prussians.

If the point was internalizing the scriptures, same again. Nothing engraves a text on the mind like a tune. Stick me in a black robe in a cold chapel and I could still sing a dozen of our psalms from memory.

But for me, the main point was the joy of rediscovering my

instrument. In my private heart I took a pride in my voice that would've been a flogging offence if I'd confessed it, since pride and private thoughts were against the Rule. I imagine all the brothers had little secrets of one sort or another. Over-fondness for wine. Drawing out an illness for one more serving of restorative meat. Artistic pride was hardly the worst of mine.

Most of the songs were texts chanted on a single, repeated pitch, with a flourish here and there as punctuation. User-friendly tunes even the most tin-eared brothers could grasp. Then there were more elaborate melodies that needed a choir of trained professionals, and sometimes a soloist. That soloist, the cantor, was Brother Rufus. The solos were where he shone. He wouldn't have let himself see it that way— Rule against pride—so I saw that way for him.

He was also basically the music library. Written notation wouldn't turn up for another three hundred years, so part of the singing master's job was to keep all the songs in his head. Every hymn and psalm and antiphon, for every Office and every Mass. I still have trouble imagining it, and I eventually *did* it.

Brother Rufus drafted me into the choir the moment I'd taken my vows. "I've satisfied the abbot that your voice is a gift from our Lord," he said with a smile of simple delight. "Singing in the choir will be part of your *laboris*." From that point, some of my bean-hoeing and goat-milking duties were replaced by rote-learning extra hymns and psalms. It was like fine ale after field work.

Two years after my arrival, Benedictus was taken with a fever and withdrew to his chamber. Constantinus announced it at the end of the Office of Prime. As we all filed out to begin our *laboris*, he and Brother Rufus held me back.

"Abbot Benedictus wants to observe the Offices in his own cell."

"I understand." Benedictus would hardly let something as earthbound as illness keep him from his holy duties.

"Including the chants." Both men looked at me expectantly.

"What?" I said.

"Well, Brother Rufus can hardly do the chants with the abbot, can he? He's needed in the community."

So for the next six days Constantinus and I attended Benedictus around the clock while his fever slowly devoured him. Our *laboris* was his palliative care. When he prayed, we prayed. When he was hungry, we fed him broth. When he slept, we watched over him, catching our own sleep in turns.

Between Matins and Lauds of the fourth day, while Constantinus dozed near the doorway, Benedictus started writhing in his sleep. I leaned in to murmur something soothing. He started awake and clutched the sleeve of my robe. "Destruction!" He stared fiercely into my eyes. "You were there, Faustinus. You tried to help. But you can't stop it."

I put my hand on his forehead. It was practically sizzling. That would account for the mixed up tenses. "What destruction, Abba? Where?"

"Here. This place." He lowered his voice, imparting a confidence. "Don't feel responsible, Faustinus." His grip relaxed, and he settled back into his pallet. "Nothing you could have done, boy. Nothing anyone can do." He drifted back to sleep.

Many of the brothers put a lot of stock in Benedictus's dreams—his visions, they called them—but I never had. I didn't that time, either. Not until much later. And then again a *very* long time after that.

But I'm getting ahead of myself again.

On the sixth day, just after the midday Office, Benedictus insisted, against our advice, that we carry him into the Oratory. He took the eucharist. He was so weak I had to hold his head up while he sipped the wine from the cup. Then Constantinus and I supported him while the three of us knelt in silent prayer. He felt like a sack of twigs.

After a few moments, he gently shook us off. He lifted his arms in praise, let out a long, soft sigh, and crumpled to the floor. And that was that.

Constantinus succeeded him as abbot. Not much changed. Why would it? The Rule was the Rule.

Eventually Brother Rufus' voice grew feeble, and I took over as cantor. When he grew too old to work at all, I took over as singing master.

And so it went.

Have you ever been in a relationship that wasn't going anywhere, but that you stayed in because it wasn't actively wrong enough for you to make the effort to leave? One that seemed to drag on, waiting on some outside force to shake it up? Thirty-five years in, that was me at Monte Cassino. I was long past needing a retreat by then, but life was just so *stable* there. Then along came the Lombards.

You see, Rome's collapse wasn't a one-time thing. The power vacuum it left was swirling with colliding interests. The Ostrogoths were only the latest Germanic tribe to stake a claim over this or that piece of the peninsula. During most my years at Cassino they were still tussling with the old Empire's eastern rump, and when that rump finally claimed victory it couldn't maintain the stability its predecessor had. There were too many neighbouring kingdoms and khanates and caliphates slavering over the old Empire's scraps. In a geopolitical mess like that, an undefended monastery on a strategically important hill was low-hanging fruit for invaders. Like the Lombards.

We'd heard vague news that a new flavour of Goths was running a pop-up kingdom somewhere to the north, though as usual, information about the outside world was sketchy. Then word filtered through that it had fragmented into warlord duchies, and we figured that would be the end of it. Our imperial overlords would mop them up, and any threat would be over.

Or not.

I was in a meeting with the abbot—Abbot Bonitus, at that point— about the hymns for the upcoming feast of Saint Somebody. Bonitus, like everyone else, assumed I was somewhere in my late fifties by then. The deception was second nature. Roughen the voice. Curl the shoulders. Whiten the temples with tinctures. He and I had finalized the hymns for Matins when we heard a cry from the direction of the gate.

"Probably just another novice gored by a goat," I said. We had a particularly spirited flock at that point, and the younger monks weren't always careful.

The abbot nodded. "The herbalist has a fresh stock of poultices. Shall we move on to Lauds?"

But the cries got closer. Soon they were accompanied by banging doors. Then the dean of novices burst in breathlessly. "Soldiers!"

The abbot rose quickly. "Whose?"

"I don't know."

"How are they dressed?" I asked.

"Tunics and capes. Fur collars. Chest armour like fish scales."

"Helmets? Shields?"

"Dome-shaped helmets, with a thing that sticks down like so—" he held his finger and thumb a couple of inches apart and drew them from his eyebrows to his nostrils "—to guard the nose. Round shields, with a metal thing in the middle." He made an eight-inch circle with his hands.

"What language?"

"Rough Latin. I could understand them, but only just."

"Goths of some kind, I imagine," the abbot said. "Are there many?"

"Dozens. Maybe more. I haven't seen outside."

"Well armed?"

"Swords and spears."

I looked around for a weapon. Next to the abbot's pallet was a thick wooden candlestick as long as my arm. I knocked the candle free and picked it up by the end opposite its heavy base. "Get everyone to the back gate."

The Dean looked awkwardly between us. What I'd said made sense, but I had no authority. Only the abbot could issue commands. "Do it," he said.

I stepped into the corridor and headed toward the gate. Bonitus followed.

"Go with the Dean."

"No. I'll reason with them. This is a place of God. They can't burst in and threaten the Lord's peace." He stayed at my elbow all the way down the corridor.

As we neared the cellar stairs we heard a shriek of pain. I peered around the corner to see a soldier pull his sword out of the cellarer, who'd been defending our stores by kneeling in front of the door in prayer. He fell over sideways. His rosary clattered to the cobbles. The abbot pushed past me. He froze at the sight of the soldier rolling the cellarer aside and kicking open the cellar door.

There were more soldiers behind him. Some followed him down the stairs, whooping at the prospect of wine kegs. Others looked at us. They didn't look receptive to the abbot's reason.

Bonitus took a step toward the cellarer. I grabbed his sleeve and stopped him.

"But I'm his abbot. He's my responsibility. He needs my help."

"He's past your help, Abba. And you have other responsibilities." I nudged back the way we'd come. "Lead the others to safety."

He took a moment to do the math. "You're right." He was a practical man. Then he gave me a curious look. I could see his mind catching up with the things he'd just seen. And the things he hadn't. A gentle, aging singing master, for example.

"What will you do?" he asked.

I hefted the heavy candlestick.

"Hold them off."

It was exhilarating.

Not that it was a challenge. They were just farm boys with fancy weapons. Disciplined troops might've been a different story. Or at least a longer one. The ending would've been much the same.

I disarmed the first one in moments. He didn't have room to get his spear into position—the corridor was too narrow and his colleagues too close—so he drew his sword and swung it at me overhand. I lifted the candlestick crosswise, a hand at each end, and smiled as his blade buried itself in the thick wood. He assumed I'd try to grab the candlestick back. A logical assumption: It was my only weapon.

I let it go.

The unexpected extra weight twisted his sword halfway out of his hand. Thanks, gravity. I snatched it before he knew what was happening.

In a single motion I kicked the candlestick from its blade and rose to the attack. I hadn't realized how much I'd missed having a sword in my hand. It was like restoring an amputated limb.

Unarmed now, the soldier lifted his round shield to defend himself. His farm-boy instinct told him to hold it snugly against his chest. A better-trained man would have held it more lightly. I kicked it upward, driving its top edge under his helmet's nose guard with a satisfying crunch. He yelped like a scalded puppy. Now his instinct told him to remove the source of the pain from his mangled nose. He dropped his shield arm. But the shield wasn't the problem. I was. And I wasn't done. Once the shoulder of his sword arm was exposed, I gave it a precise jab with my new blade, severing enough ligaments to disable it. He screamed and dropped to his knees. One down.

His colleagues had to step around him to get to me. That made them vulnerable.

By the time I withdrew I had two swords, a spear and a helmet. When I reached the storeroom where the valuables were kept, I wrenched off the lock with the butt end of the spear and scattered a trail of coins into the hallway. Soldiers lived on plunder. The ones in the cellar were probably still there, smashing wine casks and tearing smoked mutton with their teeth. A flashing neon arrow pointing to the money would slow the rest of them down better than a dozen well-armed singing masters could.

I didn't take any for myself. But I did take a book. The one book so valuable it was kept in the storeroom, wrapped in an embroidered cloth.

I spotted the monks in the woods below the back side of the hill. They looked like a flock of dark-robed rams, with Bonitus at their edge, shouting commands. I smiled at the sight. He was literally shepherding them to safety.

I knew I couldn't join them. After decades of contemplation and routine, my whole nervous system was raging with a long-forgotten freedom I couldn't say no to. But I had a last task to perform. I trotted down the hill toward Bonitus.

"This way, Aemilius," he called to one of his flock. "You'll get caught in the brambles if you go through there."

"You need a herding dog."

He turned toward me, smiling. "I *am* the herding dog." This was his element. Not the finicky Benedictine bureaucracy, though he was good at that, too; the uncluttered act of guiding and protecting the men his God had put in his charge. "Unless you're volunteering?" Then his smile dropped away.

I assumed it was because of the blood on my robe, or the sword in my hand. The Rule had no room for killing. Then I realized that the look on his face wasn't shock or disapproval. It was relief. He wasn't looking at the blood or the sword. He was looking at the cloth-wrapped bundle under my arm. He made the sign of the cross on his forehead with his thumb. "Thank you," he said softly. He wasn't talking to me. Then he looked me in the eye. "And thank you, Faustinus." Second place. I was just the instrument.

I slid my sword into my rope belt and passed him the book with both hands. "I figured you'd need it, wherever you're going. Which is where?"

He unwrapped the book. He couldn't let himself believe it until he actually saw it. The original Rule, in Benedictus' own hand.

"Rome." He balanced the book on his forearm and traced his fingers lightly over the cover. "We have brethren there we can stay with." Then his hearing caught up with what I'd said. He looked at me sternly, every inch the Abbot again. "What do you mean 'wherever *you're* going'?"

"This is where we part, Abba."

"It certainly is not." His conviction was absolute. He was my abbot. I'd sworn to obey him. That was how the world worked.

Until it didn't.

"Yes, Bonitus. It is."

"You made vows. To our Lord."

"Yes, I did." I probably owed him an explanation. But I wasn't going to give him one.

We stood in silence. Then his expression softened, just slightly. He held the book to his chest, and put a hand on my forearm. "You saved our community, Faustinus." He stroked the book. "And you saved this. Maybe that will earn you mercy from our Lord. I'll pray for it." He turned to follow the others. After a few paces he turned back to me.

"You have remarkable vigour for a man your age."

I smiled. "Abba, you don't know the half of it."

The Family

I SAW MY first victims of the pestilence in the Free Imperial City of Augsburg.

I had a good gig as a sword for hire with one of the trading guilds that would later band together as the Hanseatic League, defending shiploads of Baltic furs and English woollens between its enclaves in Hamburg and London. But I'm not keen on sailing. So when a bearded Bavarian in a wharfside tavern needed men to guard a shipment of furs and flax overland, I signed on.

As we cleared the city gate the Bavarian pulled his shirt over his nose and mouth. I looked to see what had spooked him. A group huddled in a churchyard.

"What are they up to?"

"This way. Quickly."

"Why?"

"Because you don't want to die. Especially like that."

I'd heard rumours. Hushed comments followed by the sign of the cross. Aches and fever. Black swellings. Vomiting. Gasping. Dying. I thought they were exaggerations. They weren't. By the time we reached the weavers' warehouse, we'd passed two more churchyards, each with its cluster of the stricken. The Bavarian pulled a second layer of cloth over his face. The germ theory of disease was still a century away, but even on the prevailing miasma theory—that disease was caused by "bad air"

—people were careful what they breathed. Though that wasn't the only theory.

"God curse the Jews," the Bavarian muttered.

"Sorry, what?"

"The pestilence. The Jews caused it."

Ah, the enduring pastime of the bone-headed European. Something bad is happening. I don't understand it. I can't control it. Must be the Jews. I shook my head slowly. "I don't think that's how disease works. Besides, why would they?"

"Like they need a reason."

I knew better than to try to argue. Yet I always did.

"Everyone needs a reason for what they do."

"Every Christian, maybe." He tapped his head with his finger. "They don't think like us. Plus the pestilence doesn't affect them."

The usual next step. The *non sequitur* posing as an answer.

"What makes you think it doesn't affect the Jews?"

"It's a well-known fact."

"What's your evidence for that fact?"

"You want evidence? Go back to that churchyard and check the sick people for Jews. Ask everybody there. You won't find one Jew. Not one."

"It's a Christian church!"

The Bavarian nodded sagely. "Exactly."

The weavers were expecting fully processed flax. The bundles we'd brought were only partially processed. Which affected the price. Which led to an argument in the street. I tuned it out. As security, my only concern was whether the storehouse workers reached for their knives. This was a battle of screaming, not stabbing. Both sides had a deal to strike. They couldn't strike it if one side was dead.

The Bavarian called the chief weaver the son of a scrofulous boar. Then he broke off for an aside to me. "Go down to the wine shop, will you?" His tone confirmed that my sword arm wasn't needed. This was the fun part of his job.

"Thirsty work, calling people animal names?"

"Not for *me*, you ox's rectum. Get their starting price per keg.

Something I can talk 'em down from." I must have looked puzzled. "You didn't think we'd be taking these carts back empty, did you?"

The wine stores were at the far end of a salt warehouse. Behind a wooden counter a young man surrounded by small kegs and tasting goblets looked up from his ledger. "Good day, sir," he said brightly. "Something for yourself, or are you buying for a larger household?"

"Bulk. Wholesale price by the cartload. My boss'll be along to work out the details." I glanced at the ledger to get a sense of the going rate, and tapped it with my finger. "Feel free to pinch him on price until he squeaks."

"I hear you, sir." He drew the ledger away. "For bulk you need to talk to my father." He nodded over his shoulder toward a curtained archway. "He's taking a delivery of Venetian red. Go through, if you like."

They wouldn't have any trouble filling the Bavarian's carts. The storeroom was crammed with ceiling-high stacks of kegs separated by shoulder-wide aisles. The only empty space was a receiving area to the right. Through a set of double doors to the street I could hear a heated negotiation.

I recognized the proprietor by his resemblance to his son. Same dapper figure with a little more cunning and a lot more jowl. The woman he was arguing with had her back to me. She wore travelling clothes and a linen headscarf. They were standing next to a cart full of kegs. "You want to take bread from my children's mouths?" the man said. He muttered a figure—presumably the woman's offer—with disbelief, and turned away. I did a quick calculation. If that was taking the bread from his children's mouths, it was only to make room for the roast venison and savoury pastries he'd be able to afford with his profits.

I stepped into the sunlight. "Excuse me, madam. Can I help?"

The wine merchant looked up sharply. The woman turned and held up a hand. "No, thank you, sir. I've got this."

I froze. I'd seen her face before. Long ago. Very long. It was as untouched by the passage of time as it had been in the Bamiyan valley almost nine hundred years earlier.

Her voice was dark and dense. Like syrup without the sweetness. Like vinegar syrup. "I don't have children, sir, but I do have experience in trade. I've developed a few core principles. One is that I won't be taken advantage of just because I'm a woman."

"Um ..." I started to say.

She turned back to me. Her lips were tight, but there was a flicker of amusement in her eyes. "Another, sir, is that I won't be rescued for the same reason." She was enjoying this confrontation as much as the Bavarian was enjoying his. I gave her a silent bow with an *as you wish, m'lady* sweep of my arm.

The wine seller hadn't seen what I'd seen. "I'll repeat my generous offer," he said. He did. Thirty percent below what she was asking.

She stepped to a canvas sling on the side of her cart. "I won't repeat mine. Because it's going up." She bumped her original figure by ten percent. Then she reached into the sling.

"That isn't how negotiations work. You're the seller. You don't *raise* your offer."

She drew out a sturdy axe and gestured with it toward the merchant. "And yet I just did, didn't I?"

He stumbled back, hands raised in supplication. "Hold on now. There's no need for threats."

She lowered the blade. "This isn't for *you*, you simpleton." She drew back the axe and swung it at the nearest keg in her cart. It bit into the wood and held. "It's to show you how serious I am about not being taken advantage of."

The merchant cringed at the prospect of a keg's worth of wine wasted, but he stuck to his guns. "I've made a fair offer."

She wriggled the axe free, drew it back and took another swing. The blade met the previous cut at an angle. A tidy wedge of wood dropped to the dirt. She leaned on the axe like it was a walking stick. "And mine has gone up again. Another ten percent." They stared at each other a moment. Then she shrugged and raised the axe.

"All right." The merchant's palms were raised in surrender. "I accept your price. Just ..." He waved a hand at the cart. "Just don't do *that* again."

"Of course not, sir," she said demurely. "Why would I?"

I loitered by the counter and watched them conclude their deal, counting the coins as he stacked them on the counter beside her axe. No harm in a second pair of eyes. She placed the coins in a leather pouch and concealed it in her travelling cloak.

"Thank you, sir," she said. "Pleasure."

"Likewise. Will we see you again, madam?"

"I doubt it. I'm getting out of the wine trade."

"Our loss, madam." He didn't bother disguising his relief.

She picked up her axe from the counter and pointed toward him with it. "You'll have your boy return my cart after you've unloaded it?"

"Of course. Where would you like it brought?"

She gave him the name of an inn. Then she tapped the axe against a sample cask on the counter. "And if you could draw off a bottle of this Rhenish white for me as well, I'll settle with him when he gets there."

The merchant smiled. "On the house, madam."

I walked out with her. "You aren't planning to rob me, are you?" She didn't seem much concerned. "I do still have this axe."

"No. I just wanted to tell you how much steel you seem to have gained since the Bamiyan valley."

She did a good job of almost not reacting. "I don't think I know that valley, sir. Is it in the Rhineland?"

"You know it isn't. You know exactly where it is."

She kept her composure. Pretended to remember. "Oh, of course. Bamiyan. I haven't been there for a long time, though."

"Very long. Maybe not since you were begging with your dharma sisters in the market under the Buddha statutes."

I watched with amusement as realization slowly came to her.

"Are you freakin' *kidding* me?" she said.

She came with me to the weavers' storehouse, where the Bavarian had settled on a price for his flax. I took my wages and said goodbye. It took some effort not to tell him to bugger himself with a biscuit, but I had more important things on my mind.

Her name was Nicca. Her inn was by the south wall, near a convent. I booked a bed and found us a table at a neighbouring tavern. She was bursting with questions.

"How old are you? Where are you from? Are there more like us?"

I signalled for two mugs of ale. I was as curious as she was, but not as chatty.

"My name is Ishtanu. Though I'm going by Sewastian."

"Why?"

"Um. To fit in. Different names in different places?"

"Never occurred to me. I'm always Nicca, and it's never been a problem." Then her eyes lit up again and she grabbed my arm. "But seriously, are there more of us?"

Us. I'd never thought in those terms. I probably should have. And I should have started in Bamiyan, when I'd first had the chance.

A serving girl brought our ales in tall pewter mugs. After she'd gone I dropped my voice. "You might want to be a bit more discreet about 'us.' Outsiders aren't always welcome in these parts."

"How are we outsiders? People are people."

"Tell that to the Jews."

"What do you mean?"

Newbie. "How long have you been here?"

"Just the few weeks it took to drive the cart up from Venice."

"And before that?"

"Trading between Antioch and Venice, with my husband and his company."

I felt a lump of disappointment. "And where's your husband now?"

She took a sip of ale. "Dead. Two days before we docked." She seemed strangely untroubled. "Pestilence."

"Sorry to hear it." I wasn't.

"Water under the bridge. I'd have had to move on soon anyhow. Saved me the trouble." I knew the feeling exactly. I may have been the only other person in the world who did.

"What about his company, then? Shouldn't you be running it now?"

She shook her head. "I was his second wife. Trophy wife." She took another sip. "While I was buying that load of wine in Venice for the return trip to Antioch, his sons were unloading our spices and silks and buggering off. By the time I got back to the wharf, our ship was gone. Their ship, now."

"Wow. That's harsh."

"What can you do? Like I said, time to move on." She jingled the pouch in her cloak. "At least I have something to start over with. Doesn't always work out that way, as I'm sure you know."

I did.

We exchanged edited versions of our lives, like on any first date. Being newly flush, we kept the ales coming as we talked. Neither of us felt any effects.

She was born in the Indus Valley, which I'd never heard of, during the Gupta Empire, which I'd also never heard of. She was raised Buddhist, which made Bactria a logical place to flee to once people started noticing. Sometimes she was a mendicant. Sometimes she was a wife. Sometimes she was a man, and made her living in trade. I'd never had so much in common with anyone in my life. Duh.

"Why were you alone at the wine merchant's? You didn't travel from Venice on your own, did you?" The dangers of travelling alone were in my bones.

"Well that would've been stupid. I hired a driver and a pair of thugs in Venice and sent 'em back once I got here." She gave me a mildly indulgent look. "I'm a thousand years old, Ishtanu. I negotiate risks better than any woman you've ever known." That was probably true. Apart from Tróán. "If we're going to stay together, you're going to have to adjust your thinking."

I felt an unfamiliar warmth in my chest.

It's funny how utterly normal life can seem until you get blindsided by an alternative. You think you've got most of the puzzle pieced together, and then something upends the board. That evening in Augsburg my previous existence felt crushingly lonely in a way it hadn't while I'd been living it. Life meant passing through the fleeting lives of others. That was how things worked.

Until it wasn't.

Nicca's cart was in the courtyard and her horses in the stable. The innkeeper fetched the bottle of Rhenish from a cabinet. "Couldn't just leave it out there."

We took it to her room.

For two such sexually experienced people, we were oddly coy with each other. Sometimes the most laughable clichés get it right: We sat up all night talking. We wanted to take the time to get it right.

I woke mid-morning to the sound of a crowd outside the town wall. I left Nicca sleeping and went to check on her horses. The innkeeper had given them their feed and was brushing them down. I nodded toward the wall. "Any idea what's going on?" Folks in the hospitality industry always get the gossip first.

"Mob."

"I figured as much. What kind?"

He paused his brushing. "They say a Jew in Savoy confessed to spreading the pestilence. They're going town to town, looking for other Jews."

This was chilling generally, but also personally. Never mind that I hadn't been near a synagogue in a thousand years. There was physical evidence.

"This confession. Under torture?"

"Ever hear of another kind?"

Not in Europe. "How do they say he spread the pestilence?"

"Poison in the wells."

I looked at him carefully. "What's your take?"

"Get a lot of Jewish custom here. No worse than anyone else. Better than most."

I gestured toward the nearest gate. "Any chance they'll be let in?"

"Let me put it this way. It's up to the Burgomeister. And the Burgomeister owes money to the city's Jewish bankers." He leaned toward me, frowning. "A *lot* of money."

"We have to get going." I started stuffing my few belongings into my satchel.

Nicca squirmed lazily under the blanket and stretched her arms over her head. "Mmm. Why?"

"Mob. Probably coming in today. They blame the Jews for the pestilence."

She rose on one elbow. "Can we keep them out?"

"Not likely."

"Can we help?"

"I don't think we can stay long enough. I don't want to fall into their hands."

"Why? You're not a Jew." I didn't say anything. "Or are you?" Not bothered. Just looking for information.

"Not really, no. Well. Sort of. I have a … a characteristic."

I explained.

Nicca insisted on doing what we could before we left. We bought all the salt beef and bread the innkeeper could spare and drove the cart to the nearest Jewish neighbourhood to provision those who wanted to leave. We'd given out the last of it when we heard the mob coming through the north gate. I drove us away from the roar, down a street of tenements. We had the south gate almost in sight when Nicca put a hand on my arm. "Do you hear that?"

"We need to get to the gate."

"No, stop." I did. The crying of a baby. "It's coming from that building."

"Its parents will take care of it."

"It doesn't sound like that kind of cry." She climbed down. "I'm going to look."

"Are you nuts? The mob is coming."

"We have time."

"Maybe not much."

"Enough to check on a baby." She had the same look of determination as when she'd swung the axe at the wine cask.

"Fine." I waved at the building. "Go check."

"Come with me."

"Nicca—"

"Come *with* me." I tied the horses to a doorpost and followed her inside down a darkened hall. The crying was pitiful and thin.

She was right. No parents were coming. We could tell by the smell.

The father had died first. He was tucked under a blanket, the mother across him in a last embrace. Flies buzzed around their open mouths. The cries came from a high-sided basket across the room. The baby was partially wrapped in a wool shawl. Six months old or so. Old enough to tip the basket over, if it'd had the strength. Its arms lay limp. Tears had dried to crusts around its eyes. Nicca lifted it out.

"What are you doing?"

"Checking for pestilence." She unwrapped the blanket. "He's soiled himself, but no buboes."

"Buboes?"

"Those dark patches people get. Not a pretty sight." She turned the baby this way and that. "But nothing like that on this one. Is there, little guy? Is there?" The baby's crying eased a little.

"So now what?"

"We take him with us."

"Take him *with* us?"

"It's that or leave him to die. There isn't time to get him to an orphanage. If there is one."

"He must have other family. What if they come for him?"

"Nobody's coming, Ishtanu. They'd've been here by now. There's just us. And as you keep telling me, we have to go."

So we went.

Once we were out of sight of the city we cleaned the boy up in a stream and wrapped him in one of Nicca's shawls. We bought milk from a goat farm, and Nicca dribbled it into his mouth while I drove the cart. "Where now?"

"North."

"Okay. Why?"

"You came from the south. Your husband died from the pestilence. I came from the north, and the first place I saw it was here."

She nodded. "So north is safer for the baby. It probably doesn't much matter for you or me."

"Wouldn't be the first plague I've ridden out."

And that was that. At the next crossroads we turned north. I assumed we'd drop the boy at the first disease-free monastery we came to. Maybe Nicca did too. But we kept not finding any. So we kept taking him with us.

That afternoon we passed through an area of low, rolling pasture land. Nicca was driving while I held the baby. We'd had a satisfying lunch of stew and bread at the last village. The sun was warm on my face. The rocking of the cart had soothed the boy into a cozy slumber. It was one of those God's-in-his-heaven moments. I pulled back the cloth from the baby's head to let him get some sun, and gently stroked his eyebrow with my thumb. The cliché "'soft as a baby's bottom" has it wrong, by the way. It should be soft as a baby's eyebrow. His eyes opened drowsily for a moment, and he smiled. I gave his forehead a light kiss. Nicca gave me an odd look.

"What?"

"I thought I wanted you before. But I *really* want you now."

I looked around. "Pull up behind that copse of trees."

It wasn't the kind of first time we'd had in mind. As it turned out, it wasn't the first time at all. We were barely into the preliminaries when the boy woke up and started crying.

Kids.

We stopped for the night at a town called Meitingen and checked into an inn as husband and wife. The gangly innkeeper couldn't have cared less if we were married. He spent most of the check-in process staring at Nicca's chest. His wife was more perceptive. "I'll look after the lad for a bit if you two need to rest from your journey." Her lifted eyebrow was sympathetic rather than lascivious.

It still wasn't the kind of first time we'd had in mind. Oh, it was fine. But you know how it is when you don't really know each other yet, in that way. Over time it got better.

A lot better.

We saw increased signs of pestilence as we continued north. Including in Jewish communities, of course, though the Bavarian would probably have cobbled together some explanation for that. A hoax to divert suspicion, or some such thing. The mentality of the pre-truth era. Pretty much like the post-truth era.

The first major town with no signs of pestilence was Nuremberg. I took a job as a toymaker's apprentice, Nuremberg apparently being known for the quality of its toys. That night we sat on a folded blanket in our empty room in the candlelight. I was gnawing a chicken leg. Nicca was rocking the baby. She looked up at me. "So are we really doing this?"

"Doing what?"

"This." She lifted the boy a little.

I didn't even have to think about it. "I am." It felt good to have responsibilities I couldn't shirk.

"Me too."

"Then I guess we'll have to start calling him something besides 'little guy'."

She frowned in thought. "Pythagoras?"

I leaned over and nibbled her neck. "Gilgamesh."

She set the boy down. "Vishwakarma." She slid a hand into my tunic.

By morning we'd settled on Willem.

We lasted five months before the pestilence drove us farther north.

Nicca had brought Willem to the workshop for a visit. My boss was out buying cloth for doll making while I was finishing an articulated pewter knight the castellan had ordered for his son. "Your master isn't much of a businessman." I looked up from fitting a leg pin into place. She was going through his ledger.

"Put that down." I was smiling. "He'll be back any minute."

"I could increase his profits by a third. Maybe more. Willem! No!" He'd toddled over to a drying table and was reaching for a row of clay animals. "Honestly," she said, scooping him up, "you can't take your eyes off him for a second." He stretched his hand toward the receding table with an indignant howl. Nicca balanced him on her hip. "Look what Daddy's doing."

The howling stopped as he reached for the knight. "Mah."

"No." I moved the knight gently away. "Not for Willem."

"Mah!" He squirmed to extend his reach. I raised an eyebrow at Nicca.

"I had to take him *somewhere*. We were going *nuts* back in the room." Things were different, pre-Starbucks.

The latch clicked, and my boss came in. His hands were empty.

"No cloth?"

"Not from Heinrich. He's dead."

"Dead?" Nicca shifted Willem to her other hip. "I bought a yard of linen from him two weeks ago. What happened?"

He uncorked a flask of wine from behind the counter and poured a large mug. "Pestilence."

"Here? Already?" Nicca gave me a sharp look.

"I'm afraid I may have to cut my apprenticeship a bit short," I said to my boss.

My old Hamburg contacts got us passage to London, where I bought a share in a toy stall at a market called the Cheap. The pestilence caught up in a matter of weeks.

"North?"

"North."

The market for toys in Norfolk wasn't sustainable, so I talked my way into the scriveners' guild. The switch to the more portable skill paid off when the pestilence chased us to Lincolnshire. When it caught up to us there the following Christmas, we decided to re-think our strategy. "It's probably gone from Augsburg by now," Nicca said as we watched Willem play with his unusually rich toy collection.

"So what, then? Stay put?" A felt ball from his toy trebuchet bounced off my forehead. "Head south?"

"South, I think."

Which is now we ended up in small-town Essex.

We pulled up at an inn on the high street of a town called Brentwood, on the road from London to Colchester. We liked the Ram's Head immediately. The yard had a malty smell from the shed where they brewed their ale, and the ostler was kind to our horses, which doesn't always happen. "All right if I feed 'em on spent grain from the brewing, then? It's just we're a bit light on barley until Jackie comes on Tuesday."

It was fine with us. And as we soon saw, it was clearly fine with the horses.

The ostler was also the landlord, as it turned out. He extended a hand. "Adam."

"Sten. My wife Nicca." Willem was asleep against her chest, half hidden in his sling. He was getting too big for it, but it lulled him to sleep while we travelled.

Adam took us through into the inn proper and introduced us to his wife Avice, who was hugely pregnant. "My first." She wobbled up the stairs to show us the private room. "Should be along any day, they tell me."

"Then why are you still working?" Nicca asked. "Shouldn't you be resting up?"

"And make Adam do everything? Not likely."

"Couldn't you hire some help for a few weeks?"

Avice laughed good-naturedly. "From where? The few labourers left since the pestilence have gotten used to asking for whatever wages they fancy. Which is more'n we can afford, I'll tell you that."

The room was snug and windowless, but private. We paid Avice for two nights. "Come back down and I'll find you some dinner," she said as she eased herself onto the staircase. "My latest batch of ale isn't quite ready, but we've a couple of kegs of the last one left."

"You're the brewer too?"

"Brentwood's best." She raised a teasing finger. "But don't go asking after my recipe. You want my ale, you'll come here for it."

"We're not sure how long we'll be staying."

"Where you bound, then?"

"We don't really have a destination." Nicca was less cautious than I was about giving out information. "We've just been trying to keep ahead of the pestilence." We were at the bottom of the stairs by then, where Adam had heard the conversation.

"Pestilence seems done with Brentwood for now. Haven't heard of a case in, what Avice, two or three weeks now?"

"At least. Here, come through to the kitchen and we'll see what we can find."

Willem stirred in his sling. He popped his head up to reveal one curious eye. "And who's this little fella, eh?" Adam gave Willem's cheek a gentle pinch. Willem grimaced and squirmed away.

Nicca bounced him soothingly. "This is Willem. Come on, Willem. Be nice to the man."

Adam's smile faded slightly. "Willem, is it?" His tone was so flat you could've used it to press flowers. "That a Flemish name, then?"

"Could be, I suppose," Nicca said, struggling to keep the boy still.

Avice put a hand on Nicca's arm. "Oh, no, dear, you don't want him with a Flemish name. Not 'round here." She looked over her shoulder, and then back. "Some folks don't take kindly to Flemings."

"With good reason," Adam said. "Stuck-up buggers."

"Oh, hush. Just 'cause they speak funny and have a bit of cash on hand. You're happy enough to take their coin on a Saturday night, aren't you?" She turned to us. "They do weaving, the Flemings. Very fine, it is, too." She dropped her voice. "Better than the locals, if you ask me. I think that might be the problem."

"You'll be wanting to call your boy William, I think, from now on," Adam said.

Avice brought some cold mutton shank and two tankards of ale. They sat with us at a trestle table in the dining area while we ate.

"What's your line of work, then, Sten?" Avice asked.

I chewed and swallowed. "Scrivener."

"He's one we lost, our scrivener."

I nodded sombrely, as you did by then. "Taken by pestilence?"

Adam laughed and shook his head. "Not him, no. The one over at Colchester was, though. Ours moved up there to grab his spot."

"Better pickings, I imagine," Avice said. "Big market town."

"Pah. Too full of himself, you ask me. Wants a big house and a bit of grazing land. Like he'd know one end of a cow from the other."

Avice smacked his arm lightly. "Well, he'd *hire* folks for the cow work, now wouldn't he? There's no harm in wanting to better yourself."

"He didn't have to leave us stuck the way he did, though." Adam turned to me in a man-to-man sort of way. "I mean, I ask you, how am I meant to keep my accounts for them at the manor with no one to write 'em up?" It took me a moment to realize from his look that his question wasn't rhetorical. And another moment to realize that Avice was looking at me the same way.

The next morning Nicca and I checked out the empty scrivener's shop. It was a pleasant space: a well-lit ground floor room with a work table and cabinet, and a two-room residence above.

"Did you notice the churchyard as we passed?" Nicca asked on our way back to the Ram's Head.

"Not really. What about it?"

"There was no one dying in it."

Which kind of sealed the deal.

I've never been a lawyer. I have enough trouble with the pace of change as it is. With six new laws every morning before breakfast, I'd never keep up. I often work with lawyers, though. Like the one whose advice I'm ignoring by talking to you. In fourteenth-century England, a scrivener who wanted steady work was well advised to hook up with one. In Brentwood, that meant Fisty Fitz-Smith.

I met Fisty over the paperwork for our lease on the shop. He had a precedent dropped at the Ram's Head so I could draw it up myself. I treated it as an audition. We met the next afternoon in the withdrawing room of his house off the Saint Thomas Road. He can't have been thirty, but he had the bearing and the girth of a man in his fifties.

He was the third solicitor in his line, having inherited the practice from his late father the previous year.

"Pestilence?"

Fisty shook his head as he unrolled the lease on the table. "Brained with a kettle by the kitchen maid's brother, actually. Lingered a week before he finally died."

I had trouble picturing someone of Fisty's stature below stairs, where kettles lived. "What was he doing in the kitchen?"

He peered at the page. "The kitchen maid, apparently. She couldn't stay after that, of course. Gave her a decent reference." He put the lease back down. "She's with the vicar's household now. Doing well, they say."

"And the brother?"

"Hanged." He rolled up the lease. "Can't have the villeins rising against their betters." He handed me the document. "Rents go to Sir Reginald Baltknight, the local lord who's steward for the Abbey. He'll send his boy down the first of each month. More often, if there are repairs to bill you for."

That hadn't been in the lease. "How frequent are these repairs likely to be?"

Fisty laced his fingers over his waistcoat. "That tends to depend on the state of Lord Buttnugget's gambling debts."

Sir Reginald's boy was literally his boy. Antony Baltknight can't have been more than twelve, but he was well advanced in the family extortion business. My first inking came barely a month after we'd settled in. I'd taken a midday break from copying Fisty's neighbour's farm accounts and strolled to the Ram's Head for a pork pie and ale. Avice was in a foul humour as she smacked my flagon down. Ale slopped onto the table. "Sorry," she growled.

I tried to lighten the mood. "Brentwood's best," I said, toasting her with the ale.

"Tell that to Baby Buttnugget," she said, half to herself. "He didn't seem to think so when he was in this morning."

I took a sip. "I stand by my review. And I'd say so to Tiny Tony if he were here. But I thought the manor brewed their own. What was he doing in your shop?"

"His Lordship's gone and made him the ale conner, hasn't he?"

"Ale conner?"

She wiped up the spill with a rag. "An inspector, like. Comes 'round to check the quality. Imposes a fine if it isn't up to standard. Used to be a decent local lad, 'til the pestilence took him." She smiled. "Knew his ales, that one." She stuffed the rag into her apron pocket. "Now it's young Tony, who wouldn't know barley from bacon fat."

"And Tony found this substandard?" I took another sip. Avice knew her craft. Its subtle maltiness was nicely balanced with the herb mixture she used for bittering. I suspected it included juniper, but I could never get her to tell me. "How is that possible?"

She looked at me like I was simple. "Did I mention the bit about the fine?"

Often after a tragedy things gradually go back to normal. Not after the pestilence. The carnage was historic. You couldn't take a cart ride anywhere in the county without passing an abandoned croft, or two, or six. Whole families just gone. Come autumn, even on the high street you'd catch a whiff of barley rotting in the fields for lack of workers to harvest it. Cows unmilked. Roofs unthatched. Bales of raw wool mouldering in sheds, unsold. Still, it's an ill wind. The surviving workers were in such demand they could ask for, and get, better wages. Literally a silver lining. And with all that cash about, tradesmen and artisans and other townies like me could even lift our prices a little.

But that silver didn't come from nowhere. It was an additional cost to the landowners, a lot of whom sat in Parliament. And it drew labour away from other landowners. A lot of whom sat in Parliament. You can see where this is going. Before the pestilence was even over, Parliament passed the *Ordinance of Labourers*, rolling back wages and prices to where they'd been in 1347, before the demographic shift. It was like dotty King Cnut commanding the tide not to come in.

"It's all well and good to pass a law," Fisty said over a game of Nine

Men's Morris at his garden table one afternoon. "But enforcing it?" He moved a black stone on the board. "That's a different thing."

"Why's that?" My game was rusty. I hadn't played since the Roman legions. Couldn't even remember what we'd called it back then. But I could see Fisty was positioned to make a row of three blacks on his next move, meaning he could remove one of my stones. I moved a white to block.

"Well." He moved a stone at the other corner of the board. "Enforcement's down to the manorial courts, isn't it?" He jerked his head to the east, in the direction of Sir Reginald Baltknight's manor house. "The local lords or their stewards. Which is fine if the issue is, say, the wages of a tanner's apprentice or the price of a copper pot." He smiled at the board. He had me. There was no way to stop him lining up three on his next turn. "But what about the larger economy, eh? Who benefits the most from a higher price for grain? Or wool? Or timber?" He raised an eyebrow theatrically and jerked his head to the east again.

As little boys do, William the toddler grew into William the runner and climber. Which made him a particular terror on market day.

"William! Get down from there!"

I put a calming hand on Nicca's shoulder. "Ralf's stall is sturdy enough. He'll shoo him down if there's any danger."

"Ralf shouldn't have to. He's our job." She dropped her voice. "My job."

"He's a little boy. It's what they do."

"Within limits. Which we have to set. William! Down! Now!" He smiled mischievously and lifted a knee onto the counter.

"It's fine, Nicca," Ralf said, moving a tray of eggs out of danger. "I won't let him fall."

"Not helping, Ralf."

"Come on, William," I said. "Let's go check out the sweet stall, shall we?"

He grinned and dropped to the ground.

"Oh, very nice," Nicca said. "Reward the bad behaviour."

I put my arm around her. "He's down off the stall, isn't he?"

She squirmed away. "Don't go thinking you can charm your way out of this. He'll be up there every week if he thinks it'll get him a honeyed chestnut."

"I didn't say I'd actually buy him anything, did I?" But of course I did.

Nicca was silent all the way back to the high street. I kept a close eye on our son as he danced along the road exploring the bugs in the grasses and the puddles in the ditch. When we made the turn toward the shop I said quietly: "I think you could use a job." Nicca turned with a scowl, but I held up a hand. "I mean outside the home."

The relief in her eyes was almost heartbreaking.

I was doing copy work for Fisty on a drizzly Thursday when the client himself came to see me. I almost never met Fisty's clients. The document was for the sale of a wherry—a low cargo boat common on the local rivers and marshes—with the proceeds to go to the manor in satisfaction of the seller's outstanding taxes. It was a puzzling deal, since it would take away the seller's livelihood, which was presumably the basis for the taxes in the first place. But mine was not to reason why.

The door slowly opened about a foot. A weathered man in his thirties eased his head through the gap, his hood beaded with moisture. "You Sten Scrivener?"

"Yes."

He glanced around the room uncertainly. "All right if I come in?"

I put down my pen. "Please. Take a seat. Mister ...?"

He edged through the door and gingerly closed it. "John, sir. John atte Marsh, they call me." He lowered his hood. "Mister FitzSmith said you were doing the tax papers?" The seller.

"Doing them right now."

He looked relieved. "Very good, then." Relieved, but sad. He hadn't moved from his spot just inside the door. "Will they be done soon, sir? Only I had a visit from the manor this morning. The man said—" His voice caught. He turned it into a cough. "He said if they don't get their money by Sunday they're going to lock me away, sir."

"Have a seat, John. They're nearly done. Then I'll walk them straight to Mister FitzSmith's house."

"I could take them up, sir. If that's all right, I mean."

I sympathized with his urgency. "If you like." I finished a line and started the next. He watched me earnestly. Before long I felt a need to make conversation. "This wherry. It's how you make your living?"

"Yes, sir."

"What'll you do after you sell it?"

There was an uncomfortable pause. "Plenty of farm work about." The defeat in his tone was painful to hear.

"Have you done farm work before?"

John atte Marsh shook his head. "Never, sir. Riverman from a lad. But how hard can it be, eh?"

Backbreaking, was the answer. Especially if you weren't used to it. "Runs in the family, does it? Working the rivers?"

"From my father's father's father. Maybe before that. I know every bend and shallow in the Ingrebourne all the way down to the Thames itself, at Rainford." From the light in his eyes, Rainford might have been the far reaches of the Indies. For him it probably was. Then the light went out. "I was on to teaching my boy, too. Still, farm work'll make a change. We'll keep fed."

I put down my pen again. "How did it come to this, John? How did what you owe get so far above your earnings?"

"Just how the manor works, isn't it?" He tried to chuckle, but he didn't have it in him. How ground down did a man have to be that he couldn't even manage to mock the toffs? "Plus the work dried up."

That didn't seem right. Not in the post-plague workers' economy. "Dried up how?"

"No cargo. Used to carry two, three hundred bales of wool down to the London-bound ships every shearing season." He smiled to himself at the fat times. "Had deals with three different wool-mongers. Then two of 'em just stopped coming. Passed in the pestilence, I expect. The takings dropped to what I could get from the one that was left."

It began to make sense. "But the manor expected the same amount of tax?"

"I don't know how they can do it, sir." Tears of indignation shone in his eyes. "I don't think they understand how it is for working folk." He turned away and put a hand to his face. "Sorry, sir. Sorry."

But I was still back a step. Or maybe a step ahead. "John," I said softly. "If the wool-mongers died, what happened to the wool?"

There was a pause while he thought. "Still there on the farms, I expect."

"So if a new wool-monger were to come along, there'd be plenty out there to get started with?"

He turned back to me slowly. "A full season's worth, sir. Maybe more." Then he shook his head. "But there's no one, sir."

Well. No one John atte Marsh knew of.

I pushed the papers to the side. "Let's hold off a bit on selling the wherry, shall we, John?" He looked alarmed. Sunday was looming. Bailiffs with swords. Cold stone walls. I put a hand on his forearm. "Hear me out. I'll cover your taxes for now. They won't lock you away. And if things work out the way I think they will, you'll have as much river work as you and your boy can handle."

Nicca was working out profit margins before I even finished telling her about it.

As Fisty predicted, Parliament's wage controls didn't work very well. So they tightened them up. The new *Statute of Labourers* made all workers swear an oath basically to pretend it was still 1347, and appointed new royal officials with the power to fine or imprison anyone who didn't follow through. Professionals and guild-workers like Fisty and me sighed and adjusted our rates back downward. Farm workers sucked up the pay cut and got by with less. Baked bread with acorn flour instead of rye. Put fewer beans in their oat gruel. Worked into the night at harvest time, making up for the fellows they'd lost. And through all of this government-imposed restraint, Buttnugget Manor managed to supplement its surviving villeins with a full complement of well-fed freemen. Funny how that worked.

And no one was surprised when the royal official appointed to enforce the new law in our corner of Essex was Sir Reginald Baltknight.

"So then Roger threw a rock but he missed by a mile and the frog jumped away but I saw where it landed—"

We rounded the corner of the high street on our way to the market.

"—and I snuck around but I got my boots wet but I tried to be quiet anyhow—"

William, now six, was bouncing between Nicca and me, making sure we were both following the story.

"—but Roger saw the frog too 'cause he saw me going there and he found another rock—"

Nicca seemed to be listening intently, though she was more likely working out the mark-up on this season's woollens in preparation for some amiable bargaining.

"—and he threw it but he missed again but it scared the frog again and it jumped right into my face 'cause it didn't even know I was there and it was wet and gross and I fell over and got my bum all wet—"

We arrived at the edge of the market. William raised his voice to compete with the clamour.

"—and the frog landed in my lap and I tried to grab it but it jumped away again into the reeds this time and so I couldn't see it anymore and neither could Roger—"

We came alongside Ralf's egg stall. His eighteen-month-old daughter Cecily was sitting on his lap making nonsense sounds to a rag doll I'd made her the year before.

"—but he didn't care because he was laughing because my bum was all wet and he didn't even get that it was all his *fault*." William paused and stared up earnestly at the injustice of it all.

"Quite the storyteller, your lad," called out Ralf with a grin.

"Your time will come," I said with a nod toward the little girl, who ignored us both.

"And then Roger—" William began again.

"Oh look," Nicca said quickly. "The sweet stall has marzipan animals today."

Business in Brentwood was good.

Nicca was brilliant at wool-mongering. Every shearing season her storehouse was packed to the eaves with bales, waiting on John atte Marsh and his boys to collect them for transport. William helped her with loading and unloading, and eventually with the accounts.

John was up to three sons, each learning the river trade. A second wherry, piloted by Simon, his eldest, doubled their capacity. Economies of scale.

At the Ram's Head, young Roger started helping his father behind the counter. His sisters Margery and Maud—a year apart and all but inseparable—worked the brewery and the kitchen with Avice, and switched out the straw in the bedrooms each week. Their younger brother Henry, who had a knack with horses, was already practically running the stables on his own.

Ralf's eldest daughter went into paid service at the Manor's kitchen. Five years later she came back with some savings, and they expanded the family egg business to include cakes and custard tarts.

Fisty married late, and within his rank. His wife Beatrice was the daughter of the master carpenter in Chelmsford. They cranked out four kids in six years, two of each. When we visited, Beatrice arranged them in an orderly line for us like the von Trapps before sending them off with their governess. No one does aristocratic quite like the bourgeoisie.

Tiny Tony Baltknight gradually took over some of his father's public roles. Commissioner of array. Justice of the Peace. Steward of the Abbey estates. At some point along the way he even became Sir Tiny Tony. No doubt there was a grand private celebration at the Manor when he did.

We even took a stall at the market. Not for wool, which was wholesale. For toys.

I'd made them for William when he was little. Clay animals. Wooden soldiers. Being a child, he wanted more. Which I made him. Before long he grew interested in the making, so I started to teach him. He was good at it.

We gave them out to people we knew. Dolls to Adam and Avice's girls. Wooden swords to their boys. Miniature bows to John atte Marsh's younger sons. It was John who suggested we sell them. "You and your lad could get a good return, I bet," he said as we watched his boys aim blunt-tipped arrows at a hollow in a twisted alder. Peter, his seven-year-old, sent a shot wide and into the reeds. He growled and scampered after it. "Cover your materials, at least."

"It's just for something to do." But when I mentioned it to William, his eyes lit up. He made a start on some things that were likely to be in high demand. Toy weapons, for one. All adult men were required by law to have actual weapons, in case of invasion. I still had a sword, which William had always been fascinated by. Kids basically want what grownups have. So, toy weapons and baby dolls and miniature cookware.

When William was thirteen we got him a stall at the market. A table down one of the less popular aisles, where the rents were cheaper. The one with the pie maker who picked his nose and the sketchy old woman whose rune castings always seemed to predict the painful death of someone close to you. We hung around to help at first, but that made him surly. "I know what I'm *doing*," he said, with the aggrieved belligerence of the teenage boy. So we wandered off to check out the rest of the market.

"Tell your fortune?" called the rune woman as we passed, rattling her bag of tiles.

"No thanks." I put my arm around Nicca's waist. "We're good."

We stopped at Ralf's stall for a cake. He was alone at the table.

"Cecily not helping out today?"

"She was," he said with a wry smile. "She's gone to check out a new vendor."

Cakes in hand, we took a discreet peek down the aisle where William's stall was. Cecily was standing there awkwardly. So were Margery and Maud. So were a couple of other local girls on the verge of puberty. They weren't buying. Or talking. Just standing there. They probably didn't even know why.

"Good looking boy, your William," Ralf said with a chuckle later on.

We went back at the end of the day to help William pack up his things. "Looked like quite a few girls at your stall today," Nicca said with a side wink to me.

"I *know*," he said sourly as he tied up a bundle of arrows. "That was *so* annoying. They didn't even talk to me. They just *stood* there. And nobody else would even come over. Like they thought I was busy or something."

He'd done all right. He'd sold all his wooden swords, most of his miniature cook pots, and three sets of clay farm animals.

"Pretty good for your first day," I said.

"I guess."

Business in Brentwood was good.

Until it wasn't.

The woman with the runes was bound to get it right eventually. That was the year she did. The pestilence of 1361 wasn't as severe as the earlier one, but it hit harder because it hit our most vulnerable. We didn't call it the pestilence. We called it the mortality of the children.

William did fine. Not so much as a cough. We were lucky. Others weren't. I remember sitting through the night with Adam at a table in the inn while, upstairs, Nicca and Avice mopped young Maud's brow and murmured soft words and, eventually, in the morning, wiped her clean and put her in her best dress and wrapped her in a shroud. I remember taking a cask of ale to John's cottage by Weald Brook the evening after young Peter's burial, and staying with him while he got stoically drunk. I remember the look on Ralf's face as he stood in our doorway with Cecily's old rag doll in his hand. "We just can't have it in the house anymore."

William was lucky. But he never made toys again.

Like most thirteen-year-old boys, William tried to be manly about death. But when we got home from the last of the funerals, the dam broke. I was surprised at what bothered him the most. No one had heard of survivor guilt in the fourteenth century. "Why us?" he sobbed, as Nicca held him. "Why does everyone else lose people but we're all right?"

"You've been lucky, William."

He wiped his snotty nose on his sleeve and looked up at me. "You mean us, right? We've all been lucky?"

I choked, but Nicca stepped up. "There's something we probably should have told you before now."

If you wait until your kid is thirteen to tell him he's adopted, you can expect him to take it badly. Imagine if you wait until he's thirteen to tell him he's adopted and his adoptive parents are immortal.

He didn't say anything. He just listened. First he looked puzzled, like he thought Nicca was joking. When he saw she wasn't, he looked like he'd been gut-punched. He squirmed free and ran to the door.

"No one can know," I shouted at his disappearing back. My only contribution to the discussion. Not much of one, I know.

Adam came by a little later. "Rough few months," he said. His eyes were hollow. That day's funeral hadn't been Maud's, but each one brought it all back for everyone.

"Especially for you and Avice."

He shrugged. It was a pretty expressive shrug. It said that others had been hit just as hard. That he didn't have the strength to think about it right now. That my sympathy was kind of beside the point. "Your boy is at the inn. In the stables with Roger. I gave them a bit of ale. I figured they could use it."

"Thanks, Adam." He wasn't looking at me differently. "Should I come?"

"I'd give 'em until they come out on their own. I just wanted you to know he was all right."

William came home just after dusk. "I didn't tell anyone," he said as he pushed past me through the door.

He was extra sullen for a few days. There were some barbed asides about secrets, and some full-on teen indignation about not being trusted. But kids can be pretty resilient. "Tell me," he said one day at dinner. "Everything. I need you to tell me everything." So we told him. Not everything. That would've been too much. But enough. As far as I know he kept it to himself. It must have been a huge burden, but he did it.

God, I loved that boy.

Of course I did. He was my son.

The mortality didn't just take children. One of the adults it took was Sir Reginald Baltknight. Which could've been a tiny bright spot in a dark time if it hadn't left Buttnugget Junior fully in charge.

"A fee for filing documents with the Manor?"

Fisty nodded. "That's what the notice says."

"Documents the Manor requires us to file?"

"And this surprises you why, exactly?"

Don't think everything was smooth after we told William. He was a teenager, trying to adjust to a new imbalance between him and his parents. So whenever there was any sort of conflict, that was where his scrappy teen brain tended to go. It reached its worst when he was seventeen. And it was my fault.

He was practically a full partner in the wool-mongering by then. He'd been on the circuit with Nicca as far as Havering-atte-Bower, watching her negotiate with the shepherds. He'd been with her in the office, helping her crunch the numbers and negotiate the complex taxes and fees. He'd followed the supply chain from the shearing to the storehouse to the London-bound ships on the Thames, riding shotgun with Simon atte Marsh down the Ingrebourne. He had a good head for the work. Not as good as Nicca's, but then she'd been at it a lot longer.

He was also spending a lot of time with Adam and Avice's girl Margery. She'd gone very quiet after her sister's death, but that seemed to be changing. She and William had always had the time-honoured relationship boys have with their best friend's annoying little sister. Then puberty tossed a wrench into things, as it does. William typically took out his frustrations on us.

"Can't you just *talk* to Adam?" he whined one chilly afternoon as we shifted bales in the storehouse to make room for an incoming cartload. "They never let us go *anywhere* by ourselves."

"He's just being protective."

He heaved a bale from the dirt floor onto a waist-high stack against the wall. "He doesn't *need* to be 'protective'." I actually heard the quotation marks.

Nicca chuckled as she adjusted a stack to make it more stable. "Remember that father you told me about? The Celtic one, when you were a Roman soldier?"

"That's hardly the same thing. She was practically twenty. This is more like when you were passing as that Khazar girl's uncle in—"

"Stop it!" William said. "Stop with your cutesy stories from, like, a thousand years ago. Not everything's about you." He kicked a stack of bales. "I get it. The rest of us die, and you don't. I *get* it."

Nicca turned and reached to touch his arm. "Oh, no, honey, that's not—"

He yanked his arm away. "You think you're better than us," he said.

Nicca and I spoke at the same time.

"Of course we don't," she said.

"Well, we *are*," I said.

The silence that followed was kind of awkward.

Nicca tracked me down at the inn that evening. I was on my fourth pointless pint. It had no effect, as usual. But that's what people do to get away from things, isn't it?

"He wants to set up on his own."

"Fine." I didn't look up from my ale.

"He wants to do the Billericay to Rayleigh run. As his own operation."

"Fine."

She paused.

"Something else?" I asked.

"He wants us to buy him a piece of land."

"I'll have Fisty set it up."

"As it happens," Fisty said, "I know a sub-tenant of the Abbey who's short on his taxes, and who'd be glad of the cash." That was Fisty. Finger on the pulse.

"Does he have a specific parcel available?"

"He does. Three acres on the Ingrebourne, an hour south of here. Large vegetable garden. Bit of barley. Enough pasture for a modest flock."

"Can he legally sell?" I knew English land law was riddled with risky complexities. But I also knew that those complexities were Fisty's bread and butter. And his claret, and his venison, and his cream-cakes for afters.

"Not technically. Technically the Abbey and the sub-tenant hold the land for the king." He sat back until his chair groaned. "But no one's really fussed about that in the real world. As long as we get the documents in order, your lad'll have nothing to worry about."

William barely acknowledged me when he left.

"You need to apologize," Nicca said a couple of days later.

"For what? The truth?"

"For being an asshole about it."

I went over the next morning.

"William. It's your father."

He opened the door sharply. "What?"

"I'm sorry if what I said upset you."

"You think that's an apology?" He closed the door.

"I tried," I said to Nicca when I got home.

"What did you say? Your exact words." I told her. "And you think that's an apology?"

"What else am I supposed to say?"

"That you're sorry you were an insensitive tit."

I went back the next day.

"William. It's your father again."

The door opened sharply. "What?"

"I'm sorry for what I said. I'm sorry I upset you."

"Sorry because it was wrong? Or because it upset me?"

"Because it upset you."

"But was it wrong?"

I squirmed. "Wrong to upset you."

"You know what I mean."

I knew what he wanted me to say. I just couldn't say it.

William's land was ideal for the wool business. He fixed up a shed as a storehouse, and he and Simon atte Marsh built a wherry dock in a shallow on the river frontage. After a couple of years he decided it was time to start a family. "Did you know your lad's after marrying our Margery?" Avice asked one evening at the Ram's Head, as she set down our mutton stew. The fact that she asked said a lot about my relationship with our son.

"We do." There was a hint of caution in Nicca's voice. "How are you and Adam with that?"

"About bloody time," Adam called out from behind the bar.

I was invited to the wedding, of course. I had to be. William stopped me on the chapel steps. The place was packed. He was well liked, and everyone knew Margery from the inn. He spoke quietly but firmly. "She can't know."

"Know what?"

"Really?"

"Fine." I started toward the chapel door. He stepped in front of me. "I mean it. Not her. Not her family. Not our kids, when we have them."

"I said 'fine'."

He grabbed my arm. He had a firm, workingman's grip. "You did. But I really need you to understand. This knowing what you are." I winced at "what." "It's too much. I need to protect my family from it."

I peeled his fingers from my arm. "I'm your family."

"Then act like it. I've kept your secret. Now I need—"

"You think I'm going to blurt it out to your wife? I've been keeping it—"

"Don't even say it."

I often went on Nicca's business trips. Not that she needed my protection. She always rolled her eyes when I said I was coming. But she never said no.

"I think I should expand across the river," she said one morning over breakfast.

"Into Kent, you mean?"

"No, across the Rhine into Alsace. Of course into Kent."

"Seems a long way. Tolls for the ferry. Taxes on the tolls."

"Earnings haven't come back as fast as I expected since we spun William off." She straightened her posture and sucked in her cheeks. "We have *standards*, after all." It was a chillingly precise imitation of Fisty's wife. I laughed. I always did.

"So just cold-calling over in Kent, then? 'Hey mister, wanna sell me your wool?'"

She stared at me over the top of her glasses. Or would've, if glasses had been a thing, and if she'd needed them. But you know the kind of look I mean. "I'll do my research. Maybe Fisty knows someone."

"Fisty always knows someone. The question is whether it's the kind of someone you'd want to do business with."

"I can judge that for myself. All I need from Fisty is a contact."

"I'm seeing him tomorrow. I'll ask."

She kissed my forehead. "You're too good to me."

"But I'm coming with you. To Kent. When you go."

She rolled her eyes. "Fine. But I get to come up with your backstory."

"Backstory?"

She tilted her head coyly. "New place. I thought a new story might be fun."

Fisty knew a guy. Of course he did.

"Thomas atte Raven." He wrote it on a scrap of parchment. "Destined for Parliament one day, probably. Fingers in all the pies around Rochester. Family connections in Southwark, over the river from London."

"I know where Southwark is. How far's Rochester?"

"Bit of a hike." He handed me the parchment. "Worth it, though."

It was a half-day by cart from Brentwood to the ferry at Rainham, and then the better part of a day from the river to Rochester. But Fisty was right. It was worth it.

Thomas atte Raven received us at his house in town. The decor was modest but expensive. He read the reference letter Fisty had written. It was effusive but vague, at Nicca's request. Room for story.

"FitzSmith paints an impressive picture of you, my lady." Raven gestured toward me with the letter. "Nothing about this fellow, though."

"My apologies, sir. I neglected to introduce Constantine." A name I hadn't used in a while. "My manservant." I turned in mild surprise. Her look was perfectly *faux* haughty, with a hint of mischief so slight only I could see it. Raven nodded in greeting. I opened my mouth to respond, but Nicca still wasn't done. "He's from Yorkshire." The mischief in her look went up a notch. Cute. Yorkshire was more than twenty years ago. Could I even find the accent?

"Long way from home," Raven said.

"I go where my lady needs me," I said carefully.

He frowned. "You don't sound much like a Yorkshireman."

Nicca smiled sweetly. "Give him a minute."

Raven was an excellent contact. He knew of a local wool-monger who'd grabbed up abandoned territory too fast and was overextended to the point of collapse. "He'd do better with a third fewer clients. I bet he'd hand them over for next to nothing."

Nicca nodded. "I like it. How should we proceed?"

"He's in town just now. Should I set up a meeting?"

And so Nicca and her manservant Constantine expanded into Kent.

After a year or so, William and Margery had a daughter, Isabella. I stood on the fringe while the others cooed. William took me aside as we were leaving. "Not a word."

"Leave it."

A year later they had a son, William Junior. I was oddly stung that they didn't name him for me. Which was hardly realistic. But family messes with your head.

Did I mention we were at war with France? Yeah, well. We were always at war with France. It was kind of a thing. Joan of Arc. That Shakespeare movie with Kenneth Branagh. The usual story. Your king wakes up one morning, showers and shaves, pops a bagel in the toaster, and, while he's waiting on it, says to himself: "Maybe I should be King of France." Next thing you know, historians are totting up the decades and crossing their fingers that they'll get to call it The Hundred Years' War, because wouldn't that be just, like, an awesome name?

The war didn't have much effect at the local level, apart from siphoning off a few second sons to the military and giving us a boogie man to blame for the state of things. Whatever news filtered down through official channels was always positive. King Edward was healthy and strong and Arthurian in his glory. Our lantern-jawed bowmen were unstoppable. The usual crap. Oh, sure, there'd been some famous successes. But by the seventies, Edward and his heir the Black Prince were sicker than scrofulous goats, and the French were gleefully clawing back our earlier gains. And it didn't help when the Black Prince died.

Let me correct myself. The war had one other local impact. Wars are expensive. Enter the tax system. Which had a critical design flaw: Unlike our landlords, the Crown could only tax us for the defence of the realm. You couldn't come up with a better incentive for war if you tried. Traditionally, war taxes were wealth taxes. On the value of your goods, or on the ballpark wealth of the village with the locals carving it up at the individual level. But the cost of a hundred-year vanity war adds up. If the old ways don't get you enough archers and lances and ships, you're going to look for ways that bring in more. In 1377 the Crown decided it had found one.

"What exactly *is* a 'poll tax'?" Nicca's tone said she knew she wouldn't like the answer.

"Brilliantly simple," Fisty said. "A one-time flat tax on everyone. Fourpence each, regardless of station."

"Everyone?"

"Everyone fourteen and up."

That was the medieval Crown all over. The Black Prince had owned all of Aquitaine. His younger brother John of Gaunt was richer than the two next-richest aristocrats combined. Yet they still needed fourpence a head from the rest of us so they could scrap with their cousins over the marches of Calais and the vineyards of Bordeaux.

"'One-time'?" said Nicca said skeptically.

Fisty kept his tone flat. "So they say."

Three unsurprising things flowed from the new war tax.

The first was that people hated it. "It's not that we can't manage fourpence each, you understand," Adam said. "Price of a couple of hens, really. It's just the principle of the bloody thing."

The second was that Baltknight manor got the job as its local collector. "No doubt Tiny Tony will forget to list a few of us in his accounts but keep the fourpence anyhow," Avice said. She'd never forgiven the little bugger for the ale fine. She and Adam stood to benefit, mind you. Troops *en route* to ships were a nice source of income for inns and stables. Plus by then their youngest son, Henry, was training as a longbowman with a local hobby warlord, Thomas of Woodstock. Adam was stoic about it. "Wants to be his own man, our Henry," he'd often say. Avice just went quiet when the subject came up.

The third unsurprising thing was that the one-time tax wasn't only levied one time.

To be fair, it might've been, if Edward hadn't died a couple of months later, leaving the Black Prince's eleven-year-old son Richard at the helm. That knocked the wheels off the cart. Edward was barely cold by the time the French started raiding the coast.

I'm sure John of Gaunt, who'd taken charge while his father and brother were slowly dying, scraped by as best he could on what taxes he already had. But by the spring of 1379, darned if we didn't see a fresh poll tax for an assault on Brittany.

"At least this one's a progressive tax," Fisty said archly. Not that the poor paid less. Their tax was still fourpence. But those of us with more paid more, based on an intricate chart of income and employment. Lawyers like Fisty got dinged hard. Innkeepers got dinged even harder.

"Forty pence!" Adam was beside himself. "Forty. Four zero. Can you fathom it?"

"That's what happens when you let a kid be king," Roger said. Adam's eldest boy was pretty much running the Ram's Head by then, leaving his dad plenty of time to putter in the shed and grumble about the shocking state the nation was in. But some things were beyond criticism.

"Don't go blaming young Richard, now, boy," Adam said with a shake of the finger. "He's God's anointed king. It's them so-called nobles who surround him, by Christ. Seizing the chance to make his decisions for him while he's too young to know better."

"Like John of Gaunt," Roger said with the indulgent smile of someone who's heard it all before.

"Too true, John of bloody Gaunt! Sucking us dry, that one is."

It wasn't just crabby old innkeepers who felt that way, either.

"The boy king's heart is good, but he doesn't have the experience to stand up to Gaunt and the other kleptocrats," Thomas atte Raven said to Nicca over a business lunch in Rochester one chilly autumn day.

"Can't Parliament help him with that?" Nicca speared an heirloom tomato from her quinoa salad. Or whatever.

"Too many of the kleptocrats are *in* Parliament." He scowled in deep-seated frustration. "If we could purge those self-serving bastards and let the king follow his instincts, we'd have a *real* government of the people."

At least that's how Nicca described the conversation to me later. As her manservant, I waited outside in the cart.

It was the prank that kept on pranking.

The poll taxes were so important that Sir Antony Baltknight collected them personally. For run-of-the-mill rents and fees he usually sent his man Wank. Not his real name. Just how I always thought of him. He was a serf who'd risen through the Baltknight household via mendacity and cunning to become the iron fist in Lord Buttnugget's iron glove. Any job too low or loathsome for Tiny Tony fell to Wank. You'd hear the *clop clop* of a clapped-out plough horse on the high street on some tariff collection day or other, and there he'd be in his master's oversized cast-offs. Sir Antony was indulgent enough to pass down his old breeches and tunics, but not enough to spring for a tailor to take them in, so Wank always looked a bit like a pantomime nobleman who'd shrunk in the wash.

The effect was magnified by the pair of grizzled ex-bruisers march-ing listlessly behind him, crossbows at their sides. He probably thought of them as his honour guard. I think they were there to stop him from skimming the take. Wank and his retinue did a round of the town before their first stop. Flaunting his position as the manor's Flatulent Little Turd™. Then he'd start knocking on doors, and peeking down blouses, and brushing up against bottoms. And riding on with sacks full of coin.

For the poll taxes, though, Lord Buttnugget came to town himself.

Everyone was ordered into the barn-like hall on the high street where they held the market in the winter, and where the artsy folk put on edifying theatricals on the odd Saturday night. I sang in them myself, sometimes. At one end was a tall chair with the Baltknight crest carved on its back. In front of it was the medieval equivalent of some camp stools and a folding table, where Wank and some manorial number crunchers sat with a series of strongboxes, waiting for us to file past with our fourpence per head.

Sir Antony Baltknight strode into the hall and to his seat. He had presence, I'll give him that. Not as much as he thought, but enough for a mid-level county nobleman.

"Sten the scrivener," I said when we reached the front of the line. I tossed my fourpence onto the table with a clatter. Wank scooped it up like a rat with a raisin.

"So you're the scrivener," Sir Antony said from his perch.

"I am."

"I see your boss in the manorial court from time to time. I don't much care for some of his arguments."

"I don't always care for them either. I copy what I'm paid to copy. And Mister FitzSmith isn't my boss. He's my customer."

"I don't approve of these private business relationships." Baltknight made a face like you make when you smell something sour. "In my grandfather's day everyone worked for him. Or for the church." I didn't think that was quite true. But it sounded like the kind of golden age a Baltknight would choose to believe in.

"Can't stop progress."

Baltknight smiled flatly. "Can't I?"

The second tax wasn't the success the toffs expected. People hated it so much they found creative ways to duck it. Which left Gaunt critically short of troops for his expedition. Which crashed and burned. Which made him even less popular.

Nicca and I were deeply disguising our ages by then. It was a long time to be in one place. But you make the effort for family, don't you? On the scrap land around Nicca's warehouse we kept a patch of the herb Sura taught me to use to grey my hair. Adam and Avice were our templates for how much to add each year. I grew a beard to hide my lack of jowls. Nicca wore loose, bulky clothes and cultivated a hunch.

Apart from the ongoing rift with William, life was good. Nicca's business was thriving. William's too, so I was told. He'd started teaching basic literacy to the children of some of the local serfs, which made me proud, but also concerned. Literacy was the road to ordination, and ordination included manumission from serfdom. Landowners whose workforce had taken a hit from the pestilence hardly wanted the next generation siphoned off to the church. So William kept his little tutorials discreet. So I was told.

I carried on drawing up documents for Fisty and travelling with Nicca through Essex and Kent. We developed a nice relationship with Thomas atte Raven, though before long we rarely caught him at home. As Fisty predicted, he'd become a member of Parliament.

"Nice to have friends in high places," Fisty said with a smile of satisfaction over a cup of wine at his garden table.

I tipped my cup toward him. "Better to have friends behind the scenes, I think."

He had the grace to lower his head in only partially feigned humility. "*Pas de tout*, dear boy."

Then, in the Year of Yeshu 1381, everything went sideways.

It started from the top. Gaunt and his cronies, assuming the third time would be the charm, decided that the war with France called for yet another poll tax. "Our Henry's already billeted in London with the rest of Woodstock's bowmen," Adam said. "He'll be mobilized to Brittany once the new money comes through."

It spread from the street. Because sometimes people have just had enough.

It could easily have been stopped, but it wasn't. Left hand right hand thing, maybe. Or just garden variety aristocratic greed.

The left hand took the form of young Henry. He was having a pint with his brother and dad in the Ram's Head bar when I went in to get a pork pie for lunch. "I thought you were in London," I said, "*en route* to kicking French backsides."

"Don't get him started," Roger said. "We've just had a half hour on what a cock-up it's been."

"Bloody nobles," Adam said. "Pissing away our tax dollars."

"Well, yeah, but how this time?"

"You name it," Henry said. "Billets charging manor house prices for doss house rooms. Bags of coin changing hands for ships that never show. When the profiteers dug deep enough into Woodstock's own pockets, he just told us all to bugger off home. And here I am."

"So the Brittany campaign is off, then?"

Henry lifted his flagon. "Deader than dead."

The right hand took the form of a summons to the hall on the high street. Not just Brentwood and environs this time, but villages as far away as Horndon-on-the-Hill. No one knew why. But we were sure it wasn't good. We were more sure when we saw the row of tall chairs at the end of the hall. Seven this time. Officialdom was coming in force. Our hosts filed in, flanked by soldiers. Fisty counted them off to me as they entered.

"There's the sheriff, representing the king. Sergeant-at-arms, also representing the king. This is serious, whatever it is. Wilford, the king's clerk. A couple of minor local bootlickers who you probably already know. Ah, they've even brought Grumpy Gildesburgh, our Member of Parliament. For the illusion of local consultation, no doubt, though he's basically one of Woodstock's toadies. And then ..." He peered to see the last of them enter. "Of course." Lord Buttnugget himself.

The officials took their seats. Wank called for order. The crowd settled into a taut silence. There were no pleasantries. Baltknight got straight to the point. He held up a document with a wax seal.

"This is a royal commission. It directs Sir John Gildesburgh and myself—" he nodded to the MP, who nodded back "—with the assistance of these other noble gentlemen—" he nodded vaguely at the rest of the head table "—to make good on the poll-tax here in Essex for the defence of the realm. Which begins today with the creation of a central register of names, occupations and residences of everyone fifteen years of age and older."

A buzz spread through the room.

"Poll tax?" Nicca turned to me with a frown. "But we paid that."

"We did."

"Then what's he talking about? Fisty? What's he talking about."

"Maybe it's another one? I'm actually more concerned about this central register. That's new."

Adam was stuck on the previous point. "Poll tax for what? The expedition's off. Henry's home."

"Make him show you that document up close, Fisty," Avice said. "Wrote it himself, I bet. Poll tax my eye. Him'n his pals are fixing to line their own strongboxes."

Exchanges like that were going on all around us. The general tone was puzzled indignation. It couldn't be about the old poll tax, because we'd paid it. Well, not everyone. But you didn't trot out a tableful of nobles to chase down a few deadbeats. And it couldn't be about a new poll tax, because the campaign was off. So what, then?

Indignation grew to anger. You could feel it about to erupt. Along the far wall I saw a group of men from the outlying villages in deep conversation. They seemed to reach an agreement. One of them called out to the head table. "Good gentlemen." His voice was strong. The crowd noise subsided.

Baltknight turned toward him with a frown. "Who are you?"

"Thomas Baker, sir. Of the village of Fobbing."

"Good day, master Baker. You have something to say?" His tone said anything a baker might say would be tedious, but he would endure it.

"I do, sir. I speak for my fellows here." He gestured toward them. "We've paid the poll tax. We have receipts from you, yourself, sir." There was a discreet murmuring of support from the crowd as a whole.

"You may have paid *a* poll tax, master Baker, but you have not paid *the* poll tax. Don't worry. The register we're here to create will carefully record everyone who pays this one." His eyes narrowed. "And who doesn't." He waved his hand airily over the crowd. "Organize yourselves into a line."

"So that's what they're up to," Fisty said.

"What?" William had been quiet so far.

"They've decided local records are too leaky. Too much room for folks to duck the tax. But with a centralized list ..."

A few people started toward the table. Then someone spoke. "No." Everything stopped. Everyone went quiet. It was Baker again.

"Excuse me?" Baltknight said sharply.

Baker glanced around at his friends, who nodded their support. "I said 'no', sir. We've paid the poll-tax. We have receipts. We won't pay again."

Baltknight conferred with Gildesburgh the MP, and then with the sheriff. The sheriff conferred with the sergeant-at-arms. When the conferring was over, Baltknight straightened in his chair. "Master Baker, I remind you that we have a royal commission." He waved the document. "You'll register and pay the tax, or you'll be arrested and jailed."

The room held its breath. Two hundred people or so, but it was quiet enough to hear a mouse in the wall.

"No sir." Baker moved through the crowd toward the anxious-looking nobles. "We won't register. We won't pay. And we won't be arrested." A dozen men followed him. Then a dozen more. Then some from the other side of the room. They formed a line across the front of the table, two deep. Then three. Then five. "We're done with your taxes and your tolls and your wage controls and your rents, sir. With the servitude of our fellows and their families." He lowered his head. "Sir." It was a masterfully ironic gesture, in a time before irony went viral.

I'm probably remembering his speech as more polished than it was. I've got the substance right, though. I never saw Thomas Baker of Fobbing again after that day. But I've always remembered him.

Baltknight kept his cool, I'll give him that. "Sergeant," he said to the sergeant-at-arms, "have your men arrest master Baker and his fellows."

The sergeant turned toward the armed men behind him. But

before he could speak, he froze. He'd heard something that stopped him. We'd all heard it. The rustle of bows being taken from under cloaks. A moment later half of the hundred or so men confronting the head table had arrows trained on the hapless honour guard. "No one's getting arrested today," Baker said.

Baltknight stared at the sergeant-at-arms. The sergeant stared at fifty drawn bows. He turned back to Baltknight and shook his head.

Baker smiled. "We'd like you and your men to leave now."

The local bootlickers were the first to the door. The MP wasn't far behind. Baltknight rose slowly, his eyes on Baker. "You'll regret this."

"Have your soldiers leave their weapons." The soldiers looked at the sergeant, who nodded. The men put their weapons down. Moments later, the officials and their entourage were gone. Baker started to shake. I think he would have collapsed if his friends hadn't been there to hold him up. I probably would've, in his place.

"Well, that was unexpected," Fisty said cheerily. "Won't it be interesting to see what happens next?"

It was. Because what happened next was open rebellion.

The men from Fobbing and Horndon and the rest knew they'd crossed a line they couldn't uncross. The nobles would strike back. In courts they themselves presided over. Courts that imposed capital punishment.

Unless …

If the rebels couldn't uncross the line, they'd have to push as far past it as possible and see what happened.

In the meantime, the nobles went about their work a different way. No more grand meetings where they were outnumbered. They came house by house, with Baltknight's personal guard.

William and his family were in town for Whitsunday, when Mother Church gave everyone a few days off and the town responded with church ales and pig roasts and jugglers and fiddlers. Baltknight's carriage came down the high street early in the morning, while the trestle tables were being set up in the market square and the firepit being dug for the pig. I was slicing rye bread for breakfast when I heard the pounding of a sword-pommel on the door downstairs.

"Line up for registration," Wank called in his weedy voice.

I put down the knife and gathered everyone in the ground floor office: Nicca, William, Margery, and their kids Isabella and William Junior, who were thirteen and twelve. William Junior was gnawing a heel of bread as they came down the stairs. Isabella still had bits of straw in her hair, which would've mortified her if she'd known.

Buttnugget was in my chair. Wank was leaning on my table with a pen and parchment. Two soldiers flanked the door. "Everyone fifteen and over line up there." We did. Isabella and her brother hung back against the wall.

"What about her?" Baltknight was pointing at Isabella.

"She's only ... what, William? Thirteen now?"

"Thirteen."

"Thirteen. Your list starts at fifteen, like your boy said."

"She looks fifteen to me. Put her on the register."

William tensed. "She's thirteen. Barely."

"Well that's what you'd *say*, isn't it? To keep her off the register. Dodge the tax." He shook his head. "It's like you don't even support our troops." He nodded toward Isabella. "Wank, go check."

The room froze. Even Wank went still. "Wait, what?" His expression was half baffled, half hopeful.

"Have a look under her skirts. For signs of ... adulthood."

Wank grinned.

"Like hell you will," William said. I heard Nicca gasp. I turned. William was holding my bread knife in Wank's direction.

Baltknight nodded to the soldiers. They drew their bows. "Tell your boy to stand down, scrivener."

I grasped my son's arm. "William—"

He twisted free and pointed the knife at me. "Get off! You don't have a say." He turned the knife back toward Wank, who was hovering between his master and his task, his eyes locked on the blade.

264 • K.R. WILSON

"Scrivener." Baltknight's voice was cool. "Tell your boy that if he interferes in our royal duties my men will shoot him dead."

"I heard you, you sack of pig shit." William waved the knife toward Baltknight. "Talk to me like a man. Don't go through him."

Baltknight looked at William with a hint of respect. The way he'd look at a defiant boar before running it through. "No need for vulgarity, Master William. Very well. I say to you, directly, that if you interfere in our royal duties—"

"Your royal duties don't include looking up my girl's skirts!"

The noble shook his head in *faux* regret. "Ah, but I'm afraid they do. You see, I'm charged by the Crown to document everyone over fifteen. How can I do that if I can't confirm her age?"

"You could ask me," Margery said. "I'm her mother. She's thirteen."

"And I wish I could trust you on that, madam." Baltknight was enjoying himself. "But there's been so much ... resistance here that I can't help suspecting you're all trying to hide something. So I'll need independent corroboration. Carry on, Wank."

William stepped into Wank's way. "Touch her and I cut you." His knife hand was rock steady.

Baltknight sighed theatrically. "Soldiers." They aimed at William's chest. He tensed. I could see him calculating the distances. Could he reach Wank's throat before the soldiers' bolts took him down? I was making a similar calculation. Could I knock him down before the bolts did? I felt sick. I was too far away. So was he.

Into that agonizing moment came a soft voice.

"Step back, William," Nicca said. She put a gentle hand on his shoulder. Not restraining him. Just touching him. "Come on. Just step back."

He started to shake. "But I ... but ..."

"I know. But you won't stop them, and you'll die. Your children will lose their father, and then these men will do it anyhow. So step back. Come on." Her voice was low and rhythmic and soothing. A mother's voice to her little boy. "We'll get through this. It'll be all right. Isabella's a brave girl."

William hung his head. Nicca put her arms around him. "That's it." She turned him slowly and walked him back to our little line. *Take the knife*, she mouthed at me. I did. William didn't resist.

"You married a wise woman, scrivener," Baltknight said. "Wank. You have your orders."

It was horrible. It could've been worse, but it was still horrible.

Margery stood behind Isabella, holding her supportively. Wank crouched down with a barely suppressed leer. Margery drew her daughter back beyond the man's reach. murmuring reassuringly, so softly only the girl could hear her. Isabella's hands shook as she lifted her skirts, but the look on her face was defiant.

"Hmmm," Baltknight said. "You were right after all. We'll leave her off the list." His voice hardened. "Wank, get back over here. Have some dignity, for God's sake. She's a child."

William kept to himself for the rest of the day. It felt like he blamed me, though I might have been reading that in. The rest of us went to the celebrations. Before long Isabella was laughing at the puppet theatre and chasing her brother around the food stalls, though at one point I noticed her and her mother walking slowly around the edge of the crowd in a silent embrace.

"Hear about Bocking?" Ralf asked as we waited in line at the ale tent. A town about a day's cart ride to the northwest.

"No. What about it?"

"Big gathering yesterday. Organized by some of the lads who broke up the meeting at the hall. Word is they're discussing what to do next."

Across the river in Kent, things had gone beyond discussion. A group from Lessness occupied the abbey that held their land and forced the abbot to join them "in support of the king," which was rebel shorthand for "against the rest of the nobles." While we were eating oat cakes in the sun and tossing coppers to jugglers, the Kentishmen were crossing into Essex and raising men to their cause. Serfs tired of servitude. Freemen tired of wage controls. Smallholders tired of corrupt landlords. Everyone tired of being plutocrats' playthings. It was the perfect storm for an idealistic political reformer.

"I hear Thomas atte Raven has joined the Kentish rebels," Fisty said a couple of days later at our house, over a lunch of cold mutton and pickles.

Nicca shook her head and chuckled. "That's so Raven."

Word crossed the Thames at the speed of gossip. We got broken-telephone versions of events almost as soon as they happened. Raven's group burned the house of the Justice of the Peace in Maidstone, including the documents confirming his stewardship over the surrounding lands. Spin-off mobs in Dartford and Rochester sacked the homes of stewards and officials and publicly burned all the papers they could find. That became the common theme: leases and writs and birth records and contracts of stewardship heaped onto bonfires as proxy for the domination they stood for, like sympathetic magic. Right down to the fact that it didn't actually work.

Though for a while it looked like it might.

In the beginning it was like watching the news on TV. Bocking and Kent might have been Mogadishu. In Brentwood the sun was shining and the grass was green. The Whitsun holiday ended. Work resumed.

I took a sheaf of leases to Fisty's house for his approval. He took a long time to answer the door. Then he hurried me inside. He was holding a beaker of wine. Not his first. "Something up?" I asked.

"It's spread."

"The uprising?"

He nodded.

Of course it had. I'd been through hundreds. "So we keep our heads down for a while."

Fisty paced. "I'm more concerned about keeping mine on."

"Excuse me?"

He drained the beaker. "I had a meeting with the county escheator this morning." That shouldn't have been rattling. Escheators were basically jumped-up land evaluators. Fisty met with them all the time.

"And?"

"He wasn't there."

"Stood you up?"

"Fled."

"Maybe he was just out."

"He wasn't just out."

"How do you know?"

"His clerks were there."

"And they told you he'd fled?"

"Not exactly." He poured more wine. "Their throats were cut."

"Their ... wait, their *throats* were cut?"

"Blood all over. Office ransacked. Burnt documents smouldering in the yard."

"Documents?"

"Land records, probably. Like we use to assess rents and taxes."

"So why does this worry you? You mostly represent people *against* landlords."

"You know how mobs are. They're so fed up with writs and rules they've started killing people over them. You think they care which flavour of paper-pusher gets in their way?"

Nicca insisted on business as usual. "They're shearing in Kent. I have to do my circuit."

"Tyler's mob sacked Canterbury yesterday." The name Wat Tyler had been coming up in recent reports. "They broke open the prison. The *prison*, Nicca."

"Four prisoners. Not exactly the zombie apocalypse. I'll be fine."

"I'm coming with you."

She rolled her eyes.

When we got off the ferry at Erith the village was abuzz. Raven and his men were camped nearby at Dartford, to mobilize on London. "Someone must've gotten that mixed around," I said to Nicca. "It'd be madness to move on London. The Crown's most battle-hardened troops are stationed in the Tower."

"Let's ask him when we see him."

"Who?"

"Raven."

"You want to go see Raven? We should be avoiding the mobs, not riding into the middle of them."

"We'll ask for safe passage. Then we can go where we want and not worry about the mobs."

"I'm not sure that's how mobs work."

"Of course we're moving on London." Raven looked surprised that we'd question it. "That's where the king is. We're showing him our support against the plunderers."

"Don't the plunderers control the garrisons?"

Raven made a dismissive *pfffft* sound. "Details. We take a hostage or two and force a peaceful parley. Standard diplomacy. And what do you know about the price of eels in the first place, manservant?" Raven could be oddly superior for a proto-Marxist.

"You'd be surprised," Nicca said, cutting me off before I could say anything to provoke the leader of the *de facto* army we were in the middle of. Raven eyed me as if seeing me for the first time.

There was a stir at the edge of camp. Nothing threatening, but something out of the ordinary. A young man with a farmhand's callouses approached Raven. "Woman to see your guests, Thomas." Raven turned inquiringly toward Nicca.

Nicca was puzzled. "No one knows we're here."

"Show her through."

It didn't take long. It wasn't a large camp.

The woman was Margery. She looked frightened.

Nicca embraced her. "What's going on? Why've you come?"

"It's William. He's joined those men from the north, from the trouble at Coggeshall. They're marching on London." He'd set off right after we'd left Brentwood. Margery had missed us at the ferry. She'd just crossed now, and asked around.

"William joined the … men who sacked Coggeshall?" I'd nearly said mob. "Why?"

Margery and Nicca looked at me like I was slow. Which I was.

"Because they're a big group of armed men moving on London," Nicca said.

I still wasn't getting it. "And?"

Margery connected the dots.

"And that's where Baltknight is."

I wanted to ride back to Brentwood immediately. Maybe I could still stop him.

"You'll never catch him that way. You'll lose too much time." I was surprised Nicca didn't say "we." But she'd thought it through. She and Margery would go home and defend the family. I'd go defend William.

"Well how, then?"

She raised an eyebrow toward Raven.

He smiled and nodded. "I'm heading that way. Got your own sword?"

Nicca and I had a moment alone as I loaded my things onto Margery's horse, so I asked her about the one thing that puzzled me. "Why did she come to us?"

"What do you mean?"

"She has a father and two brothers in Brentwood. One's a soldier. We were a half day's hard ride away. Why come all the way to us?"

She paused for a beat. "She knows."

"Knows what?"

"She *knows*."

"She … she *knows*? Damn it, and William made me promise—"

"William didn't tell her. He doesn't know she knows. And don't go telling him. That's up to Margery."

"But then how—?"

"What, you thought we only talked about periods and potty training?"

I let this sink in a moment.

"Damn it, he *insisted*—"

"He thinks he's protecting her. From knowledge. However that's supposed to work."

"And so you just—"

"I didn't 'just' anything. She half figured it out, and she asked me. So I told her."

"And she's fine with it?"

"She came to us, didn't she?"

I saw them off, then rejoined Raven's group. He'd drawn a rough map in the dirt. "Tyler and his men are meeting us at Blackheath." He pointed to a spot just short of London and just south of the river. "It's a three-hour march, so we'd best get on with it."

"What's the plan once we're there?"

"Get the lay of the land. Build up our numbers if we can. See about crossing into London from Southwark."

"Isn't the bridge fortified?"

"That's why we need to get the lay of the land."

Our numbers started building as soon as we set off. All along the road, men came out of the forests and fields with swords or pikes or bows. Raven would ask: "Who are you for?" A surprising number already knew the right answer: "For Richard, the true king." By the time we merged with Tyler's men at Blackheath there were hundreds of us.

They made a good pair, Tyler and Raven.

Tyler was young, charismatic and inspiring. He could charm a thousand men through a sewage lagoon to steal a nobleman's knickers. It's no accident that history refers to the uprising as Wat Tyler's Rebellion.

Raven was older, more calculating and more connected. He knew where the levers of power were, and when to pull them, and how hard. It's no accident that he was eventually pardoned for his role.

Once the revolutionary moment presented itself, they were equally determined to see it through, no matter the cost.

Blackheath was high enough above the south bank to give us a view of London and its surroundings. Tyler was scoping it out when we arrived. "That square white building there." He pointed with his sword. "Is that the Tower of London?"

Raven nodded. "It is."

"Where the mucky-mucks hide when they get skittish?"

"That's it. Why?"

"Apparently the king's in residence there."

"He knows we're here?"

"Oh yeah. We've sent a hostage to ask him to meet us here. Kept his kids as security."

"And?"

"Nothing so far. I'm not sure he's taking us seriously." Tyler stared at the walls surrounding the Tower. "Tricky to get in there, I imagine."

"Kind of the point."

The younger man chuckled. "One step at a time. That the only bridge into the city?"

"Afraid so."

"And we have to go through that town to get to it."

"Southwark, yeah."

"Any thoughts on how?"

Raven smiled coolly. "A couple."

He stuck with the approach that had worked for him so far: target the oppressors and free the oppressed.

Marshalsea prison was a brick and plaster building set back from the east side of the High Street. A narrow lane along its south wall opened into a yard, which opened to a series of footpaths across a field to the east. "Gather fifteen or twenty men in that field and wait for my signal," Raven said.

"Why not go down the High Street in force?" Tyler was big on show.

"Two reasons, Wat. First, we don't want to get bottlenecked in that narrow lane." He was right. If we met armed resistance, the lane would be a deathtrap. "And second, these people know me. If we take a mob down the High Street, they'll just see the mob. If it's me and a few others, they'll know there's nothing to worry about. That it's a targeted strike."

"But why target the prison?" Raven looked at me sharply. I was a hanger-on of no proven worth. But I wanted to know. "Isn't it risky to loose prisoners on the town?"

"Marshalsea isn't all thugs and murderers. It's mostly ordinary men who've been locked up for failing to pay their debts."

"Debts to nobles like Gaunt," Tyler said.

Raven let me ride down the High Street with him and his closer companions.

"Afternoon, Thomas," called the landlord of an inn. "Who're your friends, then?"

"Supporters of the king, Ronald. Here for a bit of mischief. Can you spread the word that we don't mean any harm to the town?"

"I'll send my boys around. Sure you've got the manpower? Happy to join in if it isn't too risky."

"Thanks, Ronald. We've got others coming. Tend to your customers."

"Won't ask twice. Good luck to you." As we rode on I saw two lads scamper from the inn and start knocking on doors.

Two streets along, a broad man with the look of a sailor called out from a bench in front of another inn, where he was sitting with three others much like him. "Thomas, lad. Didn't know you were back. Here to check on the wife's bullion?" He cackled and elbowed one of his mates.

"Here to give some good men their freedom back."

The men perked up. "Where you headed?"

"Marshalsea."

"Shameful place. My wife's brother's in there. Bloody landlord cut his wages and jacked his rent."

"It'd be a help if you could let folks know we're just after the prison, not the town."

"Done. C'mon, lads. Good excuse to hit some more taverns."

"'Wife's bullion'?" I asked as we rode on.

"Bit of an overstatement. Her father was a goldsmith here. She inherited a share of his business. That's partly why they know me."

The lane to the prison was called Mermaid Alley. We rode through in single file, our shoulders almost brushing the stone walls. When we passed into Mermaid Court we could see Tyler and his men in the field at the other end. They rode to meet us. "How'd it go?"

"Some are with us. Most of the rest are at least not against us. Hedging their bets until they see how it plays out. Hard to fault them." He nodded northward, toward the bridge. "I don't fancy having my head on a pike either."

Tyler smiled. "And yet here you are."

"Here I am. Shall we?"

Raven had it down to a science. He pounded on the heavy door. "Open up!" Faces peered cautiously around the edges of the barred windows, then drew back at the sight of our numbers. Finally someone called back. "Who's asking?" Firm but strained.

"Good men who support the king against those who would misuse him." There's always a weird formality to this stuff.

"What's your business here?"

"To free other good men, who've already been misused."

Silence. Folks inside conferring.

"Sorry, can't let you in. It's our job to keep those men locked up, right?" The formality was already breaking down. "So if we let you free 'em? Well we wouldn't be doing our job, then, would we?"

"That's fair," Raven said. "But let me ask this. Is being burned alive in your workplace part of your job?"

Another silence. "You wouldn't," the man finally said. He didn't sound confident.

"You must've heard what's been happening across Kent and Essex. Quite a lot of burning, actually. Heads coming off, too, once in a while. What's to stop us here?"

"Umm ... common human decency?"

"Showing much of that to the men inside, are you?"

After another pause, the man asked Raven to come closer to speak privately.

"Probably a trap," Tyler said. "I say we just bash the door down."

Raven climbed down from his horse. "Have a bowman line up on the door. I'll at least hear what he has to say." He went to the door. There was a grate at head height. A little door behind it opened. We could see part of a face. After a few minutes the door closed and Raven came back.

"So?" Tyler asked.

"He wants us to make a show of breaking the door down. He'll need a few minutes to weaken the drawbar."

Tyler nodded. "I can live with that."

Some of the freed prisoners joined with us. Some just went home. A few wanted to kill their jailers, but Raven talked them out of it by letting them burn the place to the ground. He supervised it himself so the fire wouldn't spread to the neighbouring structures. He'd given assurances to the town.

"Now the bridge?" Tyler asked.

"Now the bridge."

"Show of force, this time?"

The Thames frothed white in the dusk around the bridge's tapered pylons. The bridge was its own bustling high street, with multi-storey shops and taverns and grand private homes, their lantern-lit windows hovering in the dank air between us and the capital. The gatehouse bristled with the long pikes where the state mounted its enemies' heads *pour encourager les autres.*

Two men in cloaks stepped from a narrow lane, keeping to the shadows. Town aldermen, though we weren't supposed to know that. Raven and Tyler followed them to a low hut. I couldn't hear the conversation, but at one point I saw Tyler gesture to where the flames from Marshalsea lit the darkening sky.

"Well?" one of Raven's men asked when they returned.

"Formally we've been denied entry."

"And informally?"

"Remember the guy at the jail?"

We camped on the waterfront, where Southwark hosted businesses that were too dodgy for respectable London. Raven and Tyler planned the following day.

"What do we hit first?"

"We don't 'hit' anything, Wat. We're negotiating a meeting with the king."

"You expect this lot to sit quietly while men in doublets shuttle back and forth to the palace?"

"That's why we're here."

"That's why *you're* here. Me too, maybe. But these guys?" He gestured toward the dockside taverns and brothels where most of the men had gone. "They want to *wreck* something. I've heard them discussing where to find Gaunt's city palace."

"They'll do as they're told."

"Sure they will."

Raven remembered I was there. "What do you think, Constantine?"

"I'm just here to find my son."

An hour later a messenger arrived from the camp at Blackheath. The king had agreed to a meeting. "Where the hell's Rotherhithe?" Tyler asked.

"It's a manor downriver," Raven said. "About half way back to Blackheath."

"He won't come to Blackheath, then?"

"Would you?"

Raven wanted a small deputation to go to Rotherhithe, but no one would agree to stay behind. "They're hungry and frustrated and bored," Tyler said. "They've come out for action, not to sit under a tree and pick their toenails." So by the time of the meeting there were hundreds of us along the riverbank at Rotherhithe manor.

A spotter sent word that the royal barge had left the Tower. Soon we saw it approaching, bright and sleek and dotted with colourful pennants. Four others followed. The nobs were coming in force. Until they weren't.

"Hang on," Tyler said. "Why are the oarsmen reversing?"

"Check the perimeter," called Raven. "It might be a trap."

The perimeter was fine. It wasn't a trap. But for some reason it wasn't a meeting either. Not anymore. Raven was sanguine. "They probably just panicked at our numbers."

"Bullshit!" Tyler said. "They're not taking us seriously. I bet the king isn't even on that bloody barge."

They went back and forth like that for another half-hour, but what they were left with was this: Sit and do nothing, or continue trying to force a meeting. Which wasn't much of a choice.

Southwark high street echoed with the slamming of shutters and the locking of doors. The covert deal with the aldermen held: The few token shots by the archers on the gatehouse went wide, and the gate gave way easily. Tyler's men set modest fires in a couple of swankier homes on the bridge, but nothing that was in danger of spreading.

London greeted us like liberators. Men and women poured into its streets with lances and swords and kitchen knives and carpenters' hammers. They seemed to know where to go, so we followed them. To Gaunt's waterfront residence, as it turned out.

Savoy Palace was as much a corporate headquarters as a private home. It was conspicuous wealth on a deliberately intimidating scale, with a full time staff, a chapel larger than most churches, and an un-rivalled collection of furniture, tapestries, and gold-stitched tunics. I know, because I watched the people of London toss it into the street and burn it to ash. If it wouldn't burn, they chopped it up. If it wouldn't chop, they chucked it in the Thames. Then they burned the palace down, chapel and all.

London wasn't Marshalsea. Raven couldn't contain this.

I caught up with Tyler in the chaos. "Any word of the Essex men?"

"Some of them are here." He reined his horse around as an ornate headboard dropped from a third floor window and smashed on the cobbles. "But I think most of them are up at the Priory of St. John."

"A priory? Why?"

"Headquarters of the Knights Hospitaller." Their prior, a rigorous poll tax enforcer, had recently been appointed Treasurer of England. Tyler gave me directions to the priory. My "thank you" was drowned out by the sound of a wall coming down.

My route took me past the Temple, home to the city's lawyers.

Rioters were pulling roof tiles from the residences and burning books in the street. A woman danced around a bonfire chanting "away with the learning of clerks" as she fed the flames with pages from what looked like a bible.

We'd come a long way from marching for justice.

The priory was a compound of churches, barracks and administrative buildings, all on fire. I rode around until I spotted William. He was heaving books from a handcart onto a pyre near a dead monk. "You don't know Buttnugget if you think you'll find him at a priory," I said.

He turned with a start. "What are *you* doing here?"

"Keeping you from getting your throat cut." I nodded at the monk. "You do that?"

"Of course not. What do you take me for?"

"A book burner, for a start. And that monk didn't put that arrow between his own shoulders.

"Wasn't me. I'm saving that."

"For Buttnugget? Or his little weasel?"

"Whatever."

"Take it from someone who's been down this road. You think you want to kill him. You think it so hard you might even do it. But once you do, it's part of you forever."

"It should be."

"Not in a good way. You think it will be. It never is."

"It will. I feel it."

"It won't. That feeling is lying to you." I sighed. "I know you won't hear me. Because it's me. Because you're fired up on manhood and vengeance and sacramental wine. But just hear this. If the moment comes, take a beat. Doesn't have to be for long. Just long enough to see what it really is."

"I know what it really is. It isn't just about Buttnugget." He looked around. "Do you know how many serfs these monks have? Thousands. Tens of thousands, across England, living on hard bread and pond water so these bastards can kick back with a pint and a paperback."

That's me paraphrasing again. "They keep it that way by stacking the Commons with landowners whose next move will to make it illegal for people like me to teach serfs' kids to read and write!"

"All right, you're not just here for His Nuggetship. You want to improve things? Raven's brokering a meeting with the boy king. Hang out a while and see how that goes."

"The king's just like the rest."

"Word is he might not be."

Somewhere William had acquired a horse. I didn't ask. We found Raven and his men camped at the Hospital of St. Katherine just east of the Tower. The sisters were tending the wounded and passing out bread and ale.

"This your boy?"

"William, Raven. Raven, William."

"William. Doesn't your employer have a son named William?"

"Remind me to tell you about that when this is over. Any progress on a meeting?"

"We have their attention. Not quite how I wanted, mind you."

"The king's? Or his handlers'?"

"Can't tell yet. We're pretty sure they're all in there, though. The prior of the Hospitallers. Gaunt's son Bolingbroke."

"Gaunt himself?"

Raven shook his head. "Negotiating a cease-fire in Scotland. Convenient timing."

"Anyone else?" William asked. He was wondering about Baltknight.

"The Archbishop of Canterbury." William looked surprised. "He's the chancellor," Raven explained. "He's at the top of Tyler's list."

"List?"

"Tyler's sent the king a petition, asking for a bunch of heads."

"Whose heads?"

"The lot. Gaunt. Bolingbroke. The Archbishop. A dozen more. I doubt he really means it, mind you. Just another way to get the king's attention."

"Is there a Baltknight on that list?" William asked.

"Let me check." He called out down the line. "Wat! Got a Balt-knight on your death list?"

There was a stirring at the next campfire over. "Gimme a sec." A pause while Tyler checked with someone. "I think so, yeah. From Essex?"

Raven looked at William inquiringly. William nodded.

"That's the one."

"Got him right here."

William was stonefaced.

By morning we still couldn't tell where the king's mind lay. Then things moved fast. The Londoners broke open prisons at Westminster and Newgate, and the prisoners joined the uprising. The violence went up to eleven. Lawyers fled the city dressed as tinkers or cart drivers. Panic radiated from behind the Tower walls.

Mid-morning, a messenger from the Tower offered everyone the king's pardon if we'd all just go home. Raven sent a counter-offer: Arrest the men on Tyler's list, release the chancellor's books of account, and abolish serfdom. Not a lot of middle ground.

A bit later he came back with the same offer, but in writing and over the king's seal. As a sweetener, it said the king would give it all *really* serious thought and try to do what was best for everyone. Tyler stuffed the document down the messenger's codpiece and sent them both back to the Tower.

Then the third time something kind of amazing happened.

"OK, listen," the messenger said. "You know Mile End?"

Tyler turned to Raven. "Do we know Mile End?"

"Half a mile east."

"We know Mile End."

"What if the king met you there? Like, this afternoon."

Tyler turned to Raven. "Is it safe?"

"Open meadow, as far as I remember."

"Wide open," William said. "We passed it on our way from Essex."

"So no chance of ambush?"

"Shouldn't be. Open view for miles in every direction."

"What's the catch?" Tyler asked the messenger.

"None that I know of. Bit risky for the king, if you ask me. But apparently he's counting on your personal loyalty."

"He's always had that," Raven said. He and Tyler looked at each other. "Right. Tell him we're on."

"Oh, I don't speak to him directly, sir. But I'll pass it along."

Things went very differently than at Rotherhithe. Tyler—lesson learned—left most of his men behind. The king didn't turn back. He rode to Mile End with a handful of uncontroversial nobles and their equerries, plus his mother, the princess of Wales.

"His *mother*?" William said when I pointed out her carriage from our spot a half mile away.

"Shrewd negotiator, they say. Plus cut the kid a break. He's fourteen."

"You were married when you were fourteen."

"Fifteen. Different times. But point taken."

The king wore a white robe over light armour and a helmet with a gold circlet. He looked small, even for fourteen. The party on our side included Tyler and Raven, their closest advisors, and the loose leadership of the Essex men. We couldn't hear anything from where we were, but we could make out the rough dynamics. Tyler took the lead, over Raven's apparent objections. The boy king took the lead too, apparently over his mother's. Twice he made shushing motions toward her carriage. Every so often he nodded. When he did, Tyler looked back at Raven in what seemed like disbelief.

"Seems to be going well," William said.

"Suspiciously well." I looked around for surprise troops, but there weren't any. What we were seeing was what apparently we were getting: agreement. But to what? Most of the rebels' demands were unthinkable for the royals. Where were they finding middle ground?

A low cheer went up from the rebel group. One of the king's men took a bundle from the back of the carriage and rode along our ranks passing something out. There was a louder cheer. The royal party turned and left. Our men rode back to us, unfurling banners as they rode. The royal arms.

"He's abolishing serfdom!" Tyler was beaming.

"He's *what*?" I was sure I'd misheard him.

Raven rode up alongside him, also beaming. "I know it's hard to believe, but Wat's right. The king is abolishing serfdom. He's riding back now to put it in writing, with the royal seal. Local fines and fees, too. He's abolishing them all."

"He'd never do that. The nobles wouldn't let him. Does he even have the power?"

"He's the king," Tyler said. "He can do whatever he wants."

"Well, it may not be *quite* that simple," Raven said. "He can do it on his own lands. Open question whether he can do it on anyone else's."

"Everyone holds their lands from him. Besides, who cares what the lawyers and clerks say about whether he can do it? He *did* it. It's done. No more serfs. No more *serfs*." He turned it into a chant. Most of the others picked it up.

I was skeptical. But it was over, and William was in one piece. We could go.

So close.

"What's with the banners?" William asked.

"They're just safe conduct," Raven said. "So we can go home."

"Bugger that." Tyler shook his. "They're the king's authority for us to deal with Gaunt and the others."

"He didn't say that."

"Didn't he? I'm pretty sure he did." Tyler turned to one of his men. "Isn't that what the king said?"

"That's what I heard," the man said.

"That's not what happened." Raven was irritated. "You asked for their heads. He didn't agree."

"And then he gave us these banners." Tyler tapped his finger against the side of his head. "Put two and two together, eh?" With a grin, he reined his horse around and rode to the top of a small rise. "Men of Essex and Kent!" Everyone went quiet and turned to him. He held his banner high. "We act for the king, now! We have his sovereign authority to take down the traitors and deal with them according to the law."

"By cutting off their bloody heads," called out a man from the back.

The crowd looked at Tyler expectantly. He waited until he had their complete attention. "Whatever it takes!" He turned his horse and started toward London. The crowd cheered and followed him.

"That can't be good," I said to William. But he wasn't there. He was on his way with the rest.

Raven had remained behind with a couple of the Essex men. I gave him an imploring look, but he shook his head. "Nothing I can do. I have to wait here for the king's written agreement. Someone has to take care of the formalities."

I was on my own.

They'd gone to the Tower.

A low mist drifted over the water of the moat and along the mossy edge of the curtain wall. To my left, near the Tower wharf, I could see rebels surrounding a gate at the end of a fortified stone bridge. I looked for Tyler's banner—where I'd likely find William—but it wasn't there. I rode on. There was a gate where the city wall met the moat, but no one was guarding it. Four or five riderless horses were grazing on a patch of open land. No idea how they got there. In the chaos of a rebellion, sometimes things just happen.

I followed the mob sounds coming from the west side of the Tower. As I rounded the wall I saw rebels twenty or thirty deep around the Bulwark Gate. I rode up Tower Hill for a better view. Flies buzzed around darkened straw at the base of a scarred wooden chopping block. There was a short spear stuck into the ground. I took it. You never knew. From the higher ground I could see Tyler's banner down at the gate. As I scanned the rebels around it for William, I saw a group break off from the fringe and wander into the surrounding neighbourhood. Men who'd come out to smash things, and who didn't have the patience to wait on the prizes inside. I heard shouts from the side streets. Then screams.

Tyler was trying to negotiate his way past the guards on the strength of the king's banner. William was on his near side, a few men back. I shouted his name. A dozen men looked my way, including him. From five hundred feet away I could see the annoyance on his face.

Movement to the left caught my attention. On the surface of the moat, a flat boat crept from the fog. Then another. The first held three men; the second two. Both were making for the moat's north bank, to a spot out of view from either side of the Tower. I later learned that one of the men in the first boat was Gaunt's son Bolingbroke, the only noble—with one exception—not to put his trust in the Tower. If he'd stayed he'd've been just another head on a stick. Instead, not quite ten years later, he seized the throne as Henry the Fourth.

The one exception was in the second boat.

The first boat reached the bank. A man plunged a short sword into the mucky turf as a handhold and helped a second man climb ashore. The third, who'd been poling the craft, lifted his pole and pushed the second boat back. The second pilot cried in outrage. So they weren't together.

The first pilot made a shushing sound, but too late. A rebel archer ran around the far corner of the wall. He loosed an arrow. It sailed over the second boat and into the water. The men from the first boat crested the bank. They mounted three of the grazing horses and rode north. More bowmen rounded the far end of the moat.

The two men from the second boat were struggling up the bank, the smaller one pushing the larger one. They reminded me of someone. I called to William again, and gave him a vigorous *get over here* wave. I faced my horse toward the city gate and home. I wasn't concerned about the bowmen. They had no business with us.

The larger man made it to the top of the bank, leaving the smaller scrabbling up on his own. I saw a flash of rich, oversized clothing under his travelling cloak and realized why they looked familiar. Fate had given me a hook to get William away from the mob.

I waved to him again, then jabbed a finger toward the two men, who he couldn't see. I wobbled my arms at my sides to indicate Baltknight's bulk. William shook his head and pointed toward the gate. I did it again. William still didn't seem to understand, but he pushed through the rebels toward me, casting meaningful *I'm kind of busy here, you know* glances back toward them for my benefit.

Baltknight reached open ground and mounted one of the remaining horses. Arrows whizzed past him. Wank ran to his master and swung up behind him. Two bowmen circled north, cutting off the route Bolingbroke had taken. Now Baltknight's only avenue of retreat was past me. I positioned my horse across the track like a police car in an action movie. With about as much effect. The bad guys always make it past the police car. In their case, brute force and crumpled fenders. In my case, the bow Wank pulled from his cloak.

Bows are hard to shoot from horseback. But you don't want to count on that if you're facing one. I reined my horse back and raised a yielding hand. Just one. I needed the other to hold the reins. And the short spear I'd picked up.

They didn't recognize me as they rode by. Just another commoner with ideas above his station, to be forgotten once they got by. So they didn't notice me follow. Or throw the spear. It caught their horse's flank as they were entering the surrounding streets. The poor animal cried out and lurched sideways, spilling them into the dirt. They scrambled up and continued on foot. Of everything that happened that day, the one thing I regret is harming that horse.

William staggered up to me breathlessly. "Is that who I think it is?"

"Take a beat."

"Bite me." He ran into the street after them.

The cobbles were littered with spent arrows. Shop signs hung broken from their supports. A trail of blood or wine dribbled down the street and around a corner. The men who'd given up on the Tower had already made it this far and moved on.

Baltknight and Wank were a hundred feet ahead. They ducked down a lane to the right. "Could be an ambush," I said to William when we reached it. I peered around the corner. The lane was thirty feet long and strewn with rubble. Sprawled on the cobbles was a man with a bow and four arrows: three in his quiver that matched, and one in his chest that didn't. His eyes were wide and milky. Baltknight and Wank were stopped just beyond him. It didn't take long to figure out why. The lane dead-ended in a courtyard. I signalled William to follow. He drew his sword.

The air had the tang of blood and loosed bowels. More than a single sprawled body could account for. In the half obscured courtyard a mongrel hound with matted fur nosed at something out of view. Baltknight turned. He had the presence of mind to stay where he was, keeping us hemmed in. He dragged Wank in front of himself by the collar and drew a sword. Wank raised his bow and notched an arrow.

Then realization dawned. "Scrivener," he said with *faux* enthusiasm. "And your boy. How unexpected. Was that you who took down my horse?"

"It was."

"I'll let that go. Just let us pass."

"Why would we do that?"

"Seriously? My man can take you from here. Cut your losses. Save yourselves."

"No, I think we're good. At this distance he couldn't hit your fat ass."

He was smart enough not to be baited. "Maybe. But once you come closer ..."

"His bow arm will get shakier." I drew my sword with a theatrical *zinnnnng*. "The closer I get, the more he'll think about how this blade is sharp enough to shave his flaky eyebrow clean off and save his eye for dessert."

William tried to push past me. "No. The little one's mine."

"Wait for it." I eased forward a step, holding William back with my free hand. Wank took a kind of aim. As advertised, it wasn't very steady. "You got no quarrel with me," he said to William. "I never touched your girl."

"You would've, if her mother hadn't moved her back."

"You're right." He grinned. His teeth looked like broken dishes. "Got near enough for a sniff, though." He drew in a long, lascivious breath through his nose.

William snarled and pushed my arm down. Wank steadied his bow. I body-checked William into the wall and kicked a chunk of rubble toward Wank. The noise made him jerk as he fired. The arrow hit the stone wall an arm's length above us.

William rebounded from the wall toward Wank. He was so focused on the servant, he didn't see the master raise his sword. I dropped my own sword and pivoted left, snagging the dead man's bow with one hand and plucking the arrow from his chest with the other. "Back away," I said as I drew. Baltknight froze long enough for William to reach Wank. He flicked his wrist. Wank's bow string snapped, severed. The bow sprang in his hand, startling him so much he fell over onto his bottom.

William stepped back. "I took a beat," he said over his shoulder.

"I suppose that makes things a bit more even, doesn't it?" Baltknight said.

"Even? How? My bow still works."

He curled his lip, amused. "Didn't help the fellow you took it from."

"Whoever shot him is long gone."

"Dead, actually. But not long." He nodded toward the courtyard, where the hound was still snuffling. "Plenty more arrows like that back here. No one left to use them, though. Your dead friend's companions saw to that."

I risked a glance. A smear of red-brown on cobbles. A bootless foot. A shop sign knocked down and trampled, with a picture of a loom and two words. One was English. The translation of the other. Baltknight watched me stitch it together.

"Plenty of dead on a day like today," I said. "How does that even things?"

"It doesn't. Unless it makes your boy rethink your position."

"Why would a few dead Londoners make me rethink that?" William said.

"More than a few. And not really Londoners. Not to your dead friend's companions, anyhow."

"What are you on about?" William said irritably.

"You're an educated man, scrivener," Baltknight said. "You want to tell your lad what went on here?" William looked at me expectantly.

"Weavers. The broken sign. 'Weavers.' We're in a Flemish ghetto. They were doing well for themselves, I imagine."

"Why are they dead, then?"

"Because they're Flemings, boy!" Baltknight said gleefully. "Londoners hate Flemings. Don't you know that?"

"I've heard nasty comments, like anyone. Never understood why."

"Envy, boy. You heard your father. They were doing well. They make good cloth. Got stacks of the stuff myself, back at the manor. So people envy them."

"Fine, then, people might envy them. But why kill them? Who'd want to do that?"

"Your mob, of course. The common folk you've been running with these past few days. This is what the freedom you're after looks like." He waved an arm toward the courtyard. "The freedom to gut the people you envy. Nobles. Foreigners. The literate. Gingers next, for all I know. Past a certain point the target doesn't matter. Let the dogs out of their cages and they'll go after whatever's in front of them." He touched his fingertips lightly to his chest. "That's why you need us. We keep this sort of thing in check."

I wasn't about to let Lord Buttnugget run logical rings around my son. "By keeping them hungry and poor and confused."

"Yes! That's what it takes. That's how it *works.*"

"Works for you and yours. That's what troubles me. I mean, I understand order. But why do you get to make the rules and reap the benefits?"

He looked at me like I'd asked why water was wet. "Because we're better than you."

For a moment there just the snuffling of the dog. Then a triumphant little cry: "Hah!" It was William. Yes!" he said, turning to me with delight. "'Better than you.' Hah! Brilliant! How's *that* feel?"

"Really? You want to do this now?"

He didn't get a chance to respond.

While we'd been distracted, Wank had drawn a nasty-looking knife from his boot. But while the drawing of it had been subtle, the lunging with it wasn't. That got our attention. And even the nastiest knife is shorter than a basic sword, like the one William was holding.

He didn't swing it or thrust it. He just lifted it in instinctive self-defence. It slid into Wank's advancing chest. Wank dropped the knife and looked down in horror. Then he slid to the ground. William stared at the blood on his blade. "I didn't ... I mean, he ..."

Baltknight tut-tutted. "Oh, now you've done it lad. That was capital murder."

I shook my head. "Not even close. Totally self-defence."

"In whose court? You've forgotten who you're dealing with, scrivener. The law is what I say it is. And I say this was murder." He was gazing at William, but addressing me. "This will actually work out nicely. First I'll take his land, which, frankly, I'd probably take anyhow. And his life, of course. Then maybe I'll take that daughter of his. Not right away. I'm not a monster. I'll give her a year or two to ripen first."

William didn't even seem to hear him. He was still staring at the blood on his blade. But I did. "You're forgetting who has the bow," I said.

Baltknight looked amused. "The *bow*? Come now, scrivener. That would be murder, too. You couldn't even claim it was in the heat of the riot. Besides, a jumped-up serf like you doesn't have it in—" Suddenly he stopped talking.

An arrow in the throat will do that. He fell, gurgling, next to his servant.

The hound crept from the courtyard, curious about the fuss.

William turned to me in shock. "What happened to taking a beat?" His voice was at the angry edge of panic. "What happened to 'getting what it really is'?"

"I knew what it was. It was a powerful asshole threatening my family."

He started to shake. I stepped across and put a hand on his shoulder. I took his sword and wiped it on Wank's fancy clothes. Then I slipped it back into his scabbard and steered him toward the other end of the lane.

It would take him a few days to process what had happened. For now all I could do was get him home and see him settled. After a few steps he stopped. "Wait," he said. He walked back to the bodies.

He picked up the dropped knife, tugged Wank's nose taut, and sawed it off. Then he tossed it to the hound, who caught it and gobbled it down. "Right. Now we can go."

As we came out onto Tower Hill we met a cheering crowd heading toward the river. They had the head of the Archbishop of Canterbury on a pole. I didn't know the Archbishop's face, but the episcopal mitre nailed to his forehead gave it away. Wisps of the straw his head had landed in clung to the ragged edges of his neck.

"Hey," I said to a man on the edge of the crowd. "If you need another head for the bridge, there's a dead noble down a lane back there."

"It's not Gaunt, is it?" the man asked eagerly. "Is it Gaunt?"

"Sorry, mate. Gaunt's in Scotland. This is just a buttnugget from Essex."

The man didn't look fussed. He'd known it was a long shot. "Ah well. One noble's as good as the next on a pike, eh?" I didn't bother answering. I turned back to William.

"Hey," the man called as we walked off. "The noble down the lane. You kill him?"

I hesitated. "I did."

"What's your name, then?"

I frowned. "Why?"

"Seems like something a fellow ought to know, if he's gonna take a man's head."

"Jack." It was the commonest name that occurred to me.

"Jack what?"

I looked to the front of the grim procession, at the Archbishop's head bobbing its way toward London Bridge. "Straw," I said. "Jack Straw."

I learned later on that they stuck Wank's head on the bridge by mistake. They saw the clothes and just assumed.

Amazingly, my horse was where I'd left her. I climbed up, and helped my son up behind me. "Are we good now?" I asked as I steered toward the Essex Road.

"Give it time, old man."

By the time we reached Barking we were too bagged to continue, so we had bean stew and bread at the first inn we saw and crashed there for the night.

We rode into the Greater Brentwood Area the following morning. As we approached William's plot of land I could see him hoeing his cabbages in his work tunic and straw hat. The image was so convincing I forgot for a moment he was behind me.

"She's good, isn't she?"

"What?" He might've been dozing. "Who's good?"

I pointed toward the figure in the garden. "Your mother. She's got your body language down cold. Anyone passing would swear she was you."

"My mother?" He looked where I was pointing. "That's ... what's she *doing*?"

"Plausible deniability. As far as folks here know, you were never in London. You were here tending your garden." He hadn't thought through the possible consequences. But Nicca had.

"And what about you?"

"I imagine Fisty will vouch for me if I ask. There might be a fee, of course."

William was thinking things through now. The figure in the garden was visibly young and spry. "If mom's ... well, I mean, look at her. Does that mean Margery knows?"

"Knows what?"

He slapped my head.

I held up a submissive hand. This time the other only held reins. "Officially I don't know anything. But she didn't hear it from me."

And they lived happily ever after.

Well.

"Happily," sure, for the most part. I mean, there's always stuff, isn't there?

And "after" is kind of a given.

But "ever"?

That's a long time, however you cut it.

Things were dodgy in the counties for a bit. Men came back to Essex and Kent convinced that King Richard's banners gave them legal authority to hunt down traitors and execute them. Heads fell. We kept ours down. Fisty in particular. He probably wasn't really at risk, but you never knew.

Then the tide turned.

Word came that Wat Tyler had been killed near St. Bartholomew's Hospital trying to wrest more concessions from the king, which didn't surprise me. Word also spread about a rebel named Jack Straw who seemed to be everywhere and nowhere, which made me chuckle. And after a while, word came that special commissioners had been empowered to put down the rebels by any means necessary.

"How can they be rebels if they're acting in the king's name?" William Junior asked his father one morning over breakfast.

"Shut up and eat your cereal," William replied.

But by the time the commissioners came through Essex, pretty much no one was up in arms anymore. Most of those who had been were either dead or keeping quiet. The rest were easily dispersed by a handful of troops.

"Worth it in the end, though," Simon atte Marsh, the boatman's son, said. "At least the king freed the serfs. That's gotta be good for folks, eh?" And it might have been, if it had lasted.

Gaunt secured a quick truce with his Scottish hosts and came back to London to help his royal nephew with statecraft. A few days later, word went around that young Richard had taken it all back. Soon that word was made formal. Gilbert Baltknight, Sir Antony's pimply twenty-two-year-old heir, publicly read out the boy king's new proclamation: that upon sober second thought, his earlier ill-considered proclamations were revoked, quashed, invalidated and annulled. Everyone was to return to their original, regularly scheduled servitude. Four months later, Parliament confirmed it.

And that was that. *Status quo ante.* Except for the dead, of course.

And the Savoy Palace. Gaunt never rebuilt it.

Whenever he came to London after that, he couch surfed.

Life in Brentwood went on as before. Serfs served. Brewers brewed. Traders traded. Baltknight sent men with strongboxes to collect fees and fines and taxes. Not poll taxes, though. That was over. Even the nobility can take a hint when they see enough heads on sticks.

William and Margery's kids grew up and had kids of their own, who called us Granny Nicca and Grandpa Sten. They'd sit on my lap while I taught them their letters, guiding their ink-smeared hands over scraps of parchment at what was now William's work table. He'd taken over the scrivener business, leaving the wool-mongering to his kids and their spouses.

After a while, inevitably, our contemporaries started dying.

Fisty went first. The doctors said it was complications from gout. In hindsight, I suspect he was diabetic. His two eldest boys squabbled so furiously over his law practice they almost drove it into the ground. William got fed up with them both and started working for a lawyer in Billericay.

Avice went next, from probably some kind of cancer, followed eight months later by Adam, who just faded away. As husbands sometimes do.

"We can't keep this up much longer," Nicca said as we *faux*-hobbled home from John atte Marsh's funeral. So we sat down with William and Margery and came up with a plan. We invented a niece in Norfolk who wanted to go into service. We enlisted Raven's help. He'd long been pardoned, and was living on an estate near Southwark that his wife the gold merchant had inherited. We had to let him in on our secret, but there was no one apart from William and Margery whom we trusted more. He was mainly disappointed. "If I'd known you don't die, I could've made better use of you in the rebellion."

Nicca went first. She started with a cough. Over several weeks she built it into a rattling shortness of breath accompanied by fever. She spent the last few days bedridden and delirious. We buried a Nicca-sized bundle of wood and wool while she hid at Raven's estate growing out her grey-dyed hair.

I went next. Adam had set the tone. I grew listless after Nicca's death, to the point where William sent for the Norfolk niece to care for me. Re-enter Nicca, restored to glorious youth. When the Sten-shaped bundle was buried next to hers, the niece—who, against my advice, was also named Nicca—mentioned a second cousin who was literate and looking for a career. After a hair-growing-out period of my own at

Raven's, I turned up in Brentwood to apprentice in the scrivener's trade with my own son.

I have a weird life.

Not long after my rebirth, William and I took the cart to Billericay to deliver some leases to his lawyer and introduce me as his apprentice. His youngest granddaughter, Agnes—one of Grandpa Sten's better calligraphy pupils—came with us, mostly to get her out of her mother's hair. The lawyer gave us a lunch of cold beef and bread before seeing us off. On the way home we sat in a row in the cart, Agnes tucked between William and me. The sunshine and the swaying lulled us all into a comfortable doziness. As we approached William's property, Agnes closed her eyes and rested her head against my arm. "You smell like Grandpa Sten," she said after a moment.

I felt a flush of warmth so intense it was almost painful. "You remember Grandpa Sten, do you?"

"He died," she said. "He was old."

I stroked her hair gently. "Happens to all of us."

She lifted her head and frowned. Then she looked into the woods and brightened. "I saw two baby rabbits in there once."

I understood her perfectly. Youth and life. Not aging and death.

But for most people aging and death are unavoidable. Including William. He lived a fine, long life for his time. He saw King Richard grow to manhood, proclaim his independence, and negotiate a peace treaty with France, which pissed off the military-aristocratic complex. He saw him exile Bolingbroke over a petty dispute, which pissed off Gaunt. He saw him seize Gaunt's lands when the old boy finally died, which pissed off Bolingbroke enough to come back in force and rally the nobles for a coup. Politics. Ho hum. In our little town we baled our wool and drafted our documents and bought our eggs at the market on Wednesday.

When William was nearing sixty, a flu passed through Essex. It was especially hard on the very young and the very old. And in the first decade of the fifteenth century, William counted as very old.

Nicca and I and Margery—no kid herself by then—sat with him in turns, feeding him broth and mopping his brow. You're probably assuming he went in the quiet of the night, as people do in stories, but it was actually a warm, bright afternoon. We'd propped him in a chair and carried him to his garden. We sat for a couple of hours, not saying much, just savouring the sun on our faces. Then, as a grain-ripe breeze rippled in from the neighbouring fields, William smiled and reached for our hands. Margery took one. Nicca and I took the other. He looked toward Nicca and me.

"Take care of them. Promise."

"We promise," Nicca said. I just gave him a tight smile.

He turned to Margery. "I married well."

"Oh, you," she replied, giving his hand a feather-light slap.

He closed his eyes. A few minutes later his face went slack.

You want my one bottom-line piece of advice from all my centuries of life?

Don't outlive your kids.

We buried him in our plot at the churchyard, next to our own fake bodies. When we got back home after the interment, we sat together in silence. We'd raised a child together. Seen him through the stages. Watched him thrive. Watched him age. Sent him off. It had been exhilarating, and excruciating. It had been a normal life. It had been an eyeblink.

I tried to stay. I really did. I just couldn't.

Nicca threw herself into helping Isabella and William Junior with their respective kids. There was always plenty to do. That's kind of how it is with kids.

I carried on with the scrivener work. William had brought in another apprentice the previous year. The plan was for me to take the shop back when William retired or died. Now that he was gone, though, I found myself spending less and less time there. I kept half expecting him to push through the door with a smile and a bundle of fresh parchment, or to scamper down the stairs excitedly to show me the tin soldier he'd just finished assembling, or to hug me around the waist in tears over his latest indignity at Roger's hands, or to pull himself up on the table's edge and grab at the ink pot. It had all been one short, straight line.

So I left more and more work to the other apprentice, and spent my time at the Ram's Head, nursing a coffee and brioche and checking the box scores in the morning paper. But even the inn wasn't what it had been. Roger's kids, whom I barely knew, were running the place by then.

"Can you pick up Agnes after pre-school today?" Nicca asked as she pulled her dress on over her head. "I have to make the muffins for the bake sale and then get Will Junior's kids to soccer practice." Something along those lines. It was something along those lines pretty much every day. But this time the air went out of me. I slumped in my chair.

Nicca noticed. "Oh, come on. It's not that big a deal. Just get her to Isabella's and give her a fruit cup or something until her mother gets home."

"That's not it."

Nicca belted her dress and rooted around for a set of earrings. "Well, what is it then?" Briskly efficient, Nicca. Always was.

"I don't think I can do this anymore."

"Fine." It plainly wasn't. "I'll see if Will's wife can pick Agnes up, if you're too busy."

"That's not what I mean."

She caught something in my tone. She stopped what she was doing. "What *do* you mean, then? What can't you do?"

I waved my hands vaguely around the room. Around the town. "This. Just ... this. All of it."

She sat on the arm of the chair. "All of what, Ishtanu? Talk to me. What's wrong?"

It was hard to explain. And somehow not hard at all. "We buried our son, Nicca. He was our son, and he grew old, and he died, and we buried him."

She stroked the back of my neck. "We did, yes." Her voice was soft. "But we also promised him we'd take care of his wife and children."

"You promised."

The stroking stopped. "We both did."

I shook my head.

She gave this a moment's thought. "Well, you've been following through, whether you made the promise or not. But if you need some breathing space—"

"It isn't about breathing space."

"Well what, then?"

I started again. "We buried our son."

"Yes."

"And soon we'll be burying our daughter-in-law. And then her kids. And then their kids." Tears rolled onto my cheeks.

"Oh, no, Ishtanu. No. Don't think of it like that. You can't."

"How else is there to think of it? We love them and we care for them and they die. They'll always die. It doesn't matter how long we stay. Death wins."

"All right, slow down. I'm not saying anything about staying forever. Just right now. And right now is Margery and Isabella and Will Junior. And Agnes."

I twisted away. "Exactly. Agnes. I can't watch that little girl grow old and die. Or Isabella. Or maybe even Margery. I don't think I can go through that again."

"But it isn't just watching them die. It's all the other stuff. The birthday cakes and riding lessons, and teaching them to read and write ..."

"And every one of those things stabs me to the heart. Because one day we're laughing and eating cake, and the next I'm burying another one. And another, and another. William was hard enough. Don't make me keep doing that. Just don't." Tears dripped from my chin. My voice cracked. "Just *don't*."

"Whoa, whoa, my love." She stroked my neck again. "No one's making you do anything. No. No one's making you do anything."

The conversation went on a lot longer. But you get the drift.

I stayed, for a while. For Nicca. Then Margery died, and we had the conversation again. And we realized we were going to keep having it, and it was going to keep getting harder.

"I have to stay, Ishtanu. I promised William."

"I know. You have to. And I can't."

So she did. And I didn't.

I don't know how she explained why I left. That part we didn't plan together. I didn't ask before I left. I didn't ask when we saw each other centuries later, either. It was too soon.

She eventually left Brentwood, of course. I don't know when, or how, or how many lives she lived in the meantime. I know she went back to south Asia with the Dutch East India Company at some point. Maybe she went straight from Brentwood. Or maybe by then she'd been out for a hundred years. Again, I never asked.

I wish I had, now.

But of course now it's too late.

Three Weeks Ago

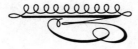

ELEVEN O'MORON DRIVES a matte black Audi with tinted windows. Of course he does.

He picked me up in front of Union Station. I always meet him somewhere public. He'd found a location for the lab, and was taking me to see it. "Excellent deal on the lease. They'll take what they can get, 'cause the building's coming down in five months for condos." He pulled away from the curb before I could get my seat belt on, cutting off a cab and nearly clipping a wide-eyed tourist's wheelie suitcase. "Even got 'em to throw in the utilities." He absently waved a middle finger at the sound of the cab's horn.

"Zoned for lab work?"

"It *is* a lab. Low rise medical building. Blood tests and that."

"Why's it closing?"

"Doctors have all gone, haven't they? Splashy new building down the road." He downshifted to pass a bread van. "Probably the same knobs who pre-bought the bloody condos."

Twenty minutes later we pulled up in front of a three-storey brick building. It was suitably, sadly anonymous, with grass growing through its cracked walkway and kinked venetian blinds in its windows. An artist's conception of the condo building took up half the ragged lawn. Glass and brushed steel at stylishly odd angles. Ground floor coffee bar with red umbrellas. No doubt a hot yoga room off the atrium and e-bike lockers in the basement. For now, though, all it needed was water and power and easily disinfected surfaces. Which it had.

"Nicely done," I said to Eleven. For all his faults, he gets the job done. It was just what I'd ordered. Epoxy resin work surfaces. Stainless steel sinks. Plenty of space for the equipment. Plus it had a lunch room.

Science has always intrigued me—especially its practical applications —but I'm not very good at it. I don't have the right analytical focus. But every so often I feel the need to hang out on its fringes.

It started when I defected from Lionheart's coalition of savages at the siege of Acre and found myself in Baghdad. The scholars at the House of Wisdom called me Satam al-Ifranj. Satam the Frank. We were all Franks to them. We hadn't made a good impression, and small wonder. Leaving aside that we'd stomped onto their lands with fire and sword, we were eons behind them in things like basic hygiene. They washed five times a day in preparation for their prayers. I was lucky if the mutton grease that ran down to my elbows at dinner took away some of the dirt from my hands.

What little I knew at that point about western "natural philosophy" was that it came from books. Really old books. Educated men could argue over them for days on end without ever looking out their own doors. In al-Islam there were advanced disciplines like astronomy and cartography and medicine based on making actual observations about the actual world. Imagine. By the time I left, I'd copied and translated enough maps and treatises that I lived comfortably in Paris for eight months just selling them a few at a time to the university.

It wasn't until Leeuwenhoek discovered sperm cells that I wondered if science might have something to say about my immortality. I started paying more attention, off and on. When you live as long as I do, pretty much everything is off and on. In the 1890s I helped arrange funding for Ehrlich's research into adaptive immunity. In the 1950s I got a lab tech position at Johns Hopkins, though they fired me six weeks later for unauthorized tinkering with some of Henrietta Lacks' immortal cervical cells. Which was kind of harsh, since that was why I'd gone there in the first place. These days I was getting interested in genetics. Late to the party, sure. Always behind the times, me. But I was determined to make up for it.

"So when do we take delivery of the equipment?"

"Patience, old son. Working out the kinks. Duties and tariffs and whatnot."

"Steer as close to legal as possible. But get it done."

"Another week. Two, tops."

"And the geneticist?"

"The paperwork is in. He'll be here before the packing crates are hauled off."

"See that he is." Eleven just stood there. "Something else?"

He gave a little *no big deal* sniff. "Project of my own I thought you might want in on." His nonchalance was a flashing amber light. "Lab-related, as it happens."

"Meaning you want to do it here?"

He rubbed his goatee. "Not necessarily *here* here ..."

I didn't have time for this. "Tell me what it is, and we'll see."

"It's shatter."

"What's shattered?"

"No, mate. Shatter. Crystallized weed oil. Wicked potent. Got a guy lined up."

I hadn't heard of shatter, but I knew a bit about weed oil. You made it with solvents like butane or benzene. If you got it wrong, it blew up.

"Not a chance. This lab is going to be legal. Or as legal as possible. And as unexploded as possible."

"We'd be careful." I knew that hurt look. It was part of the con.

"Be as careful as you like. Somewhere else."

The hurt look bloomed into the *oi, you didn't think I was serious, did you?* grin. "Right. But what if you just invested in the equipment? Silent partner, like."

"Get out of my lab."

The Composer

HAVE YOU EVER dated someone younger than you? So much younger that Pearl Jam was never new music to them? Substitute Wagner's operas for Pearl Jam and you've got my life. Richard Wagner's music was the newest of the new. The Artwork of the Future he called it, and he was pretty much right. Nearly a century after his death Stravinsky lamented the endurance of what he called its "rubbish and racket." You can still hear it in the over-the-top scores of most blockbuster movies.

I knew Wagner when he was a penniless public intellectual in Zurich, before mad King Ludwig cut him the bottomless cheque that let him set up his own opera town. Today the caring professions would probably call him a sex addict, or a narcissist, or both. He was those things and more. Magnetically egotistical. Remarkably thin-skinned. He was a philanderer, a betrayer, a visionary and a vile anti-Semite, and I loved him as I've never loved any other man.

Soldiering got me to Zurich. Music kept me there. Music and wool.

If you were young and fit and looking for work, the end of the eighteenth century was a good time to be a soldier in Europe. If you weren't fighting for the new French Republic you were probably fighting against her, and either way the pay was good and the opportunities for travel excellent.

I was fighting for her. I hadn't gotten the plum travel assignment, in Syria under General Bonaparte, although I'd lobbied hard for it. It would have been a good way to get back. Instead I was an *Adjutant-Chef* in a *demi-brigade* of light infantry in the Army of Helvetia. We were skirmishers. We skulked about trying to disrupt enemy formations before they could assemble, and created whatever other disarray we could.

I won't walk you through the battle of Zurich. Look it up online if you're interested. All you need to know is that we captured it from the Austrians and Russians before their reinforcements arrived from Italy. And that our Division was sent to chase down the fleeing Russian supply train on the road to a town called Winterthur.

The road was a confusion of burning carts, musket fire, and the cries of dying horses. A small group of riflemen protecting their comrades' retreat had stacked barrels from an upended freight wagon into an improvised wall with narrow gun slits. We looped behind them through the woods and took them easily. Some of the barrels had split open, revealing long canvas sacks. No wonder the Russians had been confident in the barrels' stopping power. The sacks were full of coins. "Notify the *Sous Lieutenant*," I said to one of my men. "We'll need more security." While we waited, we righted the cart and re-stacked the barrels.

I saw a flash of red in the forest to my right. Then another. Red collars. Russian infantrymen, escaping into the woods. A couple of my men saw them too. "Carry on with the barrels," I said. "I've got this." Chasing down stragglers had more appeal than wagon loading. It didn't take me long. They were slow and noisy, probably because they still had their knapsacks on. Which was strange. I would've discarded the excess weight. I caught up to them in a clearing and hung back out of sight. One was trying to cut his way through the brush with his sabre. "Halt," I called in perfect Russian. They turned, startled.

"Who are you?" The sabre wielder scanned the forest. "Are you one of us?"

"Put down your weapons."

The second man leaned his musket against the bushes. The first dropped his sabre and raised his musket. "Identify yourself." He peered down the gun sight toward where he'd heard my voice.

"I'm your captor. You are prisoners of the Republic of France."

His shot went horribly wide. Mine was better, but not perfect. I'd aimed for his heart; I'd shattered his hip. He screamed and dropped his weapon. The other man picked his musket up and lifted it toward my position. I leaned out long enough for him to see me, then leaned back. His fear worked to my advantage. He fired wildly. Not even close. All our muskets were now empty.

I stepped into the clearing. They were twenty paces away. The injured man's screams tapered to gasps as he slipped into shock. The other was trying to reload, but couldn't keep his hands steady. I held my musket to my left and drew my sabre.

"You don't have time." I walked toward him. "You're better off surrendering."

Powder spilled onto his trousers as he tapped it into the barrel. He got the ball and paper in, but needed to ram it into place. He fumbled to free the ramrod. Fifteen paces.

His panic was out of proportion. Capture went with the job. He'd either be ransomed back to Russia or held in decent conditions in France. Either way he was out of the fray. He glanced at his twitching comrade. He looked up at me. He took a breath and let go of the ramrod. Ten paces.

"Good choice. Now drop the musket."

He didn't. He leapt to his feet and ran at me, screaming, the bayonet on his musket levelled at my chest. I barely had time to react. I feinted left. As his bayonet swung to follow me I stepped back to the right, anchored my musket against my hip and lifted my own bayonet. It caught him below the jaw. I had a flashback to an Egyptian arrow on the plains of Qadesh. His scream stopped. He didn't even have time to look surprised. He dropped his musket and scrabbled at mine. The light left his eyes. My bayonet made a grinding sound as he dropped to his knees. I pulled it free. He flopped forward. His knapsack bounced heavily and slid down to his side. I wondered again why he hadn't left it. And why it was so heavy.

I opened it. My hands were shaking from the adrenaline high. Two canvas bags like the ones from the barrels on the cart. I cut one open. Coins cascaded into my lap. Pure silver Imperial Russian roubles, each weighing about two thirds of an ounce.

I checked the other man's knapsack. They had five bags between them.

I'd been a soldier of the Republic since just after the Revolution. I had plenty of time left before my look started to raise questions, but it'd been decades since my last retreat. I felt the weight of each one. And not just the weight of the years. Two men were dead at my hand for trying to better their lives. Countless others for resisting the Republic. I was tired. I cached the bags, marched triumphantly into the city with my men, and, after a sound night's sleep in a makeshift billet, submitted my resignation.

Zurich's banks accepted roubles without a blink. I bought a sheep pasture in the hills above a village called Adliswil, a few miles south of the city. It was forested on three sides. The fourth offered a view of the Zurichsee below and white-topped Alps in the far distance. It came with a three-room timber cottage and a flock of black-nosed sheep. I executed the documents as Torsten Staheli of Hamburg rather than *Adjutant-Chef* Etienne Chevrier (ret). Fresh start.

I hired a lad named Utz to tend the flock. He had a thick scar above his brow from a fall as a boy that had left him unable to speak. He was the third son of the local forester, a sharp-eyed villager named Gerhard, who negotiated the terms of his boy's employment shrewdly. Knowing Gerhard was watching the forests around my land gave me the security I needed for a retreat.

In the hillside behind the cottage was a brick-lined cellar for cheeses and root vegetables. I hollowed a space behind one of the bricks for my roubles and put an iron hasp and padlock on the thick wooden door. "No one in Hamburg would leave their food unsecured," I told Gerhard when he expressed his surprise.

Then I rested.

For eight years I sat by the fire, ate simple meals delivered from the village, and took solitary walks through the hills. I slept twelve to fifteen hours a day. I contracted out the milking, shearing, butchering and sales, which didn't leave much of a profit, but my land was paid for and my needs were few. I made a little money every year.

Eight years.

I didn't follow local politics, didn't read newspapers, didn't listen to village gossip. Gradually my overstuffed mind cleansed itself, editing or jettisoning the more troubling memories and packing the rest away. It was a long process. It always is.

Eight years.

The first sign that I was ready to re-engage was the desire to visit a bookshop. I'd seen a small one just off the main street in Adliswil, but I'd never gone in. One overcast morning in 1808 I did. I felt like catching up. The bookseller didn't have any books on current events. "I *do* have complete sets of the *Zürcher Zeitung*, though, bound by year of publication."

"How far back do they go?"

"Five years."

"I'll take a complete set. Plus everything you've got for this year."

I paid a couple of village boys to carry them to my cottage. By the time they did, the sky had cleared and the view down my pasture to the Zurichzee was particularly fine, so I stacked them in the sun on the bench by my door. A yearling lamb wandered over and nibbled the rough grass at the base of the bench. I scratched it gently behind the ears as I opened a volume at random. I froze.

"*Emperor* Napoleon?!"

The startled lamb scampered away down the hill.

I had some catching up to do.

One thing I wanted to catch up on was music. There hadn't been much in the army, and none during my retreat. All that was on offer in the towns around Zurich was church music. So I joined a congregation. A severe Protestant congregation. I got bored with their repertoire within weeks. I asked what else they had.

"We sing for devotion, Herr Staheli, not entertainment." Some things never change.

I thought about switching to the Catholics for their more varied playlist, but by then I was established in the Protestant camp. In small-town Switzerland it would have been easier to recharacterize myself as a woman than as a Catholic. I'd almost given up when I heard about a festival at the Grossmunster cathedral in Zurich.

I hired a cart into the city and went to the opening concert. It was the first time I'd heard an orchestra and choir in ages. They were awful. OK, that's a bit harsh. Some of the string players were professionals, though it was hard to tell through the cat-screech of those who weren't. The choir was raggedly under-rehearsed, and every so often one of the French horns made a sound like an armpit fart.

I loved every note. When it was over, I introduced myself to the conductor and told him I was a bit of a singer. He stroked his chin with his fingertips. "Are you singing anywhere now?" And so I joined Zurich's music scene.

I dumped the congregation in Adliswil like toxic waste.

I bought a second pasture and planted mulberry trees for silkworms. By 1820 I had two dozen local cottagers spinning wool and a dozen more processing silk and raw cotton from America. I rented a storehouse on the Adliswil waterfront and another off the Seefeld Quai in Zurich, where I sold yarn to weavers in Zurich and Winterthur and as far down the lake as Rapperswil. I bought a two-horse carriage and hired a part-time driver.

Singing in Zurich brought me into contact with the conductor of the *Allgemeine Musikgesellschaft Zurich* orchestra, an easygoing Belgian named Blumenthal. AMG produced, among other things, concert performances of popular operas. Blumenthal put me in the chorus, and sometimes gave me a solo. We got along great, though his performance standards were crap. One afternoon at the end of a rehearsal of *Die Zauberflote* I mentioned that the principal oboist sounded like a goose passing a gallstone. "Oh, I know," he said. "But he *tries* so hard." Zurich's concertgoers didn't seem to mind.

I started losing yarn sales to companies using mechanized spinning machines, so I bought four of them. By the end of the decade I was

running ten. "It's displacing your cottage workers," Gerhard the forester said. "They need the income from spinning, but they can't leave
their kids to work in your factory."

"What do you suggest?"

"Buy them looms. Let them pay them off in instalments. Market
your own cloth."

Six months later I bought a high end piano from Pleyel and Company in Paris.

One evening the following year I was late for a business meeting because
a work crew was blocking the city gate. Apparently the city wall was
coming down. "Progress," Blumenthal said. Progress led to development.
A handsome block of flats went up where the east wall had been, on a
new street off the Ramistrasse. "Nice location," I said as I strolled with
Blumenthal along the Hohe Promenade, discussing his proposed production of Rossini's *Moses in Egypt*. "I could use a *pied a terre* in Zurich."

"The Escher family owns the whole block. Rental units. I'll introduce you."

Another sign of progress was the redevelopment of an old monastery
church into a proper theatre, to be called the Aktientheater. "Could
you have imagined it ten years ago?" Blumenthal and I were watching
the interior walls going up in the nave. He'd been tapped to be the new
theatre's music director. Its inaugural concert opened with an overture
he wrote for the occasion, and ended with a staged performance of *Die
Zauberflote,* which I again sang in. Blumenthal took six curtain calls.
"You should meet the theatre's new director, Frau Birch-Pfeiffer," he
said to me later over drinks. "Come. I'll introduce you."

By the 1840s I knew I was going to have to jettison aging Herr Staheli
and start again. But I didn't want to. I'd built a satisfying life. I wanted
to keep it. Music stepped in, in an unexpected way.

A hundred years earlier, when *castrati* had been the musical rage,
I'd developed a convincing enough upper register to get part-time work
in the London opera houses. I decided to redevelop it. When Utz was

out of earshot across the pasture, I'd sit at my piano and do the exercises I'd done back in the day. I was far enough off the usual trekking paths to be overconfident about my privacy. One crisp Tuesday morning, though, as I was working through a contralto aria from *Giulio Cesare* there was a knock at my door. I stopped. Maybe they hadn't heard me. If I sat quietly, maybe they'd go away. Then there was another knock. More insistent.

I was going to have to answer. But how would I explain a contralto voice coming from the cottage of an aging bachelor? I adjusted my collar, checked my hairline for stubble—none, thankfully—and opened the door a hand's breadth. It was Frau Birch-Pfeiffer, wearing a sturdy hiking dress and carrying a thick walking staff. Trekking.

"*Gruss Gott*, Herr Staheli. Sorry to disturb you. But that *voice*."

"Voice?"

"From your house just now. A beautiful contralto."

I improvised wildly. "My daughter Constanze." But if I had a daughter, why wouldn't anyone have seen her? "Recently arrived from ... Luzern." I hoped Frau Birch-Pfeiffer didn't know anyone in Luzern.

"Studying voice there?"

"Ah ... yes. With a tutor. No one you'd know. Very obscure. Friend of a friend sort of thing."

"Is she studying with anyone here?"

Good question. "Just me."

"Oh no, Herr Staheli. A voice like that needs proper training." She pushed lightly against the door. "If I could speak with her?"

"I'm sorry, but Constanze is ... not presentable just now."

She looked down at her hiking costume. "Less presentable than this?"

Why wouldn't she just go away? "Even so, I must insist." I tried to close the door, but her walking staff was in the way.

"Then I too must insist." She was strangely determined. "Your daughter has a remarkable voice. I can offer her opportunities. Opportunities that may not come again. Shouldn't she have the chance to consider them herself?"

There was only one way out: play the baffled father in need of guidance. "You're right, of course. Perhaps I'm too protective. She's just so young, and my only daughter. What do you suggest?"

"Bring her to Herr Abt." A *kapellmeister* from Bernberg she'd installed as the theatre's choral conductor. "He can assess her voice. Then we can discuss her training." Training by Abt, no doubt. The good Frau's persistence was beginning to make sense. The more supplemental income she could drum up for her new choirmaster, the more likely he'd stay.

"I'll do that. Thanks." I pushed the door again, but her stick was still there.

"When?"

"Next week." I pushed. Stick.

"When next week?"

She wouldn't leave until we'd fixed a specific appointment. So we did. I made it as late in the week as I could. I'd need to get some clothing and a wig.

Frau Birch-Pfeiffer had said to meet Abt in the rehearsal room below the stage. I knew it from singing in Blumenthal's operas. At the bottom of the stairs I heard a piano from across the hall, and wondered if Abt had changed the room. I peered in. The studio was a windowless room with bare stone walls. At an upright piano a man with wire spectacles and a tidy moustache was sight-reading something hymn-like from a handwritten manuscript. A stocky young man with a beard sat next to him.

"Much improved, Herr Baumgartner. The inner voices have more interest now. If I might make one suggestion here ..." The spectacled man marked something on the top system of the second page. My skirts shifted, and the bearded man noticed me. Oh, how he noticed me. A half-distracted glance was followed by a neck-jolting stare. Then he caught himself and lowered his eyes, flushing. I knew I'd gotten the wig and make up right, but maybe I'd overstuffed the bodice. I was a little out of practice.

The pianist looked toward me with a puzzled expression.

"Herr Abt?" I asked.

"Müller. Abt is in the rehearsal room." He pointed with his pencil.

"My apologies, Herr Müller." I nodded. "Herr Baumgartner."

As I swept my skirts out of the studio doorway I smiled at how the bearded man brightened when I used his name. What the hell. If I was going to be Constanze, I might as well have fun with her.

I rapped on the door to the rehearsal room.

"Come."

This room was much larger, but still windowless. It smelled of old stone. Stacks of wooden chairs lined the walls. The piano matched the one in Müller's studio. Herr Abt was a clean-shaven man with thinning hair and thickening jowls. He stood politely and gave me a dignified bow. "Fraulein Staheli, yes?"

"*Gruss Gott*, Herr Abt."

"Will you sit?" He indicated a chair next to the piano. I did. "Frau Birch-Pfeiffer thinks you might be a good addition to our chorus. Have you done choral singing?"

"Some. School. Church choirs."

"You can read music?"

"Of course."

"Three sharps. Which key?"

"A major. Or less commonly F sharp minor."

"Not so uncommon anymore. Range?"

"Contralto."

"Yes, yes, but what *range*?"

I hesitated. My actual range would've surprised him. I gave him the range of a reasonably skilled amateur.

He nodded. "Let's have a look." He ran through a brisk G major arpeggio. "Let's start with the G above middle C." And for the next quarter-hour he ran me through a series of increasingly acrobatic vocal exercises. They would have been a challenge even if I'd been an actual contralto. Which I wasn't. But Abt seemed satisfied. "All right. Now let's try some sight reading."

Constanze was the opportunity I'd needed, however accidentally she'd presented herself. I made the rounds as Torsten to explain to my workers, customers and suppliers that I was returning to Hamburg to take over a shipping concern my family had an interest in, and that my daughter would take over in Zurich. Then I made those same rounds as Constanze, with notarized letters from Torsten where necessary. I was shocked at how different things suddenly were. Suppliers and customers I'd dealt with for decades tried to take advantage. I didn't quite know how to deal with it. I sought out Frau Birch-Pfeiffer.

"Be firm with them," she said over tea and cakes in her office. "Firmer than they expect from a man." I nodded demurely and made notes in a tiny notebook.

While I took business lessons from Frau Birch-Pfeiffer I took voice lessons from her choirmaster. I also sang in his choir, which, because it was the house choir, meant singing in Blumenthal's operas. Which made me a little anxious. He'd been touchingly saddened by Torsten's decision to leave. He'd toasted him with champagne at a farewell dinner in the dining room of the Hotel Baur au Lac, and was now dealing with his departure by harmlessly flirting with his daughter. "You look *so* much like him," he'd say, his hand on my shoulder. "And your voices. Where they overlap I can barely tell them apart."

One day Frau Birch-Pfeiffer came over, looking concerned. "Is Herr Blumenthal bothering you?" Her tone said she'd do something about it if he were.

"Thank you, no." There was a catch in my throat. "He just misses my father."

Things carried on changing, as they do. Frau Birch-Pfeiffer took a posting at the Court Theatre in Berlin. We corresponded a bit, as you do. After a while we stopped. As you do. Blumenthal retired from the AMG Orchestra, and Abt took it over. He continued teaching voice, and I continued going. If Müller the composition teacher looked up when I passed his studio, I'd nod hello, and if bearded Herr Baumgartner was there I'd give him a playful smile. Soon we were on modest speaking terms.

Abt often ran behind, so I'd wait in the green room next door. One afternoon a pretty young woman was in there ahead of me. She rose as I entered. "I'm sorry. I didn't know this room was in use."

"Not at all. This is just where I wait until Herr Abt is ready for my voice lesson."

She laughed. It was like coins tinkling into a fountain. "How splendid. This is where *I* wait until Herr Müller is ready for my composition lesson." She extended her hand eagerly. "Fraulein Hunerwadel."

I took her hand. "Fraulein Staheli. Pleased to meet you."

"Since we're waiting together, shall I get us some water?" She went to a baroque sideboard with a pitcher and a tray of tumblers. I watched the way she moved, noting for my repertoire of gestures her lift of the wrist and turn of the ankle.

"You seem quite at home here, Miss Hunerwadel." I smoothed my skirts and lowered myself into a wingback chair.

She returned with two glasses. "Please, call me Fanny." She set the glasses on a low table. "I'm new to Zurich, and there's no one here who I can use the familiar form of address with. I think I'd like to start with you, Miss Staheli. Once I learn *your* given name." There was a childlike gleam in her eye.

"That would please me Fanny. Do call me Constanze."

"Excellent. Most people I've met here through musical circles are men, and any women I've met have been too old for me to address familiarly. Until now." There was that gleam again. "And yes, I've grown quite familiar with this room. Herr Müller says the performers gather here before and after performances, but for me it's just where I wait for my chaperone after my lessons."

"And your lessons are in composition?"

"Yes."

"Aren't composers ordinarily men?"

Fanny affected a little pout. "Oh pooh. You sound like my chaperone. She thinks I should be happy to play pretty waltzes on the pianoforte and sing stern hymns on Sundays." She mimed thumping on a keyboard, her arms extended stiffly, her fingers curled into claws. "Hymns by men, and waltzes by men, and me the delicate girl following their directions." She dropped her hands to her lap and smiled brightly. "Thankfully, Father doesn't see it that way. When I say: 'But Father, why shouldn't men follow *my* directions?', he smiles and says: 'Indeed, my biscuit, why shouldn't they?' And *that* is why I'm here, studying with the pre-eminent composer in Zurich." She sat back in her chair looking entirely satisfied.

"Is Herr Müller that distinguished?"

"Oh, yes. He's at the centre of musical life in our Zurich."

"'Our Zurich'? I thought you said you were new here."

She stuck out her tongue. "Only from Lenzburg. It's barely a day's carriage ride."

I never saw Fanny in a sexual way. Not that she wasn't attractive. She was, and soon had ranks of suitors to confirm it. Being Constanze may have been part of it. But even leaving that aside, my feelings for Fanny were always more companionable than romantic.

She was a skilled pianist and singer, and although she wasn't performing publically, she did find ways of putting her music out there. One afternoon in the green room she told me she and her chaperone had just come back from a public mental asylum near Jakobsberg, where she'd gone to play for the inmates. I was aghast.

"Oh, please." She flapped her gloves at me. "It's quite safe. They're perfectly decent people. And it's helpful, I think." She leaned toward me, elbows on knees, always a sign she was about to be serious about something. "I believe music has a power for good beyond the diddlings of the salons. I intend to find it."

Before long she was following through. Her first public performances were fund-raisers for respectable social causes. I always attended, and always contributed.

"I didn't know you ran such a business empire," she said with amusement after my first contribution. "Who would've guessed, considering how puzzled you were at the idea of a woman composer?"

In 1848 a flurry of failed uprisings across Europe sent a mixed bag of agitators and intellectuals running for their freedom. Quite a few pitched up in Zurich, thanks to its generous law of asylum. They caused quite the stir. The musical community was particularly excited, because one of the refugees was a court conductor from Dresden who'd bitten the noble hands that fed him. "Have you heard Herr Müller has a houseguest?" Fanny asked when I next saw her in the green room.

"Elderly uncle come to visit?"

She slapped my shoulder with her manuscript folder. "You are *too* rude. It would serve you right if I didn't share my news."

"And how likely is that?"

She frowned prettily for a moment, then gave me her usual radiant smile. "Fine. I'll tell you." She paused for effect. "It's Herr Wagner."

Poker face. "Who's he?"

"But you must've heard of Herr Richard Wagner? He was *Kapell-meister* at the Dresden Court Opera. His operas have been produced in Munich. And now he's here." I half expected her to clap her hands.

"What post has he taken here, then? Must be a good one to tempt him from Dresden." *Kapellmeister* was a prestigious job, and a comfortable living.

"None that I know of."

"Then what brings him here?"

"An arrest warrant from the King of Saxony," Abt said from the doorway. "Which I expect you already knew, Fraulein Staheli." I smiled.

Fanny's eyes widened. "You scamp. I shall never forgive you."

By fall Wagner's wife had joined him, and they'd taken a flat in my building, the Escherhauser. Abt tweaked one of the winter chamber concerts to include some of his works, which may have been commercial shrewdness as much as generosity, since a lot of people probably came out of curiosity about the Great Man rather than interest in new music. I wasn't keen on the stuff myself, but I had to go because Fanny had been asked to sing. I took an aisle seat—so I could leave once she was done—and scanned the programme. To my dismay, she was at the end of the first half. She and an amateur bass-baritone were singing a duet from some opera about a Dutchman.

Abt escorted the Wagner party to their seats once the rest of the audience was settled. Murmurs rippled through the hall. He looked unremarkable to me. None too tall. Prominent forehead over a dark brow. He might have been one of the bankers or merchants who'd been dragged by their wives to see him, apart for his style of dress, with his hair over his ears and his emerald cravat matching the lapels of his jacket. His wife was a frosty-looking woman in last season's silks.

Four of the orchestra's strings played a quartet by Haydn, and then, with the orchestra's principal clarinettist, quintets by Mozart and Weber. Duo pianists from Winterthur bashed their way through four-hand arrangements of some of Wagner's opera overtures, which I found overblown, and the baritone sang a set of Abt's songs. Finally Fanny joined him for the duet. Her voice was lovely, though a bit young for the dreadful piece: an overwrought love duet between a gloomy sailor and his would-be beloved. I tuned out the text and focused on Fanny's voice. I slipped out during the applause.

I didn't pay much attention to Herr Wagner after that, despite Fanny's continued enthusiasm. Then, indirectly, he imposed himself. "Have you read this appalling essay that's making the rounds?" Abt asked one day at the beginning of our lesson. He opened a copy of *Neue Zeitschrift fur Musik* at an article called *Judaism in Music*.

"Is it a history of some kind?"

"A slander of some kind. Thank God Herr Mendelssohn didn't live to read such a foul thing."

I looked at the name of the author. "Herr Freethought?"

Abt snatched the journal back as if it were infectious. "No reputable writer would publish such a thing under his own name. I'm sorry I brought it up." He stuffed it under a pile of scores. "Let's start with some arpeggios." Afterward I went to Schulthess's bookshop for a copy of the *Zeitschrift*. Abt had been generous to call it appalling. Its lumpen stereotyping sent a chill through my ancient circumcision scar. I burned the journal in the grate when I was done.

Within days the buzz in Zurich was that Herr Freethought was Herr Wagner.

Over the next couple of years Wagner conducted some AMG Orchestra concerts which I didn't attend, and published some less controversial essays which I didn't read.

Fanny gave recitals in London and Paris. Zurich felt smaller when she was away.

In December of 1851 the French Republic lost its status as Europe's revolutionary consolation prize when Napoleon's nephew seized power *en route* to proclaiming the Second Empire. Or so the papers said. The coup drove Zurich's pundits into a tizzy. Or so the papers said. I just kept making yarn and cloth and music.

In the new year Fanny sent a note asking to see me on a matter of great urgency. I met her at her uncle's home, and we went for a stroll around the park near the Stadthaus Platz, our arms linked under our cloaks against the chill January air.

"So what's the urgency?"

"It's about Herr Wagner."

"What about him?"

"He's returning to the AMG to conduct a series of concerts."

"I hear he could use the money."

Fanny slapped my arm with a gloved hand. "Don't be impertinent, Constanze." She only used my full given name when pretending to be annoyed. "It's a great coup for the AMG. And for Zurich. Herr Wagner was *Kapellmeister* of the Dresden Court Opera, as you well know." Fanny could be such a fangirl.

"Yes, but we aren't actually *in* Dresden, are we? In Zurich he's a barely recognized essayist."

"You are *quite* impossible." She actually stomped her foot. "He has conducted several subscription concerts here, to great acclaim."

"Modest acclaim. And I haven't been to one."

The mischief returned to her eyes. "I'm going to change that." Her uncle had bought a block of seats for Wagner's next concert: a program of Beethoven.

"Isn't Beethoven kind of … adventurous?" I'd barely resisted saying "noisy."

Fanny gave me that dismissive look only the self-important young can pull off. "He's been dead almost a quarter of a century. He's hardly *avant garde.*"

So I went to hear Wagner conduct Beethoven.

At that point Fanny still got wound up about Zurich society. She was scanning the crowd for local notables while we were still taking our seats. "Stanzi, look. That's Herr Wesendonck and his wife." She pointed her fan at a bearded man in an evening jacket and a much younger woman showing a little more shoulder than you usually saw in Zurich.

"Who?"

"You're so provincial. Herr Otto Wesendonck and his wife Mathilde. He's *fabulously* wealthy. Uncle Johann knows him through work, don't you, Uncle?" Uncle Johann grunted noncommittally. "They're new here, and are expected to be *great* patrons of the arts. She's quite beautiful, don't you agree?"

She was pretty enough in a trophy-wifey way, but so were the wives of a lot of the bankers and industrialists in attendance. "I suppose so."

The program included an overture for a play called *Egmont* and the seventh of Beethoven's symphonies. The overture lost me immediately with its joyless opening, and although the symphony had some diverting dance-like bits, I found its harmonies baffling. Plus it was noisy.

The conductor left me colder than the music. He spent the concert tossing his hair, dipping, whirling and writhing, like the display of his emotions was more important than the music. No wonder he was better known for his essays.

After several curtain calls—with Wagner indulging in deep, dramatic bows—we made our way to the lobby. Somehow he was already there, basking in bourgeois adulation. As we inched to the exit I saw Herr Wesendonck and his wife step through the crowd to meet him. My last glimpse was of Herr Wagner touching his lips to the good Frau's gloved knuckles.

Herr Wesendonck turned out to be the European presence of his family's large New York textile importing company. I made textiles. So I set out to meet him. It wasn't hard. A passing comment to a colleague sent out the necessary ripples, and soon Wesendonck and I were meeting over a lunch of soft omelettes at the Hotel Baur au Lac. I trotted out samples of my cottons and silks during the *digestifs*. He ran an expert thumb over each, tugging it to check the tightness of the weave, angling it to check the consistency of the dye. Finally he set aside one cotton and one silk. "This and this. How much of each do you produce?"

After a bit more discussion, he agreed to take half of the cotton and all of the silk. He got them for a song. He could squeeze a *franc* tighter than anyone I ever dealt with. But I considered it a loss leader.

Later that season the AMG included Fanny in one of its subscription concerts, where she stole the show with her performance of a piano showpiece by Hummel called *Rondo Brillante*. By the time I arrived at the reception in the green room she was surrounded by young men, including Herr Baumgartner, the composition student, and Theodor Kirchner, a Winterthur organist who often performed in Zurich. Baumgartner's eyes lit up when he saw me. He strode briskly over to greet me, taking my hand lightly by the fingers. "I was glad to see you at the performance. You were impressed, yes?"

I drew my hand back and undid the bow that held my hat. "Indeed, Herr Baumgartner. Fanny was especially good, I'm sure you'll agree." My familiar way of referring to her seemed to unsettle him. They were probably on more formal terms.

"Herr Baumgartner." A man with a shovel-pointed beard was waving from a counter where a tidy man in wire spectacles was drizzling water into glasses of absinthe through a sugar cube. Baumgartner introduced me. The bearded man was Herr Sulzer, a local politician, and the absinthe-drizzler was Herr Spyri, editor of the *Eidgenossische Zeitung*. Each dutifully kissed my gloved knuckles.

"We were wondering about Herr Wagner's absence," Sulzer said. "Herr Spyri thinks he's still mourning *liberté*'s recent death in Paris." He gave the editor an amused look. "You and Wagner are close, Wilhelm. Any insights?"

Spyri interjected before Baumgartner could respond. "I only raised the possibility." He handed Baumgartner a small glass. "After all, since the collapse of liberalism everywhere *else* in Europe, poor Richard has been clinging to the Republic like a raft." Sulzer, the politician, looked slighted. Spyri raised a mollifying hand. "My apologies, Jakob. I meant everywhere else of consequence. Absinthe, Fraulein?"

I took the proffered glass and sipped it delicately.

Sulzer frowned. "Well, who could blame him, when that business in Dresden cost him his post and forced him into exile? Say what you like about his idealism, he took it to the street when called upon."

"That rather depends who he's telling the story to," Spyri said. "My point is, now that Louis Napoleon's coup has sunk Richard's raft, he could be forgiven for ... well, floundering, I suppose. If that doesn't stretch the metaphor too far."

"I think I just heard it snap from the strain." Sulzer downed his glass.

Baumgartner leaned toward me. "They're referring to last December's *coup d'etat* in Paris."

"Thank you, Herr Baumgartner. I know who Louis Napoleon is. I do read Herr Spyri's excellent newspaper." Spyri bowed. Baumgartner flushed. I took another sip of absinthe.

"What I don't understand," Sulzer said, "is why Wagner would take the failure of liberalism in Paris so earnestly when it's thriving here in Zurich, where he lives."

Spyri laughed. "Because it's *Paris*, dear Jakob. The capital city of the civilized world. And more to the point, the capital city of the *operatic* world. After all, if the aristocrats triumph in Paris, what hope can there be anywhere for poor Richard's revolution of the artists?" His tone was ironic and affectionate in equal measure. It seemed Wagner inspired loyalty even in those who recognized his foibles.

I finished my absinthe, thanked Spyri for it, and, on the pretext of spotting a business acquaintance, disengaged from the conversation. Baumgartner gazed at me wistfully as I turned to go.

Eventually Fanny made her way to where I'd found a seat and flopped breathlessly into the next chair. "What an evening!"

"You were spellbinding. *Brillante*, even."

She waved a dismissive hand. "That's the fourth or fifth time I've heard that one. I've been enduring compliments for hours now, each flatterer trying to outdo the last. Please don't add to them." But she was smiling all the same.

"Oh, poor, dear Fanny. Surrounded by adoring young men. How can you bear it?" I raised a coy eyebrow. "Tell me, is there anyone whose adoration you value more than the rest?"

She smacked my knee with her gloves. "You sound like my aunt. She has Uncle Johann bringing young bankers to the house by the cartload. She's determined to place me in the perfect bourgeois household, where I can play charming tunes for my apple-cheeked children." She shuddered. "But how can I imagine that on a night like this?" She gestured expansively toward the room. "*These* are my apple-cheeked children." She leaned back toward me. "Plus the young men in Zurich are a bit coarse, don't you think?" She nodded at a cluster of amateur pianists. "Even the artistic ones. You can see it in their eyes. They praise me, but they really want to domesticate me." She placed a hand on my knee. "Oh Stanzi, if only *you* were a man. Then everything would be solved."

My head exploded.

My business relationship with Otto Wesendonck developed nicely. I took a lease on a larger factory in Adliswil and brought in two more spinning machines.

Later that year I was on my way to my voice lesson when Fanny ran up to me in the square outside the theatre, flushed with excitement. "Stanzi, have you heard?"

"What?"

I was early, so we sat on the edge of the fountain. "Do you remember that duet I sang in, from Herr Wagner's opera *Der fliegende Hollander*?"

I remembered it was from an opera of his. "Of course. It was a triumph for you."

"Please. I was too young. But that isn't my point. Do you remember the opera it was from?"

I was in no position to fake it. "Not clearly."

"Well, here's the news. Herr Wagner is going to conduct the whole opera! Can you believe it? Here in stolid Zurich, where even a Mozart opera is considered daring!"

Zurich's stolidness was one of the things I liked about it. I didn't have to keep *adapting* to Zurich. But Fanny was so excited. "How wonderful for Zurich," I said, with all the feigned interest I could muster.

Fanny was staring at me. Apparently there was more. "What?"

"I've gotten us places in the chorus!"

Oh dear.

"Oh, Fanny, thank you. You must do it, of course. But you know I struggle with modern music."

"Oh pooh!" She swatted my shoulder. "You have to do it too. I won't hear otherwise. It's a terribly romantic story. The hero, if you can call him that, is an immortal sailor doomed to travel the seas for eternity, without—"

"Wait, what now?"

I may not have used exactly those words.

Twisted versions of my story had been around for centuries. I should just stop telling it to people. For some reason, though, suddenly they were popping up all over the place. German plays. An English operetta. A lurid French novel. Some irritatingly beautiful woodcuts by Gustav Doré that made me look like a balding Dumbledore.

Then there was the Dutchman. It was a prime example of Richard's redemption-through-love schtick, which generally meant a woman sacrificing herself to redeem a man. There's an insight into him right there.

"It's so romantic," Fanny said. "He can't die. He and his crew sail a ghost ship that only lands every seven years."

"So the opera just repeats over and over?"

She ignored me. "There's a girl in a Norwegian port who's obsessed with him. She keeps his picture on the wall of the room where she and the other girls spin wool."

"She's obsessed with a man hundreds of years older than she is?"

"He doesn't *age*, so it doesn't matter, does it? Now will you let me tell you the story?"

Doesn't it? But I waved at her to go on.

"The girl's father, a ship's captain, meets the Dutchman when their ships take shelter in the same bay after a storm. The Dutchman offers him *massive* amounts of treasure for a night's refuge, which the father of course agrees to. Then the Dutchman asks if he has a daughter."

"He offers the sailor money for his daughter? That doesn't sound respectable. I think there's even a profession built on deals like that."

"Is this how you let me tell the story?" Her voice was sharp, but her eyes were twinkling. "It isn't like that. The father just wants his daughter well provided for, like any father. Besides, the girl, Senta, is in love with the Dutchman."

"Who she's never met."

"She knows his face from his picture, and she's heard his story. He can only be redeemed by a woman who loves him unto death. She wants to be that woman."

If only it were that simple.

"That's deranged. Aren't there boys her own age in this village?"

"She has a suitor, of course, for the drama of the thing. A young hunter named Erik." She shook her head. "But Erik isn't right for her."

"Because he's a decent local boy and not a doomed immortal?"

Fanny sighed at my hopeless rationality. "No, silly. Because it isn't Erik's *story*."

Apparently the story ended with the Dutchman sailing off thinking Senta had chosen Erik, and Senta flinging herself into the sea to prove her love. "Then the sea swallows the Dutchman's ship, and he and Senta rise to the sky in a tender embrace."

"It sounds like grandiose nonsense."

Fanny smiled indulgently. "No. It sounds romantic." My silly, darling girl.

But she did persuade me to join the chorus.

Rehearsals were in the Aktientheater. For the first one, Wagner gathered everyone, including the set-builders and stage crew, into the first few rows of seats. He and his assistants, Herr Baumgartner among them, sat on the stage. Wagner's wife Minna was in the wings, discreetly keeping watch. He stood and walked grandly to the front of the stage. "There's something you need to understand before we start." His surprisingly rich voice filled the space. "This artwork isn't an opera the way the *French* use the term." The French might've been a species of crop-destroying rodent. "It isn't a display-case for aristocrats to inspect the latest ingenues. It doesn't have pretty *prima donna* showpieces for industrialists' wives to hum on the way back to their carriages. Distractions like that can be left to the Jew Meyerbeer and his collaborators in Paris."

Minna Wagner frowned. Apparently she didn't share her husband's racial views.

Wagner straightened his back. "This is German grand opera. A very different creature. It's meant to ennoble, not just to amuse. To remind us who we are." He thumped his chest with his fist. "*Our* culture." Thump. "*Our Volk.*"

Oh dear. Another grand theory of art.

I raised an eyebrow at Fanny, but she was riveted. I glanced around. Apart from the dozing old and the fidgeting young, everyone was listening raptly. The inferiority complex of the small city. Was there ever a more powerful tool in the hands of a charismatic charlatan? Alas, poor Zurich.

The Great Man went on for quite a while. His goal, he said, was to evoke the defining myths of the Germans the way ancient Athenian theatre had for the Greeks. His work was a comprehensive art, bringing the individual arts together as partners to provide hearty German fare for hardy German souls ...

I started counting the folds in the curtains.

Every time I thought he was wrapping up, he caught his breath and continued. "With this production Zurich looks to the future. A future where art doesn't just serve the money-men, living off their crumbs. Where it is *revolutionary*. Where it, not commerce, is the dominant force, as it was in Athens." His tone made it clear who the artist-king of this new society would be. Some of the crowd stirred. Talk of revolution against commerce was probably a little unsettling to the bankers' sons in the crowd whose fathers indulgently subsidized their horn playing. "Uncle Johann would *explode* if he heard talk like that," Fanny whispered. But her shining eyes never left Herr Wagner.

He went on a little longer in the same vein. "Right," he said once he was done. "Let's start. Boom, take the ladies to the rehearsal room and walk them through the Spinning Chorus." Baumgartner nodded, and gestured toward the door to the basement stairs. "Sopranos and altos, this way."

A couple of days later I ducked out of my office to see how the orchestral rehearsals were going. The orchestra was too big for the rehearsal room, so Wagner had assembled them on the stage, facing the empty seats. Because time was tight, the set painters were working too, sketching thunderheads on a semi-transparent canvas across the back of the stage. I took a seat near the front.

The orchestra was working on the scene where Senta tells her friends the Dutchman legend, with its rumbling tympani and storm-like swells in the strings. I knew it because it dovetailed with the Spinning Chorus that Baumgartner had gone through with us. The strings had just entered at the end of a chorale-like passage in the winds when Wagner waved his arms for silence. "Don't just noodle like a church accompanist. Be part of the *drama*." He flipped the pages of his score. "Back to the beginning."

I didn't see his concern. The playing was fine for a mainly amateur orchestra in the early days of rehearsal. In fact they seemed to be reining in excesses in the score that could otherwise have been a little vulgar. But soon he stopped them again.

"Close your scores. Put down your instruments." There was a baffled pause, then thumping and scraping as fiddles clunked into cases and horns clattered onto stands. Wagner waited, arms crossed, until there was silence. "When we started this project I talked about Greek drama. Do you remember?" Some silent nods. "And I assume from Zurich's revered education system that some of you know what Greek drama was?" Nods again. "Fine. Do any of you know what the *chorus* in Greek drama was for?"

The musicians looked around, waiting for someone else to respond. Eventually a third-desk cellist murmured something.

"I'm sorry, what?" Wagner cupped his hand behind his ear.

"It comments on the action." I imagined the cellist visualizing a long-ago notebook page in his schoolboy cursive.

"That's part of it. Anyone else?"

A flautist raised a hand. "It tells us about the characters?"

"Yes! It tells us about the characters. Things too subtle for dialogue. Things they may not even know themselves. And why am I asking you this?"

But he'd stumped them again. There was just fidgety, painful silence.

So I spoke. "Because *they* are the Greek chorus."

Wagner cocked his head. He couldn't tell where the voice had come from. He looked around, saw me, and stabbed a finger in my direction. "Yes. Thank you." He squinted in the dim light, trying to place me. "The women's chorus, yes?" I nodded.

He turned back to the orchestra. "There, you see? A minor singer knows your role better than you do. Because yes, you have a *role*. You're the tempest on the sea and the tempest in the Dutchman's soul. You're his longing. His redemption through Senta's love. Dialogue on its own can't show us these things. Neither can the faces of the actors, or the brushes of the scene painters—" he gestured toward the scaffold at the back "—or the stitches of the costumers. Only you can do that. So with that in mind, pick up your instruments and let's start again." As they reorganized themselves he turned back toward me. "Thank you for your help, Fraulein ...?"

I smiled demurely. "Just a minor singer." I rose, gathered my skirts and stepped lightly out of the theatre, humming as I went. Only when I emerged into the daylight did I realize I was humming the Spinning Chorus.

The Aktientheater became my refuge from the tedious aspects of the cloth business, which was why at the end of the week, after a meeting with Wesendonck about a rise in the price of indigo dye, I stopped by.

I was amazed at the progress on the set. The canvas sheet across the back now raged with dark thunderclouds. A high cliff, bright white plaster still wet on a wooden framework, filled almost a third of the stage to the right. Wagner was standing at its base, scowling at a wooden cylinder on a waist-high frame: two eighteen-inch disks connected by horizontal slats draped with a canvas panel. The wood smelled freshly cut. A sturdy crank stuck out from one end.

"Paddlewheel for a very small boat?"

Wagner looked up, startled. Then he smiled.

"Fraulein Staheli." His eyes met mine and held them. "I had to ask Baumgartner your name, since you wouldn't oblige me." His gaze was intense. Experiencing it this directly was very different from seeing it from a distance. It took effort not to look away.

"You were giving the orchestra a lesson. My name wasn't pertinent. Did they learn anything?"

"Their energy improved a bit. Time will tell."

In all my time in Zurich I'd never felt so seen. I looked down at the wooden structure. "I assume from your scowl there's some defect in this ... whatever this is?" When I looked back up the gaze was still there, but amused. I felt a tingle in my nethers.

"No, no." He shook his head. "The device is exactly right. The problem is that due to our tight orchestral budget I don't have anyone to operate it."

"Orchestral budget? This is an instrument of some kind?"

"My apologies. How would you know?" He took the crank with both hands and started to turn it. As the speed of the cylinder grew it made a sound like a strong wind. "This is our wind machine." He had to raise his voice to be heard. "The friction of the slats against the canvas generates the sound. The pitch shifts with the speed." He cranked faster, and the pitch rose. He eased off, and it subsided. "With a bit of finesse it can create a convincing storm effect." He stopped turning but left his hands resting on the crank. "The machine itself is fine."

"You just don't have anyone to ... to play it?"

"We didn't use one in Dresden. And I didn't budget for its operator here, because I didn't expect to have it. It was a surprise from the the-atre's carpenters."

"When do you need it?"

"During the storm scenes."

"Not the women's choruses?"

"No. Why?"

"Because that means I'm not busy when you need it." I faced him across the crank, put my hands next to his, and pulled. The friction of wood against canvas made it resist at first. Then it started to turn, and the wind sound rose. Wagner, too, resisted at first. Then he joined in. The sound began to fill the room. We settled into a rhythm, rising and falling, taking our cues from the movements of each other's hands, and soon we had a raging tempest echoing across the empty seats. I sang the storm motif from the overture—pum *pummm pumm*, pum *pum*, pum *pummmmm*—and Wagner laughed. His eyes were bright. "You have strong arms for a woman!" he shouted.

"You have strong arms for a composer!" I shouted back, and he laughed again.

We let the machine slow and stop, and again there was silence. I lifted my hands from the crank. They were sweating. I brushed them discreetly on my skirts. "Now you have your storm player, Herr Wagner."

He frowned. "But you're a woman. Wouldn't that be a bit un-seemly?"

I looked into his eyes. "Perhaps *I* am a bit unseemly."

This time he was the one who looked away.

The next time I visited the changes were even more astonishing. The clouds in the painted sky were darker and more threatening, and the plaster cliff—now painted in greys and greens—had been rolled into the wings. The stage was now dominated by what looked like a full-sized ship's prow, the illusion only broken by the fact that it stopped two feet from the floor, where a shallow bin ran from wing to wing.

As I stepped up onto the stage I saw that what looked like a wood-en hull was painted canvas stretched across a frame. I walked around behind it. At deck height was a sturdy platform for the singers, supported on a complex structure of angled timbers and wooden gears dark with industrial grease. At the back of the platform the ship's masts pivoted on short axles, also greased, their rough lower ends joining the mechanism below. I rested a hand on a large crank secured with a thick wooden pin and studied the structure to see how it worked.

"Choristers don't usually take this much interest in the other parts of the production." A low voice, stage left. I felt a tingle of excitement.

I turned. "Composers aren't usually so involved in set design."

He made a *pffff* sound with his lips. "Composers of Parisian confections, maybe. I keep trying to explain that this is a *unified* artwork. Someone has to oversee that union." He spread his hands in *faux* resignation, the Great Man reluctantly accepting the burden of his art.

I looked up at the back canvas. "The sky is different. Did you change your mind?"

Wagner looked puzzled. "No, this is just a different section. Ah! You haven't seen the spools. Come." He led me deeper backstage. "The canvas stretches between these tall spools, so the stage hands can change the sky to show the progress of the storm." He pointed to another crank-and-gear arrangement. "We'll have a system of covered lanterns farther back, to create a lightning effect through small holes in the canvas."

"This is ingenious." I turned in a slow circle to take in the entire set. "How do you imagine it all?"

He stepped close and brought his mouth near my ear.

"You focus your passions."

My first rehearsal with the orchestra was two days before we opened. We skipped the Overture and went straight to the storm scene with its chorus of sailors. Wagner had decided I'd operate the machine from the wings, so I could see him on the podium but the audience would be spared the spectacle of a woman in a puffy dress turning a big crank. He lifted his baton. A rocking motif—contrabasses and tubas alternating with bassoons—represented the swell of the ocean, while the wind swirled in *tremolo* quavers in the upper strings. Plus me.

Wagner cued me with a nod four bars in, once the ocean-swell figure had established itself. I turned the crank slowly at first, easing into the mix. The wind and the swells rose and grew, building to a sustained diminished chord across the entire orchestra, which then resolved and dropped away, the waves subsiding to a sextuplet figure in the strings. Here was where the wind effect surged again, rising above the orchestra to a howl. Or was supposed to.

I missed my cue.

I'd only ever seen Wagner conduct from the audience. I knew he didn't just set and maintain the tempo: He whirled and swooped and jabbed and cajoled, withdrawing to near motionlessness during soft passages, bouncing jauntily when there were dance-like rhythms, and shaking a quivering fist during climactic *fortissimi*. It'd always seemed a bit comical to me, but *chacun a son geste*. He wasn't from these parts.

That was the view from behind. Until today, I hadn't been on the receiving end.

I'd never seen a man so completely in control. At the helm of this orchestra his intensity, so palpable in conversation, was magnified beyond all expectation. They were with him, all of them, this mixed band of professionals and amateurs, right *there*, at the tip of his baton, galvanized by the force of his conviction and the authority of his stare. On this side of the baton his aggrandizing talk about unifying the arts felt like a basic truth, simply *there* before us in his perfect mastery of the elements of his creation. He might have been Prospero conjuring an actual storm within the proscenium, he was so at one with the sights and the sounds, even the *smells* of the set, the timber and pitch and sweat, like the smells of an actual ship. The sweep of an arm and the rocking motif *was* the ocean; a trickle of descending fingertips and the patterings of the violins *were* the whirl of wind and rain around a creaking mast.

All in twenty seconds, in under a dozen bars.

I was transfixed. My heart pounded. My arms tingled.

My cue passed unnoticed. And our revels ended.

His arms froze mid stroke. He turned with a savage glare. The orchestra lurched to a ragged halt. The hall was electric with silence.

"Was your cue unclear?" His voice was low but intense, his eyes blade sharp.

He was magnificent.

"No, *mein Herr*. My fault entirely. It won't happen again."

And it didn't. Spot on, every time.

By the last of the four sold-out performances Wagner had won me over. Between the intensity of his music and the grandeur of his staging, he'd turned a preposterous supernatural romance into a compelling tale of passion and redemption. I had no idea how he'd done it. Each night as the cutout of the Dutchman's ship sank behind quivering strips of sea-blue cloth while Senta and the Dutchman rose on painted ropes into the flies in their final embrace, the tears streaking my village-maiden make-up were real. I couldn't remember having been so completely and joyously taken in by a work of art.

I didn't want it to end. On the final night, when Senta hit her destination high B before flinging herself from the plaster cliff into the backstage net, I took it like a punch to the gut. I trembled as I heard the soft rattle of the stagehands securing her into the harness with the Dutchman. All I had to do at that point was stand there, but as the harp arpeggios lifted them heavenward I wasn't sure I would manage it. Somehow I did.

Before the final swell of strings and rumble of drums had ended, the audience was on its feet in frenzy. It was the hottest night of Zurich's hottest ticket, and Richard Wagner was its sovereign. He took endless curtain calls, bowing briefly each time and then spreading his arms wide, embracing the adulation.

As soon as he made it backstage he was scrummed, by the press, by the intelligentsia, by the professional hangers-on, and, here and there, even by his actual friends. Sulzer was there, and Baumgartner, of course, and Kirchner, the Winterthur organist. And tidy, bespectacled Spyri, the newspaper editor. Everyone who wanted to be anyone was desperate to touch the hem of Herr Wagner's sweat-soaked garment.

I stayed back. I was wrung out, by the passions of the production and my awareness that it was over. I couldn't bear to be in the change-room with my chattering fellow choristers, or even with dear cheerful Fanny. I needed to be alone. So I dawdled backstage, running my hand along the soon-to-be-dismantled sets, until I heard the last of the girls leave and I went down myself to change.

The rehearsal room served as the women's change room. By the time I got there the lamps had been dimmed, leaving it in shadow. I didn't bother to turn them up. I loosened my bodice laces and took a delicious deep breath. Then I sat on the *chaise longue*, removed my gloves, and started unbuttoning my boots. There were footsteps in the corridor. The latch clicked and the door swung open.

Wagner was practically pulsating with his conquest of the Zurichers. He looked taller, broader, impossibly self-assured. I could hear his breathing, long and deep. "Fraulein Staheli. I imagined I might find you here." He'd slipped his admirers to look for me. For Constanze. To look, I suddenly realized, for the spoils of his victory.

Oops.

This was going to be delicate.

"Herr Wagner."

He stood in the doorway, backlit by the lamps in the corridor. "You aren't celebrating with the rest?"

How to let him down? That was the question.

"Savouring, rather than celebrating. Away from the crowds."

How to. Not *whether* to.

Ahem.

"Thank you for making me part of this, Herr Wagner. This has been one of the most remarkable weeks of my life." Which was saying something.

"That pleases me." He bowed theatrically, eyes sweeping across my untied bodice, my exposed ankle. When he rose they looked a little darker, their pupils a little wider. Though I might have imagined that. It was a pretty dim room.

I gripped my gloves. "I had no idea music could do what I've seen yours do this week."

He gave a *faux*-modest nod. "You're most gracious. Of course it's not just about the music." He closed and latched the door. "The music has to serve the Dutchman's redemption." He approached the *chaise*. "All true art is about redemption." He was smooth, I'll give him that. He might have been concerned entirely with his theory of art and not at all with the loosened laces of my bodice. But we both knew.

Yeah, this would be delicate.

He stopped a single pace away. "Ever since I was a young man I've known that true redemption is redemption through love. Not the passionless love of the churchmen. *Personal* love." His eyes met mine. "Physical love."

I squirmed.

He stepped closer. We were almost touching. My gloves were twisted around my fingers. "I realized that when two souls join in the act of love, it lifts them from the muck of earthly existence. It *redeems* them. The ideal of that redemption drives my art." He lowered himself onto the *chaise*. "And my life."

"But surely—" My voice caught. I cleared my throat. "Surely that sort of redemption is temporary. Brief, even."

"Not necessarily *so* brief. Depending on the soul in question." He edged toward me. "And not in my art. The Dutchman's redemption is eternal. That's the ideal." He rested a hand on my knee. "And aren't we all looking for that same ideal in our lives?"

I tensed. "Wait," I said.

"Shhh." I felt his breath on my cheek, and then on my lips. His hand edged up my thigh. He was trembling.

Trembling now. Yeah. Give it a minute.

He squeezed, and I moaned. "No, really." But it was barely a murmur. My heart wasn't in it. Then his mouth was on mine, rough and wet and insistent, his hand inching higher, my skirts bunching toward my waist.

I had to stop this. It wasn't what he thought it was. But I didn't want to. I'd been with men before, of course, out of necessity or for variety or for sport. But they're not my default option. Give me the choice and I'll take the woman every time.

Every time but this one.

I wanted this. I wanted Richard, despite myself. Wanted this wild, passionate, appalling genius, right now, on this couch, with my whole body. I kissed him back, hard. His hand crept higher.

But how could I let him continue?

I tried again. "Richard—"

"Oh, yes," he said breathlessly. The poor muffin thought it was an endearment. "Yes, my own darling Constanze, yes. Let's surrender ourselves to each other." He pressed against me. "Let's *redeem* each other." His hand made its move, up my silk stocking to my lace undergarment. Slipped around and under. Arrived. Clutched.

Paused.

Froze.

The kiss stopped.

The trembling stopped.

His whole body went rigid.

He recoiled as if he'd been scalded, face pale, eyes wide. Out, up and on his feet in a single motion, backing away from the *chaise*, holding out his hand, palm up, fingers curled. One step, two. Stumbling, then stopping. Frozen. Staring. At his hand. At me. My face was hot, my throat thick. We looked at each other, one of us in shock and the other in shame. Then he spoke. His voice was dark with disbelief.

"You're a Jew," he said.

Richard's anti-Semitism was a fundamentally personal thing, which his ego expanded to universal proportions. I'm not excusing it. It was vile. I just want to be clear about its scope. For a narcissist like him, the line between the personal and the universal was blurry at best. Passing notions could blossom into grand, published theories, usually with his cockeyed sense of German cultural purity at their cores. And if you're wondering who he thought the exemplar of that culture was, then you haven't been paying attention.

Richard thought—wrongly—that Meyerbeer's influence in Paris was keeping his own works off the Parisian stage. Meyerbeer was a Jew. Richard hated the popularity of Mendelssohn's music, which he saw as a shallow facsimile of German culture. Mendelssohn was descended from Jews. But because of who Richard was, he didn't just vilify

Mendelssohn or Meyerbeer. He vilified Jewish artists in general. Any slight, any perceived betrayal by anyone Jewish, took its place in the fortress of his confirmation bias.

He felt deceived. I was a Jew. We were done.

He darted for the door. On my back with my undies in disarray, there was no way I could catch him. "Richard!" I shouted. It was like he hadn't heard me. "*Richard!*"

He reached for the latch. In an instant he'd be gone. I had no way to stop him.

Almost no way. There was still the nuclear option.

He lifted the latch.

In for a penny.

"I'm your Dutchman, Richard. In reality."

He passed through the door and closed it behind him. Didn't even glance back.

Dutchman's success was a huge boost to Wagner's profile. Familiarity with his artistic theories became the distinguishing mark of the self-conscious Zurich intellectual. His essays were the accessories of the season—*what, this? oh just a trifle I glance at in the odd spare moment*—and you couldn't attend a salon or dinner party without hearing the word *Gesamtkunstwerk* from men who last autumn wouldn't have known a bassoon from their own backside.

Wagner soaked it all up as no more than his due. Or so I heard. Then he took his wife Minna for a rustic holiday on the Zurichberg, to the east of the city. Or so I heard.

What I heard was mostly from Willi Baumgartner, whom I saw increasingly often while his mentor was away. Three or four times a week there'd be a note in the post inviting me to a chamber recital, or for coffee and cake, or for a stroll on the *Hohe Promenade*. He was nervously formal with me. Still nursing his crush. It was flattering, so I indulged it. It never crossed my mind that it could be dangerous. It should have. I was old enough and experienced enough to know better. But he was *such* a good source of gossip.

"Poor Richard," he said over a patio table at a new Viennese coffee house near the Baur au Lac. Another of little Zurich's anxious efforts at urban sophistication, like its sudden obsession with rail lines.

"Poor Richard? He has Zurich in his pocket."

"I know it seems that way. But as his fame brightens his spirits dim. Something has broken his confidence. And I think I know what it is."

My stomach clenched. Surely Richard hadn't said anything? Not to Willi, of all people. "Is it ... something he's told you in confidence?"

"Of course not. I wouldn't be so indiscreet." Then he paused, as if wondering just how indiscreet he could let himself be. He steepled his fingers and picked his way around his concerns. "Well. You know he's somewhat ... political?"

I relaxed. Political I could handle. It was better than ruinously scandalous. "So I've heard. There were some troubles in Dresden, I think."

"Yes. Some troubles." He was treating my nuanced understatement like bubble-headed superficiality. "Because of his strong convictions, of course."

"And those convictions are causing him trouble in Zurich?"

"No. It's something quite different. Do you remember a conversation at the reception after Miss Hunerwadel's performance, about Louis Napoleon?"

Of course I did. But the bubble-head card seemed to be working. "Vaguely."

"I think Herr Spyri may have been right. I think Herr Wagner is still mourning the tragic developments in France."

Which was fine with me. I was perfectly happy to have Zurich attribute Richard's depression to Louis Napoleon.

Better him than me.

Willi wasn't my only diversion during that time.

My encounter with Richard had loosened something carnal in me. Two nights after Dutchman closed, I dressed in my old Torsten clothes and went to the riverside brothels near the Limmatquai. Two or three times a week after that I'd stick on a preposterous false moustache, put on my frayed suit and ancient greatcoat, and walk from my respectable lodgings down to Zurich's queasy underbelly.

It's surprising how the persona can influence the desire. I started with men, but soon found myself inclining back toward women. The fact that there were more of them was probably a factor. That and the fact that homosexuality was a crime.

Within my means—which were considerable—I could pretty much do as I liked. Pregnancy wasn't a concern, and I wasn't affected by the French pox any more than by any other diseases. So night after night I tossed aside my Zuricher reserve and threw myself into redemption through passion. Or near enough.

Richard stuck to his rooms through the summer. I tried to visit him, but Minna turned me away. "My husband isn't receiving anyone. Certainly not *chorus* singers."

I felt responsible. But how could I make it right if he wouldn't see me?

That fall Abt left Zurich for a post at the Court Opera in Brunswick. His positions were filled by Wagner acolytes, including Willi Baumgartner.

If only I'd treated Willi better. Or at least more carefully.

One afternoon that fall I was sitting on a bench along the Hohe Promenade near my flat reading a book of peculiar stories by a Prussian named Hoffman. The trees were all but bare and the park all but empty. I glanced up to take in the view of the pewter-grey surface of the Zürichzee and saw Willi scurrying toward me from the Ramistrasse. He was carrying a paper folder. When he saw me notice him he beamed and quickened his pace. "Fraulein Staheli!" He waved the folder. "I have something to show you." He shuffled to a halt in the leaves around the bench.

"Herr Baumgartner. What's so important that it sends you racing down the Promenade like a schoolboy?" I closed my book. "Please. Sit." I shifted along the bench to give him room. He sat a proper distance away, fumbled with the folder's string, took out a sheaf of manuscript pages, and held them out to me. I set them on my lap. "Your songs. You've finished them." I leafed through the pages. A set of sixteen, for voice and piano. *Eine Fruhlingsliebe*. A Springtime Love. "Bravo." I straightened the pages and handed them back. "You must be very pleased."

"Yes, but look." He pointed to the dedication at the top. "Read it. Out loud."

My heart sank.

"Read it," he insisted.

I did, with as much of a smile as I could maintain. "Dedicated in true admiration to Fraulein Constanze Staheli."

"Brietkopf has agreed to publish them. I've just received their letter." His face was flushed. "My modest art and my admiration for you will go into the world together."

The poor, deluded boy. I looked into his eyes. "You can't."

"I will. I have. You must have noticed my ... affection for you, Fraulein Staheli. Now I will proclaim it, in the hope that you might return even a small portion."

This couldn't go on. "I refuse," I said. My tone was sharp. It had to be.

That threw him. "You ... you what?"

"I refuse. I refuse to allow you to dedicate these pieces to me."

"But ... but how can you? I wrote them for you. They are a declaration of"—he looked at me with an earnestness that pained me—"my love for you."

This couldn't happen. I had to cut it off, hard.

"I don't love you, Willi. I never have. I never will. You are an engaging friend. Nothing more. I apologize if you have thought otherwise."

His face went slack. He'd wooed me with his strongest weapon, and was incredulous at its failure. Where could he go from here? There was no way for him to salvage his dignity.

Except one.

His slack face tightened into anger. "You have toyed with my affections," he said fiercely. "You—"

"Willi, I—"

"You have led me on. I have shared my confidences with you. I ... I have opened my very heart to you. You led me to believe you ... you returned ..." His shoulders were shaking.

"Willi, I—"

"You will address me as Herr Baumgartner!" He grabbed the manuscript and stormed back down the path.

When Brietkopf published *Eine Fruhlingsliebe* a few weeks later, it was dedicated to Richard Wagner.

Shortly before Christmas Fanny sent a note inviting me to a reading of an epic poem at a private home in Mariafeld. I couldn't think of anything drearier, so I declined by the next post. Within the hour there was a sharp tap on my door. There she was, bundled in heavy woollens against the December damp. "You must come," she said as she unwound her scarf. "I won't be denied."

"Do come in." I set a kettle on the fire to make cocoa while she unlaced her boots. "I'm grateful for the invitation, but I prefer my epic poems in book form." I took two cups from the cupboard. "That way I control the dose."

She draped her coat across the arm of my couch. "Ordinarily I'd agree completely. But I thought we might make an exception for Herr Wagner."

I turned toward her, holding the empty cups in the air. "Herr Wagner?"

She sat next to her coat and stretched a languid arm along the back of the couch. "Why yes," she said with a mischievous gleam. "Didn't I mention that?"

Richard's seclusion had been productive.

"The Norse gods?" I wasn't sure I'd heard her right. "He's written a libretto about the Norse gods?"

"Four libretti, I'm told." She shook her head in amazement. "It sounds like a huge undertaking, but if anyone can do it surely he can. He hasn't written a note of music yet, mind you. Just the poems. But even so." According to Fanny, he was giving a public reading at the home of some artsy couple down the lake. She'd been invited, and wanted me to be her plus one.

"I'm not sure I'd be welcome." I pried the lid from my tin of cocoa. "As you know, he and I had a falling out after Dutchman."

"Which still mystifies me. I thought the two of you got on well."

I took my time spooning the dark powder into the cups. How far to go before she'd leave the subject alone? "Maybe too well to let it continue." Maybe that would be enough.

It wasn't. She sat forward on the couch, beaming with curiosity. "My God, Stanzi, are you *serious*? You have to tell me everything. Absolutely *everything*."

So I gave her a genital-free version of the events in the dressing room. An attempted kiss. Nothing more.

"That settles it," she said. "You *have* to attend the reading now."

Our host Herr Wille—a journalist of some sort—had the most luxuriant side-whiskers I'd ever seen, in a rainbow of blacks and greys. His wife Eliza apparently wrote novels. Their country home had a high-windowed drawing room where they'd arranged rows of chairs facing a wing-backed armchair in a well-lit window nook. Beside it was a side table with a pitcher of iced water and a glass. Beside that, holding a thick folder of papers, was Richard.

He glanced toward us as we entered. He looked away. Fanny giggled softly, so that only I would hear. "He's pretending not to see you. What fun this will be."

I was already regretting having come when Richard was joined by a familiar bearded figure. I should have expected it, but dear God, *really*?

Baumgartner glanced our way. He was in the middle of smiling a greeting at Fanny when he realized who she was with. His face hardened. He turned back to Richard. Fanny missed nothing. "My God, Stanzi," she whispered. "Herr Baumgartner too?"

"Something like that."

"My dear girl, your life is *much* more interesting than I'd imagined. And certainly more entertaining than mine. Maybe I'll live vicariously through you." We took seats in the next-to-last row, on the opposite side of the room from Baumgartner. Richard settled himself in the wing chair, took a sip of water, and opened the manuscript.

I don't know how many hours passed before he stopped reading, and I didn't care. His poems—which eventually formed his *Ring* cycle—were riveting. Historically they were nonsense, but that hardly mattered. Myth had outstripped reality to where I hardly noticed. And he'd given the myths a new potency.

It was all unproduceable, of course. No audience would accept a brother/sister love story, let alone that their union in one opera would produce the hero of the next one. Especially not an audience in Zurich, where theatre of any kind was still a guilty pleasure. Plus the technical demands would make Dutchman look like church-basement community theatre.

But oh, what a concept.

There was a reception afterward, with chilled wines and dainty *hors d'oeuvres* that contrasted sharply with the scale of what we'd just heard. I was sampling a cheese and mushroom confection on a tiny crispbread when Fanny took my arm. "Come with me." She took me to a small library, where she asked me to wait. A moment later a door on the opposite wall opened and Richard came in, looking puzzled. Someone closed it behind him. Dear naughty Fanny. What had she done?

"I'm sorry, Herr Wagner. This wasn't my idea. I'll go." I put my hand on the latch. "I was impressed by your poem, though."

"Wait." His voice was tight. "Just a moment. Now that we're here—" He swallowed. "Now that we're here, I need to ask you something."

"Of course. Ask me anything you like."

"That day in the rehearsal room. When you and I ... ah ..."

"I know the day."

"You mentioned something." His midsection gurgled. He winced. "Sorry. I haven't been well."

"It's all right." I gently touched his forearm. He jerked it away. I stepped back. "So you heard what I said, then, that day? As you were leaving?"

"I think I did."

"That I'm your Dutchman?"

"Yes. I heard that, but I can't make sense of it. I assumed I'd misheard you." He looked so bewildered it was almost comic, as if we were still in the rehearsal room with my skirts in disarray. All those feelings jostling to express themselves: anger, shame, betrayal, wonder, hope. His poor face couldn't keep up. "What does it mean?"

Could I trust him? No. But it was too late to turn back. "It means I don't die. And I don't know why."

He looked at me like a man who doesn't know whether the gift box he's opening contains a precious jewel or a poisonous snake. "What do you mean you don't die?"

"I mean I've been alive for ... for a very long time."

His gaze grew more intent. "How long?"

I nodded toward where he'd read his poem. "You know your Wotan?"

"Yes."

"I taught him how to steer a boat."

We didn't have much time. People would be wondering where he was. But his need to know more was a physical presence, like clammy air before a violent storm.

"Where can we meet? Where and when?"

"A bench on the Hohe Promenade. Tomorrow at noon." I moved toward the door.

"Wait. One more thing."

I turned. "Yes?"

"Why do you dress as a woman?"

I smiled. "Sometimes life takes you places."

Over the next year we met at least once a week. Mostly we talked about Woden and Tror. Meeting took some discretion, not only because of Minna's vigilance but also because Richard seemed uncomfortable alone with me. And fair enough.

Sometimes he took notes. "I can use this when I write the music."

Fanny spent much of that year in Italy, hobnobbing with aristocrats and studying with renowned singing teachers. Richard conducted more programs with AMG, and gave more readings of his *Nibelung* poem, to local acclaim. Zurich had finally embraced him, to the point where, that May, it hosted a series of concerts of his music, finishing up on his fortieth birthday. And because he was who he was, that meant it was time for him to start buggering it all up again. The first sign was a short piano piece.

A few days after the concerts I went to Otto Wesendonck's suite at the Baur au Lac to take payment for a shipment of silks. As we went to his desk for his chequebook I heard someone in the next room playing the piano. "What's that piece?"

"A polka Herr Wagner wrote for Mathilde. In gratitude for my sponsorship of the festival of his music, no doubt."

"You were one of the sponsors?"

"Oh, yes. Mathilde has me spending money on Herr Wagner left, right and up the middle. *Noblesse oblige.*"

"You're a fan of his music, then?"

"Well I don't really understand it, myself. But Mathilde tells me he's the future."

A month later there was another piece, more substantial. Fanny borrowed a copy of *Sonata for Mathilde Wesendonck* from Willi Baumgartner and sight-read it at the piano in my cottage. "Some of that seemed awfully passionate," she said.

"Reflecting passionate gratitude for Herr Wesendonck's financial support, no doubt." There was a beat of silence. Then we burst into slightly ungracious laughter. Though Fanny's was probably a bit less ungracious than mine.

If Richard was lusting after his patron's wife, it wasn't slowing him down creatively. He told me he was well into the piano score for the first of his *Nibelung* poems, and had started thinking about orchestration. "Do you think I could get away with anvils during the descent to the Nibelungs' forge? I think it might need actual anvils."

Constanze was getting too old to sustain for much longer. Which wasn't necessarily a big deal. I'd already revealed myself to Richard. The only compelling reason to keep Constanze around was my friendship with Fanny. I couldn't reveal myself to her. But short of leaving Zurich, I didn't know what else I could do.

Be careful what you wish for.

That summer Fanny went back to Rome for more voice lessons and life experience. She was going to be away for a year. "I'll miss you desperately," she said at the pier, where her aunt and her steamer trunks were arrayed for the journey.

I clasped her hands. "Same."

I always looked forward to her letters. Every envelope in her elegant cursive lifted my heart. Then they stopped. She contracted typhoid that spring. By the end of April it had taken her.

She's still there, in Rome. Her simple grave in the Protestant Cemetery doesn't get the attention that Shelley's or Keats's do, but it should. I go when I can. I leave a rose. I like to think it might provoke some curiosity. Her music deserves to be better known, too. What's survived includes some charming *lieder* for solo voice and piano, which I'm very fond of. I prefer them to Baumgartner's, and not just because he was such a noodle about Constanze. There's a confidence to Fanny's songs that I don't hear in his. They're subtle and moving, they sit nicely on the voice, and there's a deftness to the piano writing that sometimes reminds me of Schubert. I still occasionally sing them, though not often. They make me miss her too much.

With Fanny gone there was no reason to stretch Constanze any further, but I still didn't want to give up my comfortable life in Zurich, with its music and clean sheets and no killing. So I passed the torch again. "I am afraid I'll be leaving for Hamburg soon," I said to Otto Wesendonck one afternoon at the Baur au Lac, after we'd signed our latest set of contracts.

"Oh? For how long?"

"For good. My father is ill, and wants me to take over our businesses there."

That got his attention. "Who'll run your businesses here?"

"My younger brother Karsten. He'll be here in six weeks."

"Does he have much business experience, your brother?"

Poor Otto. Karsten was going to have *such* an advantage.

I explained my plan to Richard. He was joining Minna at a spa near Seelisberg later that day. She'd gone ahead, so we were able to meet in his study. Every flat surface was covered in orchestral sketches for *Das Rheingold*, the first of his *Nibelung* operas.

"You'll leave Zurich."

"Yes."

"Then you'll return as a man."

"Yes."

"You think people won't notice that you're the same person."

"You'd be surprised."

"And you think this will allow us to meet more freely."

"Sure it will. Minna has no reason to be suspicious of a man."

"No, but why would I associate with this newly arrived brother of yours?"

"He'll find his way into Zurich's music community."

"I hardly socialize with every new amateur musician in Zurich."

I looked around his disorderly study. "Maybe you could use a copyist."

I packed Constanze's belongings into steamer trunks and travelled to Strasbourg, where I donated them to a local charity. I bought new trunks and the wardrobe of a bourgeois young man, grew a moustache and side-whiskers, and returned to Zurich to take over my sister's rooms and business empire. Then I cheekily auditioned for one of Willi Baumgartner's choirs.

The auditions were in the familiar rehearsal room at the Aktientheater. I waited on a bench with other prospective choristers while, one by one, we were led inside by Theodor Kirchner, the organist, who was helping with the auditions. When my turn arrived he gave me a curious look. "Have we met?"

"You probably knew my sister. Constanze Staheli? They say we look alike, though I'm afraid I don't see it."

"That must be it." He held out his hand for the score I was carrying. "May I? I'll be accompanying you." He brightened when he saw the title page. "*Herbstleid*. By our Fraulein Hunerwadel."

"Yes. She and my sister were friends."

He handed it back. "I won't need this. I know it."

As we crossed the room I could see Willi recognize me, despite my whiskers. To his credit, he saw the audition through. He rejected me on the spot, of course. When Kirchner rose to walk me to the door Willi waved him down. "Sit, Theodor. I'll see Herr Staheli out." As we reached the door he gave me a hard look. "I know," he said quietly. "Not why. But I *know*."

As we'd planned, Richard took me on as a part-time copyist. Two mornings a week I'd attend his rooms after breakfast and work for a couple of hours before heading down the hill to my office. It was pleasant. Richard was happy with my ability to decipher his scribbles. By November we had a fair copy of *Rheingold*, and I was proofreading the orchestral sketches of the second opera, *Die Walkure*, which was nearly complete.

It helped that he'd been freed from the distractions of earning a living, thanks to Otto Wesendonck, who had cleared Richard's debts and promised him an annual stipend.

Then Richard's productivity hit a snag. One November morning when I called it was Minna who answered. She had her boots on, and was holding a cloth-lined basket. "He's only just gotten out of bed. He was up half the night with some book Herwegh recommended." From her tone any book from Herwegh was probably either a bomb-making manual or a collection of French pornography. She yanked a shawl into place as though it had offended her and waved toward the far door. "He's through there." She left without looking at me. Off to do Richard's breakfast shopping, no doubt.

I found him at a wash basin in his chamber, still in his shirtsleeves, drying his face with a flannel cloth. He was taking his time around his eyes, as you do after a late night. It was only when he heard Peps, his aging King Charles spaniel, trot over to sniff my feet that he looked out from behind the cloth and noticed me.

"Ah, Karsten." He ran the flannel around his jawline. "What do you know about a fellow named Schopenhauer?" Assuming as usual that whatever interested him would interest whoever he was with.

"Nothing. Is he a composer or a performer?"

Richard dried his forearms. "A philosopher. Hardly known here. He's written an extraordinary book called *The World as Will and Representation*." He wiped the backs of his hands, dropped the flannel next to the basin, and picked up a thick book from his nightstand. "The first volume." He gestured toward his study. Peps followed at his master's heels and climbed onto his special stool near the piano, looking up expectantly. Richard saw him and laughed. "No, Peps. Not now." He passed me the book and took the dog's face in both hands. "We're not composing right now. No we're *not*." The universal singsong voice of the dog-owner with his dog. He looked up at me, smiling. "This is where he sits while I work. I try out bits of *Walküre* on him before I commit them to paper." He ruffled the dog's jowls. "You're the only critic I care about, aren't you? Yes you *are*." He straightened and waved me toward his writing desk. Peps climbed down and toddled away to his bowl of water.

Richard took the padded chair, leaving me the straight-backed wooden one, and took the book back. It bristled with bits of torn paper, but he didn't open yet. He sat it on his lap and locked his fingers around its spine like it was a raft on the sea. "I can't leave this book alone. Every moment I don't spend on the *Walküre* music I spend reading and re-reading it. It's a scandal how overlooked he is by German academia."

"He thinks like you do, then?"

"That's the bizarre thing. He goes in an entirely different direction. When I first read him he infuriated me!"

"Then why are you so taken with him now?"

"I'm still working that out. He gives music a unique place among the arts, but it can't just be that. I think part of it is his starting point that all existence is suffering." Which rang a big Bactrian Buddhist bell. But I didn't interrupt. "Of course my way of dealing with that suffering has been redemption through passion." He coloured slightly. "But Schopenhauer says redemption comes through *renunciation*. Annihilation of the Will." He smacked the book. "Worlds away from my Dutchman. Or my essays. To everything I've built my reputation on. But I couldn't leave him be."

He thumbed through the pages. Not searching. Just thumbing.

"But then as I read and re-read him, I started seeing affinities with my own works! Can you imagine that feeling? What I was resisting in Schopenhauer was already in my *Nibelung* poem! His ideas made more sense of my Wotan than my own. Like he'd seen into places in my mind I hadn't seen myself."

"But you've made such a strong case for redemption through passion. In your art and in your essays." A case that was still regularly driving me to Limmatquai brothels.

"I know. But I think this has been troubling me for some time, below the surface." He glanced toward the door Minna had recently closed behind her. "Whether love is up to the task." He gave the book an affectionate pat. "Schopenhauer has shown me a way out. The love in the Dutchman's redemption is superfluous. It's the annihilation that matters."

"But that's nihilism. We can't all fling ourselves into fjords."

"No, I made that same mistake at first. But renunciation isn't nihilism." He flipped through the tabbed bits. "Here. Let me find the right passage. He talks about similarities between his ideas and an Asian philosophy called Buddhism. Have you heard of it?"

There it was.

"I have."

He spent most of the morning—apart from a breakfast of dark bread and cheese once Minna returned—walking me through Schopenhauer's notion of Buddhism. It wasn't spot on, but how could it be? There was probably only one genuine authority on Buddhism in Europe at that point. Ahem. But Schopenhauer's sense of it wasn't bad in the circumstances. And it had certainly captivated Richard. Of course Buddhist renunciation was a convenient intellectual shift for a married man in love with his benefactor's unattainable wife. But it also seemed kind of genuine.

"I need to know more."

"I can actually help you with that."

We spent the rest of the morning talking about Bactria.

Richard eventually found a few academic sources on Buddhism, too, but most of what he learned came from his next few meetings with me. He soaked it up. "I have to find a way to put this on the stage. I have to write a music drama about this Buddha."

"How would you make a music drama about renunciation? Isn't drama about conflict?"

"Please. Conflict is easy. I can find the conflict in anything."

The Buddha was the newest shiny thing, but he had a powerful rival. For all Richard's new passion for renunciation, he wasn't quite ready to let go of his passion for passion. A horndog like him doesn't manage chastity of the heart in one go. His blood had always been at a low boil over some woman or other, and December of 1854 was no different. The fact that his current infatuation was unavailable didn't mean the heat wasn't still cranked.

We were in his study, spitballing ideas for his Buddha opera, but we weren't getting anywhere. He kept going off on tangents. "Have I told you I sent my *Nibelung* libretto to Schopenhauer?" He tossed a bit of gruyère to Peps, who missed it and had to toddle over to where it landed and nibble it from the floor.

"I hadn't realized you were in contact."

Richard broke off another bit of cheese. "We aren't. It's my way of making contact." He fidgeted with the cheese, turning it in his fingers and studying its texture.

"What did you say in your covering letter?"

Richard tossed the cheese, which Peps again missed. "I didn't include one. I just inscribed it 'with reverence and gratitude.'"

"Aren't you concerned he'll find that rude?"

"He'll understand."

He didn't, as it turned out. Didn't even acknowledge receipt. The two men never met or corresponded. Richard could never have imagined that at the time, of course. They were great minds in perfect sync. What room was there for misunderstanding?

He rewrapped the cheese and took it to the cupboard. Peps trotted amiably behind him, and whimpered slightly as the cupboard door closed. Richard didn't seem to notice. "Do you know the story of Sir Tristan?"

"From the Arthurian legends?"

"That's the one."

"The one who cuckolded his king?"

He frowned disapprovingly. "Well, yes, that's where the conflict is. But the point of the story is the great love between Sir Tristan and Queen Isolde."

The conflict. That was why we weren't making progress on the Buddha opera. He was working on something else. "You aren't planning a drama about Tristan, are you? We've barely started your Buddha opera, and you're less than half way through the *Nibelung* project. You haven't even started scoring *Walkure*."

"I know. But I keep coming back to the idea of the grand passion. The consuming, redemptive love I've never managed to find in my own life."

"But why torment yourself with it? Isn't the Buddha opera about renouncing the passions?"

"I can't seem to manage that. Not yet. Their grip is too strong. I think I have to purge them first. To *monumentalize* them in a music drama." The artist sublimating his frustrated lust in his art. That was a new one. Just when we were on the verge of something genuinely revolutionary.

It turned out he'd been making notes toward a Tristan opera for a couple of months. The parallels between Tristan's frustrated passion for his queen and Richard's midlife craving for Frau Wesendonck leapt off the page. I was going to have to fight for the Buddha.

It would be a long, ragged battle.

In January Richard started scoring *Walkure.* As he finished each section I started on the fair score and the parts. He was sullen through February despite two successful conducting engagements, because he still hadn't heard from Schopenhauer. He capped that month by conducting three performances of *Tannhauser,* then left for a four-month conducting engagement in London. He barely acknowledged our Buddha project. In fact it wasn't until over a year later that he got back to it in earnest, and then only due to a serendipitous gift from his brother-in-law, a well-regarded orientalist.

We'd finished the orchestration of *Walkure,* and in celebration Richard had a group of friends to his home for a run-through of the first act "I have something to show you," he said when I arrived. "Don't leave until you've seen it." He dashed to collect chairs, leaving me wondering.

Otto and his wife were there, as were Willi Baumgartner and Theodor Kirchner, who shared piano duties. A competent amateur soprano, Frau Heim, sang the female roles, while Richard naturally sang the men. I stood at the piano and turned pages, to Willi's visible discomfort. For a cold read-through it went pretty well. Kirchner was up to the more difficult piano bits, and what Frau Heim may have lacked in rhythmic sense she made up for with rich tone and genuine musicality. The audience reacted with suitable awe at Siegmund's retrieval of the mystical sword, and if they were unsettled by the incestuous longings between Siegmund and Seiglinde they kept it to themselves.

"Bravo!" cried Willi from the piano as the final chord faded away. It really was quite good. Richard had developed a technique of using musical tidbits to represent particular characters or concepts, and was employing it with increasing skill.

"Magnificent," Otto said to Richard at the door as he lifted Mathilde's fox coat onto her shoulders. "Indeed," she agreed, giving Richard an immodest smile that her husband, behind her, couldn't see. I did, though. So did Minna. Lips tight, she turned to the cupboard and retrieved Otto's hat. Otto blustered on, oblivious. "You need the security to complete this work." He accepted his hat without even a nod. "Would an additional 250 francs per month do?"

"My dear friend," Richard said, grasping Otto's hand in both of his own. "That is most generous. How can I possibly repay you?" Minna glanced sharply at Mathilde and left the room.

"Complete your project. Promise me it'll be done, and I'll be satisfied."

"Absolutely." Richard was still holding on to Otto's hand. "You have my word."

Otto might not have been so generous if he'd known it would take Richard eighteen years to honour that word. Or that the delay would be caused by his competing project to cuckold Otto by proxy.

"At last," Richard said once everyone was gone. "Now I can show you the book I mentioned." He darted toward his bedchamber.

"A book?"

"About the Buddha. From my brother-in-law." He returned with a leather-bound volume. "I think I've found the story for my libretto."

It was an introduction to Buddhism by a French orientalist named Burnouf, which included a Buddhist legend that Richard felt had the right dramatic possibilities. "The problem is creating conflict in a story about a man who teaches letting go of conflict."

Too bad I hadn't thought of that. "I thought you said conflict was easy."

"It is, once you have the right story." Apparently the right story was a legend about the Buddha's disciple Ananda. "He's a noble who starts a relationship with a girl from the lowest caste when she offers him a drink of water at a well. I'll structure the story to parallel my own journey from passion to renunciation." Because of course everything was about Richard.

"So you'll be Ananda."

"Of course not. By that point Ananda has already accepted renunciation."

"Then who makes the journey?"

"The girl, of course. I'm thinking of calling her Prakriti."

"So, in this story you're the girl?"

I watched his face as the richness of this sank in.

The working title was *Die Sieger*. The Victors. Meaning victory over craving and illusion. Prakriti's journey would be from erotic love for Ananda to joining his community through renunciation of that love. The conflict would be with the Buddha's insistence that their community be men only, with Ananda eventually persuading him to admit her.

"You're going to create a drama where the Buddha, *as* the Buddha, starts with a deep human flaw, and overcomes it as part of the dramatic structure?"

"Yes. Exactly."

Over the following month, while I wrote out the clean orchestral parts of *Walkure*, Richard worked up a more detailed prose sketch of our Buddha project.

"Is this D sharp or D natural?"

"D sharp. What if there's a scene where Prakriti's mother magically lures Ananda to their home as a suitor for her daughter, but he withstands it because of his purity?"

The tension between Buddhist orthodoxy and the needs of Richard's narrative was beginning to tell on me. But by then I'd accepted that, no matter what I said, the tie always went to the narrative.

"Fine," I said.

Near the end of one of these evenings, as the candles I'd brought burned low and we were rewarding ourselves with a decent Neuchâtel pinot noir, which I'd also brought, I asked Richard the question that had been on my mind from the outset: "Why the Buddha?"

The light of the wall sconce highlighted his brow line, shadowing his eyes. "You know why. Schopenhauer."

"That's not what I mean. The Buddha isn't a hero of the German *Volk*. He's outside of your grand revolutionary project."

Richard massaged his expansive forehead with his fingertips. "My project is changing. Schopenhauer has changed it." He paused. "Louis Napoleon has changed it." Ah. All roads led to petulance over Paris. Except the ones that led to the other predictable place. Because Cornish Sir Tristan and Irish Queen Isolde also weren't part of the German *Volk*.

"Frau Wesendonck has changed it," I said.

He lowered his hand, but didn't speak.

I kept my voice kind. "It's not hard to see."

He took a slow sip of wine. "The Buddha's doctrine is more to my liking than Christianity. No aristocratic God punishing disobedience with eternal torment." He swirled his wine. It glinted in the candle-light. "You repeat life until you get it right, and only escape the cycle by not causing pain." His eyes followed the swirling liquid, as if he could see that cycle there in his glass. He tipped it back and drank it down. "That's 'why the Buddha'."

I nodded in silence. What I didn't ask—didn't have the nerve to ask—was why he could admit the Buddha but not the Jews. How a man who admired a life lived without causing pain could stand by a document like *Judentum in Musik*. Maybe that was what I'd meant in the first place. But I never asked him directly.

I've never reconciled Richard's embrace of the Buddha and his anti-Semitism, even now. I get that his anti-Semitism was primarily personal. And I get that it was Buddhism's metaphysics that appealed to him rather than its compassion. But those feel like simplifications. Because he also admired the Buddha's sympathy for all creatures. And he went out of his way to make his personal anti-Semitism grotesquely public.

Maybe it's just that Richard, for all his lofty ideals, was also kind of an asshole.

By May we had a fleshed-out prose sketch of *Die Sieger*. It was tight and coherent and rich with dramatic possibilities. Richard was genu-inely excited by it, and was talking it up in his letters to his friends. Then came the interruptions.

The first was in June, when he left for a spa near Geneva for a two-month water cure. "I haven't felt so well in years," he said when he re-turned. "Did I mention that we saw the Wesendoncks in Berne on our way back?"

The next interruption was a bout of melancholy when, in the same week, Brietkopf declined to publish his *Nibelung* project and the King of Saxony denied his latest amnesty request. From his comfortable home in the liberal, German-speaking city that had embraced and indulged him, Richard spent the better part of the next few days complaining to his generous patrons that he was a penniless exile.

And after that, he'd only just made a start on the music for the next *Nibelung* opera when the grandest interruption of all happened.

Franz Liszt was a rock star. His married lover, Carolyne zu Sayn-Wittgenstein, was minor Polish royalty. They were Europe's scandalous power couple. That autumn they descended on the Hotel Baur au Lac like a hipster tornado, sucking Zurich society out of its tidy burrows and into the maelstrom of their uber-celebrity. No one loves a hot virtuoso like the daughters of the conventional, and no political order fawns over a foreign aristocrat like a liberal democracy. Poor Zurich was a goner from the get go.

They were in town for a month, and I never met them. Not once, even though Liszt was one of Richard's most devoted friends. Maybe because they were such friends. Over and over during Richard's Swiss exile it had been: "Dear Franz, can you spot me a few francs?" Or: "Dear Franz, can you help me set up a music festival in Belgium?" Or: "Dear Franz, can you conduct my music in the cities I'm banished from?" And Dear Franz came through whenever he could. Especially with the money. He was dripping with the stuff. "Dear Franz, may I introduce the man whose knob I once held in my hand?" probably wasn't ever in the cards. But it still stung.

Plus it was all such a damnable interference with Richard's work. He was so taken up with Liszt's visit I barely saw him. Our work on *Nibelung* dwindled to almost nothing, and our Buddha project stopped altogether. He was too busy trotting off to Winterthur with Dear Franz to catch an organ recital, or staging another invitation-only read-through of Act I of *Walkure* with Dear Franz at the piano. Without me on the guest list. Word is that it was impressive.

While I never met the legendary couple, I did see them twice. Once was on Talstrasse in front of the Baur au Lac through a crowd of bourgeois schoolgirls, two of whom got into a hair-pulling brawl over one of Liszt's discarded cigar butts. The other was across the theatre at a performance of Halevy's opera *La Juivre*, where Liszt had popped for a block of prime balcony seats. Without me on the guest list.

There was blowback from their presence in Zurich that I did experience, though, mainly because the Wesendoncks were still living at the Baur au Lac. I was there looking for Richard. Apart from feeling snubbed, I wanted to finish my copying work on *Walkure*, which I could only do at Richard's because of the iron control he kept over the score. Minna had said he was with "Herr Liszt and his princess," so I tried the hotel. I didn't find him, but I did see Otto in the lobby, collecting a thick envelope from the desk. "Herr Staheli," he called.

"Herr Wesendonck."

"You're a man of judgment." I nodded noncommittally. Karsten had proven as shrewd in the cloth business as Constanze. Funny, that. "I have something I'd value your opinion on. Would you join me in our suite? I won't keep you long."

I glanced once around the lobby. No sign of Richard, or Liszt, or the throngs of young women who usually prefigured Liszt's appearance. "Of course."

Mathilde Wesendonck was in a padded armchair near the suite's high windows, reading a slim volume of something. "Come, Mathilde," Otto said, spreading the envelope's contents over the dining table. "See what the architects have sent." Mathilde looked irritated, but closed her book and came to see what the fuss was about.

The papers were technical plans for a two-storey villa with a columned façade. The proportions seemed good, with arches on the upper level fronting a long balcony above a recessed ground-level entryway. "Very nice," I said. "Is this the residence you're building?" All of Zurich knew Otto had bought a plot of land in Enge, over the river, where he planned to build a permanent home.

"Yes. The basic structure is underway, but this revision includes some exterior changes to accommodate concerns my dear wife had." He smiled indulgently.

She seemed to notice me for the first time. "You're Richard's friend, aren't you?"

"I do some copying work for him, yes."

Otto chuckled. "Mathilde thinks we should offer Herr Wagner and his wife the existing building on the property."

"I didn't realize there was already a residence there."

"It was quite the issue. I hadn't intended to buy the land it's on, but some head doctor was planning to build an asylum there." He frowned. "We could hardly have *that*, could we? Not with the *children*." He gave me a look of complicit normality. "So I bought that parcel too. At a premium, but what can one do?"

His wife nudged him affectionately. "Perhaps Herr Wagner and his family could take *asylum* in it."

"Indeed." Either he didn't get her little joke, or didn't care. "Now, Herr Staheli. These recent improvements. Do the costs seem reasonable to you in the current market?" We spent the next quarter of an hour going over the details, which Otto seemed to think I'd have some insight into because my family was more established in the area. I didn't, but I provided what noncommittal nods and grunts I could. Mathilde spent the whole time eyeing me as if assessing what use I might be to her social advancement. Given how abandoned by Richard I was feeling, I found her attentions more than a little flattering.

The other consequence for me of Liszt's visit was its effect on Zurich's sex trade, which had been strained by the influx of overstimulated visitors. At that point my search for redemption through passion was focussed on a disinherited country girl named Ariette, whose schedule suddenly seemed to have less room for me. "I need to be with you," I said one evening in the antechamber of her workplace.

"You'll have to pick another time," said the Bernese businessman whose trousers she was fondling. No doubt he had a Liszt-enflamed wife back at his hotel who might have done trouser duty if not for the candlelit baths she was taking in the company of the virtuoso's photograph.

"When can I see you then?"

"How's Friday morning?" Ariette said as she undid his fly-buttons.

In mid-November Richard saw Liszt to the border at Sankt Gallen, where they had a tag-team conducting gig. When he returned, he got back to work on *Siegfried*, which meant I was finally able to work on the last of the orchestral parts from *Walkure*.

"It would've been nice to meet Liszt," I said at one point.

"Be sure to give enough space to that run of semiquavers in the third bassoon," he replied.

I completed the last of the orchestral parts just before the new year. After that I didn't see much of Richard until the end of March, when he finished the orchestral score of Act I of *Siegfried* and I was able to start working on the fair copy. The balance of that year was devoted to *Siegfried*. We spent long periods in his home while he wrote, I copied, and once in a while he idly picked my brain about the Aesir.

"Did Wotan have the dignity I've given him in this Wanderer *motif*?"

I finished inking a complicated dotted rhythm in the violas. "Wotan was the most dignified man I had ever met." A half-truth at best. But tie goes to the narrative.

My only complaint during that time was that he didn't have any time for the Buddha project. Before long I'd have other complaints.

By Christmas Richard's progress on *Siegfried* had slowed, which worried me at first, but by January I discovered that the reason was a good one. I was in his study working on the *Siegfried* orchestral parts when he said, "I think I'll call her Savitri."

"Who?" It was a bit late to be renaming characters in *Siegfried*.

"Prakriti. In *Die Sieger*. Savitri sings better."

I looked up from the third clarinet part. It was the first time in months he'd mentioned our Buddha project. "You've been working on *Die Sieger*?"

"A little. Not on the actual poem. Just refining the dramatic structure."

I put my pen down. "Tell me."

"Well, for the audience to appreciate Savitri's progress from passion to renunciation, they have to *see* the depths of her passion. I have an image of her in the forest, soaking up the whole of nature as she waits for Ananda. Flowers, sun, birds, forest, water. The sets and the music will be voluptuous, to show how powerfully sensual the experience is, and how tied it is to her anticipation of Ananda's arrival." I could see it on his face, see him picturing the young woman's passion in swells of strings and rumbles of tympani. His breath was quickening at the thought. Our eyes met, and we connected, just for an instant, over the imaginary desires of Richard's young avatar. I felt his breath on my neck in the post-Dutchman dressing room, his hand climbing my thigh …

He looked away sharply.

That was the high water mark of our Buddha project.

It was also the high water mark of my redemption through passion. "I'm sorry," I said to Ariette, "but I'm afraid I won't be returning."

She didn't look up from adjusting her garter. "Leave the money on the table."

In the spring, as construction on Villa Wesendonck neared completion, Richard and his family moved into the smaller building Otto had saved from becoming an asylum. Richard's standard unfunny joke, no doubt picked up from Mathilde, was that he'd taken a kind of asylum there himself. He repeated it to the point where the building actually became known as the Asyl. I hated the place. It meant my visits required a forty-minute carriage ride rather than a two-minute walk within the Escherhauser.

The first time my carriage lurched up the rutted track to Richard's new home I was struck by the magnificence of its setting. The Wesendonck estate sprawled across a high suburban bluff with a commanding view of the city and of the Zurichberg beyond. It was nice to know the *centimes* Otto was squeezing from me were going to impressive use. Nothing but the best for pretty Mathilde. Her pet composer even came pre-installed at the foot of her garden.

The Asyl itself—a tall half-timbered lump with stacked wooden balconies and uneven floors—was less impressive, though it had the advantage of space. Richard's music room was far enough from Minna's bedchamber that he could work all night without disturbing her sullen slumbers. "The Villa looks nearly ready, apart from the landscaping," I said as Richard took my hat and gloves.

"And the road, of course. Plus there's still a lot to be done inside. They're bringing in stucco-workers from Paris. But Mathilde still thinks they'll be able to move in by August." Mathilde. Not Frau Wesendonck.

"I'm sure they'll be glad to. It's been a long process, and the Baur au Lac can't have been cheap."

Richard made a *pffft* sound. "Money means nothing to Otto. He just turns on the tap and lets it flow. I'm one or two good conversations away from getting him to produce my entire *Nibelung* saga." Which seemed as likely as Richard's dumping Minna to marry me, but I kept my mouth shut.

When we reached the music room he took a scant few sheets of the *Siegfried* manuscript from his piano bench and handed them to me. "Would you mind working on these in the room through there? There's ink and paper on the table. I have something else on the go just now."

I looked at the papers on his desk. Dialogue. Pages of the stuff. I felt a flush of excitement. "Is that the libretto for *Die Sieger*?"

He looked puzzled. "Oh, that," he finally said. "No. This is the Tristan poem."

Before long his work on *Siegfried* dried up completely and he no longer needed me at the Asyl.

By the end of the summer the Villa Wesendonck was finished and Otto had moved his family in. In the Asyl, by the time the leaves turned Richard had finished his Tristan poem. I learned about it from Otto.

"You seem quiet," I said at the end of a meeting. "Is everything all right?"

"My apologies. I'm preoccupied with Herr Wagner's latest enthusiasm."

"His Tristan opera?"

He nodded irritably. "He gave a reading of the poem to some of us last night."

"He's finished it, then?"

"Oh, he's finished it, all right."

"And you disapprove?" I asked absently. I was prickling at having been excluded.

"I certainly do. It is an unashamed celebration of adultery."

"That's hardly daring for Herr Wagner. After all, his last opera was basically a celebration of brother-sister incest."

"Yes, but I doubt Herr Wagner was contemplating incest with another man's wife."

There it was.

Richard had made it so obvious that even single-minded Otto could see it.

Within the week I received a note. My services were needed at the Asyl.

"So you've resumed work on *Siegfried*?" I asked as Richard took my coat.

"No. I've started the *Tristan* music."

Vintage Richard. For all his lofty talk about renunciation, he couldn't keep from following his knob into disaster.

This new music pushed even his boundaries. I was grudgingly impressed. And yet we'd hardly begun when he let himself get distracted. On a frost-crusted morning in November he greeted me at the door of the Asyl with an apology. "I'm afraid I don't have anything for you today, Karsten. I should've sent a note."

"You haven't been writing?" That was unusual when the muse was on him.

"I've been writing. Just not *Tristan*."

My hopes rose. "*Siegfried*?"

He snorted. It created a puff of steam in the chill air. "Stop pushing *Siegfried*, Karsten. If you must know, I've been writing some *lieder* for soprano solo."

This surprised me. "What for?"

"Good day, Karsten. I'll contact you when you're needed."

I soon learned what he'd been up to.

"His presumption knows no bounds," Otto said. "Do you know he's written my wife a set of songs?" It seemed Richard's mysterious *lieder* were settings of some of the least worst of Mathilde's poems.

I tried to mollify him. "I'm sure they're just a token of gratitude for your support."

His stare would've hardened steel. "Can you really believe that?"

Shortly before Christmas Otto had to go to New York to deal with a crisis in the US money markets. He came to see me before he left. I'd never seen him look so vulnerable. "It was a mistake to let Herr Wagner live in the Asyl. I know you spend time there, Karsten, with the work you do for him." It was the first time he'd used my given name. "I hesitate to ask, but I can't think of anyone else. Would it compromise your association if I asked you to keep an eye on Mathilde while I'm away?"

I gave him a reassuring smile. "Not at all."

Otto was right to be concerned. He was barely beyond the horizon when Richard started the next stage of his campaign. Prudently, he played to his strengths as composer, arranger and impresario. Imprudently, he involved me. "I've arranged some of my works for a small ensemble." He handed me an untidy stack of music paper. "Can you have the parts done by the weekend? I'd do them myself, but I have to organize the musicians."

I took the pages. "What's this for?"

"A birthday recital for Frau Wesendonck. A week from today."

That wasn't much time to pull off a recital from scratch. "Have you booked a hall? Performance space is scarce this time of year."

"Not in a hall, Karsten. In her home."

That set me back. "While her husband is away?"

Richard waved a dismissive hand. "Otto won't mind."

He pulled it off. I worked day and night to get the parts done on the condition that I could attend the recital, and Richard had agreed. "You can help Minna with the refreshments." He'd enlisted his unwitting wife in his grand seduction.

He put together a pick-up band of strings and winds and secretly rehearsed them in one of the Asyl's larger rooms. On Mathilde's birthday, with the complicity of her servants, he smuggled the performers into her drawing room and waited in careful silence. When he heard her skirts approaching he raised his baton.

Frau Wesendonck was visibly startled at the crowd of musicians in the little room, but when she recognized the opening motif of Richard's setting of one of her poems she beamed with joy. As I brought her a chair she mouthed *Oh, Richard*, and he nodded in acknowledgement. He was lucky Minna wasn't positioned to see the adoration in his eyes, or the game would have been up. When the final chord tapered away Frau Wesendonck leapt up and applauded. "Bravo to all of you." She ran to Richard and took his hands. "What an unexpected treat this has been."

Richard cut her off with a wag of his finger. "It isn't over." He lifted his baton, and the ensemble started a march from his opera *Rienzi*.

The concert went well for something so rushed. It wasn't perfect, but there were no false starts or other gross errors, and Frau Wesendonck was plainly enchanted by the whole elaborate gesture. Minna seemed strangely untroubled by her husband's attention to their hostess. But she'd been vague the whole morning. I'd literally had to snap my fingers in front of her eyes to get her attention when the teapots ran dry. "Oh," she'd said, with a wobble of her hand toward a corner door. "There are servants through there who will get more water for you."

I put it down to the competing tensions of an impossible situation. The Wagners' tenancy on the estate was at Otto's pleasure, which, realistically, meant his wife's pleasure. Which meant Minna had a painful interest in not noticing certain things.

As I gathered the scores at the end, Frau Wesendonck stepped away from Richard with a light touch on his elbow and came over to speak to me. "You're Herr Staheli?"

"I am." Always at the furthest edge of her awareness.

"You have a sister, I think?" She glanced at Richard, who was thankfully, paying some attention to his own wife. "Who Richard was rather fond of?"

I stiffened. What had she seen? Or had Richard been talking?

I straightened the scores into a neat pile. "She did mention him in her letters sometimes, before I came to Zurich."

She smiled coyly. "You and I must chat one day soon, I think." For the first time since the Limmatquai brothels I felt a stirring.

I bowed slightly. "At your service, *meine Frau*."

When Otto got back from America, financial crisis averted, he was furious. "In my own home! The nerve of the man. He *knew* I was away."

I had to defuse this. If Otto withdrew his patronage, what would happen to *Siegfried*, or *Die Sieger*? "There was nothing to it. It was just a concert. A birthday present. Minna was even there, for God's sake. Really, Otto, would a man bring his own wife to an attempted seduction?"

That last bit seemed to help. Yet even as Otto's fury wound down, a whiff of petulance remained. "The little bugger has never acknowledged *my* birthday."

"You have to give a concert for Otto."

"Otto? Whatever for?"

"Domestic harmony."

It took a while to make him understand.

Always the only smart one in the room, our Richard.

By the time we got it organized we'd missed Otto's birthday by a couple of weeks, but we went ahead. Setting up in the drawing room was easier with Mathilde's help. The performances—a few of Otto's favourite movements from Beethoven's symphonies—went off without a hitch. Minna didn't attend.

Otto was tickled. Guessing my role, he gave me a grateful nod. "You're a good friend, Herr Staheli."

While I gathered the scores, Mathilde came over to speak to me. "We haven't had that chat about your sister yet." Her smile was sly and inviting.

"Pick a day."

I went the following afternoon, while Otto was at work. So much for being a good friend. We met in the drawing room, its furniture back in place. She sat on an embroidered couch and leaned lightly against its arm. I took a straight-backed chair.

"Oh no, Herr Staheli." She delicately removed a glove. "That won't do." She leaned toward the low table in front of her. I caught a glimpse of décolletage as she lifted the stopper from a lapis-tinted bottle of scent. She raised her eyes, caught my gaze, and smiled. I felt myself redden. She drew the stopper across a bare fingertip. It left a thin smear of moisture. She replaced the stopper and touched her finger to each side of her neck, at the pulse points. "Sit here, on the couch." She stroked the embroidered cushion. I'd seen that couch seat four adults. She wasn't gesturing toward the far end or the middle. She was directing me to sit next to her.

I rose and crossed toward her. Her eyes stayed on mine. "Just here, so I can see you properly." Only when I was at her knee did she lift her hand from the spot where I was to sit. Which I did.

The scent was dark musk and rose petals. From Paris via New York, probably. The fruits of one of Otto's business trips. "Shall we have tea?" Her bare hand lighted on my knee, her scented fingertip lingering for an instant as she drew it slowly away again. Marking me. "Or shall we be daring and risk an aperitif this early in the day?"

"Let's be daring." I placed my hand on her thigh.

She lifted it away with a cool smile. "Oh no, Herr Staheli. I'm a married woman. We're here to discuss your sister." But she stayed right there next to me on the couch.

Smiling.

My head cleared. It all made sense. Loin-addled Richard, dancing to the teasing tune of this cunning little *bourgeoise*. A merchant's wife, leading the boldest artist of the age around by his own blue balls. And the things she drew out of him! Hiring an orchestra for her birthday. Turning her crap poems into songs. Putting his *Nibelung* project on hold—and abandoning our Buddha opera entirely!—to write a trifle about a love triangle, just so *his* proxy could win *her* proxy from *Otto's* proxy and then die in a thundering orchestral orgasm before it all had the chance to degenerate into *who left the lid off the jam pot?* and *how much can it cost, really, to hire a decent maid?*

All right, fair enough. *Tristan* isn't a trifle.

But I was pissed. How dare she.

This couldn't go on.

About a week later I trudged through the spring muck to the door of the Asyl to work on the latest pages of *Tristan*. Richard opened the door before I could knock. "I heard your carriage," he said softly. "Listen, before we begin, I need you to do something for me."

"Of course. What is it?"

He handed me a bound set of pages. "Take this to Frau Wesendonck." He glanced back nervously. "Minna reacts badly when I go to the main house these days."

"I can't imagine why."

"Don't make light of this. Her doctor has her on laudanum." There was concern in his eyes. "I think she's taking too much." I thought of how vague she'd been at Mathilde's birthday concert. No wonder she'd handled it so well.

I looked at the pages. A draft of the *Tristan* prelude, in Richard's own hand. "Surely a servant could take this over. Why me?"

He glanced around again, then bent back the first page.

There was a sealed letter inside.

I took the carriage toward the main house, and opened the letter once I was out of Richard's sight. It was pretty innocuous. He seemed to be trying to get in the last word in some argument over *Faust* he'd had the night before with some Italian intellectual in Mathilde's salon circle. But it was, after all, a *secret* letter. With the right amount of spin …

I dropped the score with Mathilde's housemaid and returned to the Asyl with the letter in my breast pocket. Around mid-day Richard decided to take a break. "Will you join me for a walk down to the river?"

I nodded at the pages in front of me. "I'll keep going for now."

"Suit yourself."

I watched from the window until I was sure he was gone.

Then I went to find Minna.

The only way to get Richard back on track was to scupper his obsession with Mathilde Wesendonck. The simplest way was through Minna. Through Otto was too risky. His patronage was crucial. But Minna had the clout to bring it to its necessary end.

It took some effort to get her there.

"Surely this is just about Goethe," she said.

"But Richard is so adamant. It reads like a duel, with Frau Wesendonck as the prize."

"Richard is often adamant."

"But generally for a reason. What is it here? Why does he care whether Frau Wesendonck agrees with this Italian or not? Unless he sees the Italian as a rival?"

Her opiate-clouded eyes stared off into the room. "I just don't know."

"Look, here. He says that when he looks into her eyes he can't even speak. Those are the words of a lover."

"Why are you rubbing my nose in this muck, Herr Staheli?" Her voice was almost lifeless. "I thought you were Richard's friend."

I took her hand. "I am. But I can't bear to see him treat you this way."

She dropped the letter and shook her head. "But what can I do?" It wasn't rhetorical. "I'm asking you, Herr Staheli. Advise me. What can I do?"

I let out a contrived sigh. "Confront him. Make him give her up."

When I heard Richard return I slipped out the back way. It was between them now. I couldn't give him the opportunity to make it about me. My time would come. When it did, there was a good chance my relationship with him would be over. But his art was worth that risk.

Things didn't go the way I expected them to.

First there was silence. After about a week, the buzz was that Frau Wagner had left Zurich for another water cure. That she'd grown horribly dependent on laudanum. That there'd been a shrieking confrontation with Frau Wesendonck. The buzz didn't say much about Richard yet.

When Otto came to my office, unannounced, he was discreet. "There's been a bit of conflict. I'm leaving for Italy this afternoon with Frau Wesendonck and the children. You won't be able to reach me for a while."

"And Herr Wagner?"

"Still at the Asyl. For now."

The Wesendoncks returned to their Villa in June. Minna came back in July. After their mutual time-outs they could have normalized relations and gone on. But Richard couldn't leave it alone.

"I'm sending Mathilde to Munich," Otto told me shortly after Minna's return.

"Things still tense with Frau Wagner?"

"Yes, but she isn't the problem. It's that odious husband of hers. I apologize, Karsten, I know you are friends—"

"Not so much these days."

"Well. Regardless. He's gone unspeakably far."

"What, in his attentions to your wife?"

"Oh, yes. His *attentions* now include asking her to run off with him! Can you believe it? When I've supported him and his strange music so completely."

I had a hard time believing it, actually. Surely even Richard had the sense not to foul his own nest so completely. "Frau Wesendonck refused, of course?"

"Damn right. Came straight to me with it."

"But you're sending her away?"

"Not as punishment. To keep her clear of that dreadful man. And of the gossip." He placed a hand on my shoulder. "You'll keep this between us, yes?"

"Naturally." And I did. Not that it did any good. The buzz was all over the canton within days. Minna had filed for divorce, it said. Or Otto had. Or Richard and Mathilde had disappeared together. None of which was true, but why would that matter? A good scandal never lets the truth get in its way.

Life in musical Zurich went on. In July the city hosted a national choral festival, which Baumgartner chaired. For three days the streets around the Grossmunster and the Aktientheater were jammed with choirs from across the country, wandering the streets in their frock coats and breaking into spontaneous motets on the patios of the coffee houses. I'd pulled out of my own choir well in advance, to keep my head down. I needn't have. No one ever publicly associated me with the scandal. Privately, though ...

I was crossing the Grossmunsterplatz after a mediocre performance of French songs by a choir from Lausanne when I found myself face to face with Richard. "You." His voice was flat. A bare acknowledgement.

"Hello, Richard. You look well." It was feeble, but I had to say something.

"I have to go." He turned away.

This was the moment. The only chance I'd get. "You had to be freed from her."

He turned back. "I would've been. Mathilde would have freed me from her eventually. But not anymore. You saw to that." The poor boy thought I meant Minna.

Getting it all tragically wrong as usual, Richard disappeared into the crowd.

I never saw him again. Within the month he'd left Zurich for good.

With Fanny and Richard gone there wasn't much keeping me in Zurich, but I had a comfortable life and a reasonably new persona, and maybe that was enough. I could've retreated to the sheep pasture, but the thought of solitude made me sad. Everything to its season.

A week or so after Richard's departure, as I sat under my tree on the Hohe Promenade looking over some music for the choir I'd rejoined, I saw movement from the corner of my eye. Striding toward me as he had years before was Willi Baumgartner. It was like a flashback, except this time I was wearing trousers instead of a dress and he was carrying gloves instead of an envelope of unmemorable songs. And this time he looked livid instead of nervous.

"Willi, what—"

He slapped me with his gloves. "I challenge you." He was vibrating with fury. He smelled of brandy. "I will have satisfaction."

"Satisfaction for what? How have I wronged you? Publically, I mean?" That was petty. But the man had just slapped me with his gloves.

"You've wronged me and all of Zurich by your betrayal of Herr Richard Wagner. And I will have satisfaction." He'd probably rehearsed this in front of his mirror. It had probably gone better there.

"Betrayal? How? I've always been devoted to Herr Wagner. I'm as troubled to see him go as anyone." That last bit, sadly, was all too true.

"Liar!" He flung his gloves at my feet. "You engineered his public humiliation. You forced him from this city, which nurtured him in his exile and which, in his gratitude, he served so well." Mirror. No question.

"I did no such thing." I kept my voice soft and level, like a trauma therapist or a hostage negotiator. "As I understand it, Frau Wagner went to Herr Wesendonck with—"

"With a letter Herr Wagner entrusted to *you*." There it was. Richard had blabbed to his lackey. Now the lackey was gunning for me.

"Listen, Willi—"

"You will address me as Herr Baumgartner."

"Very well, Herr Baumgartner." I closed the score in my lap. "What satisfaction do you propose to obtain from me here this afternoon, on behalf of your city?"

He snarled. You almost never see anyone actually snarl, but damned if Willi Baumgartner didn't do it just then. "Not here and not this afternoon. At first light tomorrow, in the rehearsal room of the Aktientheater."

"And what will happen then?"

Willi straightened and snapped his heels together in what he probably imagined was the manner of a proud Prussian officer. He looked more like he had a gooseberry up his bum. "Satisfaction. Pistols or swords. Your choice, as the challenged."

Oh dear God. "Really, Willi, you can't—"

"You will address me as Herr Baumgartner!"

Poor dear Willi. I'd studied swordplay with experts from a dozen eras, and I could probably put three holes through his hat while he was still figuring out how to cock his pistol. The closest he'd ever been to a sword or a gun was seeing wooden stage props from the wings. But he was determined.

I sighed. "You really want to do this?"

"It is my duty as a man." Where do boys get this stuff?

"Very well. Swords."

I could hardly let him blast a hole through the theatre's rehearsal piano, could I?

He was there when I arrived in the dusk of the following morning, along with Kirchner, who was presumably meant to be his second. There was a pitcher of water on the upright piano and a velvet-lined case with a set of illicit Italian duelling sabres across two hard-backed chairs. They were examining the weapons cautiously, like they were worried they might leap out of the case on their own. Kirchner noticed me first. He gave me an apologetic look as I entered the lamplit room. "Herr Staheli."

Willi looked up. "Where is your second?"

"Haven't brought one. Don't need one."

This seemed to bewilder him. "But ... but you have to have a second." He picked up a creased document from the sword case. "It's in the rules."

I deliberately didn't look at it. "The *Code Duello* of 1777?" The standard across Europe, though not many non-duellists would've known that. The fact that I did surprised him, as I intended. "I waive my right to a second." I stepped to the case and selected a sabre. Flat, unadorned blades with simple steel guards around the knuckles. Tools for genuine duelling, not drawing room display.

My waiver didn't help Willi's bafflement. He stared at his document, presumably looking for authority for dispensing with a second. A good rule-bound German Swiss. I tried a few practice passes. The sword had decent balance and a comfortable grip. Kirchner looked concerned at my ease with it, so I addressed him rather than Willi. "There's still time to call this off."

Willi flushed angrily. "No! You will not deprive me of satisfaction so easily."

Kirchner frowned.

Willi took the other sabre and waved it vaguely about. Kirchner took him aside. There was a whispered conversation. Willi became increasingly irritated and finally said: "Enough! Let's begin." Kirchner looked at me and shook his head. Then he marked off two chalk lines on the floor, about four paces apart.

I draped my jacket across a chair at the edge of the room. Willi struggled out of his, not quite sure how to manage it while holding a sword, and handed it to Kirchner. We took our positions. Kirchner raised his eyebrows at Willi in a last plea, but Willi shook his head. "*Allez*," Kirchner said, and stepped back.

Willi lunged at me like a bear climbing out of a bathtub. I drove the point of his sword down to the floor with a twist of my wrist, stepped on it to hold it there, and tapped him on each cheek with the flat of my blade. "You really don't have to do this."

"It is my honour to do this." He lifted his blade and lunged again.

I tapped it away to the left, away to the left, away to the left. No matter where he tried to move it, away it went to the left. Then to the right, once, twice. He was expecting a third, so I knocked it upward, hard. Before he could recover I sliced the top button from his waistcoat. "Fly buttons next," I said amiably. "I'll try to be as accurate."

He swung wildly, throwing himself off balance. I slapped my blade on his backside. "Really, Willi, you should just—"

He spun, breathing hard. "You will address me. As Herr. *Baumgartner!*"

The duel, if you can call it one, went on like that for another ten minutes. I wondered if Willi might end it if I nicked him, so I did. When he brought a bloodied hand away from the nape of his neck I thought maybe we were done, but it spurred him on. He swung more furiously, and I dodged him more easily.

Kirchner had had enough. "Time!"

Willi stopped in the middle of a backswing. "What do you mean 'time'?"

"A break. To catch your breath. Take a glass of water."

Willi's chest was heaving. "The *Code* doesn't say anything about *breaks*."

"And yet I've called one."

Willi seemed torn between his need to follow the rules and his need for a rest. With a dramatic sigh, he lowered his sword. I lowered mine. Kirchner handed us each a glass of water. Mine came with a piece of folded paper. While Willi was wiping the sweat from his eyes I unfolded it. *You must lose*, it said.

I looked over at Kirchner. He tilted his head toward Willi and raised an eyebrow. His meaning was plain. Willi wouldn't yield, and wouldn't accept a mere apology. He was prepared to see this through to the death. It was up to me to find a way to end it short of that. I nodded. Kirchner looked relieved.

I sipped my water and thought about the *Code Duello*.

I took off my waistcoat.

We re-took our places at the chalk lines, and Kirchner called *Allez*. At first I toyed with Willi as before. Then I took an extra beat to dodge his thrust and turned just enough that it grazed my forearm and drew a little blood.

"Right." I held out my arm. "We're both blooded. Will you retire?"

Wounding me seemed to energize him. "On scrapes like these?"

I let him give me two more minor cuts, but each time he insisted on continuing.

There was only one way out. I parried his blade to my left and then drew mine back in a ridiculously wide arc to my right, leaving my side exposed. I was afraid I'd been too obvious, but he beamed. He thought he'd created the advantage himself. I had to hover like an ungainly boob to keep his opening open, and adjust my posture to make sure he didn't hit any organs.

Willi's sword went in above my left hip. I let out a cry. Kirchner let out a sharper one as the blade tented the back of my shirt and then poked through, smeared bright red. I waited until Willi withdrew it, his eyes wide, before I dropped my own sword and collapsed to the floor. "Ah!" I shouted. "I am undone!"

Maybe that was overdoing it.

I rolled to my right to highlight the spreading stains front and back. Surely he would stop now. But instead he lifted his sabre for a killing blow to my neck.

Oops.

I couldn't reach my own sword in time to parry, and with my injured side I couldn't roll away fast enough or far enough. The sabre reached the top of its arc. I was about to die at the hands of the least competent swordsman I'd faced in a thousand years. I took a moment to appreciate the irony. Then Kirchner stepped in and grabbed Willi's arm. "No, Wilhelm. You mustn't."

Willi glared at him, his pupils as wide as copper coins. "Why not? He's a vile, sinful creature."

"Because it's against the rules."

Rule 5 of the *Code* says the challenger may not kill an opponent who's been "well blooded, disabled or disarmed." He has to lay his sword on his opponent's shoulder and say: "I spare your life." He also gets to break the other guy's sword, but since ours were borrowed there wasn't much point to that. Willi mumbled the words so quietly I was tempted to ask him to say them again, but I didn't. I needed to bind up my side. Thankfully Kirchner had had the foresight to bring a roll of bandages. He helped dress my injuries while Willi stood staring at nothing.

As I was retrieving my jacket, I heard a clatter and a thump. I turned. Willi had dropped his sabre and fallen to his knees, trembling and sobbing. I limped over to him. "Normal reaction after a duel. You'll be all right."

He wiped snot from his nose with his sleeve. "You will leave Zurich now." It wasn't a command, or a question. Just a statement, made with complete conviction.

I nodded. "Sounds about right." I draped my jacket over my shoulders. Sleeves seemed like too much effort.

"I'll take you to a surgeon," Kirchner said.

I shook my head and turned toward the door. "I'm fine."

I walked out of the Aktientheater for the final time, into the dim Zurich dawn.

It took a few weeks to settle my affairs. In the meantime I gave up my flat and moved back to Adliswil. Utz was long dead, but his successors had kept the rooms dusted and the weeds trimmed. I took my meals in the village and spent my evenings reading by the fire.

I sold off my assets to my competitors, including Otto Wesendonck, who gave me a better price than he needed to. My looms, land and flocks were in high demand as Switzerland's growing rail network opened new markets for its textiles. I was getting out of the business at the wrong time, but I didn't care. I parked my profits in a numbered account at Credit Suisse and, with just a small suitcase and a large letter of credit, took the first train elsewhere.

Richard never did write his Buddha opera. Instead he cannibalized it for his interminable final work about Sir Percival, the knight whose vacuous innocence leads him to the Holy Grail. I discreetly attended its premiere in 1882. Its conductor, Hermann Levi, was the son of a rabbi.

I didn't appreciate the darker side of Richard's ambivalence toward me until *Parsifal*. It's there in the backstory: King Amfortas has fallen from grace via his seduction by a cursed Semitic immortal named Kundry. Nudge nudge. The overarching theme, as in our Buddha project, is redemption through renunciation. The music for the scene where Parsifal resists Kundry's seduction could easily have been for Savitri's rapture in the forest. Maybe it had been ripening in Richard's mind the whole time.

Even Kundry gets her redemption in the end. As the opera winds down she just dies, for no apparent reason, while the Grail Knights revel around her in smug purity. Her death has been seen as misogynist —punishment for her sins while the men are all saved—but to me it feels more like a letting go, a release from the merry-go-round of eternal rebirth. It breaks my heart every time I see it. It's almost worth enduring its wearisome four-hour preamble.

Wagner's vision of redemption from eternal wandering is his legacy to me, whether he meant it to be or not. It reassures me that my own Kundry moment is out there. I attend productions of *Parsifal* whenever I can.

Though I generally wait in the bar until Act Three.

There's one other, even clearer sign of Richard's attitude toward me. Although he published his thoughts with a relentlessness unmatched before the development of social media, he never mentioned me in his writings. Not anywhere. Not even once.

Thanks a bunch, asshole.

Ten Days Ago

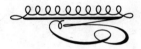

I MET ELEVEN at a coffee bar on the ground floor of the Reference Library. You've seen my library, of course. Probably the first place you went. Sorry it was in such a state. I spend a lot of my time there. Spent, I guess, now. It's the part of the house I've devoted the most thought to. The watercolour on the mantle is the Asyl, by the way. I found it in a bazaar in Morocco. When I bought the place in the 1920s it was a billiard room. Fifty years later I sold the billiard table to my neighbour and used the proceeds to put in the glass-fronted shelving. Five hundred linear feet. You do a lot of reading when you're me.

I see that look. Someone's gone through my books. Books about Buddhism, and Wagner, and the Peasants' Revolt, and the Battle of Qadesh. Your conventional mind is starting to relax. *He got it all out of his books*, you're thinking. *Sitting in his bay window with his glass of port.* I bet that's a satisfying feeling. But what if you've got it back to front? Wouldn't I be intrigued to see how historians have cobbled together the times I've lived through? Imagine the amusement value. In my bay window with my glass of port.

You've sent the sword for testing, I assume. It's the one I made in Wales in the sixties. A replica of the one I pulled out of the ruins of Troy and carried up the Danube and the Vltava and the Elbe. You should've seen it in its spot over the mantle. In the halogen lighting it seemed to glow from inside.

Say what you like about stainless steel. Polished bronze is lovely stuff.

The coffee bar was busy, so we sat at a long table between some students with stickered laptops and a herd of yoga moms. I went up for the coffees, to pre-empt any pointless conflict between Eleven and the counter staff. I brought him four packets of sugar. He put three in his cup and one in his pocket.

"Still time for you to invest in—" he glanced around like a pantomime spy "—in that, ah, other project of mine." He cupped his hand

and mimed putting a joint to his lips, which was a good move if he wanted to tip off everyone in the room rather than just everyone at our table. If he weren't so good at his job I'd be done with him. Which I guess I am now.

"Still not interested. Don't want to know anything about it."

Which wasn't strictly true. I wanted to know enough to keep it from blowing back on me. But I already did. His guy was a portly stoner named Sully whose gelled-up hair made him look like an exotic chicken. Their lab was a shed behind an empty house in Cabbagetown.

"Your loss." He unlocked his phone and drew it slowly away from himself in the international sign for being too vain for reading glasses. "The equipment's in bond at Pearson Airport. Ordinarily we could just pick it up, but the broker says there's a hold on it. He says it's nothing to worry about. Random check, probably."

"How long is that likely to last?"

"Depends what they're checking for. You didn't slip a couple kilos of coke in there, did you?" He was joking. Of course I didn't. But maybe his leash needed a yank.

"What if I did? Who'd be on the hook? Me? Or you and Jeremy and Wayne?"

His grin vanished. He went pale. "Jesus, Murray—"

"No names."

I let him twist a moment. Dog training, basically. Then I let him go. "It's all legitimate. Nothing illicit. Nothing hidden."

His face sagged with relief. "Christ, mate. Don't do that to me."

"Then don't cack around. Find out what the hold is about."

He tapped his screen. "Done."

"Good. What about my Chechen?"

He scrolled down. "Something odd there, too."

"Odd how?"

"Not sure. My guy says the approvals should've come through by now, but they haven't. He doesn't know why."

One bureaucratic glitch was normal. Two made me wonder. "Tell him to find out."

In the meantime I'd be wise to update my exit strategy.

The Cabaret

AFTER THE MECHANIZED butchery of the Great War I swore off soldiering for good. So when World War II started ramping up, I took refuge in a familiar place where I could sit it out in safety. Saint Benedict's monastery at Monte Cassino. Shows what I know.

When American bombers flattened the place, those of us who'd taken shelter in the vaults crept out and caught a lift in a three-ton truck. I should've gone with the others to Sant'Anselmo in Rome. Instead I melted into the countryside and spent the rest of the war trying to get to my money in Zurich. Fat chance. Paranoia was high and borders tight. It got worse when the war ended. In a shattered Europe jammed with the displaced, all I could do was ride the currents. Which took me to Berlin.

I don't know how the people around me coped: hollow-eyed Jews who'd seen their families shot or gassed or starved; women, thousands of them, with haunting stories of brutalization by the advancing Russian troops. I'd been a German, and a Russian. And a brute. But I couldn't comprehend where impulses like that had come from. I'd been a Jew too, sort of. I'd seen the scapegoating and the persecution and the pogroms. But not like this. This was a different order of magnitude.

Apparently there was a nugget of naiveté in me that three thousand years of cynicism hadn't dug out.

In Berlin I ate when there were handouts and slept in bombed-out ruins. When bucket brigades of energetic young women came to clear the rubble from my resting place I moved down the street. There were always more ruins. Slowly the city stuck itself back together. Slowly so did I. My thoughts returned to my accounts in Zurich. Maybe I could get there now. But not looking and smelling the way I did. And not without money for transport and lodgings and bribes.

I turned my attention to the world around me. Tensions among the occupying powers. Posturing. Wariness. Cravings for intel. I could work with that.

I found work at the Budapester Kabarett. I'd washed in a pond in the Tiergarten and stolen a shirt and trousers from a clothesline behind a French barracks. The cabaret took care of my work wardrobe. Including wigs and makeup.

With the Nazis gone, the cabaret scene was re-emerging. The neighbourhood around Nollendorfplatz was dotted with clubs where women and men in gowns sang and served drinks and danced with patrons for a fee. The Budapester wasn't as *luxe* as the Eden or the Eldorado. Our clients were workingmen and squaddies rather than officers and attachés. Like the other clubs we had a gay clientele, but we also attracted groups of straight men and couples looking for live music and the *frisson* of the unfamiliar.

Some nights there'd be soldiers on day leave who'd misread the nature of the club. A lot of them were American, so our playlist leaned toward Cole Porter and Irving Berlin. Every night one or two crew-cuts from Pittsburgh or Pensacola would point out how hilarious it was that we were singing Irving Berlin in, like, you know, Berlin? In case we hadn't made the connection.

But as long as they kept buying dances and drinks, we kept laughing.

I'd been working there about a week when Ilsa leaned toward me. "The SIS is back." Not so long ago she'd been a tank driver with a crew cut and a clipped moustache. There was nowhere like post-war Berlin for reinventing yourself. I don't think I'd felt more comfortable anywhere.

We were near the beer taps, placing our customers' orders. A fat man with a patchy beard and a threadbare jacket had taken a seat at the other end of the bar. He lit a cigarette and waved at Klaus the bartender. Klaus ignored him and strained whisky sours into the glasses on Ilsa's tray.

"What's SIS?"

Ilsa stared. "How long have you been in Berlin?"

"Not long enough, apparently."

The cook grunted from the pass-through. Klaus put two plates of bockwurst and boiled potatoes next to the cocktails. Ilsa dropped her voice to a husky whisper. "Secret Intelligence Service." She smiled conspiratorially. "English spies."

She had my attention. I wasn't going to get to Zurich dancing with GIs for tokens and tips. I'd assumed I'd have to work my way up to the Eldorado to meet anyone with marketable information. Maybe I'd been wrong. "If it's so secret, how do you know he's part of it?"

Ilsa gave me a world-weary sigh. "This is Berlin, sweetie. Secrets here are like sausages." She balanced her tray on one hand. "You can spot them anywhere if you know what you're looking for." She gave my crotch a playful grab, laughed lightly, and headed to her table.

Klaus was still pointedly ignoring the new arrival. I caught his eye, raised an eyebrow and gave a nod toward the man. Klaus responded with a *whatever you like* shrug. So over I went. "Take your order, sir?"

He looked me up and down. Not the way most of the men did. Just taking in information. "New here, are you?" he asked in a lumpy Flemish accent. "What's your name, then?"

"Betty. Yours?" I rested my elbow on his shoulder.

"Vlaming. Jan Vlaming. You can take your arm away. That's not why I'm here."

I left my elbow where it was. "And why *are* you here, then, Mr. Vlaming?"

"For a half-litre of lager and a pretzel. If your Bolshie bartender would be so kind."

I turned to Klaus. He nodded. He'd heard. Which meant he'd been listening. I filed that away. He tossed the smallest pretzel from the basket onto a plate. Then he drew the glass of lager, taking care to give it an extra couple of inches of foam. I set them in front of Vlaming. "Anything else?"

"Mustard."

As I turned to get the mustard pot, Vlaming put his hand on my arm. "Maybe one other thing." I looked back at him. "You *girls*—" he resisted the word, but saw it through "—sometimes hear things, yes?"

I pursed my lips noncommittally. "Hmmm."

"Sometimes people say things of value. If you were to hear such a thing, I might be able to arrange a small fee."

I felt Klaus' presence behind my shoulder. "Bite me," I said. Or something to that effect. But with a wink Klaus couldn't see. I didn't want to close off any options. Vlaming sipped his lager as if he hadn't seen the wink. But I knew he had.

"Good call," Klaus said when I went for my table's order. "Damned English spies."

"He doesn't sound very English."

"You work for the English, you're English."

I picked up my tray. This time it was Klaus who put a hand on my arm. "He's right about information, though. Sometimes you hear things."

This day was getting interesting. "And?"

"And if you do, I may know some people who appreciate its value."

"People?"

He turned his face away from Vlaming. "HVA."

"What's HVA?"

He gave me the look Ilsa had given me when I'd asked about SIS. "The intelligence service of the German Democratic Republic."

"East German spies?"

"Collectors of information. Supporters of the cause."

Whatever. I gave him a complicit nod and headed to my table.

The future was starting to look profitable.

A couple of weeks later a group of men turned up as I was about to take the stage. Half a dozen, in civilian jackets and ties, with an assortment of regional English accents but American military crew cuts. My radar crackled. I asked Ilsa to take my set. "Gentlemen," I said to them in English. "Anything I can do for you?" It was clear what I meant. They already had a round of drinks and a basket of pretzels, but their stack of dance tokens was untouched.

"Let us get a pint in first, eh love?" said a red-faced Brummie who plainly thought he was their ringleader. "Pacing ourselves, yeah?" He nudged his mates and cackled. They laughed, but without much enthusiasm. There's always one, isn't there?

The one who drew my attention was a quiet lad with dirt under his nails. He had a quivery look of anticipation and dread. With a little finesse, I could open a boy like that right up. But not just yet.

"Enjoy yourselves." As I wandered to the next table I gave the quiet lad a smile. He reddened and glanced down.

I made eye contact with the boy a couple of times while I danced with other patrons, and during my next set I looked at him through the final chorus of *Blaue Nacht am Hafen*. He smiled shyly. Starting to play along. When I eventually came back to their table, during the band's first instrumental set, they treated me like an old friend.

"Oi, what's your name, love?" the Brummie asked through a mouthful of potato salad.

"Betty."

"Betty, is it?" He laughed and looked around the table. "More like Bertie, eh lads?" This drew some tepid chuckles. The boy missed his meaning entirely.

"You haven't spent any of your dance tokens." I directed this to the whole table, but with my fingertips on my young target's shoulder. "Don't English boys dance?"

The boy swallowed. The Brummie noticed, and saw his chance for a bit of fun. "Go on, Nige. Have a dance with the lady." He gave this last word just enough stress to show off his worldliness without tipping his hand to young Nigel. The boy stayed quiet.

I reached across the table for a token, brushing Nigel's shoulder with my bosom. "I can only have this if someone dances with me. Surely you brave English soldiers wouldn't deprive a poor cabaret girl of her income, would you?"

"We ain't soldiers, miss," a wiry ginger said. "Civilians, us." He, too, had dirt under his nails.

"That's right." The Brummie again. "Administration. Keeping the lights on sort of thing."

"My mistake." I waggled the token. "Then you brave English *administrators* wouldn't deprive me of my income, yes?"

Nigel looked from me to his mates, uncertain what to do. The ginger sighed and gave him a gentle nudge. "Right, Nige, off you go. It's just a dance, eh?" The Brummie grinned deliciously. I could have gutted him. But I had work to do. I held out a hand. Nigel took it and rose shakily to his feet.

"Steady on, Nige." The Brummie's eyes glittered with mischief.

I turned the boy away toward the dance floor. "Ignore your friend. I wouldn't dance with him for all the tokens on your table." I felt him relax a little. The band was playing *Wunderland bei Nacht*. He didn't know what to do, so I put his right hand on my hip and held his left near my bare shoulder. I swayed to the lazy sound of the muted trumpet. After a moment he picked up the rhythm and swayed along.

"So." My mouth was next to his ear. "You keep the lights on, do you?"

"Um. Yeah. You know. Shuffle paper. See the bills get paid."

"Dirty work, shuffling paper?"

"What do you mean?"

I pressed myself against his chest. "Nothing. Just the dirt under your fingernails."

He jerked his hand from my hip and looked at it.

"Shhhhh." I guided his hand back. "Never mind. Idle curiosity."

He was sweating. "That's from, ah, gardening. I help with the gardening."

"Of course." I wriggled slightly. "What do you grow in your garden, Nigel? Tulips? Potatoes?"

"Potatoes, yeah. Potatoes and carrots. Patch of land behind the offices." He was heartbreakingly transparent.

"Mmmm-hmmm. And where are these offices?"

"I can't say." He drew a breath. "Security."

That bit I believed. But it was all I believed. Wherever the dirt under his nails was from, it wasn't a potato garden. The song ended.

"Thank you, Nigel."

"Thank you, miss." His face shone. I steered him back to his table, one hand on his shoulder, half hating myself for it when I saw the Brummie's sly grin. "Anyone else?" They shook their heads. I bowed slightly. "Enjoy your evening."

As I walked to the wings for my next set, I glanced back. I saw the Brummie gleefully whisper something to Nigel. Saw the boy's face blanch with shock. Saw it cave in on itself as he looked over at me. I looked away.

They stayed until closing. I avoided their table. But when they headed for the door, I rushed to where Ilsa was turning in her tokens. "Can I borrow your scooter?" She had a battered white Vespa she'd bought on the black market.

"What for?" I gave her a little leer and glanced toward the door. "Ooooh, *darling*." She fished out her key and handed it to me. "If you promise to give me the details later."

"I promise." I took the key and slipped outside in time to see the Englishmen climb into the back of a US Army truck. My radar had been right. I hiked up my gown and kicked the Vespa into life.

I held well back from the truck and kept the scooter's light off, to be as discreet as someone in an evening gown on a Vespa could be. I didn't know Berlin's roads well, but we seemed to be in the American sector. I memorized the turns so I could find my way back. After a while the truck slowed. I kept my distance. It pulled up at a gatehouse in a high chain fence. The gate opened and the truck drove in. I parked the Vespa and crept toward the enclosure, staying beyond the reach of its lights. There were three main buildings. None looked like the kind of administrative offices where people shuffled paper to keep the lights on. I risked getting close enough to see the sign near the gate. A US radar station.

Why would Brits be working at an American military radar station? And why claim security concerns when there was a sign announcing the site's purpose? It didn't fit. The only thing that *did* fit was the thing I'd been most suspicious about: a rectangular green patch that just might have been a potato garden.

"You look disappointed," Ilsa said when I dropped off her Vespa the next day.

"Misunderstanding."

The Brits came back a couple of times over the next month or so. All except Nigel. Sometimes I'd catch the Brummie smiling at me smugly. Then they stopped coming at all.

Over the next few months the mystery of the radar station receded. Ilsa had been right about secrets. They were easy once I learned how to look. Small, but easy. A Soviet Warrant Officer's unguarded criticism of Krushchev during his sixth vodka. A glimpse of a French *Sous-lieutenant*'s cache of forged travel passes. Some I took to Klaus and some to Vlaming. The pay was pocket change, but it added up.

"These trifles are getting tiresome," Vlaming said one day, pocketing the slip of paper I'd put in his pretzel basket. It was Klaus' day off. Presumably he was enjoying whatever bonuses the HVA gave its lesser assets. A pork steak and a cigar, maybe.

"Steer me toward something better and I'll get it for you."

Vlaming pushed back his stool and heaved himself to his feet. "Not my job." He brushed crumbs from his spotty waistcoat. "You find. I pay."

The tip he left included my fee. When I got home I added it to my travel fund.

That winter a new group of Americans turned up at the cabaret. GIs in Signals Service uniforms. I was on stage, singing *I've Got You Under My Skin*. They were led by a tall, blond man with a thin scar on his left cheekbone, whose bearing said he'd chosen the venue, and knew what it was. While he seated them at a pair of floor-side tables our eyes met. He smiled. He wasn't there for a half-litre of lager and a pretzel.

We didn't dance that night. But he came back a week later on his own, in civvies, and sat at the bar. "I'm Jack," he said when I approached him.

"Betty." I extended a hand. He didn't shake it. He drew it forward and kissed it. We danced three times that night. He danced with Ilsa once, too. "For form's sake," he told me later after I'd comped him a bierwurst. Not a euphemism. An actual bierwurst.

We never went beyond dancing and the occasional fondle. Maybe he wouldn't have. I can't be sure. But as winter softened into spring, his visits felt like chapters in a seasonal romance. A calculated one, on my part. The Signals Service probably had marketable intel. Jack got a six-hour pass once a week, but didn't come to the cabaret every time. "Gotta go to the regular bars with the boys." Appearances. I understood. I could've ratted him out to Klaus for a pittance, but I didn't. I wanted to see what more I could get. Plus I kind of liked him.

March was sunny that year. Colour returned to people's faces after the grey of winter. Except to Jack's. One night after a set I joined him on a dim banquette and stroked his cheek. "You look pale."

He smiled and nuzzled my hand. "Too much time underground."

I stopped breathing. "Underground?"

"Indoors. I meant indoors."

I let it go. But I filed it away. Two weeks later, during a close dance, I rested my head on his shoulder and said, offhand: "I don't even know where you go when you aren't here. What you do."

"Nothing very interesting. Mostly sitting in a room watching a screen."

"A screen?"

"A radar screen."

"At one of the airports?"

"At a radar station."

I drew away slightly so he wouldn't feel my heart beating faster, covering it by looking up at him. "But where would there be a radar station besides an airport?" I aimed for adorably puzzled rather than suspiciously curious.

Jack laughed. "Couple miles that way, for one." He nodded vaguely to the south east. He smiled as if I were a mischievous puppy. "But that's all I can say."

"Oh, I'm sorry. I shouldn't have asked."

"It's all right." He put a finger under my chin and tilted my face toward his. "I haven't said more than I should."

But he'd said enough.

"Do we have a map of the city?" I asked Klaus after we closed up.

"Why?"

"Just … do we have one?"

"On the wall in the office, but it's pretty out of date. Have a look if you like." He took me to the room behind the kitchen and unlocked it. On the wall over a metal desk was a faded Post Office map. He peered at the bottom corner. "Nineteen thirty-nine."

"It'll do. Where are we?"

He stabbed the map with a finger. "Here."

I thought back to the route I'd taken when I'd followed the truck-load of Brits. I traced it with my eyes to where the American radar station was, in a southern suburb called Rudow. More than a couple of miles, if it was the same one. But Jack might've been deliberately imprecise. To the right of the station, the Schönefelder Chaussee ran north to south. Parallel to it was a symbol I didn't recognize. I checked the legend.

Underground telephone cables.

My heart was racing.

"Where's the sector border in this area?" I gestured vaguely toward Rudow.

Klaus was an HVA asset. He knew the borders as well as anyone. He drew a line down the map with his finger. "There."

Right between the radar station and the cables.

He tapped to the left of the line. "American sector." To the right. "Soviet sector."

The pieces clicked into place. A fenced American radar station sat five hundred metres from a buried Soviet phone network. A year ago there were British civilians there, with GI haircuts and dirt under their nails. Now there were US Signals Service officers working underground. In Berlin. Where information was gold.

"Klaus, I need you to set up a meeting."

He wanted me to give what I had to him, the way I usually did.

"No. This is different. Bigger. I want something specific in return."

I laid out my terms. I kept them reasonable. Train ticket to Zurich, with the date left open. Travel documents. Cash for a week's food and lodging. "After that I'll look after myself."

"They'll need to be sure it's worth it."

"Have them bring what I need. Once I tell them, they'll hand it over. They won't believe the bargain they're getting."

When I cashed in my dance tokens that Saturday night, Klaus gave me a slip of paper with an address on it. "Tuesday afternoon at four. You'll be meeting a woman. Veles." He said the name with a kind of reverence.

The room, at the top of a narrow stairway, was empty apart from a plain table, two hard-backed chairs and the smell of disuse. I slid the window up to let some air in. You could step through to the roof of the adjacent building, like stepping onto a balcony. From the cigarette butts and empty bottles, people did. Not recently, though.

Forty minutes later I heard a creak on the landing. The door opened. A woman in black came in and kicked it shut behind her. Her dark hair was pulled back severely. She peered at me over a Tokarev pistol, held at eye height with both hands. Something about her half-hidden face looked familiar. Something in the focus of that peering eye. The eye widened, and she lowered the gun. "Ishtanu? My God, is it really you?"

They say old memories are more durable than new ones. That's true even for me. Even if the memories are three thousand years old.

I'd last seen Tróán as she rode into the Thracian woods, just before her presumed death sent Tror on his bloody rampage. But her face was as clear to me as if I'd seen her last week. "You're one of us?" she said. "How could I have missed that?"

"Us?"

She holstered the gun. "Us. People who don't die."

"'There are more?"

"Who can say? But you and me, and presumably Tror. This is fantastic! Now we can find him together."

My gut flipped. "Tror?"

"You can't have forgotten. I know it was a long time ago, but ..."

"I haven't forgotten. But why would Tror be alive after all this time?"

She placed a brown leather satchel on the table. "He's my son. I don't die. Why would he? And the legends call him a god. There has to be a reason for that."

Not as direct a reason as she supposed.

My brain caught up a couple of steps. "Wait, you can have children? How can you have children?"

"How is that a surprise? You were there when Tror was born."

"But we can't reproduce."

Tróán frowned. "Well obviously I did. Though Tror was the only time."

"And you haven't seen him since Thrace?"

"No. After I faked my ambush I went south, to the land of the Achaeans." I recognized her sly smile. "I did some damage."

I gestured to the satchel, mostly to get the conversation away from Tror. "Is that my money and travel documents?"

"What?" It was like she'd forgotten why we were there. "Well sure, but does it matter now? Whatever your plans were, this changes them."

It didn't, since my plans were to reunite myself with my money. Especially when the alternative was joining a cold-blooded warrior woman whose son's head I'd cut off. But how to ease away?

"It's been thousands of years, Tróán. Wouldn't you have found him by now?"

"Tróán." She repeated the name softly. "How long since anyone called me that? These days I'm Teresia. I stay close to my original name. It helps me keep track."

"Yeah, me too. I'm Konstantin. When I'm not Betty. But I thought your name was Veles."

"That's a code name. Betty?"

"Never mind. Do you want my intel?" I really wanted to pass it on. I planned to attribute it to the Brummie who'd been cruel to young Nigel. Maybe there'd be blowback.

"Later. First let's plan where we go from here."

"To find Tror."

"To find Tror."

"Again, it's been three thousand years. Don't you think by now—"

"I haven't spent it *all* looking. I'd have gone mad. But every so often I find a lead."

"You're following a lead?"

"A dead end. There were rumours of a Thor near Jüterbog, with great destructive power. Turned out it was the nickname of a massive howitzer. But by then I'd wormed my way into the HVA, and decided to stay. It's an intelligence agency. With links to a larger one. If my son is in Europe, what better place to look for him?"

"That's a pretty big 'if'."

"Maybe. But every few lifetimes it seizes me and I can't let go. I heal from everything. He must, too."

I had to play this carefully. "There was a war. Could he heal from a bomb? Or a bullet to the heart? Or decapitation?"

Damn. Why would I say decapitation?

"He'd know how to look after himself. And why would anyone decapitate him?"

"No reason. Just, er … hypothetically." I could feel the damp of my armpits soaking into my shirt.

"Do you know something you're not telling me?" Sweat beaded on my forehead. She unholstered the Tokarev and raised it. "You know I'll get it from you."

I did. I was over three thousand years old, but Tróán was older. She'd always been older. She'd known me—and dominated me—when I was basically a kid. All these centuries later that was still her place in my psyche. This time the mic drop was hers.

"Um," I said. "Well. Interesting story, actually."

I kept it simple. Explained the position I'd been in. Tried to make her see. Knowing I was wasting what might be my last breaths. She was his mother, and I'd killed him. Beyond that, not much mattered.

She didn't say a word. Didn't shout or rail at me. Didn't move a muscle. Except in her trigger finger. She didn't move it far. But she didn't have to. That's kind of how triggers work.

Things happened fast. A loud noise. A sharp pain in my chest. The room tilted. I slid to the floor. Tróán stood over me. Aimed the Tokarev at my head. Darkness crept around the edge of my vision.

Something crashed against the door behind her. She turned her head. I turned mine. The doorframe splintered. Two uniformed British soldiers came through, rifles raised. "Don't move," one shouted. In the corridor I saw the shabby outline of Jan Vlaming.

Tróán fired her second shot before she'd finished turning back to me. The bullet hit the floor where my head had been. No time for another. She glanced at my bleeding chest. *That'll do*, said her expression. She was through the window before either soldier could get a bead on her.

Pain howled through my chest. It was consuming. It was everything, and yet not quite. There was something else. Something missing. As the darkness swallowed me I realized what it was. My heartbeat.

For the first time in more than three thousand years, I didn't have one.

A gunshot wound isn't the red dot you see on TV. A gunshot wound is catastrophic. But I caught some breaks. The bullet hadn't hit bone, for one thing. Bone splinters were a complication I didn't need. Plus I must've twitched to one side while it was in flight. If it had gone straight in at the entry wound—as Tróán apparently thought—it would've hit my heart smack in the middle, but can't have done more than nick the edge. That's an educated guess. But it's the only possibility. If my heart had taken a direct hit, it wouldn't have healed in time to save me.

The other break I caught was that Jan Vlaming knew what to do.

I woke up with a field dressing on my chest. It was dark outside. Vlaming was on one of the chairs, smoking a stale cigarette and reading a paperback copy of *To Have and Have Not* in Dutch. The door was back in its splintered frame. The soldiers were gone. "You're awake." He held the book toward me. "You know this Hemingway?"

"Not personally."

"That was weak, even for you. I'll blame it on your trauma." He closed the book, thumb holding his place, and peered at the cover. "A bit Marxist for my taste. But in some men that's a side effect of being anti-fascist."

I took a breath. Pain hit my chest like a hammer.

"Your lung is compromised. I applied pressure to keep it from collapsing until the medic arrived with a chest seal. I'll have to get you to a proper medical facility." He dog-eared his spot in the book and set it on the table. "But first we must have a chat." He dropped his cigarette and crushed it with his boot. "I thought you were dead at first. I couldn't find a pulse. Then I could. Thin, but there. Lucky man."

"Unlucky shot."

"Maybe. Not my concern." He leaned over me with his elbows on his knees. "My concern is why you were here."

"Getting information for you. From the HVA. You wanted something bigger."

He nodded. "Nice. A lie, but nice. No, the agent who shot you isn't a source of information. She's a gatherer of information. At a high level."

"So you followed her here?"

"Veles doesn't let herself be followed. We followed you."

"Me? Why?"

"Because you were careless. You're playing with professionals. You don't even see it. We feed you a snippet of false intel, only to you, and later it surfaces through your friend Klaus's handler. So we know. We keep an eye. Lucky for you. A sucking chest wound doesn't clear up on its own." He rubbed his chin. "Which makes me wonder. Why would Veles shoot you? Did you try to cheat her?"

"Previous life. Nothing to do with the HVA. Or the SIS."

He stared at me. "I think I believe you."

"So you'll get me to a hospital now?"

He shook his head. "Not yet. We haven't discussed why you were here. What you were trading to Veles for—" he opened the satchel Tróán had left on the table, and his eyes went wide "—for a train ticket and some travel documents? That's it?"

"And cash. There should be some cash."

"Not much. Your intel can't be very valuable. And yet it drew out an important HVA agent. So satisfy my curiosity. What do you have that warrants Veles's personal attention?"

"Nothing. Suspected homosexuals. People open to blackmail."

Vlaming sighed. "Please." He rested the sole of his shoe on my dressing. "Anyone with two eyeballs could spend a quarter hour in your cabaret and make a list of fifty suspected homosexuals. One eyeball, even." He pressed down, just a little. Pain spiked from my chest through my arm. "You have something better than that. Tell me what it is."

"What's it worth to you?"

He pressed harder. The pain got sharper. "It's worth lifting my foot." His tone was conversational. "Maybe even worth letting you keep the bag with the ticket and the documents. Though perhaps not the cash."

"Throw in the cash and you have a deal."

He considered this. "Half the cash." More pressure. More pain.

"All right," I said through clenched teeth.

He lifted his foot and spread his hands. "Well?"

It took me a moment to catch my breath. "It's the tunnel."

"What tunnel?"

"The phone tap. In Rudow. At the radar station. I'm right, aren't I?"

He looked surprised. Surprised and amused.

"The … the phone lines? In Rudow? Hah!" He laughed out loud. It made him jiggle like a blancmange. "That's your information? Oh, dear God, this is too good."

I didn't know what was so funny, so I went on. "I can't be sure, but it's the only thing that fits. The location. The Brits with the dirty nails.

I figured it'd be easy enough for the HVA to check, once I told them where to look."

"Stop," said Vlaming, his body still shaking. "Enough."

"But you wanted to know."

"Yes, I did. And now I do. So does everyone. You're luckier than you know."

Lucky? I'd been shot in the chest, and my customer had literally gone out the window. "What do you mean, everyone knows? I've only just told you." A chilling thought hit me. "Did Klaus figure it out?"

Vlaming wiped his eyes with his hanky. "Your Klaus isn't that clever. But your timing is very good. A day earlier and I would've had no idea what you were talking about. A day later and your intel would've been worthless. But this afternoon?" He angled his head at Tróán's satchel on the table. "This afternoon brought you a windfall."

"I don't understand."

"Of course not. But I'll tell you." He sat back like a grandfather starting a bedtime story. "You're right about the tunnel. It was a sophisticated phone tap, and apparently ran for many months. I myself had no idea. It was need-to-know, and I didn't."

"So why do you know now?"

"Because the Soviets stumbled upon it two nights ago. Red Army workers checking for flood-damaged cables. This very evening the Soviet military commandant took Berlin's journalists on a guided tour. It's on every radio station in every language. Tomorrow it will be in all the papers." He laughed and shook his head. "Timing."

I thought about Tróán. Thirty-three hundred years, and when we finally met again she had a gun on me. Timing.

Vlaming slapped his knees. "So. Shall we go?"

"Go where?"

"The hospital. Not a public one. Somewhere more secure."

"That's it?"

He stood. "That's it. Now that I know what your intel was." He chuckled. "The tunnel."

"Can we get my things from the cabaret first?"

"Oh, you won't be going back to the cabaret. You're no use there now. To either side."

Well, wasn't *that* a little self-absorbed? "It isn't just an intelligence market, you know. It's my income."

"Pah!" He waved the comment away with a flick of his hand. "You don't need an income. You'll be staying with us." He made it sound like an invitation to a spot of hunting at the family estate. What ho.

"At the hospital."

"At first, yes."

"And then?"

He sighed deeply. "Can you really be so dim? And then you'll be telling us whatever you passed to friend Klaus, of course. Every scrap. However long it takes."

My body sagged. I nodded at the satchel. "And Zurich?"

"I keep my word. You'll get your passage to Zurich." He slung the satchel over his shoulder. "Eventually."

They expected me to be an invalid for at least a month. That made them careless. On day eight I teased the location of Tróán's bag from a sweet Bavarian nurse. Five hours and two picked locks later, I had it. Twenty minutes after that I had an ill-fitting tweed suit and a pre-war BMW motorbike. I was gone before sunrise.

I knew they'd be looking for me on the Zurich train, so I cashed in the ticket, gassed up the bike and headed east toward Poland.

Last Weekend

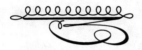

THE NIGHT BEFORE the Chechen was supposed to arrive he called me in a panic. "They never heard of me," he said. "There's no paperwork."

"What do you mean? My guy put it all through."

"Nothing is put through. My name is nowhere. My flight is in two hours, and even the airline doesn't know me."

"Give me an hour. I'll see what I can find out."

I called Eleven's cell. No answer. I left a message. I didn't wait to hear back. I'd linked his phone's GPS to my locater app. I love my phone apps. Best new thing this lifetime. I have them for everything. Time management. Home security. Language learning. Keeping tabs on my people.

The icon on the map was at his shatter lab.

A light snowfall was starting as I pulled up. I checked the dashboard clock. Eleven. How did time get so tight? I parked in the driveway and crossed the dark lawn to the shed. The door was unlocked. Stainless steel devices shone under an overhead bulb. Shatter equipment, presumably. A faint smell of butane. I turned off the bulb at the wall switch. Butane vapour and a live incandescent filament made me uneasy.

I heard a soft moan. I turned on my LED flashlight. Eleven was in an armchair in the corner, head lolling. His shadow danced as I approached. "Eleven." No response. A scorched glass pipe sat next to a half-empty mickey of scotch and a plate of amber shards that looked like the world's thinnest peanut brittle. "Eleven. I need your help sorting out the Chechen."

His eyelids fluttered. "The forehead is the ceiling of the face."

The butane smell worried me. "We're getting out of here." I slipped my arm behind his shoulders. "The last thing I need is to get caught in a drug lab."

Yeah, I know. Looks good by comparison now, doesn't it?

We'd reached my car when my phone bleeped. Not the e-mail bleep or the text message bleep. The home security bleep. I draped Eleven over the hood and took out the phone. The home screen showed an intruder alert message. I entered my password and swiped through the camera feeds. Foyer. Living room. Kitchen.

I nearly missed it. The library. My wing chair was the wrong way around. It was facing the bay window, away from the camera. I couldn't tell who was in it. All I could see was a curve of dark hair.

Now I had to go home. Like I didn't have enough on my plate. But what to do with Eleven? I gave him a shake. "Wake up. I don't have time for this."

"Bismuth," he said.

I couldn't drag him back to his explosive shed. And I couldn't leave him in the driveway to freeze. Damn. I opened the back door and wrestled him onto the seat. I didn't want him knowing where I lived, but it didn't seem likely he'd notice much. Not for a while.

I pulled onto the gravel pad behind my house and went in through the side door. I slipped out of my shoes and crept down the hall in my socks. The library door was open. I could hear the crackle of a fire in the fireplace and the Finale of *Parsifal* on the stereo. Someone had a sense of occasion.

I thought about getting a weapon before going in, but decided not to bother. The best weapon in the house was the sword over the mantel. I'd have time to get to it if I needed to. But I didn't think I would.

I stepped through the door. Curve of dark hair. Sandaled foot. Slim, braceleted wrist. There was a click as she set her glass of port on my wine table. "Your Chechen isn't coming."

"I know. He called. Is that why you followed me to Kyiv?"

Nicca rose from the chair. "I was there a day ahead, actually. I wanted you to see me. A warning shot." The recording reached the choral entry. She cocked her head. "Is this the part where Kundry sinks to the stage and dies?"

"Near enough. You timed it well."

"I put it on a loop. I didn't know how long you'd take to get here."

"Still, I'm surprised you remembered."

"I'm surprised you're surprised. Wagner was practically all you could talk about, that night at *Les Deux Magots* in Paris."

"That was nearly a hundred years ago."

"When it comes to you, Ishtanu, I remember things."

She'd been shadowing me online for two years, using Latvian hackers.

"Why?"

"Curiosity, at first. And the challenge of seeing if I could find you."

"And later?"

"I saw you sending out feelers to biomedical departments in out-of-the-way places. Myanmar. The Philippines. Ukraine."

"I was making a list. Geneticists with grand ambitions and limited opportunities."

"And flexible medical ethics. I know. I have that list."

"How?" I could hear a tightness in my voice.

"My people know their job."

"That's how you knew I'd be in Kyiv?"

"I'd told my people to alert me if you booked a flight to an airport within a day's drive of anyone on the list. Your Chechen was the first."

"So you beat me there. And went to the sculpture park."

"Just to let you know I was watching."

"You overestimated me. It never occurred to me that was why you were there." Because it never occurred to me I was under her surveillance. The idea of it was starting to make me angry.

"I also wanted to confirm why you were there. Which I did when you met with the Chechen on the patio near the Maidan."

"I didn't see you there."

"Your Chechen did. He looked me over pretty thoroughly."

"When?"

"Before you arrived. I was at the next table. He was so focused on my cleavage he didn't notice me press a listening device under the window frame between our tables as I left."

I flashed back to my conversation with the Chechen. What had I said? What had Nicca heard? Damn her. How *dare* she?

"Don't worry. You mostly talked about visas and money. There was frustratingly little about what he was going to be doing for you."

"I'm glad I maintained *some* privacy." It came out more bitterly than I'd intended.

"Not as much as you think. I wasn't done looking."

I gave her a cold stare. "What else do you know?"

"I know you bought three kinds of DNA sequencers from three companies in three non-NATO countries. Two of which are now stuck in customs because their online documentation disappeared."

"That was you."

"Of course. The order for the third one has vanished altogether, by the way."

"Like the Chechen's travel clearance."

"Exactly like the Chechen's travel clearance."

"Why would you do that to me?"

"Let me ask you a question first. Any number of public companies would sequence your genome. Why set up your own shop?"

Could I trust her? No. She'd just proved I couldn't. But she'd worked most of it out already. For all I knew, her people had the Chechen in a room right now, spilling the rest of it. Or selling it. "I don't just want it sequenced. I want it copied."

I knew the expression that crossed her face then. The sad satisfaction of being right when you want to be wrong. "Do you even know anything about genetics?"

"That's what the Chechen is for."

"To find you the immortality gene."

"Yes."

"And reproduce it. Make more people who don't die."

I nodded. I couldn't say it out loud.

"Why? What's your end game?" She waved an arm around the room, as if the Chechen, the lab, the equipment were all there with us. "Secret society? Ruling class?" She lifted an eyebrow. "Master race?"

Her words hit me like a slap. "No. How could you …?" I turned away at her incomprehension. At how the woman I'd raised a family with could think that. A woman who knew me better than anyone. I turned back and looked her in the eye. "Not a master race. A family."

I expected sympathy. I didn't get it. "Family? " She slapped my face. An actual slap, this time. "You son of a bitch. You *had* a family."

"And they died. And they would've kept on dying." How could she not get this? "I don't want a family of goddamn mayflies." My cheek really stung. "I want a family I don't outlive."

"You *had* that. You had *me*. You didn't outlive me. You *left* me." She was shouting into my face. "Left me to deal with it. All the dying and the burying and the grieving. While you went on your merry way."

Like I said. I should've dealt with it better at the time.

"I messed that up. I should've stayed. But you're here now. I'm here." I reached for her hand. "What if we picked things up again? Fresh start?"

She turned and walked to the mantle. Adjusted the watercolour. "It's too late."

"No, it isn't." I followed her and put a hand on her shoulder. "We aren't the people we were. And if my work pans out, it won't just be the two of us."

"Your *work*?" She turned to me with a look I'd never seen. "Your *work* isn't going to pan out, Ishtanu. Ask your Chechen, if you ever get him here. Ask him if there's an immortality gene sitting there waiting to be spotted with some off-the-shelf equipment in an abandoned medical lab."

"What other explanation can there be? It has to be genetics. My whole life I've tried to figure it out. Now I'm on the road to finding it."

"Poor, dear Ishtanu. Always just a little behind the times." She touched my cheek. "Thinking there's something simple out there that'll explain you to yourself. A divine purpose. A squiggle under a microscope. A single gene. If that's what your Chechen is telling you, then you're being scammed."

"What? No. He … I mean …" I couldn't put words together. "What?"

"There won't be an immortality gene. There'll be some complex interaction of random genes spread across your DNA strands. Triggered by some unreproducible series of childhood events." She lowered her hand to my shoulder. "Whatever caused you, Ishtanu, your Chechen isn't going to find it, no matter how well you pay him."

I felt my blood pressure rise. "No, you're wrong. Maybe it takes time. But we have time." I could salvage this. "We'll need a dedicated lab. Long term. More staff. In the meantime maybe we start with cloning. See if our combination of genes is enough."

She took her hand away. "Not mine. And not yours either."

I felt a flush from my chest up into my neck. "Why not?"

"Because I'm not going to let you do this." Her eyes were like slate. "I'm not going to let you inflict this hell on anyone else."

"Hell?" My voice cracked. "It's a *gift*. It's a *blessing*."

She slapped my face again. It was making me angry. "Wake up, Ishtanu. It isn't a blessing. It's an affliction. And it doesn't need to be reproduced. It needs to *end*."

The edge of my vision glowed red. "But I *need* this. It's my life's work." My voice was jagged in my own ears.

"*You* need it? Just like *you* need to walk away when it gets hard. Like *you* need playmates who don't die. What about what I need?" She pushed my chest with both hands. I stumbled. My shoulder hit the mantle. "Did you ever ask what *I* need?"

"Fine! What, Nicca? What do you need?"

"I need out! I need it to be over. *That's* what I need!"

My temples were pounding. Somehow the grip of my bronze sword was in my hand. I don't remember reaching for it. But I remember lifting it.

It takes a lot.

It took a lot.

Nicca got out. She got the Kundry moment.

It wasn't an act of violence. It was an act of love.

Wasn't it?

Now

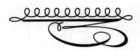

YOU KNOW THE rest, or most of it. Blood. Then silence. Then Eleven O'Moron screaming outside my bay window. I'd forgotten he was there.

He'll have been your anonymous 911 caller. He ran off so fast that by the time I reached the street all I could see of him was his phone screen bobbing in the dark, two blocks away. Then I heard the sirens.

Your boys must've been close. I was only halfway back to the house when they pulled into my driveway. And here I am.

Did your people clean up the blood, or do I have to arrange for that?

I don't suppose there's a chance of getting a sample for the Chechen, is there?

Ah, well. Had to ask, didn't I?

So there it is. That's as much of a confession as you're going to get. More than you wanted, probably. And less. I hope it at least makes what happened intelligible, if not forgivable. Or not. I don't much care anymore. On my timeline, understanding and forgiveness are always a couple of steps behind the next great wave of chaos and sin.

You're wondering why I've told you so much. About so many other misdeeds. You of all people. A cop. Here's why.

Because I haven't given you the details you'd need to pin any of them on me. No dates, no account numbers, no specific locations. No names of banks or brokers or shipping companies. Or people. I mean, Eleven O'Moron? Really? And the Chechen? *So* not a Chechen.

Because my story is so preposterous that your supervisor will never approve the resources to follow it up. Because you'll never hold me. Because when I'm gone you'll never find me.

And because every few lives I just have to let someone in on it all.

Epilogue

The Post Imperator

Wounded inmate missing

TORONTO—An inmate facing a murder charge went missing yesterday while en route to hospital for treatment of multiple stab wounds. Stan Tarnen, 26, was assaulted by an unknown attacker while in remand custody and was rushed to hospital suffering from "extreme trauma." Almost an hour later the hospital alerted the jail that the ambulance carrying Tarnen hadn't arrived. Police found it in an alley with the driver and paramedics unconscious.

"There must have been a gang of them," said a jail official on condition of anonymity. "There's no way he got out on his own. He was cut bad. He was barely breathing when he left here."

Reports that ambulance staff were injected with opiates from their own supplies could not be confirmed at press time.

Tarnen is charged with the murder last week of Nicca Kumar, a financial analyst from Amsterdam. The circumstances of the murder have not yet been made public.

Acknowledgements

As always, I'm grateful beyond possible expression to my wife and daughter for their love and support. Also as always, I'm specifically grateful to my wife for her invaluable input as first reader. *Call Me Stan* would be a lesser book without that input.

Thanks to Michael Mirolla at Guernica Editions for seeing this book's possibilities, and to him and the rest of the Guernica team—Connie McParland, Anna van Valkenburg, Margo LaPierre and Dylan Curran—for giving it the green light and seeing it through. Thanks to Julie Roorda for her kind words and gentle edits, and to David Moratto for his stunning cover design.

This book wouldn't be what it is without the support and encouragement of those who read it in fragments along the way: Graham Mariacci, Laura K. McRae, I.H. Smythe and Tracy Urquhart. Never doubt that your interest and enthusiasm feed the flame.

Special thanks to Sean Michaels for flagging an important issue late in the process. Special thanks to Helen Robertson for her thoughtful and valuable Trans sensitivity read. Any issues that remain are mine alone.

Because historical fiction—even the weird kind—necessarily depends on the work of actual historians, I'd also like to give due credit to those I relied on the most.

My main resources for *The Hatti* were *Hittite Warrior* by Trevor Bryce (illustrations by Adam Hook), and *Qadesh 1300 BC: Clash of the Warrior Kings* by Mark Healy. For trade patterns and other period context I relied on the wonderfully illuminative *1177 B.C.: The Year Civilization Collapsed*, by Eric. H. Cline. Elements of Stan's polytheism were inspired by Nicholas Wade's *The Faith Instinct: How Religion Evolved and Why It Endures*.

The rationalization by Christianized Vikings that the chief Norse gods, or Aesir, were actually Trojan refugees has long been debunked (along with any connection between 'Aesir' and 'Asia'), but it was just too good a story to resist. I came upon it—and much more that I relied on—in John Lindow's excellent book *Norse Mythology*.

For the Trojan war and its aftermath—including the notion that Troy's city wall may have been breached by an earthquake attributed to Poseidon—I relied mainly on Eric H. Cline's *The Trojan War: A Very Short Introduction*. For Tror's time in Thrace I drew on *The Thracians: 700 BC–AD 46* by Christopher Webber (illustrations by Angus McBride). For Thracian herbalism and ceremony I relied on *Thracian Magic* by Georgi Mishev. For information on the Ore Mountains I mainly relied on Wikipedia, which was indispensable at all stages for any number of details, including, later on, things like whether Europe in the 1850s had upright pianos (yes), lead pencils (yes) or doorknobs (no).

The Dharma grew out of the Taliban's 2001 destruction of the massive Buddha statues in Afghanistan's Bamiyan Valley, and my amazement that Buddhism had once been that dominant that far west. My resources were mainly *Religions of the Silk Road* by Richard Foltz and *What the Buddha Taught* by Walpola Rahula. Oh, and don't tweet me to tell me Stan has impermanence wrong. That was an authorial choice. Plus, cute story: In Buddhist writings, the Pali word for impermanence is *anicca*. The 'a' at the beginning essentially means 'non-'. So ...

The Teacher grew out of my lifelong, mostly secular interest in the Jesus story, and from my more specific interest in how the Buddhist elements that some scholars have seen in his teachings might've got there. I mainly drew on the gospels for this chapter, though I also relied on the maps in J.R. Porter's *The Illustrated Guide to the Bible*. I don't remember at this point where I came upon the camel/gamla thing, but it's all over the internet if you want to look for it.

My main resources for *The Abbot* were Rev. Boniface Verheyen's translation of *The Rule* (including Hugh Ford's biography of St. Benedict appended to it) and Roger Rosewell's *The Medieval Monastery*. I also drew on *History of the City of Rome in the Middle Ages, Vol. I* by Ferdinand Gregorovius. Also, again and always, Wikipedia.

The first part of *The Family* draws mainly on *In the Wake of the Plague* by Norman F. Cantor, and the second part mainly on *1381: The Year of the Peasants' Revolt* by Juliet Barker, along with some bits from *The Time Traveler's Guide to Medieval England* by Ian Mortimer. With respect to the revolt, I've conflated some historical characters, moved some events around to suit my own narrative, and clumsily oversimplified the laws and courts of the time. That's entirely on me, not on Ms. Barker or Mr. Mortimer.

The Composer was inspired by my decades-long difficulty reconciling Richard Wagner's vile antisemitism with his interest in the Buddha. It relies heavily on three excellent books: Chris Walton's *Richard Wagner's Zurich: The Muse of Place*, Brian Magee's *The Tristan Chord: Wagner and Philosophy*, and Urs App's *Wagner and Buddhism*. I've probably taken some of Mr. Walton's thoughts on Mathilde Wesendonck a bit further than he would have, but, again, that's on me. Plus Wilhelm Baumgartner almost certainly wasn't the buffoon I've turned him into. That's just who fictional Willi insisted on being. Again, apologies to the actual Herr Baumgartner.

The Cabaret was inspired by the Berlin chapter in Ian Fleming's quirky travel book *Thrilling Cities*, which is why I gave a version of his name—though nothing else about him—to my slightly shabby British spy. For the details of the Allied tunnel and its discovery I relied on David Stafford's *Spies Beneath Berlin*, and on a reproduction of a 1945 Berlin *Allied Intelligence Map of Key Buildings*.

James May's delightful book *How to Land an A330 Airbus and Other Vital Skills for the Modern Man* was an invaluable resource on both dueling and childbirth. No, really.

About the Author

K.R. Wilson's debut novel *An Idea About My Dead Uncle* received the inaugural Guernica Prize for an unpublished manuscript in 2018. *Call Me Stan* is his second novel. He has a Bachelor of Music degree in Theory and Composition from the University of Calgary, which probably explains why there's so damn much music in his books. He lives with his wife and daughter in Toronto, where he is working on another book about Ishtanu. He can be found at www.krwilson.ca, on Twitter at @krwilson8, and on Instagram at @krwbooks.

Printed in July 2021
by Gauvin Press,
Gatineau, Québec